Dennis Lehane was born and raised in Dorchester, Massachusetts. He has won and been shortlisted for several awards for his writing and three of his books have been made into films. He lives in the Boston area.

DENNIS LEHANE

LIVE BY NIGHT

ABACUS

First published in the United States in 2012 by William Morrow,
an imprint of HarperCollins US
First published in Great Britain in 2012 by Little, Brown
This paperback edition published in 2013 by Abacus

A CIP catalogue record for this book
is available from the British Library.

ISBN 978-0-349-12369-1

Printed and bound in Great Britain by
Clays Ltd, St Ives plc

Papers used by Abacus are from well-managed forests
and other responsible sources.

MIX
Paper from
responsible sources
FSC® C104740

Abacus
An imprint of
Little, Brown Book Group
100 Victoria Embankment
London EC4Y 0DY

An Hachette UK Company
www.hachette.co.uk

www.littlebrown.co.uk

For Angie
I'd drive all night . . .

Men of God and men of war have strange affinities.

CORMAC MCCARTHY, *BLOOD MERIDIAN*

It's too late to be good.

LUCKY LUCIANO

PART I

Boston

1926–1929

CHAPTER ONE

A Twelve O'Clock Fella
in a Nine O'Clock Town

Some years later, on a tugboat in the Gulf of Mexico, Joe Coughlin's feet were placed in a tub of cement. Twelve gunmen stood waiting until they got far enough out to sea to throw him overboard, while Joe listened to the engine chug and watched the water churn white at the stern. And it occurred to him that almost everything of note that had ever happened in his life – good or bad – had been set in motion the morning he first crossed paths with Emma Gould.

They met shortly after dawn in 1926, when Joe and the Bartolo brothers robbed the gaming room at the back of an Albert White speakeasy in South Boston. Before they entered it, Joe and the Bartolos had no idea the speakeasy belonged to Albert White. If they had, they would have beat a retreat in three separate directions to make the trail all the harder to follow.

They came down the back stairs smoothly enough. They

passed through the empty bar area without incident. The bar and casino took up the rear of a furniture warehouse along the waterfront that Joe's boss, Tim Hickey, had assured him was owned by some harmless Greeks recently arrived from Maryland. But when they walked into the back room, they found a poker game in full swing, the five players drinking amber Canadian from heavy crystal glasses, a gray carpet of cigarette smoke hanging overhead. A pile of money rose from the center of the table.

Not one of the men looked Greek. Or harmless. They had hung their suit jackets over the backs of their chairs, which left the guns on their hips exposed. When Joe, Dion, and Paolo walked in with pistols extended, none of the men went for the guns, but Joe could tell a couple were thinking about it.

A woman had been serving drinks to the table. She put the tray aside, lifted her cigarette out of an ashtray and took a drag, looked about to yawn with three guns pointed at her. Like she might ask to see something more impressive for an encore.

Joe and the Bartolos wore hats pulled down over their eyes, and black handkerchiefs covered the lower halves of their faces. Which was a good thing because if anyone in this crowd recognized them, they'd have about half a day left to live.

A walk in the park, Tim Hickey had said. Hit them at dawn when the only people left in the place would be a couple of mokes in the counting room.

As opposed to five gun thugs playing poker.

One of the players said, 'You know whose place this is?'

4

Joe didn't recognize the guy, but he knew the guy next to him – Brenny Loomis, ex-boxer and a member of the Albert White Mob, Tim Hickey's biggest rival in the bootlegging business. Lately, Albert was rumored to be stockpiling Thompson machine guns for an impending war. The word was out – choose a side or choose a headstone.

Joe said, 'Everyone does as they're told, no one gets so much as a scratch.'

The guy beside Loomis ran his mouth again. 'I asked you know whose game this was, you fucking dunce.'

Dion Bartolo hit him in the mouth with his pistol. Hit him hard enough to knock him out of his chair and draw some blood. Got everyone else thinking how much better it was to be the one who wasn't getting pistol-whipped than the one who was.

Joe said, 'Everyone but the girl, get on your knees. Put your hands behind your head and lace the fingers.'

Brenny Loomis locked eyes with Joe. 'I'll call your mother when this is over, boy. Suggest a nice dark suit for your coffin.'

Loomis, a former club boxer at Mechanics Hall and sparring partner for Mean Mo Mullins, was said to have a punch like a bag of cue balls. He killed people for Albert White. Not for a living, exclusively, but rumor was he wanted Albert to know, should it ever become a full-time position, he had seniority.

Joe had never experienced fear like he did looking into Loomis's tiny brown eyes, but he gestured at the floor with his gun nonetheless, quite surprised that his hand didn't shake. Brendan Loomis laced his hands behind his head and got on his knees. Once he did, the others did the same.

Joe said to the girl, 'Come over here, miss. We won't harm you.'

She stubbed out her cigarette and looked at him like she was thinking about lighting another, maybe freshening her drink. She crossed to him, a girl near his own age, maybe twenty or so, with winter eyes and skin so pale he could almost see through it to the blood and tissue underneath.

He watched her come as the Bartolo brothers relieved the cardplayers of their weapons. The pistols made heavy thumps as they tossed them onto a nearby blackjack table, but the girl didn't even flinch. In her eyes, firelights danced behind the gray.

She stepped up to his gun and said, 'And what will the gentleman be having with his robbery this morning?'

Joe handed her one of the two canvas sacks he'd carried in. 'The money on the table, please.'

'Coming right up, sir.'

As she crossed back to the table, he pulled one pair of handcuffs from the other sack, then tossed the sack to Paolo. Paolo bent by the first cardplayer and handcuffed his wrists at the small of his back, then moved on to the next.

The girl swept the pot off the center of the table – Joe noting not just bills but watches and jewelry in there too – then gathered up everyone's stakes. Paolo finished cuffing the men on the floor and went to work gagging them.

Joe scanned the room – the roulette wheel behind him, the craps table against the wall under the stairs. He counted three blackjack tables and one baccarat table. Six slot machines took up the rear wall. A low table with a dozen phones on top constituted the wire service, a board behind it listing the horses from last night's twelfth race at Readville. The only other door besides the one they'd come through was chalk-marked with a *T* for *toilet*, which made sense, because people had to piss when they drank.

Except that when Joe had come through the bar, he'd seen two bathrooms, which would certainly suffice. And this bathroom had a padlock on it.

He looked over at Brenny Loomis, lying on the floor with a gag in his mouth but watching the wheels turn in Joe's head. Joe watched the wheels in Loomis's head do their own turning. And he knew what he'd known the moment he saw that padlock – the bathroom wasn't a bathroom.

It was the counting room.

Albert White's counting room.

Judging by the business Hickey casinos had done the past two days – the first chilly weekend of October – Joe suspected a small fortune sat behind that door.

Albert White's small fortune.

The girl came back to him with the bag of poker swag. 'Your dessert, sir,' she said and handed him the bag. He couldn't get over how level her gaze was. She didn't just stare at him, she stared through him. He was certain she could see his face behind the handkerchief and the low hat. Some morning he'd pass her walking to get cigarettes, hear her yell, 'That's him!' He wouldn't even have time to close his eyes before the bullets hit him.

He took the sack and dangled the set of cuffs from his finger. 'Turn around.'

'Yes, sir. Right away, sir.' She turned her back to him and crossed her arms behind her. Her knuckles pressed against the small of her back, the fingertips dangling over her ass, Joe realizing the last thing he should be doing was concentrating on anyone's ass, period.

He snapped the first cuff around her wrist. 'I'll be gentle.'

'Don't put yourself out on my account.' She looked back over her shoulder at him. 'Just try not to leave marks.'

Jesus.

'What's your name?'

'Emma Gould,' she said. 'What's yours?'

'Wanted.'

'By all the girls or just the law?'

He couldn't keep up with her and cover the room at the same time, so he turned her to him and pulled the gag out of his pocket. The gags were men's socks that Paolo Bartolo had stolen from the Woolworth's where he worked.

'You're going to put a sock in my mouth.'

'Yes.'

'A sock. In my mouth.'

'Never been used before,' Joe said. 'I promise.'

She cocked one eyebrow. It was the same tarnished-brass color as her hair and soft and shiny as ermine.

'I wouldn't lie to you,' Joe said and felt, in that moment, as if he were telling the truth.

'That's usually what liars say.' She opened her mouth like a child resigned to a spoonful of medicine, and he thought of saying something else to her but couldn't think of what. He thought of asking her something, just so he could hear her voice again.

Her eyes pulsed a bit when he pushed the sock into her

8

mouth and then she tried to spit it out – they usually did – shaking her head as she saw the twine in his hand, but he was ready for her. He drew it tight across her mouth and back along the sides of her face. As he tied it off at the back of her head, she looked at him as if, until this point, the whole transaction had been perfectly honorable – a kick, even – but now he'd gone and sullied it.

'It's half silk,' he said.

Another arch of her eyebrow.

'The sock,' he said. 'Go join your friends.'

She knelt by Brendan Loomis, who'd never taken his eyes off Joe, not once the whole time.

Joe looked at the door to the counting room, looked at the padlock on the door. He let Loomis follow his gaze and then he looked Loomis in the eyes. Loomis's eyes went dull as he waited to see what the next move would be.

Joe held his gaze and said, 'Let's go, boys. We're done.'

Loomis blinked once, slowly, and Joe decided to take that as a peace offering – or the possibility of one – and got the hell out of there.

When they left, they drove along the waterfront. The sky was a hard blue streaked with hard yellow. The gulls rose and fell, cawing. The bucket of a ship crane swung in hard over the wharf road, then swung back with a scream as Paolo drove over its shadow. Longshoremen, stevedores, and teamsters stood at their pilings, smoking in the bright cold. A group of them threw rocks at the gulls.

Joe rolled down his window, took the cold air on his face, against his eyes. It smelled like salt, fish blood, and gasoline.

Dion Bartolo looked back at him from the front seat. 'You asked the doll her name?'

Joe said, 'Making conversation.'

'You cuff her hands like you're putting a pin on her, asking her to the dance?'

Joe leaned his head out the open window for a minute, sucked the dirty air in as deep as he could. Paolo drove off the docks and up toward Broadway, the Nash Roadster doing thirty miles an hour easy.

'I seen her before,' Paolo said.

Joe pulled his head back in the car. 'Where?'

'I don't know. But I did. I know it.' He bounced the Nash onto Broadway and they all bounced with it. 'You should write her a poem maybe.'

'Write her a fucking poem,' Joe said. 'Why don't you slow down and stop driving like we did something?'

Dion turned toward Joe, placed his arm on the seat back. 'He actually wrote a poem to a girl once, my brother.'

'No kidding?'

Paolo met his eyes in the rearview mirror and gave him a solemn nod.

'What happened?'

'Nothing,' Dion said. 'She couldn't read.'

They headed south toward Dorchester and got stuck in traffic by a horse that dropped dead just outside Andrew Square. Traffic had to be routed around it and its overturned ice cart. Shards of ice glistened in the cobblestone cracks like metal shavings, and the iceman stood beside the carcass, kicking the horse in the ribs. Joe thought about her the whole way. Her hands had been dry and soft. They were very small and pink at the base of the palms. The veins in her wrist were violet. She had a black freckle on the back of her right ear but not on her left.

The Bartolo brothers lived on Dorchester Avenue above a butcher and a cobbler. The butcher and the cobbler had married sisters and hated each other only slightly less than they hated their wives. This didn't stop them, however, from running a speakeasy in their shared basement. Nightly, people came from the other sixteen parishes of Dorchester, as well as from parishes as far away as the North Shore, to drink the best liquor south of Montreal and hear a Negro songstress named Delilah Deluth sing about heartbreak in a place whose unofficial name was The Shoelace, which infuriated the butcher so much he'd gone bald over it. The Bartolo brothers were in The Shoelace almost every night, which was fine, but going so far as to reside above the place seemed idiotic to Joe. It would only take one legitimate raid by honest cops or T-Men, however unlikely that might be, and it would be nothing for them to kick in Dion and Paolo's door and discover money, guns, and jewelry that two wops who worked in a grocery store and a department store, respectively, could never account for.

True, the jewelry usually went right back out the door to Hymie Drago, the fence they'd been using since they were fifteen, but the money usually went no further than a gaming table in the back of The Shoelace, or into their mattresses.

Joe leaned against the icebox and watched Paolo put his and his brother's split there that morning, just pulling back the sweat-yellowed sheet to reveal one of a series of slits they'd cut into the side, Dion handing the stacks of bills to Paolo and Paolo shoving them in like he was stuffing a holiday bird.

At twenty-three, Paolo was the oldest of them. Dion, younger by two years, seemed older, however, maybe because he was smarter or maybe because he was meaner. Joe, who would turn twenty next month, was the youngest of them but had been acknowledged as the brains of the operation since they'd joined forces to knock over newsstands when Joe was thirteen.

Paolo rose from the floor. 'I know where I seen her.' He slapped the dust off his knees.

Joe came off the icebox. 'Where?'

'But he's not sweet on her,' Dion said.

'Where?' Joe repeated.

Paolo pointed at the floor. 'Downstairs.'

'In The Shoelace?'

Paolo nodded. 'She come in with Albert.'

'Albert who?'

'Albert, the King of Montenegro,' Dion said. 'Albert Who Do You Think?'

Unfortunately, there was only one Albert in Boston who could be referred to without a last name. Albert White, the guy they'd just robbed.

Albert was a former hero of the Philippine Moro Wars and a former policeman, who'd lost his job, like Joe's own brother, after the strike in '19. Currently he was the owner of White Garage and Automotive Glass Repair (formerly Halloran's Tire and Automotive), White's Downtown Café (formerly Halloran's Lunch Counter), and White's Freight and Transcontinental Shipping (formerly Halloran's Trucking). Rumored to have personally rubbed out Bitsy Halloran. Bitsy got himself shot eleven times in an oak phone booth inside a Rexall Drugstore in Egleston Square. So many shots fired at such close range, they set the booth on fire. It was rumored Albert had bought the charred remains of the phone booth, restored it, and kept it in the study of the home he owned on Ashmont Hill, made all his calls from it.

'So she's Albert's girl.' It deflated Joe to think of her as just another gangster's moll. He'd already had visions of them racing across the country in a stolen car, unencumbered by a past or a future, chasing a red sky and a setting sun all the way to Mexico.

'I seen them together three times,' Paolo said.

'So now it's three times.'

Paolo looked down at his fingers for confirmation. 'Yeah.'

'What's she doing fetching drinks at his poker games then?'

'What else she going to do?' Dion said. 'Retire?'

'No, but . . .'

'Albert's married,' Dion said. 'Who's to say how long a party gal lasts on his arm?'

'She strike you as a party gal?'

Dion slowly thumbed the cap off a bottle of Canadian gin, his flat eyes on Joe. 'She didn't strike me as anything but a gal bagged up our money. I couldn't even tell you what color her hair was. I couldn't—'

'Dark blond. Almost light brown, but not quite.'

'She's Albert's girl.' Dion poured them all a drink.

'So she is,' Joe said.

'Bad enough we just knocked over the man's joint. Don't go getting any ideas about taking anything else from him. All right?'

Joe didn't say anything.

'All right?' Dion repeated.

'All right.' Joe reached for his drink. 'Fine.'

She didn't come into The Shoelace for the next three nights. Joe was sure of it – he'd been there, open to close, every night.

Albert came in, wearing one of his signature pinstripe off-white suits. Like he was in Lisbon or something. He wore them with brown fedoras that matched his brown shoes which matched the brown pinstripes. When the snow came, he wore brown suits with off-white pinstripes, an off-white hat, and white-and-brown spats. When February rolled around, he went in for dark brown suits and dark brown shoes with a black hat, but Joe imagined, for the most part, he'd be easy to gun down at night. Shoot him in an alley from twenty yards away with a cheap pistol. You wouldn't even need a streetlamp to see that white turn red.

Albert, Albert, Joe thought as Albert glided past his bar stool in The Shoelace on the third night, I could kill you if I knew the first thing about killing.

Problem was, Albert didn't go into alleys much, and when he did he had four bodyguards with him. And even if you did get through them and you did kill him – and Joe, no killer, wondered why the fuck he found himself thinking about killing Albert White in the first place – all you'd manage to do would be to derail a business empire for Albert

White's partners, who included the police, the Italians, the Jew mobs in Mattapan, and several legitimate businessmen, including bankers and investors with interests in Cuban and Florida sugarcane. Derailing business like that in a city this small would be like feeding zoo animals with fresh cuts on your hand.

Albert looked at him once. Looked at him in such a way that Joe thought, He knows, he knows. He knows I robbed him. Knows I want his girl. He knows.

But Albert said, 'Got a light?'

Joe struck a match off the bar and lit Albert White's cigarette.

When Albert blew out the match, he blew smoke into Joe's face. He said, 'Thanks, kid,' and walked away, the man's flesh as white as his suit, the man's lips as red as the blood that flowed in and out of his heart.

The fourth day after the robbery, Joe played a hunch and went back to the furniture warehouse. He almost missed her; apparently the secretaries ended their shift the same time as the laborers, and the secretaries ran small while the forklift operators and stevedores cast wider shadows. The men came out with their longshoremen's hooks hanging from the shoulders of their dirty jackets, talking loud and swarming the young women, whistling and telling jokes only they laughed at. The women must have been used to it, though, because they managed to move their own circle out of the larger one, and some of the men stayed behind, and others straggled, and a few more broke off to head toward the worst-kept secret on the docks – a houseboat that had been serving alcohol since the first sun to rise on Boston under Prohibition.

The pack of women stayed tight and moved smoothly up the dock. Joe only saw her because another girl with the same color hair stopped to adjust her heel and Emma's face took her place in the crowd.

Joe left the spot where he'd been standing, near the loading dock of the Gillette Company, and fell into step about fifty yards behind the group. He told himself she was Albert White's girl. Told himself he was out of his mind and he needed to stop this now. Not only should he not be following Albert White's girl along the waterfront of South Boston, he shouldn't even be in the state until he learned for sure whether or not anyone could finger him for the poker game robbery. Tim Hickey was down south on a rum deal and couldn't fill in the blanks about how they'd ended up knocking over the wrong card game, and the Bartolo brothers were keeping their heads down and noses clean until they heard what was what, but here was Joe, supposedly the smart one, sniffing around Emma Gould like a starving dog following the scent of a cook fire.

Walk away, walk away, walk away.

Joe knew the voice was right. The voice was reason. And if not reason, then his guardian angel.

Problem was, he wasn't interested in guardian angels today. He was interested in her.

The group of women walked off the waterfront and dispersed at Broadway Station. Most walked to a bench on the streetcar side, but Emma descended into the subway. Joe gave her a head start, then followed her through the turnstiles and down another set of steps and onto a north-bound train. It was crowded on the train and hot but he never took his eyes off her, which was a good thing because she left the train one stop later, at South Station.

South Station was a transfer station where three subway lines, two el lines, a streetcar line, two bus lines, and the commuter rail all converged. Stepping out of the car and onto the platform turned him into a billiards ball on the break – he was bounced, pinned, and bounced again. He lost sight of her. He was not a tall man like his brothers, one of whom was tall and the other abnormally so. But thank God he wasn't short, just medium. He stepped up on his toes and tried to press through the throng that way. It made the going slower, but he got a flash of her butterscotch hair bobbing by the transfer tunnel to the Atlantic Avenue Elevated.

He reached the platform just as the cars arrived. She stood two doors ahead of him in the same car when the train left the station and the city opened up in front of them, its blues and browns and brick red deepening in the onset of dusk. Windows in the office buildings had turned yellow. Street-lamps came on, block by block. The harbor bled out from the edges of the skyline. Emma leaned against a window and Joe watched it all unfurl behind her. She stared out blankly at the crowded car, her eyes alighting on nothing but wary just the same. They were so pale, her eyes, paler even than her skin. The pale of very cold gin. Her jaw and nose were both slightly pointed and dusted with freckles. Nothing about her invited approach. She seemed locked behind her own cold and beautiful face.

And what will the gentleman be having with his robbery this morning?

Just try not to leave marks.

That's usually what liars say.

When they passed through Batterymarch Station and rattled over the North End, Joe looked down at the ghetto, teeming with Italians – Italian people, Italian dialects, Italian customs and food – and he couldn't help but think of his oldest brother, Danny, the Irish cop who'd loved the Italian ghetto so much he'd lived and worked there. Danny was a big man, taller than just about anyone Joe had ever met. He'd been a hell of a boxer, a hell of a cop, and he knew little of fear. An organizer and vice president of the policemen's union, he'd met the fate of every cop who'd chosen to go out on strike in September 1919 – he'd lost his job without hope of reinstatement and been blackballed from all law enforcement positions on the Eastern Seaboard. It broke him. Or so the story went. He'd ended up in a Negro section of Tulsa, Oklahoma, that had burned to the ground in a riot five years ago. Since then, Joe's family had heard only rumors about his whereabouts and those of his wife, Nora – Austin, Baltimore, Philadelphia.

Growing up, Joe had adored his brother. Then he'd come to hate him. Now, he mostly didn't think about him. When he did, he had to admit, he missed his laugh.

Down the other end of the car, Emma Gould said 'Excuse me, excuse me' as she worked her way toward the doors. Joe looked out the window and saw that they were approaching City Square in Charlestown.

Charlestown. No wonder she hadn't gotten rattled with a

gun pointed at her. In Charlestown, they brought .38s to the dinner table, used the barrels to stir their coffee.

He followed her to a two-story house at the end of Union Street. Just before she reached the house, she took a right down a pathway that ran along the side, and by the time Joe got to the alley behind the house, she was gone. He looked up and down the alley – nothing but similar two-story houses, most of them saltbox shacks with rotting window frames and tar patches in the roof. She could've gone into any of them, but she'd chosen the last walkway on the block. He assumed hers was the blue-gray one he was facing with steel doors over a wooden bulkhead.

Just past the house was a wooden gate. It was locked, so he grabbed the top of it, hoisted himself up, and took a look at another alley, narrower than the one he was in. Aside from a few trash cans, it was empty. He let himself back down and searched his pocket for one of the hairpins he rarely left home without.

Half a minute later he stood on the other side of the gate and waited.

It didn't take long. This time of day – quitting time – it never did. Two pairs of footsteps came up the alley, two men talking about the latest plane that had gone down trying to cross the Atlantic, no sign of the pilot, an Englishman, or the wreckage. One second it was in the air, the next it was gone for good. One of the men knocked on the bulkhead, and after a few seconds, Joe heard him say, 'Blacksmith.'

One of the bulkhead doors was pulled back with a whine

and then a few moments later, it was dropped back in place and locked.

Joe waited five minutes, clocking it, and then he exited the second alley and knocked on the bulkhead.

A muffled voice said, 'What?'

'Blacksmith.'

There was a ratcheting sound as someone threw the bolt back and Joe lifted the bulkhead door. He climbed into the small stairwell and let himself down it, lowering the bulkhead door as he went. At the bottom of the stairwell, he faced a second door. It opened as he was reaching for it. An old baldy guy with a cauliflower nose and blown blood vessels splayed across his cheekbones waved him inside, a grim scowl on his face.

It was an unfinished basement with a wood bar in the center of the dirt floor. The tables were wooden barrels, the chairs made of the cheapest pine.

At the bar, Joe sat down at the end closest to the door, where a woman with fat that hung off her arms like pregnant bellies served him a bucket of warm beer that tasted a little of soap and a little of sawdust, but not a lot like beer or a lot like alcohol. He looked for Emma Gould in the basement gloom, saw only dockworkers, a couple of sailors, and a few working girls. A piano sat against the brick wall under the stairs, unused, a few keys broken. This was not the kind of speak that went in for entertainment much beyond the bar fight that would open up between the sailors and the dockworkers once they realized they were short two working girls.

She came out the door behind the bar, tying a kerchief

off behind her head. She'd traded her blouse and skirt for an off-white fisherman's sweater and brown tweed trousers. She walked the bar, emptying ashtrays and wiping spills, and the woman who'd served Joe his drink removed her apron and went back through the door behind the bar.

When she reached Joe, her eyes flicked on his near-empty bucket. 'You want another?'

'Sure.'

She glanced at his face and didn't seem fond of the result. 'Who told you about the place?'

'Dinny Cooper.'

'Don't know him,' she said.

That makes two of us, Joe thought, wondering where the fuck he'd come up with such a stupid name. *Dinny?* Why didn't he call the guy 'Lunch'?

'He's from Everett.'

She wiped the bar in front of him, still not moving to get his drink. 'Yeah?'

'Yeah. We worked the Chelsea side of the Mystic last week. Dredge work?'

She shook her head.

'Anyway, Dinny pointed across the river, told me about this place. Said you served good beer.'

'Now I know you're lying.'

'Because someone said you serve good beer?'

She stared at him the way she had in the payroll office, like she could see the intestines curled inside him, the pink of his lungs, the thoughts that journeyed among the folds of his brain.

'The beer's not *that* bad,' he said and raised his bucket. 'I had some once in this place this one time? I swear to you it—'

'Butter doesn't melt on your tongue, does it?' she said.

'Miss?'

'Does it?'

He decided to try resigned indignation. 'I'm not lying, miss. But I can go. I can certainly go.' He stood. 'What do I owe you for the first one?'

'Two dimes.'

She held out her hand and he placed the coins in them and she placed them in the pocket of her man's trousers. 'You won't do it.'

'What?' he said.

'Leave. You want me to be so impressed that you *said* you'd leave that I'll decide you're a Clear-Talk Charlie and ask you to stay.'

'Nope.' He shrugged into his coat. 'I'm really going.'

She leaned into the bar. 'Come here.'

He cocked his head.

She crooked a finger at him. 'Come here.'

He moved a couple of stools out of the way and leaned into the bar.

'You see those fellas in the corner, sitting by the table made out of the apple barrel?'

He didn't need to turn his head. He'd seen them the moment he walked in – three of them. Dockworkers by the look of them, ship masts for shoulders, rocks for hands, eyes you didn't want to catch.

'I see 'em.'

'They're my cousins. You see a family resemblance, don't you?'

'No.'

She shrugged. 'You know what they do for work?'

Their lips were close enough that if they'd opened their mouths and unfurled their tongues, the tips would have met.

'I have no idea.'

'They find guys like you who lie about guys named Dinny and they beat them to death.' She inched her elbows forward and their faces grew even closer. 'Then they throw them in the river.'

Joe's scalp and the backs of his ears itched. 'Quite the occupation.'

'Beats robbing poker games, though, doesn't it?'

For a moment Joe forgot how to move his face.

'Say something clever,' Emma Gould said. 'Maybe about that sock you put in my mouth. I want to hear something slick and clever.'

Joe said nothing.

'And while you're thinking of things,' Emma Gould said, 'think of this – they're watching us right now. If I tug this earlobe? You won't make the stairs.'

He looked at the earlobe she'd indicated with a flick of her pale eyes. The right one. It looked like a chickpea, but softer. He wondered what it would taste like first thing in the morning.

Joe glanced down at the bar. 'And if I pull this trigger?'

She followed his gaze, saw the pistol he'd placed between them.

'You won't *reach* your earlobe,' he said.

Her eyes left the pistol and rose up his forearm in such a way he could feel the hairs parting. She sculled across the center of his chest and then up his throat and over his chin. When she found his eyes, hers were fuller and sharper, lit with something that had entered the world centuries before civilized things.

'I get off at midnight,' she said.

CHAPTER TWO

The Lack in Her

Joe lived on the top floor of a boardinghouse in the West End, just a short walk from the riot of Scollay Square. The boardinghouse was owned and operated by the Tim Hickey Mob, which had long had a presence in the city but had flourished in the six years since the Eighteenth Amendment took effect.

The first floor was usually occupied by Paddys right off the boat with woolen brogues and bodies of gristle. One of Joe's jobs was to meet them at the docks and lead them to Hickey-owned soup kitchens, give them brown bread and white chowder and gray potatoes. He brought them back to the boardinghouse where they were packed three to a room on firm, clean mattresses while their clothes were laundered in the basement by the older whores. After a week or so, once they'd gotten some strength back and freed their hair of nits and their mouths of poisoned teeth, they'd sign voter registration cards and pledge bottomless support to Hickey candidates in next year's elections. Then they were set loose with the names and addresses of other immigrants from the same villages or counties back home who might be counted on to find them jobs straightaway.

On the second floor of the boardinghouse, accessible only by a separate entrance, was the casino. The third was the whore floor. Joe lived on the fourth, in a room at the end of the hall. There was a nice bathroom on the floor that he shared with whichever high rollers were in town at the moment and Penny Palumbo, the star whore of Tim Hickey's stable. Penny was twenty-five but looked seventeen and her hair was the color bottled honey got when the sun moved through it. A man had jumped off a roof over Penny Palumbo; another had stepped off a boat; a third, instead of killing himself, killed another guy. Joe liked her well enough; she was nice and wonderful to look at. But if her face looked seventeen, he'd bet her brain looked ten. It was solely occupied, as far as Joe could tell, by three songs and some vague wishes about becoming a dressmaker.

Some mornings, depending on who got down to the casino first, one brought the other coffee. This morning, she brought it to him and they sat by the window in his room looking out at Scollay Square with its striped awnings and tall billboards as the first milk trucks puttered along Tremont Row. Penny told him that last night a fortune-teller had assured her she was destined to either die young or become a Trinitarian Pentecostal in Kansas. When Joe asked her if she was worried about dying, she said sure, but not half as much as moving to Kansas.

When she left, he heard her talking to someone in the hall,

and then Tim Hickey was standing in his doorway. Tim wore a dark pinstripe vest, unbuttoned, matching trousers, and a white shirt with the collar unbuttoned and no tie. Tim was a trim man with a fine head of white hair and the sad, helpless eyes of a death row chaplain.

'Mr Hickey, sir.'

'Morning, Joe.' He drank coffee from an old-fashioned glass that caught the morning light rising off the sills. 'That bank in Pittsfield?'

'Yeah?' Joe said.

'The guy you want to see comes in here Thursdays, but you'll find him at the Upham's Corner place most other nights. He'll keep a homburg on the bar to the right of his drink. He'll give you the lay of the building and the out-route too.'

'Thanks, Mr Hickey.'

Hickey acknowledged that with a tip of his glass. 'Another thing – 'member that dealer we discussed last month?'

'Carl,' Joe said, 'yeah.'

'He's up to it again.'

Carl Laubner, one of their blackjack dealers, had come from a joint that ran dirty games, and they couldn't convince him to run a clean game here, not if any of the players in question looked less than 100 percent white. So if an Italian or a Greek sat down at the table, forget it. Carl magically pulled tens and aces for hole cards all night, or at least until the swarthier gents left the table.

'Fire him,' Hickey said. 'Soon as he comes in.'

'Yes, sir.'

'We don't run that horseshit here. Agreed?'

'Absolutely, Mr Hickey. Absolutely.'

'And fix the twelve slot, will you? It's running loose. We might run a straight house, but we're not a fucking charity, are we, Joe?'

Joe wrote himself a note. 'No, sir, we are not.'

Tim Hickey ran one of the few clean casinos in Boston, which made it one of the most popular casinos in town, particularly for the high-class play. Tim had taught Joe that rigged games fleeced a chump maybe two, three times at the most before he got wise and stopped playing. Tim didn't want to fleece someone a couple of times; he wanted to drain them for the rest of their lives. Keep 'em playing, keep 'em drinking, he told Joe, and they will fork over all their green and thank you for relieving them of the weight.

'The people we service?' Tim said more than once. 'They visit the night. But we live in it. They rent what we own. That means when they come to play in our sandbox, we make a profit off every grain.'

Tim Hickey was one of the smarter men Joe had ever known. At the start of Prohibition, when the mobs in the city were split down ethnic lines – Italians mixing only with Italians, Jews mixing only with Jews, Irish mixing only with Irish – Hickey mixed with everyone. He aligned himself with Giancarlo Calabrese, who ran the Pescatore Mob while old man Pescatore was in prison, and together they started dealing in Caribbean rum when everyone else was dealing in whiskey. By the time the Detroit and New York gangs had leveraged their power to turn everyone else into subcontractors in the whiskey trade, the Hickey and Pescatore mobs had cornered the market on sugar and molasses. The product came out of Cuba mostly, crossed the Florida Straits, got turned into rum on U.S. soil, and took midnight runs up the Eastern Seaboard to be sold at an 80 percent markup.

As soon as Tim had returned from his most recent trip to Tampa, he'd discussed the botched job at the Southie furniture warehouse with Joe. He commended Joe on being smart enough not to go for the house take in the counting room ('That avoided a war right there,' Tim said), and told him when he got to the bottom of why they'd been given such a dangerously bad tip, someone was going to hang from rafters as high as the Custom House spire.

Joe wanted to believe him because the alternative was to believe Tim had sent them to that warehouse because he'd *wanted* to start a war with Albert White. It wouldn't be beyond Tim to sacrifice men he'd mentored since they were boys with the aim of cornering the rum market for good. In fact, nothing was beyond Tim. Absolutely nothing. That's what it took to stay on top in the rackets – everyone had to know you'd long ago amputated your conscience.

In Joe's room now, Tim added a spot of rum from his flask to his coffee and took a sip. He offered the flask to Joe, but Joe shook his head. Tim returned the flask to his pocket. 'Where you been lately?'

'I been here.'

Hickey held his gaze. 'You've been out every night this week and the week before. You got a girl?'

Joe thought about lying but couldn't see the point. 'I do, yeah.'

'She a nice girl?'

'She's lively. She's' – Joe couldn't think of the precise word – 'something.'

Hickey came off the doorjamb. 'You got yourself a blood sticker, huh?' He mimed a needle plunging into his arm. 'I can see it.' He came over and clamped a hand on the back of Joe's neck. 'You don't get many shots at the good ones. Not in our line. She cook?'

'She does.' Truth was, Joe had no idea.

'That's important. Not if they're good or bad, just that they're willing to do it.' Hickey let go of his neck and walked back to the doorway. 'Talk to that fella about the Pittsfield thing.'

'I will, sir.'

'Good man,' Tim said and headed downstairs to the office he kept behind the casino cashier.

Carl Laubner ended up working two more nights before Joe remembered to fire him. Joe had forgotten a few things lately, including two appointments with Hymie Drago to move the merch' from the Karshman Furs job. He had remembered to get to the slot machine and tighten the wheels good, but by the time Laubner came in on his shift that night, Joe was off with Emma Gould again.

Since that night at the basement speakeasy in Charlestown, he and Emma had seen each other most nights. Most, not every. The other nights she was with Albert White, a situation Joe had thus far managed to characterize as annoying, though it was fast approaching the intolerable.

When Joe wasn't with Emma, all he could think about was when he would be. And then when they did meet, keeping their hands off each other went from an unlikely proposition to an impossible one. When her uncle's speakeasy was closed, they had sex in it. When her parents and siblings were out of the apartment she shared with them, they had sex in it. They had sex in Joe's car and sex in his room after he'd snuck her up the back stairs. They had sex on a cold hill, in a stand of bare trees overlooking the Mystic River, and on a cold November beach overlooking Savin Hill Cove in Dorchester. Standing, sitting, lying down – it didn't make much difference to them. Inside, outside – same thing. When they had the luxury of an hour together, they filled it with as many new tricks and new positions as they could dream up. But when they had only a few minutes, then a few minutes would do.

What they rarely did was talk. At least not about anything outside the borders of their seemingly bottomless addiction to each other.

Behind Emma's pale eyes and pale skin lay something coiled and caged. And not caged in a way that it wanted to come out. Caged in a way that demanded nothing come in. The cage opened when she took him inside her and for as long as they could sustain their lovemaking. In those moments, her eyes were open and searching and he could see her soul back there and the red light of her heart and what-ever dreams she may have clung to as a child, temporarily untethered and freed of their cellar and its dark walls and padlocked door.

Once he'd pulled out of her, though, and her breathing slowed to normal, he would watch those things recede like the tide.

Didn't matter, though. He was starting to suspect he was in love with her. In those rare moments when the cage opened and he was invited in, he found a person desperate to trust, desperate to love, hell, desperate to live. She just needed to see he was worthy of risking that trust, that love, that life.

And he would be.

He turned twenty years old that winter and he knew what he wanted to do with the rest of his life. He wanted to become the one man Emma Gould put all her faith in.

As the winter wore on, they risked appearing in public together a few times. Only on the nights when she had it on good authority that Albert White and his key men were out of town and only at establishments that were owned by Tim Hickey or his partners.

One of Tim's partners was Phil Cregger, who owned the Venetian Garden restaurant on the first floor of the Bromfield Hotel. Joe and Emma went there on a frigid night that smelled of snow even though the sky was clear. They'd just checked their coats and hats when a group exited the private room behind the kitchen and Joe knew them for what they were by their cigar smoke and the practiced bonhomie in their voices before he ever saw their faces – pols.

Aldermen and selectmen and city councillors and fire captains and police captains and prosecutors – the shiny, smiling, grubby battery that kept the city's lights on, barely. Kept the trains running and the traffic signals working, barely. Kept the populace ever aware that those services and a thousand more, big and small, could end – *would* end – were it not for their constant vigilance.

He saw his father at the same moment his father noticed him. It was, as it usually was if they hadn't seen each other in a while, unsettling if for no other reason than how completely they mirrored each other. Joe's father was sixty. He'd sired Joe late after producing two sons at a more respectably youthful age. But whereas Connor and Danny carried the genetic strains of both parents in their faces and bodies and certainly their height (which came from the Fennessey side of the family, where the men grew tall), Joe had come out the spitting image of his old man. Same height, same build, same hard jawline, same nose and sharp cheekbones and eyes sunk back in their sockets just a little farther than normal, which made it all the harder for people to read what he was thinking. The only difference between Joe and his father was one of color. Joe's eyes were blue whereas his father's were green; Joe's hair was the color of wheat, his father's the color of flax. Otherwise, Joe's father looked at him and saw his own youth mocking him. Joe looked at his father and saw liver spots and loose flesh, Death standing at the end of his bed at 3 A.M., tapping an impatient foot.

After a few farewell handshakes and backslaps, his father broke from the crowd as the men lined up for their coats. He stood before his son. He thrust out his hand. 'How are you?'

Joe shook his hand. 'Not bad, sir. You?'

'Tip-top. I was promoted last month.'

'Deputy superintendent of the BPD,' Joe said. 'I heard.'

'And you? Where are you working these days?'

You'd have to have known Thomas Coughlin a long time to spot the effects of alcohol on him. It was never to be found in his speech, which remained smooth and firm and of consistent volume even after half a bottle of good Irish. It wasn't to be found in any glassiness of the eyes. But if you knew where to look for it, you could find something predatory and mischievous in the glow of his handsome face, something that sized you up, found your weaknesses, and debated whether to dine on them.

'Dad,' Joe said, 'this is Emma Gould.'

Thomas Coughlin took her hand and kissed the knuckles. 'A pleasure, Miss Gould.' He tilted his head to the maître d'. 'The corner table, Gerard, please.' He smiled at Joe and Emma. 'Do you mind if I join you? I'm famished.'

They got through the salads pleasantly enough.

Thomas told stories of Joe's childhood, the point of which was invariably what a scamp Joe had been, how irrepressible and full of beans. In his father's retelling, they were whimsical stories fit for the Hal Roach shorts at a Saturday matinee. His father left out how the stories had usually ended – with a slap or the strap.

Emma smiled and chuckled at all the right places, but Joe could see she was pretending. They were all pretending. Joe and Thomas pretended to be bound by the love between a father and son and Emma pretended not to notice that they weren't.

After the story about six-year-old Joe in his father's garden – a story told so many times over the years Joe could predict to a breath his father's pauses – Thomas asked Emma where her family hailed from.

'Charlestown,' she said, and Joe worried he heard a hint of defiance in her voice.

34

'No, I mean before they came here. You're clearly Irish. Do you know where your ancestors were born?'

The waiter cleared the salad plates as Emma said, 'My mother's father was from Kerry and my father's mother was from Cork.'

'I'm from just outside Cork,' Thomas said with uncommon delight.

Emma sipped her water but didn't say anything, a part of her missing suddenly. Joe had seen this before – she had a way of disconnecting from a situation if it wasn't to her liking. Her body remained, like something left behind in the chair during her escape, but the essence of her, whatever made Emma *Emma,* was gone.

'What was her maiden name, your grandmother?'

'I don't know,' she said.

'You don't *know?*'

Emma shrugged. 'She's dead.'

'But it's your heritage.' Thomas was flummoxed.

Emma gave that another shrug. She lit a cigarette. Thomas showed no reaction but Joe knew he was aghast. Flappers appalled him on countless levels – women smoking, flashing thigh, lowering necklines, appearing drunk in public without shame or fear of civic scorn.

'How long have you known my son?' Thomas smiled.

'Few months.'

'Are you two—?'

'Dad.'

'Joseph?'

'We don't know what we are.'

Secretly he'd hoped Emma would take the opportunity to

clarify what, in fact, they were, but instead she shot him a quick look that asked how much longer they had to sit here and went back to smoking, her eyes drifting, anchorless, around the grand room.

The entrées reached the table, and they passed the next twenty minutes talking about the quality of the steaks and the béarnaise sauce and the new carpeting Cregger had recently installed.

During dessert, Thomas lit his own cigarette. 'So what is it you do, dear?'

'I work at Papadikis Furniture.'

'Which department?'

'Secretarial.'

'Did my son pilfer a couch? Is that how you met?'

'Dad,' Joe said.

'I'm just wondering how you met,' his father said.

Emma lit a cigarette and looked out at the room. 'This is a real swank place.'

'It's just that I'm well aware how my son earns a living. I can only assume that if you've come into contact with him, it was either during a crime or in an establishment populated by rough characters.'

'Dad,' Joe said, 'I was hoping we'd have a nice dinner.'

'I thought we just did. Miss Gould?'

Emma looked over at him.

'Have my questions this evening made you uncomfortable?'

Emma locked him in that cool gaze of hers, the one that could freeze a fresh coat of roofing tar. 'I don't know what you're on about. And I don't particularly care.'

Thomas leaned back in his chair and sipped his coffee. 'I'm on about you being the type of lass who consorts with criminals, which may not be the best thing for your reputation. The fact that the criminal in question happens to be my son isn't the issue. It's that my son, criminal or no, is still my son and I have paternal feelings for him, feelings that cause me to question the wisdom of his consorting with the type of woman who knowingly consorts with criminals.' Thomas placed his coffee cup back on the saucer and smiled at her. 'Did you follow all that?'

Joe stood. 'Okay, we're going.'

But Emma didn't move. She dropped her chin to the heel of her hand and considered Thomas for some time, the cigarette smoldering next to her ear. 'My uncle mentioned a copper he has on his payroll, name of Coughlin. That you?' She gave him a tight smile to match his own and took a drag off her cigarette.

'This uncle would be your Uncle Robert, the one everyone calls Bobo?'

She flicked her eyelids in the affirmative.

'The police officer to whom you refer is named Elmore Conklin, Miss Gould. He's stationed in Charlestown and is known to collect shakedown payments from illegal establishments like Bobo's. I rarely get over to Charlestown, myself. But as deputy superintendent, I'd be happy to take a more focused interest in your uncle's establishment.' Thomas stubbed out his cigarette. 'Would that please you, dear?'

Emma held out her hand to Joe. 'I need to powder.'

Joe gave her tip money for the ladies'-room attendant and

they watched her cross the restaurant. Joe wondered if she'd return to the table or grab her coat and just keep walking.

His father removed his pocket watch from his vest and flicked it open. Snapped it closed just as quickly and returned it to its pocket. The watch was the old man's most prized possession, an eighteen-karat Patek Philippe given to him over two decades ago by a grateful bank president.

Joe asked him, 'Was any of that necessary?'

'I didn't start the fight, Joseph, so don't criticize how I finished it.' His father sat back in his chair and crossed one leg over the other. Some men wore their power as if it were a coat they couldn't get to fit or to stop itching. Thomas Coughlin wore his like it had been tailored for him in London. He surveyed the room and nodded at a few people he knew before looking back at his son. 'If I thought you were just making your way in the world on an unconventional path, do you think I'd take issue with it?'

'Yes,' Joe said, 'I do.'

His father gave that a soft smile and a softer shrug. 'I've been a police officer for thirty-seven years and I've learned one thing above all else.'

'That crime never pays,' Joe said, 'unless you do it at an institutional level.'

Another soft smile and a small tip of the head. 'No, Joseph. No. What I've learned is that violence procreates. And the children your violence produces will return to you as savage, mindless things. You won't recognize them as yours, but they'll recognize you. They'll mark you as deserving of their punishment.'

Joe had heard variations of this speech over the years.

What his father failed to recognize – besides the fact that he was repeating himself – was that general theories need not apply to particular people. Not if the people – or person – in question was determined enough to make his own rules and smart enough to get everyone else to play by them.

Joe was only twenty, but he already knew he was that type of person.

But to humor the old man, if for no other reason, he asked, 'And what exactly are these violent offspring punishing me for again?'

'The carelessness of their reproduction.' His father leaned forward, elbows on the table, palms pressed together. 'Joseph.'

'Joe.'

'Joseph, violence breeds violence. It's an absolute.' He unclasped his hands and looked at his son. 'What you put out into the world will always come back for you.'

'Yeah, Dad, I read my catechism.'

His father tipped his head in recognition as Emma came out of the powder room and crossed to the coat-check room. His eyes tracking her, he said to Joe, 'But it never comes back in a way you can predict.'

'I'm sure it doesn't.'

'You're not sure of anything except your own certainty. Confidence you haven't earned always has the brightest glow.' Thomas watched Emma hand her ticket to the coat-check girl. 'She's quite easy on the eyes.'

Joe said nothing.

'Outside of that, though,' his father said, 'I fail to grasp what you see in her.'

'Because she's from Charlestown?'

'Well, that doesn't help,' his father said. 'Her father was a pimp back in the old days and her uncle has killed at least two men that we know of. But I could overlook all that, Joseph, if she weren't so ...'

'What?'

'Dead inside.' His father consulted his watch again and barely suppressed the shudder of a yawn. 'It's late.'

'She's not dead inside,' Joe said. 'Something in her is just sleeping.'

'That something?' his father said as Emma returned with their coats. 'It never wakes up again, son.'

On the street, walking to his car, Joe said, 'You couldn't have been a little more ... ?'

'What?'

'Engaged in the conversation? Social?'

'All the time we been together,' she said, 'all you ever talk about is how much you hate that man.'

'Is it *all* the time?'

'Pretty much.'

Joe shook his head. 'And I've never said I hate my father.'

'Then what have you said?'

'That we don't get along. We've never gotten along.'

'And why's that?'

'Because we're too fucking alike.'

'Or because you hate him.'

'I don't hate him,' Joe said, knowing it, above all things, to be true.

'Then maybe you should climb under his covers tonight.'

'What?'

'He sits there and looks at me like I'm trash? Asks about my family like he knows we're no good all the way back to the Old Country? Calls me fucking *dear*?' She stood on the sidewalk shaking as the first snowflakes appeared from the black above them. The tears in her voice began to fall from her eyes. 'We're not people. We're not respectable. We're just the Goulds from Union Street. Charlestown trash. We tat the lace for *your* fucking curtains.'

Joe held up his hands. 'Where is this coming from?' He reached for her and she took a step back.

'Don't touch me.'

'Okay.'

'It comes from a lifetime, okay, of getting the high hat and the icy mitt from people like your father. People who, who, who ... who confuse being lucky with being better. We're not less than you. We're not shit.'

'I didn't say you were.'

'*He did.*'

'No.'

'I'm not shit,' she whispered, her mouth half open to the night, the snow mingling with the tears streaming down her face.

He put his arms out and stepped in close. 'May I?'

She stepped into his embrace but kept her own arms by her sides. He held her to him and she wept into his chest and he told her repeatedly that she was not shit, she was not less than anyone, and he loved her, he loved her.

Later, they lay in his bed while thick, wet snowflakes flung themselves at the window like moths.

'That was weak,' she said.

'What?'

'On the street. I was weak.'

'You weren't weak. You were honest.'

'I don't cry in front of people.'

'Well, you can with me.'

'You said you loved me.'

'Yeah.'

'Do you?'

He looked in her pale, pale eyes. 'Yes.'

After a minute she said, 'I can't say it back.'

He told himself that wasn't the same as saying she didn't feel it.

'Okay.'

'Is it really okay? Because some guys need to hear it back.'

Some guys? How many guys had told her they loved her before he came along?

'I'm tougher than them,' he said and wished it were true.

The window rattled in the dark February gusts and a foghorn bayed and down in Scollay Square several horns beeped in anger.

'What do you want?' he asked her.

She shrugged and bit a hangnail and stared across his body out the window.

'For a lot of things to never have happened to me.'

'What things?'

She shook her head, drifting away from him now.

'And sun,' she mumbled after a while, her lips sleep swollen. 'Lots and lots of sun.'

CHAPTER THREE

Hickey's Termite

Tim Hickey once told Joe the smallest mistake sometimes casts the longest shadow. Joe wondered what Tim would have said about daydreaming behind the wheel of a getaway car while you were parked outside a bank. Maybe not daydreaming – fixating. On a woman's back. More specifically, on Emma's back. On the birthmark he'd seen there. Tim probably would have said, then again, sometimes it's the biggest mistakes that cast the longest shadows, you moron.

Another thing Tim was fond of saying was when a house falls down, the first termite to bite into it is just as much to blame as the last. Joe didn't get that one – the first termite would be long fucking dead by the time the last termite got his teeth into the wood. Wouldn't he? Every time Tim made the analogy, Joe resolved to look into termite life expectancy, but then he'd forget to do it until the next time Tim brought it up, usually when he was drunk and there was a lull in the conversation, and everyone at the table would get the same look on their faces: What is it with Tim and the fucking termites already?

Tim Hickey got his hair cut once a week at Aslem's on Charles Street. One Tuesday, some of those hairs ended up in his mouth when he was shot in the back of the head on his way to the barber's chair. He lay on the checkerboard tile as the blood rolled past the tip of his nose and the shooter emerged from behind the coatrack, shaky and wide-eyed. The coatrack clattered to the tile and one of the barbers jumped in place. The shooter stepped over Tim Hickey's corpse and gave the witnesses a hunched series of nods, as if embarrassed, and let himself out.

When Joe heard, he was in bed with Emma. After he hung up the phone, Emma sat up in bed while he told her. She rolled a cigarette and looked at Joe while she licked the paper – she always looked at him when she licked the paper – and then she lit it. 'Did he mean anything to you? Tim?'

'I don't know,' Joe said.

'How don't you know?'

'It's not one thing or the other, I guess.'

Tim had found Joe and the Bartolo brothers when they were kids setting fire to newsstands. One morning they'd take money from the *Globe* to burn down one of the *Standard*'s stands. The next day they'd take a payoff from the *American* to torch the *Globe*'s. Tim hired them to burn down the 51 Café. They graduated to late-afternoon home rips in Beacon Hill, the back doors left unlocked by cleaning women or handymen on Tim's payroll. When they worked a job Tim gave them, he set a flat price, but if they worked their own jobs, they paid Tim his tribute and took the lion's share for themselves. In that regard, Tim had been a great boss.

Joe had watched him strangle Harvey Boule, though. It had been over opium, a woman, or a German shorthaired pointer; to this day Joe had only heard rumors. But Harvey had walked into the casino and he and Tim got to talking and then Tim snapped the electric cord off one of the green banker's lamps and wrapped it around Harvey's neck. Harvey was a huge guy and he carried Tim around the casino floor for about a minute, all the whores running for cover, all of Hickey's gun monkeys pointing their guns right at Harvey. Joe watched the realization dawn in Harvey Boule's eyes – even if he got Tim to stop strangling him, Tim's goons would empty four revolvers and one automatic into him. He dropped to his knees and soiled himself with a loud venting sound. He lay on his stomach, gasping, as Tim pressed his knee between his shoulder blades and wrapped the excess cord tight around one hand. He twisted and pulled back all the harder and Harvey kicked hard enough to knock off both shoes.

Tim snapped his fingers. One of his gun monkeys handed him a pistol and Tim put it to Harvey's ear. A whore said, 'Oh, God,' but just as Tim went to pull the trigger, Harvey's eyes turned hopeless and confused, and he moaned his final breath into the imitation Oriental. Tim sat back on Harvey's spine and handed the gun back to his goon. He peered at the profile of the man he'd killed.

Joe had never seen anyone die before. Less than two minutes before, Harvey had asked the girl who brought him his martini to get him the score of the Sox game. Tipped her good too. Checked his watch and slipped it back into his vest. Took a sip of his martini. Less than two minutes before, and now he was fucking *gone*? To where? No one knew. To God, to the devil, to purgatory, or worse, maybe to nowhere. Tim stood and smoothed his snow-white hair and pointed in a vague way at the casino manager. 'Freshen everyone's drinks. On Harvey.'

A couple of people laughed nervously but most everyone else looked sick.

That wasn't the only person Tim had killed or ordered killed in the last four years, but it had been the one Joe witnessed.

And now Tim himself. Gone. Not coming back. As if he'd never been.

'You ever see anyone killed?' Joe asked Emma.

She looked back at him steadily for a bit, smoking the cigarette, chewing a hangnail. 'Yeah.'

'Where do you think they go?'

'The funeral home.'

He stared at her until she smiled that tiny smile of hers, her curls dangling in front of her eyes.

'I think they go nowhere,' she said.

'I'm starting to think that too,' Joe said. He sat up and gave her a hard kiss and she returned it just as hard. Her ankles crossed at his back. She ran her hand through his hair and he looked into her, feeling if he stopped looking at her, he'd miss something, something important that would happen in her face, something he'd never forget.

'What if there is no After? And *this*' – she ground herself down on him – 'is all we get?'

'I love this,' he said.

She laughed. 'I love this too.'

'In general? Or with me?'

She put her cigarette out. She took his face in her hands when she kissed him. She rocked back and forth. 'With you.'

But he wasn't the only one she did this with, was he?

There was still Albert. Still Albert.

A couple days later, in the billiards room off the casino, Joe was shooting pool alone when Albert White walked in with the confidence of someone who expected an obstacle to be removed before he reached it. Walking in beside him was his chief gun monkey, Brenny Loomis, Loomis looking right at Joe like he'd looked at him from the floor of the gaming room.

Joe's heart folded itself around the blade of a knife. And stopped.

Albert White said, 'You must be Joe.'

Joe willed himself to move. He met Albert's outstretched hand. 'Joe Coughlin, yeah. Nice to meet you.'

'Good to put a face to a name, Joe.' Albert pumped his hand like the pumping would get water to a fire.

'Yes, sir.'

'This is Brendan Loomis,' Albert said, 'a friend of mine.'

Joe shook Loomis's hand, and it was like putting his hand between two cars as they backed into each other. Loomis cocked his head and his small brown eyes roamed over Joe's face. When Joe got the hand back, he had to resist the urge to wring it. Loomis, meanwhile, wiped his own hand with a silk handkerchief, his face a rock. His eyes left Joe and looked around the room like he had plans for it. He was good with a gun, they said, and great with a knife, but most of his victims he just beat to death.

Albert said, 'I've seen you before, right?'

Joe searched his face for signs of mirth. 'I don't think so.'

'No, I have. Bren', you seen this guy before?'

Brenny Loomis picked up the nine ball and examined it. 'No.'

Joe felt a relief so overpowering he worried he might lose control of his bladder.

'The Shoelace.' Albert snapped his fingers. 'You're in there sometimes, aren't you?'

'I am,' Joe said.

'That's it, that's it.' Albert clapped Joe on the shoulder. 'I run this house now. You know what that means?'

'I don't.'

'Means I need you to pack up the room where you've been living.' He raised an index finger. 'But I don't want you to feel like I'm putting you on the street.'

'Okay.'

'It's just this is a swell joint. We have a lot of ideas for it.'

'Absolutely.'

Albert put a hand on Joe's arm just above the elbow. His wedding band flashed under the light. It was silver. Celtic snake patterns were etched into it. A couple of diamonds too, small ones.

'You think about what kind of earner you want to be. Okay? Just think about it. Take some time. But know this – you can't work on your own. Not in this town. Not anymore.'

Joe turned his gaze away from the wedding band and the hand on his arm, looked Albert White in his friendly eyes. 'I have no desire to work on my own, sir. I paid tribute to Tim Hickey, rain or shine.'

Albert White got a look like he didn't like hearing Tim Hickey's name uttered in the place he now owned. He patted Joe's arm. 'I know you did. I know you did good work too. Top-notch. But we don't do business with outsiders. And an independent contractor? That's an outsider. We're building a great team, Joe. I promise you – an *amazing* team.' He poured himself a drink from Tim's decanter, didn't offer anyone else one. He carried it over to the pool table and hoisted himself up on the rail, looked at Joe. 'Let me just say one thing plain – you're too smart for the stuff you've been pulling. You're nickel-and-diming with two dumb guineas – hey, they're great friends, I'm sure, but they're stupid and they're wops and they'll be dead before they're thirty. You? You can keep on the path you're on. No commitments, but no friends. A house, but no home.' He slid off the pool table. 'If you don't want a home, that's fine. I promise. But you can't operate anywhere in the city limits. You want to carve something out on the South Shore, go ahead. Try the North Shore, if the Italians let you live once they hear about you. But the city?' He pointed at the floor. 'That's organized now, Joe. No tributes, just employees. And employers. Is there any part of this I've been unclear on?'

'No.'

'Vague about?'

'No, Mr White.'

Albert White crossed his arms and nodded, looked at his

shoes. 'You got anything lined up? Any jobs I should know about?'

Joe had spent the last of Tim Hickey's money to pay the guy who'd given him the info he needed for the Pittsfield job.

'No,' Joe said. 'Nothing lined up.'

'You need money?'

'Mr White, sir?'

'Money.' Albert reached into his pocket with a hand that had run over Emma's pubic bone. Gripped her hair. He peeled two ten spots off his wad and slapped them into Joe's palm. 'I don't want you thinking on an empty stomach.'

'Thanks.'

Albert patted Joe's cheek with that same hand. 'I hope this ends well.'

'We could leave,' Emma said.

'Leave?' he said. 'Like together?'

They were in her bedroom in the middle of the day, the only time her house was empty of the three sisters and the three brothers and the bitter mother and angry father.

'We could leave,' she said again, as if she didn't believe it herself.

'And go where? Live on what? And do you mean together?'

She didn't say anything. Twice he'd asked the question, twice she'd ignored it.

'I don't know much about honest work,' he said.

'Who said it needs to be honest?'

He looked around the grim room she shared with two

sisters. The wallpaper had come off the horsehair plaster by the window and two of the panes were cracked. They could see their breath in here.

'We'd have to go pretty far,' he said. 'New York's a closed town. Philly too. Detroit, forget about it. Chicago, KC, Milwaukee – all shut to a guy like me unless I want to join a mob as low man on the totem.'

'So we go west, as the man said. Or down south.' She nuzzled her nose into the side of his neck and took a deep breath, a softness seeming to grow in her. 'We'll need stake money.'

'We got this job lined up for Saturday. You free Saturday?'

'To leave?'

'Yeah.'

'I've got to see You Know Who Saturday night.'

'Fuck him.'

'Well, yeah,' she said, 'that's the general plan.'

'No, I mean—'

'I know what you mean.'

'He's a bad fucking guy,' Joe said, his eyes on her back, on that birthmark the color of wet sand.

She looked at him with a mild disappointment that was all the more dismissive for being so mild. 'No, he's not.'

'You stick up for him?'

'I'll tell you he's not a bad guy. He's not *my* guy. He's not someone I love or admire or anything. But he's not *bad*. Don't always try to make things so simple.'

'He killed Tim. Or ordered him killed.'

'And Tim, he, what, he made his living handing out turkeys to orphans?'

'No, but—'

'But what? No one's good, no one's bad. Everyone's just trying to make their way.' She lit a cigarette and shook the match until it was black and smoldering. 'Stop fucking judging everyone.'

He couldn't stop looking at her birthmark, getting lost in its sand, swirling with it. 'You're still going to see him.'

'Don't start. If we're truly leaving town, then—'

'We're leaving town.' Joe would leave the country if it meant no man ever touched her again.

'Where?'

'Biloxi,' he said, realizing as he said it that it actually wasn't a bad idea. 'Tim had a lot of friends there. Guys I met. Rum guys. Albert gets his supply from Canada. He's a whiskey guy. So if we get to the Gulf Coast – Biloxi, Mobile, maybe even New Orleans, if we buy off the right people – we might be okay. That's rum country.'

She thought about it a bit, that birthmark rippling every time she stretched up the bed to tap ash off her cigarette. 'I'm supposed to see him for that new hotel opening. The one on Providence Street?'

'The Statler?'

She nodded. 'Supposed to have radios in every room. Marble from Italy.'

'And?'

'And if I go to that, he'll be with his wife. He just wants me there 'cuz I, I dunno, 'cuz it excites him to see me when his wife's on his arm. And after that, I know for a fact he's going to Detroit for a few days to talk to new suppliers.'

'So?'

'So, it'll buy us all the time we need. By the time he comes looking for me again, we'll have a three- or four-day head start.'

Joe thought it through. 'Not bad.'

'I know,' she said with another smile. 'You think you can clean yourself up, get over to the Statler Saturday? Say, about seven?'

'Absolutely.'

'Then we're gone,' she said and looked over her shoulder at him. 'But no more talk about Albert being a bad guy. My brother's got a job 'cuz of him. Last winter, he bought my mother a coat.'

'Well, then.'

'I don't want to fight.'

Joe didn't want to fight either. Every time they did, he lost, found himself apologizing for things he hadn't even done, hadn't even thought of doing, found himself apologizing for not doing them, for not thinking of doing them. It hurt his fucking head.

He kissed her shoulder. 'So we won't fight.'

She gave him a flutter of eyelashes. 'Hooray.'

Leaving the First National job in Pittsfield, Dion and Paolo had just jumped in the car when Joe backed into the lamppost because he'd been thinking about the birthmark. The wet sand color of it and the way it moved between her shoulder blades when she looked back at him and told him she might love him, how it did the same thing when she said Albert White wasn't such a bad guy. A fucking peach actually was ol' Albert. Friend of the common man, buy your mother a winter coat as long as you used your body to keep *him* warm. The birthmark was the shape of a butterfly but jagged and sharp around the edges, Joe thinking that might sum up Emma too, and then telling himself forget it, they were leaving town tonight, all their problems solved. She loved him. Wasn't that the point? Everything else was heading for the rearview mirror. Whatever Emma Gould had, he wanted it for breakfast, lunch, dinner, and snacks. He wanted it for the rest of his life – the freckles along her collarbone and the bridge of her nose, the hum that left her throat after she'd finished laughing, the way she turned 'four' into a two-syllable word.

Dion and Paolo ran out of the bank.

They climbed in the back.

'*Drive,*' Dion said.

A tall, bald guy with a gray shirt and black suspenders came out of the bank, armed with a club. A club wasn't a gun, but it could still cause trouble if the guy got close enough.

Joe rammed the gearshift into first with the heel of his hand and hit the gas, but the car went backward instead of forward. Fifteen feet backward. The eyes of the guy with the club popped in surprise.

Dion shouted, 'Whoa! Whoa!'

Joe stomped the brake and the clutch. He rammed the shift out of reverse and into first, but they still hit the lamppost. The impact wasn't bad, just embarrassing. The yokel with the suspenders would tell his wife and friends for the rest of his life how he'd scared three gun thugs so bad they'd reversed a getaway car to get away from *him*.

When the car lurched forward, the tires kicked dust and small rocks off the dirt road and into the face of the man with the club. By now, another guy stood in front of the bank. He wore a white shirt and brown pants. He extended his arm. Joe saw the guy in the rearview mirror, his arm jumping. For a moment, Joe couldn't comprehend why, and then he understood. He said, 'Get down,' and Dion and Paolo dropped in the backseat. The guy's arm jerked up again, then jerked a third or fourth time, and the side-view mirror shattered and the glass fell to the dirt street.

Joe turned onto East Street and found the alley they'd scouted last week, banged a left into it, and stood on the gas pedal. For several blocks he drove parallel to the railroad tracks that ran behind the mills. By now they could assume the police were involved, not enough so that they were setting up roadblocks or anything, but enough that they could follow tire tracks off the dirt road by the bank, know the general direction in which they'd headed.

They'd stolen three cars that morning, all in Chicopee, about sixty miles south. They'd picked up the Auburn they were in now, as well as a black Cole with bald tires and a '24 Essex Coach with a raspy engine.

Joe crossed the railroad tracks and drove another mile along Silver Lake to a foundry that had burned down some years before, the black shell of it listing to the right in a field of weeds and cattails. Both cars were waiting for them when Joe pulled into the back of the building, where the wall was long gone, and they parked beside the Cole and got out of the Auburn.

Dion lifted Joe by his overcoat lapels and pushed him against the Auburn's hood. 'What the fuck is wrong with you?'

'It was a mistake,' Joe said.

'*Last week* it was a mistake,' Dion said. 'This week it's a fucking pattern.'

Joe couldn't argue. But he still said, 'Take your hands off me.'

Dion let go of Joe's lapels. He breathed heavily through his nostrils and pointed a stiff finger at Joe. 'You're fucking up.'

Joe took the hats and the kerchiefs and the guns and put them in a bag with the money. He put the bag in the back of the Essex Coach. 'I know it.'

Dion held out his fat hands. 'We've been partners since we were little fucking kids, but this is bad.'

'Yeah.' Joe agreed because he didn't see the point in lying about the obvious.

The police cars – four of them – came through a wall of brown weeds on the edge of the field behind the foundry. The weeds were the color of a riverbed and stood six or seven feet tall. The cruisers flattened them and revealed a small tent community behind them. A woman in a gray shawl and her baby leaned over a recently doused campfire, trying to scoop whatever heat was left into their coats.

Joe jumped into the Essex and drove out of the foundry. The Bartolo brothers drove past him in their Cole, the back end sliding away from them as they hit a patch of dry red dirt. The dirt spewed onto Joe's windshield and covered it. He leaned out the window and wiped at the dirt with his left arm while he drove with his right. The Essex bounced high off the uneven ground and something took a bite out of Joe's ear. When he pulled his head back in, he could see a lot better, but blood poured from his ear, sluicing under his collar and down his chest.

A series of pings and thunks hit the back window, the sound of someone skipping coins off a tin roof, and then the window blew out and a bullet sparked off the dashboard. A cruiser appeared on Joe's left and then another on his right. The one to his right had a cop in the backseat who rested the barrel of a Thompson on the window frame and opened fire. Joe stepped on the brakes so hard the steel coils of his seat pressed against his back ribs. The passenger windows exploded. Then the front window. The dashboard spit pieces of itself all over Joe and the front seat.

The cruiser to his right tried to brake as it turned in toward him. It rose on its nose and left the ground like something lifted by a gust. Joe had time to see it land on its side before the other cruiser rammed the back of his Essex and a boulder appeared out of the weeds just before the tree line.

The front of the Essex collapsed and the rest of it snapped to the right, Joe snapping with it. He never felt himself leave the car until he hit the tree. He lay there for a long time, covered in glass pebbles and pine needles, sticky with his own blood. He thought of Emma and he thought of his father. The woods smelled like burning hair, and he checked his arm hair and head just in case, but he was fine. He sat in the pine needles and waited for the Pittsfield police to arrest him. Smoke drifted through the trees. It was black and oily and not too thick. It moved around the tree trunks like it was looking for someone. After a while, he realized the police might not be coming.

When he stood and looked past the mangled Essex, he couldn't see the second cruiser anywhere. He could see the first, the one that had fired the tommy gun at him; it lay on its side in the field, a good twenty yards from where he'd last seen it bounce.

His hands had been chewed up by glass or fragments flying around inside the car. His legs were fine. His ear continued to bleed. When he found the rear window along the driver's side of the Essex intact, he looked at his reflection and saw why – no more left earlobe. It had been removed as if by a flick of the barber's blade. Past his reflection, Joe saw the leather satchel that held the money and the guns. The door wouldn't open right away, and he had to put both feet on the driver's door, which was unrecognizable as a door. He pulled hard though, pulled until he felt nauseated and light-headed. Just when he was thinking he should probably go find a rock, the door opened with a loud groan.

He took the bag and walked away from the field and deeper into the woods. He came upon a small, dry tree that was aflame, its two largest branches curving toward the fire-ball in its center, like a man trying to pat out his own burning head. A pair of oily black tire tracks flattened the brush in front of him, and some burning leaves listed in the air. He found a second burning tree and a small bush, and the black tire tracks grew blacker and more oily. After about fifty yards, he arrived at a pond. Steam curled along its edges and wisped off the surface, and at first Joe couldn't tell what he was seeing. The police cruiser that had rammed him had entered the water on fire, and now it sat in the middle of the pond, the water up to its windowsills, the rest of it charred, a few greasy blue flames still dancing on the roof. The windows had blown out. The holes the Thompson gun had made in the rear panel looked like the butts of flattened beer cans. The driver hung halfway out his door. The only part of him that wasn't black was his eyes, all the whiter for the charring of the rest of him.

Joe walked into the pond until he was standing on the passenger side of the cruiser, the water just below his waist. There was no one else inside the car. He stuck his head in through the passenger window even though it meant getting that much closer to the body. The heat radiated off the driver's roasted flesh in waves. He leaned back out of the car, certain he'd seen two cops in that cruiser as they'd raced across the field. He got another whiff of cooked flesh and lowered his head.

The other cop lay in the pond at his feet. He looked up from the sandy floor, the left side of his body as blackened as his partner's, the flesh on the right curdled but still white. He was about Joe's age, maybe a year older. His right arm pointed up. He'd probably used it to pull himself out of the burning car and fell into the water on his back, and it had stayed that way when he died.

But it still looked like he was pointing at Joe, the message clear:

You did this.

You. No one else. No one living anyway.

You're the first termite.

CHAPTER FOUR

A Hole at the
Center of Things

Back in the city, he dumped the car he'd stolen in Lenox and replaced it with a Dodge 126 he found parked along Pleasant Street in Dorchester. He drove it to K Street in South Boston and sat down the street from the house he'd grown up in while he considered his options. There weren't many. By the time night fell, he'd probably be out of them.

It was in all the late editions:

THREE PITTSFIELD POLICEMEN CUT DOWN
(*The Boston Globe*)
3 MASS. POLICE OFFICERS BRUTALLY SLAIN
(*The Evening Standard*)
COP SLAUGHTER IN WESTERN MASS.
(*The American*)

The two men Joe had come across in the pond were identified as Donald Belinski and Virgil Orten. Both had left wives behind. Orten had left two children. After studying their photos for a bit, Joe decided that Orten had been the one driving the car and Belinski had been the one who pointed up at him from the water.

He knew the real reason they were dead was because one of their brother lawmen had been stupid enough to fire a fucking tommy gun from a car bouncing across uneven ground. He knew that. He also knew that he was Hickey's termite and Donald and Virgil never would have been in that field if he and the Bartolo brothers hadn't come to their small city to rob one of their small banks.

The third dead cop, Jacob Zobe, was a state trooper who'd pulled over a car along the edge of the October Mountain State Forest. He'd been shot once in the stomach, which bent him over, and once through the top of his skull, which finished him off. The killer or killers ran over his ankle as they sped away, snapping the bone in half.

The shooting sounded like Dion. It was how he fought – punched a guy in the stomach to fold him in half and then worked the head until he went down for good. Dion, to the best of Joe's knowledge, had never killed a man before, but he'd come close a few times, and he hated cops.

Investigators had yet to identify any suspects, at least publicly. Two of the suspects were described as 'heavyset' and 'of foreign descent and odor,' while the third – possibly a foreigner as well – had been shot in the face. Joe looked at his reflection in the rearview mirror. Technically, he supposed, it was true; the earlobe was attached to the face. Or, in his case, it had been.

Even though no one had their names yet, a sketch artist with the Pittsfield Police Department had rendered their likenesses. So while most papers ran pictures of the three dead cops below the fold, above it they printed sketches of Dion, Paolo, and Joe. Dion and Paolo looked more jowly than normal and Joe would have to ask Emma if his face looked that thin and wolfish in the flesh, but otherwise, the resemblance was remarkable.

A four-state dragnet was in effect. The Bureau of Investigation had been consulted and was said to be joining the pursuit.

By now his father would have seen the papers. His father, Thomas Coughlin, deputy superintendent of the Boston Police Department.

His son, party to a cop killing.

Since Joe's mother had passed two years ago, his father worked himself to numb exhaustion six days a week. With a dragnet in effect for his own son, he'd have a cot brought into his office, probably not come home until they closed the case.

The family home was a four-story row house. It was an impressive structure, a redbrick bowfront where all the center rooms looked out at the street and boasted curved window seats. It was a house of mahogany staircases, pocket doors, and parquet floors, six bedrooms, two bathrooms, both with indoor plumbing, a dining room fit for the great hall of an English castle.

When a woman once asked Joe how he could come from

62

such a magnificent home and such a good family and still become a gangster, Joe's answer was two-pronged: (a) he wasn't a gangster, he was an outlaw; (b) he came from a magnificent house, not a magnificent home.

Joe let himself into his father's house. From the phone in the kitchen, he called the Gould household and got no answer. The satchel he'd carried into the house with him contained sixty-two thousand dollars. Even split three ways, it was enough to last any reasonably frugal man ten years, maybe fifteen. Joe wasn't a frugal man, so he figured it'd last him four regular years. But on the run, it would last him eighteen months. No more. By then, he'd figure something out. It was what he was good at, thinking on the fly.

Unquestionably, a voice that sounded suspiciously like his oldest brother's said. *It's worked out so well so far.*

He called Uncle Bobo's blind pig but got the same result as the Gould house. Then he remembered that Emma was attending the opening soiree at the Hotel Statler tonight at six. Joe pulled his watch from his vest: ten minutes to four.

Two hours to kill in a city that was, by now, looking to kill him.

That was far too much time out in the open. In that time they'd learn his name, his address, and come up with a list of his known associates and favorite haunts. They'd lock down all the train and bus stations, even the rural ones, and put up every last roadblock.

But that could cut both ways. The roadblocks would prohibit entry into the city under the logic that he was still outside it. No one would ever assume he was here, planning

63

to slip right back out again. And they wouldn't assume that because only the world's dumbest criminal would risk returning to the only city he'd ever called home after committing the biggest crime the region had seen in five or six years.

Which made him the dumbest criminal in the world.

Or the smartest. Because pretty much the only place they *weren't* searching right now was the place right under their noses.

Or so he told himself.

What he could still do – what he should have done in Pittsfield – was vanish. Not in two hours. Now. Not wait around for a woman who might choose not to join him under the present circumstances. Just leave with the shirt on his back and a bag of money in his hand. The roads were all being watched, yes. Same for trains and buses. And even if he could get out to the farmlands south and west of the city and steal a horse, it wouldn't do him any good because he didn't know how to ride one.

That left the sea.

He'd need a boat, but not a pleasure craft and not an obvious rumrunner like a sea skiff or a garvey. He'd need a worker's boat, one with rusted cleats and frayed tackle, a deck piled high with dented lobster traps. Something moored in Hull or Green Harbor or Gloucester. If he boarded by seven, it would probably be three or four in the morning before the fisherman noticed it missing.

So now he was stealing from workingmen.

Except the boat would be registered. Would have to be, or he'd move on to another. He'd get the address off the registration, mail the owner enough money to buy two boats or just get the fuck out of the lobster business altogether.

It occurred to him that thinking like this could explain why, even after all the jobs he'd pulled, he rarely had much money in his pockets. Sometimes it seemed like he stole money from one place just to give it away somewhere else. But he also stole because it was fun and he was good at it and it led to other things he was good at like bootlegging and rum-running, which is why he knew his way around boats in the first place. Last June, he'd run a boat from a no-name fishing village in Ontario across Lake Huron to Bay City, Michigan, another from Jacksonville to Baltimore in October, and just last winter ferried cases of newly distilled rum out of Sarasota and across the Gulf of Mexico to New Orleans, where he'd blown his entire profit one weekend in the French Quarter on sins that, even now, he could only remember in fragments.

So he could pilot most boats, which meant he could steal most boats. He could walk out this door and be on the South Shore in thirty minutes. The North Shore would take a little longer, but this time of year there'd probably be more boats up there to choose from. If he set out from Gloucester or Rockport, he could reach Nova Scotia in three to four days. And then he'd send for Emma after a couple of months.

Which seemed a bit long.

But she'd wait for him. She loved him. She'd never said it, true, but he could feel her wanting to. She loved him. He loved her.

She'd wait.

Maybe he'd just swing by the hotel. Pop his head in real

quick, see if he could spot her. If they both vanished, they'd be impossible to trace. But if he disappeared and then sent for her, by that point, the cops or the BI could have figured out who she was and what she meant to him and she'd show up in Halifax with a posse on her tail. He'd open the door to greet her, they'd both go down in bullet rain.

She wouldn't wait.

He either went with her now or without her forever.

He looked at himself in the glass of his mother's china cabinet and remembered why he'd come here in the first place – no matter where he decided to go, he wouldn't get far dressed like this. The left shoulder of his coat was black with blood, his shoes and trouser cuffs were caked in mud, his shirt torn from the woods and speckled with blood.

In the kitchen, he opened the bread box and pulled out a bottle of A. Finke's Widow Rum. Or, as most called it, Finke's. He removed his shoes and carried them and the rum with him up the service stairs to his father's bedroom. In the bathroom, he washed as much of the dried blood from his ear as he could, careful not to disturb the heart of the scab. When he was certain it wasn't going to bleed, he took a few steps back and appraised it in relation to the other ear and the rest of his face. As deformities went, it wasn't going to make anyone look twice once the scab fell away. And even now, the majority of the black scab clung to the underside of his ear; it was noticeable, no question, but not in the way a black eye or broken nose would have been.

He had a few sips of the Finke's while he chose a suit from his father's closet. There were fifteen of them, about thirteen too many for a policeman's salary. Same with the shoes, the shirts, the ties and hats. Joe chose a striped malacca tan single-breasted suit from Hart Schaffner & Marx with a white Arrow shirt. The silk tie was black with diagonal red stripes every four inches or so, the shoes a pair of black Nettletons, and the hat a Knapp-Felt, as smooth as a dove's breast. He stripped off his own clothes and folded them neatly on the floor. He placed his pistol and his shoes on top and changed into his father's clothes, then returned the pistol to the waistband at the small of his back.

Judging by the length of the trousers, he and his father weren't exactly the same height after all. His father was a little taller. And his hat size a bit smaller than Joe's. Joe dealt with the hat problem by tilting it back off the crown a bit so it looked jaunty. As for the length of his trousers, he double-rolled the cuffs and used safety pins from his late mother's sewing table to hold them in place.

He carried his old clothes and the bottle of good rum down into his father's study. Even now he couldn't deny that crossing the threshold into that room when his father wasn't present felt sacrilegious. He stood at the threshold and listened to the house – the ticking of its cast-iron radiators, the scratch of the chime hammers in the grandfather clock down the hall as they prepared to strike four. Even though he was positive the house was empty, he felt watched.

When the hammers did, in fact, fall on the chimes, Joe entered the office.

The desk sat in front of tall bay windows overlooking the street. It was an ornate Victorian partners desk, built in Dublin in the middle of the last century. The kind of desk no tenant farmer's son from the shitheel side of Clonakilty could have reasonably expected to ever grace his home. The same could be said for the matching credenza under the window, the Oriental rug, the thick, amber drapes, the Waterford decanters, the oak bookshelves and leather-bound books his father never bothered to read, the bronze curtain rods, the antique leather sofa and armchairs, the walnut humidor.

Joe opened one of the cabinets beneath the bookshelves and crouched to confront the safe he found there. He dialed the combination – 3-12-10, the months in which he and his two brothers had been born – and opened the safe. Some of his mother's jewelry was in it, five hundred dollars in cash, the deed to the house, his parents' birth certificates, a stack of papers Joe didn't bother examining, and a little more than a thousand dollars in treasury bonds. Joe removed it all and placed it on the floor to the right of the cabinet door. At the back of the safe was a wall made of the same thick steel as the rest of it. Joe popped it off by pressing his thumbs hard against the upper corners and lay it on the floor of the first safe while he faced the dial of the second.

The combination here had been much harder to figure out. He'd tried all the birthdays in the family and got nowhere. He tried the numbers of the stationhouses where his father had worked over the years. Same result. When he recalled that his father sometimes said good luck, bad luck, and death all came in threes, he tried every permutation of that number. No luck. He'd started the process when he was fourteen. One day when he was seventeen, he'd noticed some correspondence his father had left out on his desk – a letter to a friend who'd become fire chief in Lewiston,

Maine. The letter was typed on his father's Underwood and filled with lies that wrapped 'round and 'round the paper like ribbon – 'Ellen and I are blessed, still as smitten as the day we met ...' 'Aiden recovered quite well from the dark events of 9/19 ...' 'Connor has made remarkable strides with his infirmity ...' and 'Looks like Joseph will enter Boston College in the fall. He speaks of working in the bond trade ...' At the bottom of all this bullshit, he'd signed it *Yours, TXC.* It was the way he signed everything. Never wrote out his full name, as if to do so would somehow compromise him.

TXC.

Thomas Xavier Coughlin.

TXC.

20-24-3.

Joe dialed the numbers now and the second safe opened with a sharp peep of the hinges.

It was roughly two feet deep. A foot and a half of that was filled with money. Bricks of it, tightly bound in red rubber bands. Some of the bills had entered the safe before Joe was born and some had probably been placed there in the last week. A lifetime of payoffs and kickbacks and graft. His father – a pillar of the City on the Hill, the Athens of America, the Hub of the Universe – was more a criminal than Joe could ever aspire to be. Because Joe had never figured out how to show more than one face to the world, whereas his father had so many faces at his disposal the question was which of them was the original and which the imitations.

Joe knew that if he cleaned out the safe tonight, he'd have

enough to live on the run for ten years. Or, if he got to somewhere far enough that they stopped looking, he could buy his way into the refining of Cuban sugar and/or the distilling of molasses, turn himself into a pirate king within three years, never have to worry about shelter or a hot meal the rest of his days.

But he didn't want his father's money. He'd stolen his clothes because the idea of leaving the city dressed as the old son of a bitch appealed to him, but he'd break his own hands before he'd spend his father's cash with them.

He placed his neatly folded clothes and muddy shoes on top of his father's dirty money. He thought of leaving a note, but he couldn't think of anything else he'd want to say, so he closed the door and spun the dial. He replaced the fake wall of the first safe and locked that up too.

He walked around the office for a minute, mulling it over one last time. To try to get to Emma during a function that most of the city's luminaries would attend, where the guests would arrive by limousine and invitation only, would be the pinnacle of insanity. In the cool of his father's study, maybe some of the old man's pragmatism, merciless as it was, finally rubbed off. Joe had to take what the gods had given him – an exit route out of the very city he was expected to enter. Time was not on his side, though. He had to go out this front door, hop into the purloined Dodge, and scoot north like the road itself had caught fire.

He looked out the window at K Street on a damp spring evening and reminded himself that she loved him and she'd wait.

*

Out on the street, he sat in the Dodge and stared back at the house of his birth, the house that had shaped the man he was now. By Boston Irish standards, he'd grown up in the lap of luxury. He'd never gone to bed hungry, never felt the street press through the soles of his shoes. He'd been educated, first by the nuns, then by the Jesuits until he dropped out in eleventh grade. Compared to most he met in his line of work, his upbringing had been positively cushy.

But there was a hole at the center of it, a great distance between Joe and his parents that reflected the distance between his mother and his father and his mother and the world at large. His parents had fought a war before he was born, a war that had ended in a peace so fragile that to acknowledge its existence could cause it to shatter, so no one ever discussed it. But the battlefield had still lain between them; she sat on her side, he sat on his. And Joe sat out in the middle, between the trenches, in the scorched dirt. The hole at the center of his house had been a hole at the center of his parents and one day the hole had found the center of Joe. There was a time, several full years during his childhood actually, when he'd hoped things could be different. But he couldn't remember anymore why he'd felt that way. Things weren't ever what they were supposed to be; they were what they were, and that was the simple truth of it, a truth that didn't change just because you wanted it to.

He drove over to the East Coast Bus Line Terminal on St James. It was a small yellow-brick building surrounded by much taller ones, and Joe gambled that any laws looking for him would be stationed by the bus terminals on the northern side of the building, not the lockers in the southwestern corner.

He slipped in through the exit door there and right into the rush-hour crowd. He let the crowd work for him, never bucking the flow, never trying to edge past anyone. And for once he had no complaints about not being tall. As soon as he got into the thick of the throngs, his was just another head bobbing alongside so many others. He counted two cops near the doors to the terminals and one in the crowd about sixty feet away.

He popped out of the streaming crowd into the quiet of the locker bank. This was where, simply by dint of being alone, he was most noticeable. He'd already removed three thousand dollars from the satchel and buckled it back up. He had the key to locker 217 in his right hand, the bag in his left. Inside 217 was $7,435, twelve pocket watches and thirteen wristwatches, two sterling silver money clips, a gold tie pin, and assorted women's jewelry he'd never gotten around to selling because he'd suspected the fences were trying to fleece him. He took smooth strides to the locker, raised his right hand, which only trembled slightly, and opened it.

Behind him, someone called, 'Hey!'

Joe kept his eyes straight ahead. The tremor in his hand turned into a spasm as he swung the locker door back.

'I said, "Hey!"'

Joe pushed the satchel into the locker, closed the door.

'Hey, you! Hey!'

Joe turned the key, locked the door, and pocketed the key.

'Hey!'

Joe turned, picturing the cop waiting for him, service revolver drawn, probably young, probably jumpy. . . .

A wino sat on the floor by a trash barrel. Bone thin, nothing to him but red eyes, red cheeks, and sinew. His jaw jutted in Joe's direction.

'The fuck you looking at?' he asked.

The laugh left Joe's mouth like a bark. He reached in his pocket, came back with a ten spot. He stooped and handed it to the old wino.

'Looking at you, Pops. Looking at you.'

The guy belched at that, but Joe was already moving away, lost in the crowd.

Outside, he walked east on St James toward the two klieg lights crossing back and forth in the low clouds above the new hotel. It calmed him for a moment to imagine his money sitting safe and sound in the locker until he chose to return for it. A decision, he thought as he turned onto Essex Street, that was a bit unorthodox when a fella was planning a lifetime on the run.

If you're leaving the country, why leave the money here?
So I can come back for it.
Why would you need to come back for it?
In case I don't make it out tonight.
There's your answer.
There's no answer. What answer?
You didn't want them to find the money on you.
Exactly.
Because you know you're going to get caught.

CHAPTER FIVE

Rough Work

He entered the Hotel Statler through the employee entrance. When a porter and then a dishwasher gave him curious glances, he lifted his hat and shot them confident smiles and two-finger salutes, a bon vivant avoiding the crowds out front, and they gave him nods and smiles in return.

Going through the kitchen, he could hear a piano, a peppy clarinet, and a steady bass coming from the lobby. He climbed a dark concrete staircase. He opened the door up top and came out by a marble staircase into a kingdom of light and smoke and music.

Joe had been in a few swank hotel lobbies in his time, but he'd never seen anything like this. The clarinetist and the cellist stood near brass entrance doors so unblemished the light bouncing off them turned the dust motes in the air gold. Corinthian columns rose from marble floors to wrought iron balconies. The molding was creamy alabaster, and every ten yards a heavy chandelier descended, the same pendant shape as the candelabras in their six-foot stands. Blood-dark couches perched on Oriental rugs. Two grand pianos, submerged in white flowers, sat on either side of the lobby. The pianists lightly tinkled the keys and carried on repartee with the crowd and each other.

In front of the center staircase, WBZ had placed three radiophones in their black stands. A large woman in a light blue dress stood by one of them, consulting with a man in a beige suit and yellow bow tie. The woman patted the buns of her hair repeatedly and sipped from a glass of pale, foggy liquid.

Most men in the crowd wore tuxedos or dinner jackets. There were a few in suits, so Joe wasn't the only sore thumb in the gathering, but he was the only one still wearing a hat. He thought of removing it, but that would put the face on the front page of everyone's evening edition in clear view. He glanced up at the mezzanine; there were plenty of hats up there because that's where all the reporters and photographers mingled with the swells.

He dipped his chin and headed for the nearest staircase. It was slow going, the crowd pushing together, now that they'd seen the radiophones and the round woman in the blue dress. Even with his head down, he noticed Chappie Geygan and Boob Fowler talking with Red Ruffing. Joe, a Red Sox fanatic as long as he could remember, had to remind himself that it might not be a good idea for a wanted man to walk up to three baseball players and chat about their batting averages. He squeezed his way around the back of them, though, hoping he might hear a snippet to clear up the trade rumors about Geygan and Fowler, but all he heard was talk about the stock market, Geygan saying the only way to make real money was to buy on margin, any other way was for suckers who wanted to stay poor. That's when the large woman in the light blue dress stepped up to the microphone and cleared her throat. The man beside her stepped to the other radiophone and raised an arm to the crowd.

'Ladies and gentlemen, for your listening pleasure,' the man said, 'WBZ Radio, Boston, 1030 on your dial, is here live from the Grand Lobby of the landmark Hotel Statler. I'm Edwin Mulver and it gives me great pleasure to present to you Mademoiselle Florence Ferrel, mezzo-soprano with the San Francisco Opera.'

Edwin Mulver stepped back, his chin tilted up, as Florence Ferrel patted the buns of her hair one more time and then exhaled into her radiophone. The exhalation turned, without warning, into a mountain peak of a high note that thrummed through the crowd and climbed three stories to the ceiling. It was a sound so extravagant and yet so authentic it filled Joe with an awful loneliness. She was bearing forth something from the gods, and as it moved from her body into his, Joe realized he would die someday. He knew it in a different way than he'd known it coming through the door. Coming through the door, it had been a distant possibility. Now, it was a callous fact, indifferent to his dismay. In the face of such clear evidence of the otherworldly, he knew, beyond argument, that he was mortal and insignificant and had been taking steps out of the world since the day he'd entered it.

As she ventured deeper into the aria, the notes grew ever higher, ever longer, and Joe pictured her voice as a dark ocean, beyond end, beyond depth. He looked around at the men in their tuxedos and the women in their glittering taffeta and silk sheaths and lace wreaths, at the champagne flowing from a fountain in the center of the lobby. He recognized a judge and Mayor Curley and Governor Fuller and another infielder for the Sox, Baby Doll Jacobson. By one of the pianos, he saw Constance Flagstead, a local stage star, flirting with Ira Bumtroth, a known numbers man. Some people were laughing, and others tried so hard to look respectable it was laughable. He saw stern men with muttonchop sideburns and wizened matrons with skirts the shape of church bells. He identified Brahmins and blue bloods and Daughters of the American Revolution. He noted bootleggers and bootlegger lawyers and even the tennis player Rory Johannsen, who'd made it to the quarterfinals at Wimbledon last year before being knocked out by the Frenchman Henri Cochet. He saw bespectacled intellectuals trying not to get caught looking at frivolous flappers with insipid conversational skills but sparkling eyes and dazzling legs ... and all of them soon to vanish from the earth. Fifty years from now, someone could look at a photograph of this night and most of the people in the room would be dead, and the rest would be on their way.

As Florence Ferrel finished her aria, he looked up toward the mezzanine and saw Albert White. Standing dutifully behind his right elbow was his wife. She was middle-aged and twig-thin, carrying none of the ample weight of a well-to-do matron. Her eyes were the biggest part of her, noticeable even from where Joe stood. They were bulging and frantic, even as she smiled at something Albert said to a chuckling Mayor Curley, who'd found his way up there with a glass of scotch.

Joe looked a few yards down the balcony and there was Emma. She wore a silver sheath dress and stood in a crowd near the wrought iron railing, a glass of champagne in her left hand. In this light, her skin was the white of the alabaster, and she looked stricken and alone, lost in a private grief. Was this who she was when she didn't think he was looking? Was there some unnameable loss grafted to her heart? For a moment he feared she'd jump over the balcony rail, but then the sickness in her face turned to a smile. And he realized what had placed the grief in her face: she'd never expected to see him again.

Her smile widened and she covered it with her hand. It was the same hand that held the champagne glass, so the glass tipped and a few drops fell into the crowd below. One man looked up and touched the back of his head. A portly woman wiped at her brow then blinked her right eye several times.

Emma leaned back from the rail and tilted her head toward the staircase on his side of the lobby. Joe nodded. She moved away from the railing.

He lost her in the crowd above as he worked his way through the one below. He had noticed that most of the reporters on the mezzanine wore their hats back on their heads and their tie knots were crooked. So he pushed his hat back and loosened his tie as he squeezed through the last cluster of people and reached the staircase.

Officer Donald Belinski ran down toward him, a ghost who'd somehow risen from the pond floor, scraped the burned flesh from his bones, and now trotted down the staircase toward Joe – same blond hair, same blotchy complexion, same ridiculously red lips and pale eyes. No wait, this guy was fleshier, and his blond hair had already begun to recede and leaned a bit more toward red than pure blond. And even though Joe had only seen Belinski lying on his back, he was fairly certain the cop had been taller than this man. And probably smelled better too, this guy smelling of onions, Joe that close to him as they passed in the stairwell, the guy's eyes narrowing. He swept a hank of oily red-blond hair off his forehead, his hat in his free hand, a *Boston Examiner* press ID tucked inside the grosgrain ribbon. Joe sidestepped him at the last moment, and the man fumbled with his hat.

Joe said, 'Excuse me.'

The guy said, 'My apologies,' but Joe could feel his eyes on him as he moved up the stairs fast, stunned at his own stupidity not only to have looked someone directly in the face but also to have looked a reporter directly in the face.

The guy called up the stairwell, 'Excuse me, excuse me. You dropped something,' but Joe hadn't dropped shit. He kept going, and a group entered the stairwell above him, already tipsy, one woman draped over another like a loose robe, and then Joe was passing through them and not looking back, not looking back, looking only forward.

At her.

She held a small purse that matched her dress and the silver feather and silver band in her hair. A small vein pulsed in her throat. Her shoulders rippled; her eyes flashed. It was all he could do not to clutch those shoulders and lift her off her feet until she wrapped her legs around his back and lowered her face to his. But instead he kept moving past her and said, 'Guy just recognized me. Gotta move.'

She fell in beside him as he walked a red carpet past the main ballroom. The crowds were thick up here but not as jammed in as down below. You could move along the perimeter of the crowd easily enough.

'There's a service elevator just past the next balcony,' she said. 'Goes to the basement. I can't believe you came.'

He took the right at the next opening, his head down, and pushed his hat to his forehead, pulled it down tight. 'What else was I going to do?'

'Run.'

'To what?'

'I don't know. Jesus. It's what people do.'

'It's not what I do.'

The crowd grew thicker as they passed along the back of the mezzanine. Down below, the governor had taken the radiophone and was proclaiming today Hotel Statler Day in the Commonwealth of Massachusetts, and a cheer went up, the crowd good and drunk now as Emma came abreast of him and nudged him to the left with her elbow.

He saw it now, past where their corridor intersected with another – a dark nook behind the banquet tables and the lights and the marble and red carpet.

Downstairs, a brass band struck its horns and the throngs in the mezzanine kicked up their heels and the flashbulbs flashed and popped and hissed. He wondered if any of the staff photographers would get back to their newsrooms and notice the guy in the background of some of their shots, the guy in the tan suit with the bounty on his head.

'Left, left,' Emma said.

He turned left between two banquet tables and the marble floor gave way to thin black tile. Another couple of steps and he reached the elevator. He pressed the down button.

Four drunken men passed along the edge of the mezzanine. They were a couple years older than Joe and singing 'Soldiers Field.'

'O'er the stands of flaming Crimson,' the men crooned off-key, 'the Harvard banners fly.'

Joe pressed the down button again.

One of the men met his eyes, then leered at Emma's ass. He nudged a buddy as they continued to sing, 'Cheer on cheer like volleyed thunder echoes to the sky.'

Emma grazed the side of his hand with her own. She said, 'Shit, shit, shit.'

He pressed the button again.

A waiter banged through the two kitchen doors to their left, a large tray held aloft. He passed within three feet of them but never looked their way.

The Harvard guys had passed but they could still hear them:

'Then fight, fight, fight! For we win tonight.'

Emma reached past him and pressed the down button.

'Old Harvard forevermore!'

Joe considered slipping through the kitchen, but he suspected it was a box with, at best, a dumbwaiter to bring up food from the main kitchen two stories down. In retrospect, the smart thing would have been for Emma to come to him, not the other way around. If only he'd been thinking clearly, but he couldn't remember the last time he'd done that.

He reached for the button again, but then he heard the car rising toward them.

'If there's anyone in it, just show them your back,' he said. 'They'll be in a rush.'

'Not once they see my back,' she said, and he smiled in spite of the weight of his worry.

The car arrived and he waited but the doors stayed closed. He counted five beats of his own heart. He slid back the gate. He opened the door on an empty car. He looked back over his shoulder at Emma. She stepped in ahead of him and he followed. He closed the gate and then the door. He turned the crank and they began their descent.

She placed the flat of her palm to his cock and it immediately hardened as she covered his mouth with her own. He slid his free hand under her dress and between the heat of her thighs and she groaned into his mouth. Her tears fell on his cheekbones.

'Why're you crying?'

'Because I might love you.'

'Might?'

'Yes.'

'Then laugh.'

'I can't, I can't,' she said.

'You know the bus station on St James?'

She narrowed her eyes at him. 'What? Sure. Of course.'

He placed the locker key in her hand. 'In case anything happens.'

'What?'

'Between here and freedom.'

'No, no, no, no,' she said. 'No, no. You take this. I don't want it.'

He waved it off. 'Put it in your purse.'

'Joe, I don't want this.'

'It's money.'

'I know what it is and I don't want it.' She tried handing it to him, but he held his hands high.

'Hold on to it.'

'No,' she said. 'We'll spend it together. I'm with you now. I'm with you, Joe. Take the key.'

She tried handing it to him again but they'd reached the basement.

The window in the door was black because the lights were off for some reason.

They weren't off for 'some' reason, Joe realized. There was only one reason.

He reached for the crank as the gate was thrown open from the other side and Brendan Loomis reached in and pulled Joe out of the car by his tie. He pulled Joe's pistol free of the small of his back and tossed it off into the dark along the cement floor. Then he punched Joe in the face and the side of his head more times than Joe could count, all of it happening so fast Joe barely got his hands up.

Once he did, he reached back for Emma, thinking somehow he could protect her. But Brendan Loomis had a fist like a butcher's mallet. Every time it hit Joe's head – bap bap bap bap – Joe felt his brain go numb and his vision white out. His eyes slid through the white, unable to fix on anything. He heard his own nose break and then – bap bap bap – Loomis hit him in the same spot three more times.

When Loomis let go of his tie, Joe fell to all fours on the cement floor. He heard a series of steady drips, like leaky faucets, and opened his eyes to see his own blood dripping to the cement, the drops the size of nickels, but piling up so fast they turned into amoebas and the amoebas became puddles. He turned his head to see if somehow, some way, Emma had used his beating to slam the elevator door shut and make a run for it, but the elevator wasn't where he'd left it, or he wasn't where he'd left the elevator, because all he saw was a cement wall.

That's when Brendan Loomis kicked him in the stomach hard enough to lift him off the floor. When he landed in a fetal position, he couldn't find air. He gulped for it, but it wouldn't come. He tried to rise to his knees, but his legs slid away from him, so he used his elbows to lift his chest off the cement and gulped like a fish, trying to get something down his windpipe but seeing his chest as a black stone, without openings, without gaps, nothing in there but the stone, no room for anything else, because he could not fucking breathe.

It pushed up his esophagus like a balloon through a fountain pen, squeezing his heart, crushing his lungs, closing off his throat, but then, finally, it punched up past his tonsils and out through his mouth. It had a whistle at its tail, a whistle and several gasps, but that was okay, that was fine, because he could breathe again, at least he could breathe.

Loomis kicked him in the groin from behind.

Joe ground his head into the cement floor and coughed

and might have puked, he had no idea, the pain something he couldn't have imagined prior to this. His balls were stuffed into his intestines; flames licked the walls of his stomach; his heart beat so fast it had to give out soon, just had to; his skull felt like someone had pried it open with their hands; his eyes bled. He vomited, vomited for certain, vomited bile and fire onto the floor. He thought he was done and then he did it again. He fell onto his back and looked up at Brendan Loomis.

'You look' – Loomis lit a cigarette – 'unfortunate.'

Brendan swung from side to side with the room. Joe stayed where he was, but everything else was on a pendulum. Brendan looked down at Joe as he pulled on a pair of black gloves and flexed his fingers in them until they fit to his liking. Albert White appeared beside him, Albert on the same pendulum, and they both looked down at Joe.

Albert said, 'I have to turn you into a message, I'm afraid.'

Joe looked up through the blood in his eyes at Albert in his white dinner jacket.

'To everyone out there who thinks it's okay to disregard what I say.'

Joe looked for Emma, but he couldn't find the elevator in all the swinging and swaying.

'It's not going to be a nice message,' Albert White said. 'And I'm sorry about that.' He squatted in front of Joe, his face sad, weary. 'My mother always said everything happens for a reason. I'm not sure she was right, but I do think people often become what they're supposed to be. I thought I was supposed to be a cop but then the city took my job and I became this. And most times I don't like it, Joe. I fucking

85

hate it to tell the truth, but I can't deny that it comes natural to me. It fits. What comes natural to you, I'm afraid, is fucking up. All you had to do was run but you didn't. And I'm sure – look at me.'

Joe's head had lolled to the left. He rolled it back, met Albert's kind gaze.

'I'm sure, as you die, you'll tell yourself you did it for love.' Albert gave Joe a rueful smile. 'But that's not why you fucked up. You fucked up because it's your nature. Because deep down you feel guilty about what you do, so you want to get caught. But in this line of work, you face your guilt at the end of every night. You turn it over in your hands, you make a ball of it. And then you pitch it into the fire. But *you,* you don't do that, so you've spent your short life hoping someone will punish you for your sins. Well, I'm that someone.'

Albert rose from his crouch and Joe lost focus for a moment, everything turning to a blur. He caught a flash of silver and then another and he narrowed his eyes until the blurring sharpened and everything came into focus again.

And he wished it hadn't.

Albert and Brendan still shimmied a bit, but the pendulum was gone. Emma stood beside Albert, her hand on his arm.

For a moment, Joe didn't understand. And then he did.

He looked up at Emma and it no longer mattered what they did to him. He was okay with dying because living hurt too much.

'I'm sorry,' she whispered. 'I'm sorry.'

'She's sorry,' Albert White said. 'We're all sorry.' He

gestured toward somebody Joe couldn't see. 'Take her out of here.'

A beefy guy in a coarse wool jacket and knit hat pulled down on his forehead put his hands on Emma's arm.

'You said you wouldn't kill him,' Emma said to Albert. Albert shrugged.

'Albert,' Emma said. 'That was the deal.'

'And I'll honor it,' Albert said. 'Don't you worry.'

'Albert,' she said, her voice catching in her throat.

'Dear?' Albert's voice was far too calm.

'I never would have led him here if—'

Albert slapped her face with one hand and smoothed his shirt with the other. Slapped her hard enough to split her lips.

He looked down at his shirt. 'You think *you're* safe? You think I'm going to be humiliated by a whore? You're under the impression I'm mush for you. Maybe I was yesterday, but I've been up all night. And I've already replaced you. Get me? You'll see.'

'You said—'

Albert wiped her blood off his hand with a kerchief. 'Put her in the fucking car, Donnie. Now, Donnie.'

The beefy guy wrapped Emma in a bear hug and started walking backward. 'Joe! Please don't hurt him anymore! Joe, I'm sorry. I'm sorry.' She screamed and kicked and scratched Donnie's head. 'Joe, I love you! I love you!'

The elevator gate slammed shut and the car rose out of the basement.

Albert squatted beside him and put a cigarette between his lips. A match flared and the tobacco cackled and he said, 'Inhale. You'll get your wits back faster.'

87

Joe did. For a minute, he sat on the floor and smoked and Albert crouched beside him and smoked his own cigarette and Brendan Loomis stood there watching.

'What're you going to do with her?' Joe asked once he trusted himself to speak.

'With her? She just sold you down the river.'

'For a good reason, I bet.' He looked at Albert. 'There was a good reason, right?'

Albert chuckled. 'You're some kind of rube, aren't you?'

Joe raised a split eyebrow and the blood fell in his eye. He wiped at it. 'What're you going to do with her?'

'You should be more worried about what I'm going to do to you.'

'I am,' Joe admitted, 'but I'm asking what you're going to do with her.'

'Don't know yet.' Albert shrugged and pulled a speck of tobacco off his tongue, flicked it away. 'But you, Joe, you're going to be the message.' He turned to Brendan. 'Get him up.'

'What message?' Joe said as Brendan Loomis slipped his arms under him from behind and hoisted him to his feet.

'What happened to Joe Coughlin is what will happen to you if you cross Albert White and his crew.'

Joe said nothing. Nothing occurred to him. He was twenty years old. That's all he was going to get in this world – twenty years. He hadn't wept since he was fourteen but it was all he could do, looking into Albert's eyes, not to break down and beg for his life.

Albert's face softened. 'I can't let you live, Joe. If I could see any way I could, I'd try to make it work. And it's not about the girl, if that helps. I can get whores anywhere. Got a pretty new one waiting for me as soon as I'm done with you.' He studied his hands for a moment. 'But you shot up a small town and stole sixty thousand dollars without my permission and left three cops dead. That brings a shit-brown rain down on all of us. Because now every cop in New England thinks Boston gangsters are mad dogs to be put down like mad dogs. And I need to make everyone understand that's just not true.' He said to Loomis. 'Where's Bones?'

Bones was Julian Bones, another of Albert's gun monkeys.

'In the alley, engine running.'

'Let's go.'

Albert led the way to the elevator and opened the gate and Brendan Loomis dragged Joe into the car.

'Turn him around.'

Joe was spun in place and the cigarette fell from his lips when Loomis gripped the back of his head and pushed his face into the wall. They pulled his hands behind his back. Coarse rope snaked around his wrists, Loomis pulling it tight with every loop before he tied off the ends. Joe, something of an expert on the subject, knew a secure knot when he felt one. They could leave him alone in this elevator and not come back till April and he still wouldn't have freed himself.

Loomis spun him back around, then went to work the crank, and Albert pulled a fresh cigarette from a pewter case and put it between Joe's lips and lit it for him. In the flare of the match, Joe could see that Albert took no joy from any of this, that when Joe was sinking to the bottom of the Mystic River with a leather noose around his head and sacks full of rocks tied to his ankles, Albert would rue the price of doing business in a dirty world.

For tonight anyway.

On the first floor, they left the elevator and walked down an empty service corridor, the sounds of the party reaching them through the walls – dueling pianos and a horn section going full blast and lots of gay laughter.

They reached the door at the end of the corridor. DELIVERIES had been stamped across the center in fresh yellow paint.

'I'll make sure it's clear.' Loomis opened the door onto a March night that had grown much rawer. A light sprinkle fell and gave a tinfoil smell to the iron fire escapes. Joe could also smell the building, the newness of the exterior, as if limestone dust kicked up by the drills still hung in the air.

Albert turned Joe to him and fixed his tie. He licked both his palms and smoothed Joe's hair. He looked bereft. 'I never wanted to grow up to be a man who kills people to maintain my profit margin, and yet I am. I never get a single night's decent sleep – not fucking one, Joe. I get up every day in fear and lay my head back to the pillow at night the same way.' He straightened Joe's collar. 'You?'

'What?'

'Ever wanted to be anything else?'

'No.'

Albert picked something off Joe's shoulder, flicked it away with his finger. 'I told her if she delivered you to us, I wouldn't kill you. Nobody else believed you'd be stupid enough to show up tonight, but I hedged my bets. So she agreed to lead you to me to save you. Or so she told herself.

But you and I know I have to kill you, don't we, Joe?' He looked at Joe with heartbroken eyes, glassy with moisture. 'Don't we?'

Joe nodded.

Albert nodded as well. He leaned in and whispered in Joe's ear, 'And then I'm going to kill her too.'

'What?'

'Because I loved her too.' Albert raised his eyebrows up and down. 'And because the only way you could have known to knock over my poker game on that particular morning? Would be if she tipped you.'

Joe said, 'Wait.' He said, 'Look. She didn't tip me to anything.'

'What else would you say?' Albert fixed his collar, smoothed his shirt. 'Look at it this way – if what you sweethearts have *is* true love? Then you'll meet tonight in heaven.'

He buried a fist in Joe's stomach, driving it up to the solar plexus. Joe doubled over and lost all his oxygen again. He jerked at the rope around his wrists and tried to butt Albert with his head, but Albert merely slapped his face away and opened the door to the alley.

He grabbed Joe by the hair and straightened him up, so Joe could see the car waiting for him, the back door open, Julian Bones standing by it. Loomis crossed the alley and grabbed Joe's elbow, and they dragged him over the threshold. Joe could smell the backseat foot wells now. He could smell the oil rags and dirt.

Just as they were about to hoist him in, they dropped him. He fell to his knees on the cobblestones and he heard Albert yell, 'Go! Go! Go!' and their footsteps on the cobblestones.

Maybe they'd already shot him in the back of the head because the heavens descended in bars of light.

His face was saturated in white, and the buildings along the alley erupted in blue and red, and tires squealed and somebody shouted something through a megaphone and someone fired a gun and then another gun.

A man walked through the white light toward Joe, a trim and confident man, a man who wore command like a birthmark.

His father.

More men walked out of the white behind him, and Joe was soon surrounded by a dozen members of the Boston Police Department.

His father cocked his head. 'So you're a cop killer now, Joseph.'

Joe said, 'I didn't kill anybody.'

His father ignored that. 'Looks like your accomplices were about to take you on the dead man's drive. Did they decide you were too much of a liability?'

Several of the policemen had removed their billy clubs.

'Emma's in the back of a car. They're going to kill her.'

'Who?'

'Albert White, Brendan Loomis, Julian Bones, and some guy named Donnie.'

On the streets beyond the alley, several women screamed. A car horn blared, followed by the solid thump of a crash. More screams. In the alley, the rain turned from a drizzle to a heavy downpour.

His father looked at his men, then back at Joe. 'Fine company you keep, son. Any other fairy tales you have for me?'

'It's not a fairy tale.' Joe spit blood from his mouth. 'They're going to kill her, Dad.'

'Well, *we* won't kill you, Joseph. In fact, I won't touch you a'tall. But some of my coworkers would like a word.'

Thomas Coughlin leaned forward, hands on his knees, and stared at his son.

Somewhere behind that gaze of iron lived a man who'd slept on the floor of Joe's hospital room for three days when Joe had the fever back in 1911, who'd read each of the city's eight newspapers to him, cover to cover, who told him he loved him, who told him if God wanted his son, He'd have to go through him, Thomas Xavier Coughlin, and God would know, sure, what a rough proposition that could turn out to be.

'Dad, listen to me. She's—'

His father spit in his face.

'He's all yours,' he said to his men and walked away.

'Find the car!' Joe screamed. 'Find Donnie! She's in a car with Donnie!'

The first blow – a fist – connected with Joe's jaw. The second, a shot from a billy club, he was pretty sure, hit his temple. After that, all light disappeared from the night.

CHAPTER SIX

All the Sinners Saints

The ambulance driver gave Thomas his first hint of the publicity nightmare about to descend on the BPD.

As they strapped Joe to a wooden gurney and lifted him into the back of the ambulance, the driver said, 'You throw this kid off the roof?'

The rain came down in a clatter so loud they all had to shout.

Thomas's aide and driver, Sergeant Michael Pooley, said, 'His injuries were sustained before we arrived.'

'Yeah?' The ambulance driver looked from one to the other, water pouring from the black brim of his white cap. 'Horseshit.'

Thomas could feel the temperature rising in the alley, even in the rain, so he pointed at his son on the gurney. 'This man was involved in the murders of those three police officers in New Hampshire.'

Sergeant Pooley said, 'Feel better now, asshole?'

The ambulance driver was checking Joe's pulse, eyes on his wristwatch. 'I read the papers. All I do most days – sit up in my cab and read the fucking papers. And this kid was the driver. And while they were chasing him, they shot another police car all to hell.' He placed Joe's wrist on his chest. '*He* didn't do it, though.'

Thomas looked at Joe's face – torn black lips, flattened nose, eyes swelled shut, a collapsed cheekbone, black blood crusted in his eyes and ears and nose and the corners of his mouth. Blood of Thomas's blood. His creation.

'But if he hadn't robbed the bank,' Thomas said, 'they wouldn't be dead.'

'If the other cops hadn't used a fucking machine gun, they wouldn't be dead.' The driver closed the doors, looked at Pooley and Thomas, and Thomas was surprised by the revulsion in his eyes. 'Your guys probably just beat this kid to death. But *he's* the criminal?'

Two guard units pulled in behind the ambulance, and all three vehicles drove off into the night. Thomas had to keep reminding himself to think of the beaten man in the ambulance as 'Joe.' Thinking of him as 'son' was too overwhelming. His flesh and blood, and a lot of that blood and some of that flesh lay in this alley.

He said to Pooley, 'You put that APB out on Albert White?'

Pooley nodded. 'And Loomis and Bones and Donnie No Last Name, but we assume it's Donnie Gishler, one of White's guys.'

'Make Gishler a priority. Get it out to all units that he might have a woman in the car. Where's Forman?'

Pooley chin-gestured. 'Up the alley.'

Thomas started walking and Pooley fell in line. When they reached the crowd of policemen by the service door, Thomas avoided looking at the puddle of Joe's blood near his right foot, a puddle rich enough to receive the rain and still remain a bright red. Instead, he focused on his chief of detectives, Steve Forman.

'You got anything on the cars?'

Forman flipped open his steno notebook. 'Dishwasher said there was a Cole Roadster parked in the alley between eight-fifteen and eight-thirty. After that, dishwasher said it was gone, said this Dodge replaced it.'

The Dodge was what they'd been trying to drag Joe into when Thomas and the cavalry had arrived.

'I want a priority APB on the Roadster,' Thomas said. 'It's being driven by Donald Gishler. There might be a woman in the backseat, Emma Gould. Steve, she's of the Charlestown Goulds. Know who I mean?'

'Oh, yeah,' Forman said.

'Not Bobo's kid. She's Ollie Gould's.'

'Okay.'

'Send someone to make sure she's not safe and sound in bed on Union Street. Sergeant Pooley?'

'Yes, sir.'

'Have you seen this Donnie Gishler in the flesh?'

Pooley nodded. 'He's about five-six, a hundred ninety pounds. Usually wears black knit caps. Had a handlebar mustache last time I saw him. The One-Six would have his mug shot.'

'Send someone to get it. And get out the description to all units.'

He looked at the puddle of his son's blood. A tooth floated in it.

He and his eldest son, Aiden, hadn't spoken in years, though he did receive the occasional letter filled with bland facts but no personal reflections. He didn't know where he lived or even if he was alive or dead. His middle son, Connor, had been blinded during the police strike riots of '19. Physically, he'd adapted to his infirmity with commendable speed, but mentally it had set ablaze his inclination toward self-pity, and he'd quickly turned to alcohol. After he'd failed to drink himself to death, he found religion. Shortly after he abandoned that flirtation (God apparently demanded more from his worshippers than a love affair with martyrdom), he took up residence at the Silas Abbotsford School for the Blind and Crippled. They gave him a custodian's job – this, for a man who'd been the youngest assistant district attorney in state history assigned as lead prosecutor on a capital case – and he lived out his days there, mopping floors he couldn't see. Every now and then he was offered a teaching job at the school, but he'd declined them all under the pretense of shyness. There was nothing shy about any of Thomas's sons. Connor had simply decided to shutter himself away from all who loved him. Which, in his case, meant Thomas.

And here now was his youngest son, given over to a life of crime, a life of whores and bootleggers and gun thugs. A life that always seemed to promise glamour and riches but rarely delivered either. And now, because of his compatriots and Thomas's own men, he might not live through the night.

Thomas stood in the rain and could smell nothing but the stink of his own horrid self.

'Find the girl,' he said to Pooley and Forman.

A patrol officer in Salem spotted Donnie Gishler and Emma Gould. By the time the chase ended, nine cruisers were involved, all from small North Shore towns – Beverly, Peabody, Marblehead. Several of the policemen saw a woman in the backseat of the car; several didn't; one claimed he saw two or three girls back there, but they later confirmed he'd been drinking. After Donnie Gishler had driven two cruisers off the road at high speed, damaging both, and after the officers had taken his fire (however poorly aimed), they'd fired back.

Donnie Gishler's Cole Roadster left the road at 9:50 P.M. in heavy rain. They were racing down Ocean Avenue in Marblehead alongside Lady's Cove when one of the policemen either fired a lucky shot into Gishler's tire or – more likely at forty miles an hour in the rain – the tire simply blew out from wear and tear. At that part of Ocean Avenue, there was very little avenue and endless ocean. The Cole left the road on three wheels, dipped over the shoulder, and snapped back out, its tires no longer touching ground. It entered eight feet of water with two of its windows shot out and sank before most of the policemen had left their vehicles.

A patrolman from Beverly, Lew Burleigh, stripped down to his skivvies and dove in, but it was dark, even after someone got the idea to point the cruisers' headlamps at the water. Lew Burleigh dove into the frigid water four times, enough to suffer hypothermia that landed him in the hospital for a day, but he never found the car.

The divers found it the next afternoon, shortly after two, Gishler still behind the wheel. A piece of the steering wheel had snapped off and entered his body through his armpit. The gearshift had perforated his groin. That's not what killed him, though. One of the more than fifty bullets fired by police that night had hit the back of his head. Even if the tire hadn't blown out, the car would have entered the water.

They found a silver band and matching feather stuck to the ceiling of the car but no other evidence of Emma Gould.

The gunfire exchanged between the police and three gangsters behind the Hotel Statler entered the city's historic mist about ten minutes after it happened. This, even though no one was hit and, in all the confusion, few bullets were actually fired. The criminals had the good fortune to flee the alley just as the theater crowd exited the restaurants and headed toward the Colonial or the Plymouth. A revival of *Pygmalion* had been sold out at the Colonial for three weeks, and the Plymouth had incurred the wrath of the Watch and Ward Society by staging *The Playboy of the Western World*. The Watch and Ward dispatched dozens of protesters, dowdy women with lemon-sucker lips and tireless vocal cords, but this just drew attention to the play. The women's loud and strident presence wasn't only a boon for business; it was also a godsend for the gangsters. The trio came pinwheeling out of the alley and the police crashed out onto the street not far behind, but when the Watch and Ward women saw the guns, they screamed and shrieked and pointed. Several couples on their way to the theater took awkward, violent cover in doorways, and a chauffeur swerved his employer's Pierce-Arrow into a streetlamp as a light drizzle turned suddenly into a heavy downpour. By the time the officers got their wits back, the gangsters had commandeered a car on Piedmont Street and slipped off into a city pelted by relentless rain.

The 'Statler Shootout' made for good copy. The narrative started simply – hero coppers shoot it out with cop-killer thugs and subdue and arrest one. It soon grew more complicated, however. Oscar Fayette, an ambulance driver, reported that the thug under arrest had been so severely beaten by the police that he might not live through the night. Shortly after midnight, unconfirmed rumors spread through the newsrooms along Washington Street that a woman had been seen locked in a car that had entered the waters of Lady's Cove in Marblehead at top speed and sank to the bottom in less than a minute.

Then word went round that one of the gangsters involved in the Statler Shootout was none other than Albert White, the businessman. Albert White had, until this point, occupied an enviable position in the Boston social scene – that of a *possible* bootlegger, a *likely* rumrunner, a *probable* outlaw. Everyone assumed he had a hand in the rackets, but most could believe he managed to stay above the mayhem now plaguing the streets of every major city. Albert White was considered a 'good' bootlegger. A gracious provider of a harmless vice who cut a striking figure in his pale suits and could regale a crowd with tales of his war heroics and his days as a policeman. But after the Statler Shootout (a moniker E. M. Statler tried, unsuccessfully, to get the papers to reconsider), that sentiment vanished. Police filed a warrant for Albert's arrest. Whether he eventually beat the rap or not, his days of hobnobbing with respectable people were over. Thrills born of the vicarious and the salacious, it was acknowledged in the parlors and drawing rooms of Beacon Hill, had limits.

Then there was the fate that befell Deputy Police Superintendent Thomas Coughlin, once considered a shoo-in for commissioner and quite possibly the State House. When it was revealed in the next day's late editions that the thug arrested and beaten at the scene was Coughlin's own son, most readers refrained from judging him on issues of paternity because most knew the travails of trying to raise virtuous children in such a Gomorrahan age. But then the *Examiner* columnist Billy Kelleher wrote of his encounter with Joseph Coughlin on the staircase at the Statler. It was Kelleher who'd called the police and reported his sighting and Kelleher who reached the alley in time to see Thomas Coughlin feed his son to the lions under his command. The public recoiled – failing to raise your child properly was one thing. Ordering him beaten into a coma was quite another.

By the time Thomas was called to the commissioner's office in Pemberton Square, he knew he'd never occupy it.

Commissioner Herbert Wilson stood behind his desk and waved Thomas to a chair. Wilson had run the department since 1922, after the previous commissioner, Edwin Upton Curtis, who'd done more damage to it than the Kaiser had done to Belgium, graciously died of a heart attack. 'Have a seat, Tom.'

Thomas Coughlin hated being called Tom, hated the diminutive nature of it, the callous familiarity.

He took the seat.

'How's your son?' Commissioner Wilson asked him.

'In a coma.'

Wilson nodded and exhaled slowly through his nostrils. 'And every day he remains that way, Tom, the more he resembles a saint.' The commissioner peered across the desk at him. 'You look terrible. You've been sleeping?'

Thomas shook his head. 'Not since . . .' He'd spent the last two nights at his son's hospital bed, counting his sins and praying to a God he scarcely believed in anymore. Joe's doctor had told him that even if Joe came out of the coma, brain damage was a possibility. Thomas, in a rage – that white-hot rage of which everyone from his shit of a father to his wife to his sons had been justifiably frightened – had ordered other men to bludgeon his own son. Now he pictured his shame as a blade left on hot coals until the steel was black and serpent-coils of smoke slithered along the edges. The point entered his abdomen below the rib cage and moved through his insides, cutting and cutting until he couldn't see or breathe.

'Any more information on the other two, the Bartolos?' the commissioner asked.

'I would've thought you'd heard by now.'

Wilson shook his head. 'I've been in budget meetings all morning.'

'Just came over the Teletype. They got Paolo Bartolo.'

'Who's they?'

'Vermont State Police.'

'Alive?'

Thomas shook his head.

For some reason they might never understand, Paolo Bartolo had been driving a car stuffed with canned hams; they filled the back and were piled up in the foot well of the passenger seat. When he rolled a red light on South Main Street in St Albans, about fifteen miles shy of the Canadian border, a state trooper tried to pull him over. Paolo took off. The trooper gave chase and other staties joined in and they eventually drove the car off the road near a dairy farm in Enosburg Falls.

Whether Paolo pulled a gun as he exited his car on a fine spring afternoon was still being ascertained. It was possible that he reached for his waistband. Also possible that he simply didn't raise his hands fast enough. Given that either Paolo or his brother Dion had executed state trooper Jacob Zobe on the side of a road very similar to this one, the troopers took no chances. Every officer fired his service revolver at least twice.

'How many cops responded?' Wilson asked.

'Seven, I believe, sir.'

'And how many bullets struck the felon?'

'Eleven is the number I heard, but the truth awaits a proper autopsy.'

'And Dion Bartolo?'

'Holed up in Montreal, I'd assume. Or nearby. Dion was always the smarter of the two. Paolo's the one you'd expect to stick his head up.'

The commissioner lifted a sheet of paper off one small pile on his desk and placed it atop another small pile. He looked out the window, seemed entranced by the Custom House spire a few blocks away. 'The department can't let you walk back out of this office carrying the same rank you carried in, Tom. You understand that?'

'I do, yes.' Thomas glanced around the office he'd coveted for the past ten years and felt no sense of loss.

'And if I demoted you to captain, I'd have to have a division house to hand over to you.'

'Which you don't.'

'Which I don't.' The commissioner leaned forward, his hands clasped together. 'You can pray exclusively for your son now, Thomas, because your career just reached its highest floor.'

'She's not dead,' Joe said.

He'd come out of the coma four hours before. Thomas had arrived at Mass. General ten minutes after the doctor called. He'd brought the attorney Jack D'Jarvis with him. Jack D'Jarvis was a small, elderly man who wore wool suits of the most forgettable colors – tree bark brown, damp sand gray, blacks that appeared to have been left in the sun too long. His ties usually matched the suits; the collars of his shirts were yellowed, and on the rare occasions he wore a hat, it seemed too big for his head and perched on the tops of his ears. Jack D'Jarvis looked ready to be put out to pasture, and he'd looked that way for the better part of three decades, but no one but a stranger was stupid enough to believe it. He was the best criminal defense lawyer in the city, and few could name a close second. Over the years Jack D'Jarvis had dismantled at least two dozen ironclad cases Thomas had brought to the DA. It was said that when Jack D'Jarvis died, he'd spend his time in heaven springing all his former clients from hell.

The doctors examined Joe for two hours while Thomas and D'Jarvis cooled their heels in the corridor with the young patrolman manning the door.

'I can't get him off,' D'Jarvis said.

'I know that.'

'Rest assured, though, the second-degree murder charge is a farce and the state's attorney knows it. But your son will have to do time.'

'How much?'

D'Jarvis shrugged. 'Ten years would be my guess.'

'In Charlestown?' Thomas shook his head. 'There'll be nothing left of him to walk back out those doors.'

'Three police officers are dead, Thomas.'

'But he didn't kill them.'

'Which is why he won't get the chair. But pretend this is anyone else but your son and *you'd* want him to get twenty years.'

'But he is my son,' Thomas said.

The doctors exited the room.

One of them stopped to talk to Thomas. 'I don't know what his skull is made of, but we're guessing it's not bone.'

'Doctor?'

'He's fine. No cranial bleeding, no loss of memory or speech disability. His nose and half his ribs are broken, and it'll be some time before he urinates without seeing blood in the bowl, but no brain damage that I can see.'

Thomas and Jack D'Jarvis went in and sat by Joe's bed and he considered them through his swollen black eyes.

'I was wrong,' Thomas said. 'Dead wrong. And, sure, there's no excuse for it.'

Joe spoke through black lips crisscrossed with sutures. 'You shouldn't have let them beat me?'

Thomas nodded. 'I shouldn't have.'

'You going soft on me, old man?'

Thomas shook his head. 'I should've done it myself.'

Joe's soft chuckle traveled through his nostrils. 'With all due respect, sir, I'm happy your men did it. If you'd done it, I might be dead.'

Thomas smiled. 'So you don't hate me?'

'First time I remember liking you in ten years.' Joe tried to raise himself off the pillow but failed. 'Where's Emma?'

Jack D'Jarvis opened his mouth, but Thomas waved him off. He looked his son steadily in the face as he told him what had happened in Marblehead.

Joe sat with the information for a bit, turning it over. He said, somewhat desperately, 'She's not dead.'

'She is, son. And even if we'd acted immediately that night, Donnie Gishler was not of the disposition to be taken alive. She was dead as soon as she got in that car.'

'There's no body,' Joe said. 'So she's not dead.'

'Joseph, they never found half the bodies on *Titanic,* but the poor souls are no longer with us just the same.'

'I won't believe it.'

'You won't? Or you don't?'

'It's the same thing.'

'Far from it.' Thomas shook his head. 'We've pieced together some of what happened that night. She was Albert White's moll. She betrayed you.'

'She did,' Joe said.

'And?'

Joe smiled, sutured lips and all. 'And I don't give a shit. I'm crazy about her.'

'"Crazy" isn't love,' his father said.

'No, what is it?'

'Crazy.'

'All due respect, Dad, I witnessed your marriage for eighteen years, and that wasn't love.'

'No,' his father agreed, 'it wasn't. So I know whereof I speak.' He sighed. 'Either way, she's gone, son. As dead as your mother, God rest her.'

Joe said, 'What about Albert?'

Thomas sat on the side of the bed. 'In the wind.'

Jack D'Jarvis said, 'But rumored to be negotiating his return.'

Thomas looked over at him, and D'Jarvis nodded.

'Who're you?' Joe asked D'Jarvis.

The lawyer extended his hand. 'John D'Jarvis, Mr Coughlin. Most people call me Jack.'

Joe's swollen eyes opened as wide as they had since Thomas and Jack had entered the room.

'Damn,' he said. 'Heard of you.'

'I've heard of you too,' D'Jarvis said. 'Unfortunately, so has the whole state. On the other hand, one of the worst decisions your father has ever made could end up being the best thing that could have happened to you.'

'How so?' Thomas asked.

'By beating him to a pulp, you turned him into a victim. The state's attorney isn't going to want to prosecute. He *will* but he won't want to.'

'Bondurant is state's attorney these days, right?' Joe asked.

D'Jarvis nodded. 'You know him?'

'I know of him,' Joe said, the fear apparent on his bruised face.

'Thomas,' D'Jarvis asked, watching him carefully, 'do you know Bondurant?'

Thomas said, 'I do, yes.'

Calvin Bondurant had married a Lenox of Beacon Hill and had produced three willowy daughters, one of whom had recently married a Lodge to great notice in the society pages. Bondurant was a tireless advocate of Prohibition, a fearless crusader against all manner of vice, which he proclaimed was a product of the lower classes and inferior races who'd been washing ashore in this great land the last seventy years. The last seventy years of immigration had been primarily limited to two races – the Irish and the Italians – so Bondurant's message wasn't particularly subtle. But when he ran for governor in a few years, his donors on Beacon Hill and in Back Bay would know he was the right man.

Bondurant's secretary ushered Thomas into his office on Kirkby and closed the doors behind them. Bondurant turned from where he stood by the window and gave Thomas an emotionless gaze.

'I've been expecting you.'

Ten years ago, Thomas had swept Calvin Bondurant up in a raid on a rooming house. Bondurant had been keeping time with several bottles of champagne and a naked young man of Mexican descent. In addition to a burgeoning career in prostitution, the Mexican turned out to be a former member of Pancho Villa's División del Norte who was wanted in his homeland on charges of treason. Thomas had deported the revolutionary back to Chihuahua and allowed Bondurant's name to vanish from the arrest logs.

'Well, here I am,' Thomas said.

'You turned your son the criminal into a victim. That's an amazing trick. Are you that smart, Deputy Superintendent?'

Thomas said, 'Nobody's that smart.'

Bondurant shook his head. 'Not true. A few people are. And you might be one of them. Tell him to plead. There are three dead cops in that town. Their funerals will be all over the front pages tomorrow. If he pleads to the bank robbery and, I don't know, reckless endangerment, I'll recommend twelve.'

'Years?'

'For three dead cops? That's light, Thomas.'

'Five.'

'Excuse me?'

'Five,' Thomas said.

'Not a chance.' Bondurant shook his head.

Thomas sat in his chair and didn't move.

Bondurant shook his head again.

Thomas crossed his legs at the ankle.

Bondurant said, 'Look.'

Thomas cocked his head slightly.

'Let me disabuse you of a notion or two, Deputy Superintendent.'

'Chief inspector.'

'I'm sorry?'

'I was demoted yesterday to chief inspector.'

The smile never reached Bondurant's lips but it slipped through his eyes. A glint and then gone. 'Then we can leave unsaid the notion I was going to dispel for you.'

'I have no notions or illusions,' Thomas said. 'I'm a

practical man.' He removed a photograph from his pocket and placed it on Bondurant's desk.

Bondurant looked down at the picture. A door, faded red, the number 29 in its center. It was the door to a row house in Back Bay. What fluttered through Bondurant's eyes this time was the opposite of mirth.

Thomas placed one finger on the man's desk. 'If you move to another building for your liaisons, I'll know within an hour. I understand you're building quite the war chest for your run for the governor's office. Make it deep, counselor. A man with a deep war chest can take on all comers.' Thomas placed his hat on his head. He tugged at the center of the brim until he was sure it sat straight.

Bondurant looked at the piece of paper on his desk. 'I'll see what I can do.'

'*Seeing* what you can do is of little interest to me.'

'I'm one man.'

'Five years,' Thomas said. 'He gets five years.'

It was another two weeks before a woman's forearm washed up in Nahant. Three days after that, a fisherman off the coast of Lynn pulled a femur into his net. The medical examiner determined that the femur and the forearm came from the same person – a woman in her early twenties, probably of Northern European stock, freckle-skinned and pale of flesh.

In *The Commonwealth of Massachusetts v. Joseph Coughlin*, Joe pled guilty to aiding and abetting an armed robbery. He was sentenced to five years and four months in prison.

*

He knew she was alive.

He knew it because the alternative was something he couldn't live with. He had faith in her existence because not to believe left him feeling stripped and flayed.

'She's gone,' his father said to him just before they transferred him from the Suffolk County Jail to Charlestown Penitentiary.

'No, she's not.'

'Listen to yourself.'

'No one saw her in the car when it went off the road.'

'At high speed in the rain at night? They put her in the car, son. The car went off the road. She died and floated off into the ocean.'

'Not until I see a body.'

'The *parts* of the body weren't enough?' His father held a hand up in apology. When he spoke again, his voice was softer. 'What will it take for you to accept reason?'

'It's not reason that she's dead. Not when I know she's alive.'

The more Joe said it, the more he knew she was dead. He could feel it in the same way he could feel that she'd loved him, even as she'd betrayed him. But if he admitted it, if he faced it, what did he have left but five years in the worst prison in the Northeast? No friends, no God, no family.

'She's alive, Dad.'

His father considered him for some time. 'What did you love about her?'

'I'm sorry?'

'What did you love about this woman?'

Joe searched for the words. Eventually, he stumbled over

a few that felt less inadequate than the rest. 'She was becoming something with me that was different than what she showed to the rest of the world. Something, I dunno, softer.'

'That's loving a potential, not a person.'

'How would you know?'

His father cocked his head at that. 'You were the child that was supposed to fill the distance between your mother and me. Were you aware of that?'

Joe said, 'I knew about the distance.'

'Then you saw how well that plan worked out. People don't fix each other, Joseph. And they never become anything but what they've always been.'

Joe said, 'I don't believe that.'

'Don't? Or won't?' His father closed his eyes. 'Every breath, son, is luck.' He opened his eyes and they were pink in the corners. 'Achievement? Depends on luck – to be born in the right place at the right time and be of the right color. To live long enough to be in the right place at the right time to make one's fortune. Yes, yes, hard work and talent make up the difference. They are crucial, and you know I'd never argue different. But the *foundation* of all lives is luck. Good or bad. Luck is life and life is luck. And it's leaking from the moment it lands in your hand. Don't waste yours pining for a dead woman who wasn't worthy of you in the first place.'

Joe's jaw clenched, but all he said was, 'You make your luck, Dad.'

'Sometimes,' his father said. 'But other times it makes you.'

They sat in silence for a bit. Joe's heart had never beat so hard. It punched at his chest, a frantic fist. He felt for it the way he'd feel for something outside himself, a stray dog on a wet night, perhaps.

His father looked at his watch, put it back in his vest. 'Someone will probably threaten you your first week behind the walls. No later than the second. You'll see what he wants in his eyes, whether he says it or not.'

Joe's mouth felt very dry.

'Someone else – a real good egg of a fella – will stand up for you in the yard or in the mess hall. And after he backs the other man down, he'll offer you his protection for the length of your sentence. Joe? Listen to me. That's the man you hurt. You hurt him so he can't get strong enough again to hurt you. You take his elbow or his kneecap. Or both.'

Joe's heartbeat found an artery in his throat. 'And then they'll leave me alone?'

His father gave him a tight smile and started to nod, but the smile went away and the nod went with it. 'No, they won't.'

'So what will make them stop?'

His father looked away for a moment, his jaw working. When he looked back his eyes were dry. 'Nothing.'

CHAPTER SEVEN

The Mouth of It

The distance from Suffolk County Jail to the Charlestown Penitentiary was a little more than a mile. They could have walked it in the time it took to load them into the bus and bolt their ankle manacles to the floor. Four of them went over that morning – a thin Negro and a fat Russian whose names Joe never learned, Norman, a soft and shaky white kid, and Joe. Norman and Joe had chatted a few times in jail because Norman's cell was across from Joe's. Norman had had the misfortune to fall under the spell of the daughter of the man whose livery stable he tended on Pinckney Street in the flat of Beacon Hill. The girl, fifteen, got pregnant, and Norman, seventeen and orphaned since he was twelve, got three years in a maximum security prison for rape.

He told Joe he'd been reading his Bible and was ready to atone for his transgressions. Told Joe the Lord would be with him and that there was good in every man, not the least of which could be found in the lowest of men, and that he suspected he might even find more good behind those walls than he'd found on this side of them.

Joe had never met a more terrified creature.

As the bus bounced along the Charles River Road, a guard rechecked their manacles and introduced himself as Mr Hammond. He informed them that they would be housed in East Wing, except, of course, for the nigger, who would be housed in South Wing with his own kind.

'But the rules apply to all of you, no matter what your color or creed. Never look a guard in the eyes. Never question a guard's order. Never cross over the dirt track that runs along the wall. Never touch yourselves or one another in an unwholesome manner. Just do your time like good fish, without complaint or ill will, and we'll find harmonious accord along the pathway to your restitution.'

The prison was more than a hundred years old; its original dark granite buildings had been joined by redbrick structures of more recent vintage. Designed in cruciform style, the heart of it was comprised of four wings branching off a central tower. Atop the tower was a cupola, manned at all times by four guards with rifles, one for each direction a prisoner could run. It was surrounded by train tracks and factories, foundries, and mills that stretched from the North End down the river to Somerville. The factories made stoves and the mills made textiles and the foundries reeked of magnesium and copper and cast-iron gases. When the bus dropped down the hill and into the flats, the sky took cover behind a ceiling of smoke. An Eastern Freight train blew its whistle, and they had to wait for it to rattle past them before they could cross the tracks and travel the final three hundred yards onto the prison grounds.

The bus pulled to a stop and Mr Hammond and another guard unlocked their manacles and Norman started to shiver and then he blubbered, the tears dripping off his jaw like sweat.

Joe said, 'Norman.'

Norman looked across at him.

'Don't do that.'

But Norman couldn't stop.

His cell was on the top tier of East Wing. It baked in the sun all day long and held the heat through the night. There was no electricity in the cells themselves. They reserved that for the corridors, the mess hall, and the killing chair in the Death House. Cells were lit by candlelight. Indoor plumbing had yet to come to Charlestown Penitentiary, so cell mates pissed and shat in wooden buckets. His cell was built for a single prisoner, but they'd stacked four beds in it. His three cell mates were named Oliver, Eugene, and Tooms. Oliver and Eugene were garden-variety stickup guys from Revere and Quincy, respectively. They'd both done business with the Hickey Mob. They'd never had a chance to work with Joe or even hear about him, but after they all passed a few names back and forth, they knew he was legit enough not to turn him out just to make a point.

Tooms was older and quieter. He had stringy hair and stringy limbs, and something foul lived behind his eyes that you didn't want to look at. As the sun set on their first night, he sat on his top bunk, legs dangling over the edge, and every now and then Joe found Tooms's blank stare turned in his direction, and it was all he could do to meet it and then casually move off it.

Joe slept on one of the low bunks, across from Oliver. He had the worst mattress and the bunk sagged, and his sheet was coarse and moth-eaten and smelled like wet fur. He dozed fitfully but he never slept.

In the morning, Norman approached him in the yard. Both of his eyes were black and his nose looked to be broken and Joe was about to ask him about it when Norman scowled, bit down on his lower lip, and punched Joe in the neck. Joe two-stepped to his right and ignored the sting and thought of asking why, but he didn't have enough time. Norman came for him, both arms awkwardly raised. If Norman avoided his head and started punching his body, Joe was done. His ribs weren't healed; sitting up in the morning still hurt so much he saw stars. He shuffled, his heels scrabbling the dirt. High above them, the guards in their watchtowers watched the river to the west or the ocean to the east. Norman drilled a punch into the other side of his neck and Joe raised his foot and brought it down on Norman's kneecap.

Norman fell onto his back, his right leg at an awkward angle. He rolled in the dirt, then used his elbow to try to stand. When Joe stomped the knee a second time, half the yard heard Norman's leg break. The sound that left his mouth wasn't quite a scream. It was something softer and deeper, a huffing noise, something a dog would make after it crawled under a house to die.

Norman lay in the dirt and his arms fell to his sides, and

the tears leaked from his eyes into his ears. Joe knew he could help Norman up, now that he was no danger, but that would be seen as weakness. He walked away. He walked across the yard, already sweltering at 9 A.M., and felt the eyes on him, more than he could count, everyone looking, deciding what the next test would be, how long they'd toy with the mouse before they took a real swipe with their claws.

Norman was nothing. Norman was a warm-up. And if anyone here got a sense of how badly Joe's ribs were damaged – it hurt to fucking breathe at the moment; it hurt to walk – there'd be nothing but bones left by morning.

Joe had seen Oliver and Eugene over by the west wall, but now he watched their backs melt into a crowd. They wanted no part of him until they saw how this played out. So now he was walking toward a group of men he didn't know. If he stopped suddenly and looked around, he'd look foolish. And foolish in here was the same thing as weak.

He reached the group of men and the far side of the yard, by the wall, but they walked away too.

It went that way all day – no one would talk to him. Whatever he had, no one wanted to catch it.

He returned that night to an empty cell. His mattress – the lumpy one – lay on the floor. The other mattresses were gone. The bunks had been removed. Everything had been removed except the mattress, the scratchy sheet, and the shit bucket. Joe looked back at Mr Hammond as he locked the door behind him.

'Where'd everyone else go?'

'They went,' Mr Hammond said and walked down the tier.

For the second night in a row, Joe lay in the hot room and barely slept. It wasn't just his ribs and it wasn't simply fear – the reek of the prison was matched only by the reek of the factories outside. There was a small window at the top of the cell, ten feet up. Maybe the thought behind placing it there had been to give the prisoner a merciful taste of the outside world. But now it was just a conduit for the factory smoke, for the stench of textiles and burning coal. In the heat of the cell, as vermin scuttled along the walls and men groaned in the night, Joe could not fathom how he could survive five days here, never mind five years. He'd lost Emma, he'd lost his freedom, and now he could feel his soul beginning to flicker and wane. What they were taking from him was all he had.

The next day, more of the same. And the day after that. Anyone he approached walked away from him. Anyone he made eye contact with looked away. But he could feel them watching as soon as his gaze moved on. It was all they did, every man in the prison – they watched him.

Waiting.

'For what?' he said at lights-out as Mr Hammond turned the key in the cell door. 'What are they waiting for?'

Mr Hammond stared through the bars at him with his lightless eyes.

'The thing is,' Joe said, 'I'm happy to straighten things out with whoever I offended. If I did, in fact, offend somebody. Because if I did, I didn't do so knowingly. So I'm willing to—'

'You're in the mouth of it,' Mr Hammond said. He looked up at the tiers arrayed above and behind him. 'It decides to roll you around on its tongue. Or it bites down real hardlike, grind its teeth into you. Or it lets you climb over them teeth and jump out. But it decides. Not you.' Mr Hammond swung his enormous ring of keys in a circle before hooking them to his belt. 'You wait.'

'For how long?' Joe asked.

'Till it says so.' Mr Hammond walked up the tier.

The boy who came for him next was just that, a boy. Trembling and jump-eyed and no less dangerous for it. Joe was walking to the Saturday shower when the kid dislodged himself from the line about ten men up and walked down toward Joe.

Joe knew from the moment the kid left the line that he was coming for him, but there was nothing he could do to stop it. The kid wore his striped prison pants and coat and carried his towel and soap bar like the rest of them, but he also had a potato peeler in his right hand, its edges sharpened by a whetstone.

Joe stepped to meet the kid and the kid acted like he was moving on, but then he dropped his towel and soap, planted his foot, and swung his arm at Joe's head. Joe feinted to his right and the kid must have anticipated that because he went to his left and sank the potato peeler into Joe's inner thigh. Joe didn't have time to register the pain before he heard the kid pull it back out. It was the sound that enraged him. It sounded like fish parts sucked into a drain. His flesh, his blood, his meat hung off the edges of the weapon.

On his next pass, the kid lunged for Joe's abdomen or groin: Joe couldn't tell in all the ragged breathing and left-right, right-left scrabbling. He stepped inside the kid's arms and gripped the back of his head and pulled it to his chest. The kid stabbed him again, this time in the hip, but it was a feeble stab with no momentum behind it. Still hurt worse than a dog bite. When the kid pulled his arm back to get a better thrust, Joe ran him backward until he cracked the kid's head against the granite wall.

The kid sighed and dropped the potato peeler, and Joe banged his head off the wall twice more to be sure. The kid slid to the floor.

Joe had never seen him before.

In the infirmary, a doctor cleaned his wounds, sutured the one in his thigh, and wrapped it tightly in gauze. The doctor, who smelled of something chemical, told him to keep off the leg and the hip for a while.

'How do I do that?' Joe asked.

The doctor went on as if Joe had never spoken. 'And keep the wounds clean. Change the dressing twice a day.'

'Do you have more dressing for me?'

'No,' the doctor said, as if embittered by the stupidity of the question.

'So . . .'

'Good as new,' the doctor said and stepped back.

He waited for the guards to come and mete out their punishment for the fight. He waited to hear if the boy who'd attacked him was alive or dead. But no one said anything to him. It was as if he'd imagined the whole incident.

At lights-out, he asked Mr Hammond if he'd heard about the fight on the way to the showers.

'No.'

'No, you didn't hear?' Joe asked. 'Or, no, it didn't happen?'

'No,' Mr Hammond said and walked away.

A few days after the stabbing, an inmate spoke to him. There was little special about the man's voice – it was lightly accented (Italian, he guessed) and a bit gravelly – but after a week of almost total silence it sounded so beautiful that Joe's throat closed up and his chest filled.

He was an old man with thick glasses too big for his face. He approached Joe in the yard as Joe limped across it. He'd been in the line to the showers on Saturday. Joe remembered him because he'd looked so frail one could only imagine the horrors this place had foisted upon him over the years.

'Do you think they'll run out of men to fight you soon?'

He was about Joe's height. He was bald up top, a shade of silver on the sides that matched his pencil-thin mustache. Long legs and a short, pudgy torso. Tiny hands. Something delicate about the way he moved, almost tiptoeing, like a cat burglar, but eyes as innocent and hopeful as a child's on his first day of school.

'I don't think they can run out,' Joe said. 'Lot of candidates.'

'Won't you get tired?'

'Sure,' Joe said. 'But I'll go as long as I can, I guess.'

'You're very fast.'

'I'm fast, I'm not *very* fast.'

'You are, though.' The old man opened a small canvas pouch and removed two cigarettes. He handed one to Joe.

'I've seen both your fights. You're so fast most of these men haven't noticed you're protecting your ribs.'

Joe stopped as the man lit their cigarettes with a match he struck off his thumbnail. 'I'm not protecting anything.'

The old man smiled. 'A long time ago, in another life, before this' – he gestured past the walls and the wire – 'I promoted a few boxers. A few wrestlers too. I never made much money, but I met a lot of pretty women. Boxers attract pretty women. And pretty women travel with other pretty women.' He shrugged as they began walking again. 'So I know when a man is protecting his ribs. Are they broken?'

Joe said, 'There's nothing wrong with them.'

'I promise,' the old man said, 'if they send me to fight you, I'll limit myself to grasping your ankles and holding on tight.'

Joe chuckled. 'Just the ankles, uh?'

'Maybe the nose, if I sense an advantage.'

Joe looked over at him. He must have been here so long he'd seen every hope die and experienced every degradation, and now they left him alone because he'd survived all they'd thrown at him. Or because he was just a bag of wrinkles, unappealing for purposes of trade. Harmless.

'Well, to protect my nose . . .' Joe took a long drag off the cigarette. He'd forgotten how good one could taste if you didn't know where your next one was coming from. 'A few months ago, I broke six ribs and fractured or sprained the rest.'

'A few months ago. That leaves you only a couple months to go.'

'No. Really?'

The old man nodded. 'Broken ribs are like broken hearts – at least six months before they heal.'

Is that how long it takes? Joe thought.

'If only meals lasted as long.' The old man rubbed his small paunch. 'What do they call you?'

'Joe.'

'Never Joseph?'

'Just my father.'

The man nodded and exhaled a stream of smoke with slow relish. 'This is such a hopeless place. Even in your limited time here, I'm sure you've come to the same conclusion.'

Joe nodded.

'It eats men. It doesn't even spit them back out.'

'How long have you been here?'

'Oh,' the old man said, 'I stopped counting years ago.' He looked up at the greasy blue sky and spit a piece of tobacco off his tongue. 'There's nothing about this place I don't know. If you need help comprehending it, just ask.'

Joe doubted the old fella was as tuned to the pulse of the place he imagined himself to be, but he saw no harm in saying, 'I will. Thank you. I appreciate your offer.'

They reached the end of the yard. As they turned to walk back the way they'd come, the old man placed his arm around Joe's shoulders.

The whole yard watched.

The old man flicked his cigarette into the dust and held out his hand. Joe shook it.

'My name is Tommaso Pescatore, but everyone calls me Maso. Consider yourself under my care.'

Joe knew the name. Maso Pescatore ran the North End

and most of the gambling and women on the North Shore. From behind these walls, he controlled a lot of the liquor coming up from Florida. Tim Hickey had done a lot of work with him over the years and usually mentioned that extreme caution was the only sensible course of action when dealing with the man.

'I didn't ask to be under your care, Maso.'

'How many things in life – good and bad – come to us whether we ask for them or not?' Maso removed his arm from Joe's shoulders and placed a hand over his eyebrows to block the sun. Where Joe had just seen innocence in his eyes, he now saw cunning. 'Call me Mr Pescatore from now on, Joseph. And give this to your father next time you see him.' Maso slipped a piece of paper into Joe's hand.

Joe looked at the address scrawled there: *1417 Blue Hill Ave.* That was it – no name, no telephone number, just an address.

'Hand it to your father. Just this once. It's all I'll ask of you.'

'What if I don't?' Joe asked.

Maso seemed genuinely confused by the question. He tilted his head to one side and looked at Joe and a small and curious smile found his lips. The smile widened and turned into a soft laugh. He shook his head several times. He gave Joe a two-finger salute and walked back to the wall where his men stood waiting.

In the visiting room, Thomas watched his son limp across the floor and take his seat.

'What happened?'

'Guy stabbed me in the leg.'

'Why?'

Joe shook his head. He slid his palm across the table, and Thomas saw the piece of paper under it. He closed his hand over his son's for a moment, relishing the contact and trying to remember why he'd refrained from initiating it for over a decade. He took the piece of paper and placed it in his pocket. He looked at his son, at his dark-ringed eyes and sullied spirit, and he saw the whole of it suddenly.

'I'm to do someone's bidding,' he said.

Joe looked up from the table and met his eyes.

'Whose bidding, Joseph?'

'Maso Pescatore's.'

Thomas sat back and asked himself just how much he loved his son.

Joe read the question in his eyes. 'Don't try to tell me you're clean, Dad.'

'I do civilized business with civilized people. You're asking me to get under the thumb of a bunch of dagos one generation removed from a cave.'

'It's not under their thumb.'

'No? What's on the piece of paper?'

'An address.'

'Just an address?'

'Yeah. I don't know any more than that.'

His father nodded several times, his breath exiting through his nostrils. 'Because you're a child. Some wop gives you an address to give your father, a member of police command, and you don't grasp that the only thing that address could be is the location of a rival's illicit supply.'

'Of what?'

'Most likely a warehouse filled to the bursting with liquor.' His father stared up at the ceiling and ran a hand over his trim white hair.

'He said just this once.'

His father gave him a malevolent smile. 'And you believed him.'

He left the prison.

He walked down the path toward his car, surrounded by the smell of chemicals. Smoke rose from the factory stacks. It was dark gray in most places but it turned the sky brown and the earth black. Trains chugged along the outskirts; for some odd reason, they reminded Thomas of wolves circling a medical tent.

He had sent at least a thousand men here over the course of his career. Many of them had died behind the granite walls. If they arrived with any illusions about human decency, they lost those straightaway. There were too many prisoners and too few guards for the prison to run as anything but what it was – a dumping ground, and then a proving ground, for animals. If you went in a man, you left a beast. If you went in an animal, you honed your skills.

He feared his son was too soft. For all his transgressions over the years, his lawlessness, his inability to obey Thomas or the rules or much of anything, Joseph was the most open of his sons. You could see his heart through the heaviest winter coat.

Thomas reached a call box at the end of the path. His key was attached to his watch chain and he used it now to open the box. He looked at the address in his hand: 1417 Blue Hill Avenue in Mattapan. Jew Country. Which meant the warehouse was probably owned by Jacob Rosen, a known supplier of Albert White.

White was back in the city now. He'd never spent a night in jail, probably because he'd hired Jack D'Jarvis to handle his defense.

Thomas looked back at the prison his son called home. A tragedy but not surprising. His son had chosen the path that had led him here over years of Thomas's strenuous objection and disapproval. If Thomas used this call box, he was wedded to the Pescatore mob for life, to a race of people who had brought to the shores of this country anarchism and its bombers, assassins, and the Black Hand and now, organized in something rumored to be called *omertà organiza*, they had overtaken by force the entire business of illegal liquor.

And he was supposed to give them more?

Work for them?

Kiss their rings?

He closed the call box door, returned his watch to his pocket, and walked to his car.

For two days, he considered the piece of paper. For two days, he prayed to the God he feared didn't exist. Prayed for guidance. Prayed for his son behind those granite walls.

Saturday was his day off, and Thomas was up on a ladder, repainting the black trim of the windowsills of the K Street row house, when the man called up for directions. It was a hot and humid afternoon, a few purple clouds undulating in his direction. He looked through a window on the third floor into what had once been Aiden's room. It had stood empty for three years before his wife, Ellen, had taken it over as a sewing room. She had passed in her sleep two years ago, so now it sat empty except for a pedal-charged sewing machine and a wooden rack from which hung the items that had been awaiting mending two years ago. Thomas dipped his brush into the can. It would always be Aiden's room.

'I'm a bit turned around.'

Thomas looked down the ladder at the man standing on the sidewalk thirty feet below. He wore a light blue seer-sucker, white shirt, and a red bow tie, no hat.

'How can I help?' Thomas said.

'I'm looking for the L Street Bathhouse.'

From up here, Thomas could see the bathhouse, and not just the roof – the whole of its brick edifice. He could see the small lagoon beyond it, and beyond the lagoon, the Atlantic, stretching all the way to the land of his birth.

'End of the street.' Thomas pointed, gave the man a nod, and turned back to his paintbrush.

The man said, 'Right down the end of the street, huh? Right down there?'

Thomas turned back and nodded, his eyes on the man now.

'Sometimes, I can't get out of my own way,' the man said. 'Ever happen to you? You know what you should do, but you just can't get out of your own way?'

The man was blond and bland, handsome in a forgettable way. Neither tall nor short, fat nor thin.

'They won't kill him,' he said pleasantly.

Thomas said, 'Excuse me?' and dropped the brush into the paint can.

The man put his hand on the ladder.

From there, it wouldn't take much.

The man squinted up at Thomas and then looked down the street. 'They'll make him wish they did, though. Make him wish that every day of his life.'

'You understand my rank with the Boston Police Department,' Thomas said.

'He'll think about suicide,' the man said. 'Of course he will. But they'll keep him alive by promising to kill you if he does. And every day? They'll think of a new thing to try on him.'

A black Model T pulled off the curb and idled in the middle of the street. The man left the sidewalk, climbed in, and they drove away, taking the first left they found.

Thomas climbed down, surprised to see the shakes in his forearms even after he entered his house. He was getting old, very old. He shouldn't be up on ladders. He shouldn't be standing on principle.

The way of the old was to allow the new to push you aside with as much grace as you could muster.

He called Kenny Donlan, the captain of the Third District in Mattapan. For five years, Kenny had been Thomas's lieutenant at the Sixth in South Boston. Like many of the department command staff, he owed his success to Thomas.

'And on your day off no less,' Kenny said when his secretary patched Thomas through.

'Ah, there's no days off for the likes of us, boy.'

'That's the truth of it,' Kenny said. 'How can I help you, Thomas?'

'One-four-one-seven Blue Hill Avenue,' Thomas said. 'It's a warehouse, supposedly for gaming parlor equipment.'

'But that's not what's in there,' Kenny said.

'No.'

'How hard do you want it hit?'

'Down to the last bottle,' Thomas said, and something inside him cried out as it died. 'Down to the last drop.'

CHAPTER EIGHT

In the Gloaming

That summer at Charlestown Penitentiary the Commonwealth of Massachusetts prepared to execute two famous anarchists. Global protests didn't deter the state from its mission, nor did a flurry of last-minute appeals, stays, and further appeals. In the weeks after Sacco and Vanzetti were taken to Charlestown from Dedham and housed in the Death House to await the electric chair, Joe's sleep was interrupted by throngs of outraged citizens gathered on the other side of the dark granite walls. Sometimes they remained there through the night, singing songs and shouting through megaphones and chanting their slogans. Several nights Joe assumed they brought torches to add a medieval flavor to the proceedings because he'd wake to the smell of burning pitch.

Other than a few nights of fitful sleep, however, the fate of the two doomed men had no effect on the lives of Joe or anyone he knew except for Maso Pescatore, who'd been forced to sacrifice his nightly strolls atop the prison walls until the world stopped watching.

On that famous night in late August, the excess voltage used on the hapless Italians sapped the rest of the electricity in the prison, and the lights on the tiers flickered and dimmed or snapped off entirely. The dead anarchists were taken to Forest Hills and cremated. The protestors dwindled and then went away.

Maso returned to the nightly routine he'd been following for ten years – walking the tops of the walls along the thick, curled wire and the dark watchtowers that overlooked the yard within and the blasted landscape of factories and slums without.

He often took Joe with him. To his surprise, Joe had become some kind of symbol to Maso – whether as the trophy scalp of the high-ranking police officer now under his thumb or as a potential member of his organization or as a puppy, Joe didn't know, and he didn't ask. Why ask when his presence on the wall beside Maso at night clearly stated one thing above all others – he was protected.

'Do you think they were guilty?' Joe asked one night.

Maso shrugged. 'It doesn't matter. What matters is the message.'

'What message? They executed two fellas who might have been innocent.'

'That was the message,' Maso said. 'And every anarchist in the world heard it.'

Charlestown Penitentiary spilled blood all over itself that summer. Joe first believed the savagery to be innate, the pointless dog-eat-dog viciousness of men killing each other over pride – in your place in line, in your right to continue walking to the yard on the path you'd chosen, in not being jostled or elbowed or having the toe of your shoe scuffed.

It turned out to be more complicated than that.

An inmate in East Wing lost his eyes when someone clapped handfuls of glass into them. In South Wing, guards found a guy stabbed a dozen times below his ribs, entrance wounds that, judging by the odor, had perforated his liver. Inmates two tiers down smelled the guy die. Joe heard of all-night rape parties on the Lawson block, the block so named because three generations of the Lawson family – the grandfather, one of his sons, and three grandsons – had all been jailed there at the same time. The last one, Emil Lawson, had once been the youngest of the Lawson inmates but always the worst of them, and he was never getting out. His sentences added up to 114 years. Good news for Boston, bad news for Charlestown Pen. When he wasn't leading gang rapes of new fish, Emil Lawson did murder for whoever paid him, though he was rumored to be working exclusively for Maso during the recent troubles.

The war was fought over rum. It was fought on the outside, of course, to some public consternation, but also on the inside, where no one thought to look and wouldn't have shed a tear if they had. Albert White, an importer of whiskey from the north, had decided to branch out into importing rum from the south before Maso Pescatore was released from prison. Tim Hickey had been the first casualty in the White-Pescatore war. By the end of the summer, though, he was one of a dozen.

On the whiskey end of things, they shot it out in Boston

and Portland and along the back roads that branched off the Canadian border. Drivers were run off roads in towns like Massena, New York; Derby, Vermont; and Allagash, Maine. Some were hijacked with just a beating, though one of White's fastest drivers was forced to his knees in a bed of pine needles and had his jaw blown off at the hinge because he'd talked sass.

As for rum, the battle was waged to keep it out. Trucks were waylaid as far south as the Carolinas and as far north as Rhode Island. After they were coaxed to the shoulder and the drivers were convinced to vacate their cabs, White's gangs set fire to the trucks. Rum trucks burned like Viking funeral boats, yellowing the underside of the night sky for miles in every direction.

'He's got a stockpile somewhere,' Maso said on one of their walks. 'He's waiting until he's bled New England of rum, and then he'll ride in, the savior, with his own supply.'

'Who'd be stupid enough to supply him?' Joe knew of most of the suppliers in South Florida.

'It's not stupid,' Maso said. 'It's smart. It's what I'd do if I had to choose between a slick operator like Albert and an old man who's been inside since before the czar lost Russia.'

'But you've got eyes and ears everywhere.'

The old man nodded. 'But they're not *exactly* my eyes and they're not *exactly* my ears so they're not connected to my hand. And my hand wields the power.'

That night, one of the guards on Maso's payroll was off duty in a South End speakeasy when he left with a woman no one had ever seen before. A real looker, though, and definitely a pro. The guard was found three hours later in

Franklin Square, sitting on a bench, a canyon cut through his Adam's apple, deader than Thomas Jefferson.

Maso's sentence ended in three months, and it was all starting to feel a bit desperate on Albert's part, and the desperation only made things more dangerous. Just last night, Boyd Holter, Maso's best forger, had been tossed off the Ames Building downtown. He'd landed on his tailbone, pieces of his spine spitting up into his brainpan like gravel.

Maso's people responded by blowing up one of Albert's fronts, a butcher's shop on Morton Street. The hairdresser and the haberdashery on either side of the butcher also burned to the ground, and several cars along the street lost their windows and paint.

So far, no winner, just a lot of mess.

Along the wall, Joe and Maso stopped to watch an orange moon as big as the sky itself rise over the factory smokestacks and the fields of ash and black poison, and Maso handed Joe a folded piece of paper.

Joe didn't look at them anymore, just folded them another couple of times and hid them in a slot he'd cut in the sole of his shoe until he saw his father next.

'Open it,' Maso said before Joe could pocket it.

Joe looked at him, the moon making it feel like daylight up here.

Maso nodded.

Joe turned the piece of paper in his hand and thumbed the top edge back. At first, he couldn't make sense of the two words he saw there:

Brendan Loomis.

Maso said, 'He was arrested last night. Beat a man outside

of Filene's. Because they both wanted to buy the same coat. Because he's a savage who doesn't think. The victim has friends, so Albert White's right hand is not returning to Albert's wrist anytime in the immediate future.' He looked at Joe, the moon turning his flesh orange. 'You hate him?'

Joe said, 'Of course.'

'Good.' Maso patted his arm once. 'Give the note to your father.'

At the bottom of the copper mesh screen between Joe and his father was a gap big enough to slide notes back and forth. Joe meant to place Maso's note on his side of the gap and push, but he couldn't bring himself to lift it off his knee.

That summer his father's face had grown translucent, like onion skin, and the veins in his hands had turned unreasonably bright – bright blue, bright red. His eyes and shoulders sagged. His hair had thinned. He looked every day and more of his sixty years.

But that morning something had put a bit of snap back into his speech and some life into the broken green of his eyes.

'You'll never guess who's coming to town,' he said.

'Who?'

'Your brother Aiden himself.'

Ah. That explained it. The favorite son. The beloved prodigal.

'Danny's coming, uh? Where's he been?'

Thomas said, 'Oh, he's been all over. He wrote me a letter that took fifteen minutes to read. He's been to Tulsa and

Austin and even Mexico. Of late, he's apparently been in New York. But he's coming to town tomorrow.'

'With Nora?'

'He didn't mention her,' Thomas said in a tone that suggested he would prefer to do the same.

'Did he say why he was coming to town?'

Thomas shook his head. 'Just said he'd be passing through.' His voice trailed off as he looked around at the walls like he couldn't get used to them. And he probably couldn't. Who could, unless they had to? 'You holding up?'

'I'm ...' Joe shrugged.

'What?'

'Trying, Dad. Trying.'

'Well, that's all you can do.'

'Yeah.'

They stared through the mesh at each other and Joe found the courage to remove the note from his knee and push it across to his father.

His father unfolded it and looked at the name there. For a long moment, Joe wasn't sure if he was still breathing. And then ...

'No.'

'What?'

'No.' Thomas pushed the note back across the table and said it again. 'No.'

'"No" isn't a word Maso likes, Dad.'

'So it's "Maso" now.'

Joe said nothing.

'I don't do murder for hire, Joseph.'

'That's not what they're asking,' Joe said, thinking, *Is it?*

'How naive can you be before it becomes unforgivable?' His father's breath exited through his nostrils. 'If they give you the name of a man in police custody, then they want that man found hanging in his cell or shot in the back "trying to escape." So, Joseph, given the degree of ignorance you seem willfully to cling to in such matters, I need you to hear exactly what I have to say.'

Joe met his father's stare, surprised by the depths of love and loss he saw there. His father, it seemed quite clear, now sat at the culmination of a life's journey, and the words about to leave his mouth were a summation of it.

'I will not take the life of another without cause.'

'Even a killer?' Joe said.

'Even a killer.'

'And the man responsible for the death of a woman I loved.'

'You told me you think she's alive.'

'That's not the point,' Joe said.

'No,' his father agreed, 'it's not. The point is that I don't engage in murder. Not for anyone. Certainly not for that dago devil you've sworn your allegiance to.'

'I've got to survive in here,' Joe said. 'In *here*.'

'And you do what you have to.' His father nodded, his green eyes brighter than usual. 'And I'll never judge you for it. But I won't commit homicide.'

'Even for me?'

'Especially for you.'

'Then I'll die in here, Dad.'

'That's possible, yes.'

Joe looked down at the table, the wood blurring, everything blurring. 'Soon.'

'And if that happens' – his father's voice was a whisper – 'I'll die soon after of a broken heart. But I won't murder for you, son. Kill for you? Yes. But murder? Never.'

Joe looked up. He was ashamed how wet his voice sounded when he said, 'Please.'

His father shook his head. Softly. Slowly.

Well, then. There was nothing left to say.

Joe went to stand.

His father said, 'Wait.'

'What?'

His father looked at the guard standing by the door behind Joe. 'That screw, is he in Maso's pocket?'

'Yeah. Why?'

His father removed his watch from his vest. He removed the chain from the watch.

'No, Dad. No.'

Thomas dropped the chain back into his pocket and slid the watch across the table.

Joe tried to keep the tears in his eyes from falling. 'I can't.'

'You can. You will.' His father stared through the screen at him like something on fire, all the exhaustion swept from his face, all the hopelessness too. 'It's worth a fortune, that piece of metal. But that's all it is – a piece of metal. You buy your life with it. You hear me? You give it to that dago devil and buy your life.'

Joe closed his hand over the watch and it was still warm from his father's pocket, ticking against his palm like a heart.

*

He told Maso in the mess hall. He hadn't intended to; he hadn't guessed it would come up. He thought he'd have time. During meals, Joe sat with members of the Pescatore crew, but not with the ones at the first table who sat with Maso himself. Joe sat at the next one over with guys like Rico Gastemeyer, who ran the daily number, and Larry Kahn, who made toilet gin in the basement of the guards' quarters. He came back from his meeting with his father and took a seat across from Rico and Ernie Rowland, a counterfeiter from Saugus, but they were pushed down the bench by Hippo Fasini, one of the soldiers closest to Maso, and Joe was left looking across the table at Maso himself, flanked on one side by Naldo Aliente and on the other by Hippo Fasini.

'So when will it happen?' Maso asked.

'Sir?'

Maso looked frustrated, as he always did when asked to repeat himself. 'Joseph.'

Joe felt his chest and throat clench around his answer. 'He won't do it.'

Naldo Aliente chuckled softly and shook his head.

Maso said, 'He refused?'

Joe nodded.

Maso looked at Naldo, then at Hippo Fasini. No one said anything for some time. Joe looked down at his food, aware that it was growing cold, aware he should eat it because if you skipped a meal in here, you'd grow weak very fast.

'Joseph, look at me.'

Joe looked across the table. The face staring back at him seemed amused and curious, like a wolf who'd come upon a nest of newborn chicks where he'd least expected.

'Why weren't you more convincing with your father?'

Joe said, 'Mr Pescatore, I tried.'

Maso looked back and forth between his men. 'He tried.'

When Naldo Aliente smiled he exposed a row of teeth that looked like bats hanging in a cave. 'Not hard enough.'

'Look,' Joe said, 'he gave me something.'

'He . . . ?' Maso put a hand behind his ear.

'Gave me something to give to you.' Joe handed the watch across the table.

Maso took note of the gold cover. He opened it and considered the timepiece itself and then the inside of the dust cover where *Patek Philippe* had been engraved in the most graceful script. His eyebrows rose in approval.

'It's the 1902, eighteen karat,' he said to Naldo. He turned to Joe. 'Only two thousand ever made. It's worth more than my house. How's a copper come to own it?'

'Broke up a bank robbery in '08,' Joe said, repeating a story his Uncle Eddie had told a hundred times, though his father never discussed it. 'It was in Codman Square. He killed one of the robbers before the guy could kill the bank manager.'

'And the bank manager gave him this watch?'

Joe shook his head. 'Bank president did. The manager was his son.'

'So now he gives it to me to save his own son?'

Joe nodded.

'I got three sons, myself. You know that?'

Joe said, 'I heard that, yeah.'

'So I know something about fathers and how they love their sons.'

Maso sat back and looked at the watch for a bit. Eventually he sighed and pocketed the watch. He reached across the table and patted Joe's hand three times. 'You get back in touch with your old man. Tell him thanks for the gift.' Maso stood from the table. 'And then tell him to do what I fucking told him to do.'

Maso's men all stood together and they left the mess hall.

When he returned to his cell after work detail in the chain shop, Joe was hot, filthy, and three men he'd never seen before waited inside for him. The bunk beds were still gone but the mattresses had been returned to the floor. The men sat on the mattresses. His mattress lay beyond them, against the wall under the high window, farthest from the bars. Two of the fellas he'd never seen before, he was sure of it, but the third looked familiar. He was about thirty, short, but with a very long face, and a chin as pointy as his nose and the tips of his ears. Joe ratcheted through all the names and faces he'd learned in this prison and realized he was looking across at Basil Chigis, one of Emil Lawson's crew, a lifer like his boss, no possibility of parole. Alleged to have eaten the fingers of a boy he'd killed in a Chelsea basement.

Joe looked at each of the men long enough to show he wasn't frightened, though he was, and they stared back at him, blinking occasionally but never speaking. So he didn't speak either.

At some point, the men seemed to tire of the staring and played cards. The currency was bones. Small bones, the bones of quail or young chickens or minor birds of prey. The men carried the bones in small canvas sacks. Boiled white, they clacked when they were gathered up in a winning pot. When the light dimmed, the men continued playing, never speaking except to say, 'Raise,' or 'See ya,' or 'Fold.' Every now and then one of them would glance at Joe but never for very long, and then he'd go back to playing cards.

When full dark descended, the lights along the tiers were shut off. The three men tried to finish their hand but then Basil Chigis's voice floated out of the black – 'Fuck this' – and cards scraped as they gathered them off the floor and the bones clicked as they returned them to their sacks.

They sat in the dark, breathing.

Time wasn't something Joe knew how to measure that night. He could have sat in the dark thirty minutes or two hours. He had no idea. The men sat in a half circle across from him, and he could smell their breath and their body odor. The one to his right smelled particularly bad, like dried sweat so old it had turned to vinegar.

As his eyes adjusted, he could see them, and the deep black became a gloaming. They sat with their arms across their knees, their legs crossed at the ankles. Their eyes were fixed on him.

In one of the factories behind him, a whistle blew.

Even if he'd had a shank, he doubted he could have stabbed all three of them. Given that he'd never stabbed anyone in his life, he might not have been able to get to one of them before they took it away and used it on him.

He knew they were waiting for him to speak. He didn't know how he knew, but he knew. That would be the signal for them to do whatever they intended to do to him. If he spoke, he'd be begging. Even if he never asked for anything or pleaded for his life, speaking to these men would be a plea in itself. And they'd laugh at him before they killed him.

Basil Chigis's eyes were the blue a river got not long before it froze. In the dark, it took a while for the color to return, but eventually it did. Joe imagined feeling the burn of that color on his thumbs when he drove them into Basil's eyes.

They're men, he told himself, not demons. A man can be killed. Even three men. You just need to act.

Staring into Basil Chigis's pale blue flames, he felt their sway over him diminish the more he reminded himself these men held no special powers, no more so than he anyway – the mind and the limbs and willpower, all working as one – and so it was entirely possible that he could overpower them.

But then what? Where would he go? His cell was seven feet long and eleven feet wide.

You have to be willing to kill them. Strike now. Before they do. And after they're down, snap their fucking necks.

Even as he imagined it, he knew it was impossible. If it was just one man and he acted before one assumed he would, he *might* have had a chance. But to successfully attack three of them from a sitting position?

The fear spread down through his intestines and up through his throat. It squeezed his brain like a hand. He couldn't stop sweating and his arms trembled against his sleeves.

The movement came from the right and left simultaneously. By the time he sensed it, the tips of the shanks were pressed against his eardrums. He couldn't see the shanks but he could see the one Basil Chigis pulled from the folds of his prison uniform. It was a slim metal rod, half the length of a pool cue, and Basil had to cock his elbow when he placed the tip to the base of Joe's throat. He reached behind him and pulled something out of the back of his waistband, and Joe wanted to un-see it because he didn't want to believe it was in the room with them. Basil Chigis raised a mallet high behind the butt end of the long shank.

Hail Mary, Joe thought, full of grace . . .

He forgot the rest of it. He'd been an altar boy for six years and he forgot.

Basil Chigis's eyes had not changed. There was no clear intent in them. His left fist gripped the shaft of the metal rod. His right clenched the mallet handle. One swing of his arm and the metal tip would puncture Joe's throat and drive straight down into his heart.

. . . the Lord is with thee. Bless us, O Lord, and these thy gifts . . .

No, no. That was grace, something you said over dinner. The Hail Mary went differently. It went . . .

He couldn't remember.

Our Father, who art in Heaven, forgive us our trespasses as we—

The door to the cell opened and Emil Lawson entered. He crossed to the circle, knelt to the right of Basil Chigis, and cocked his head at Joe.

'I heard you were pretty,' he said. 'They didn't lie.' He stroked the stubble on his cheeks. 'Can you think of anything I *can't* take from you right now?'

My soul? Joe wondered. But in this place, this dark, they could probably get that too.

Damned if he'd answer, though.

Emil Lawson said, 'You answer the question or I'll pluck an eye out and feed it to Basil.'

'No,' Joe said, 'nothing you can't take.'

Emil Lawson wiped the floor with a palm before sitting. 'You want us to go away? Leave your cell tonight?'

'Yeah, I do.'

'You were asked to do something for Mr Pescatore and you refused.'

'I didn't refuse. The final decision wasn't up to me.'

The shank against Joe's throat slipped in his sweat and bumped along the side of his neck, taking some skin with it. Basil Chigis returned it to the base of his throat again.

'Your daddy.' Emil Lawson nodded. 'The copper. What was he supposed to do?'

What?

'You know what he was supposed to do.'

'Pretend I don't and answer the question.'

Joe took a long, slow breath. 'Brendan Loomis.'

'What about him?'

'He's in custody. He gets arraigned day after tomorrow.'

Emil Lawson laced his hands behind his head and smiled. 'And your daddy was supposed to kill him but he said no.'

'Yeah.'

'No, he said yes.'

'He said no.'

Emil Lawson shook his head. 'You're going to tell the first Pescatore hood you see that your father got word back to you through a guard. He'll take care of Brenny Loomis. He also found out where Albert White's been sleeping at night. And you've got the address to give to Old Man

Pescatore. But only face-to-face. You following me so far, pretty boy?'

Joe nodded.

Emil Lawson handed Joe something wrapped in oilcloth. Joe unwrapped it – another shank, almost as thin as a needle. It had been a screwdriver at one point, the kind people used on the hinges of their eyeglasses. But those weren't sharp like this. The tip was like a rose thorn. Joe ran his palm over it lightly and cut a path there.

They removed the shanks from his ears and throat.

Emil leaned in close. 'When you get close enough to whisper that address in Pescatore's ear, you drive that shank right through his fucking brain.' He shrugged. 'Or his throat. Whatever kills him.'

'I thought you worked for him,' Joe said.

'I work for me.' Emil Lawson shook his head. 'I did some jobs for his crew when I was paid to. Now someone else is paying.'

'Albert White,' Joe said.

'That's my boss.' Emil Lawson leaned forward and lightly slapped Joe's cheek. 'And now he's your boss too.'

In the small spit of land behind his house on K Street, Thomas Coughlin kept a garden. His efforts with it had, over the years, met with varying degrees of success and failure, but in the two years since Ellen had passed on, he'd had nothing but time; now the bounty of it was such that he made a small profit every year when he sold the surplus.

Years ago, when he was five or six, Joe had decided to help his father harvest in early July. Thomas had been sleeping off a double shift and the several nightcaps he'd consumed with Eddie McKenna afterward. He woke to the sound of his son talking in the backyard. Joe had talked to himself a lot back then, or maybe he spoke to an imagined friend. Either way, he'd had to talk to somebody, Thomas could admit to himself now, because he certainly wasn't being spoken to much around the house. Thomas worked too much, and Ellen, well, by that point Ellen had firmly established her fondness for Tincture No. 23, a cure-all first introduced to her after one of the miscarriages that had preceded Joe's birth. Back then, No. 23 wasn't yet the problem it would become for Ellen, or so Thomas had told himself. But he must have second-guessed that assessment more than he liked to admit because he'd known without asking that Joe was unattended that morning. He lay in bed listening to his youngest jabbering to himself as he tramped back and forth to the porch, and Thomas started to wonder what he tramped back and forth *from*.

He rose from bed and put on a robe and found his slippers. He walked through the kitchen (where Ellen, dull-eyed but smiling, sat with her cup of tea) and pushed open the back door.

When he saw the porch, his first instinct was to scream. Literally. To drop to his knees and rage at the heavens. His carrots and parsnips and tomatoes – all still green as grass – lay on the porch, their roots splayed like hair across the dirt and wood. Joe came walking up from the garden with another crop in his hands – the beets, this time. He'd transformed into a mole, his skin and hair caked with dirt. The only white left on him could be found in his eyes and his teeth when he smiled, which he did as soon as he saw Thomas.

'Hi, Daddy.'

Thomas was speechless.

'I'm helping you, Daddy.' Joe placed a beet at Thomas's feet and went back for more.

Thomas, a year's work ruined, an autumn's profit vanished, watched his son march off to finish the destruction, and the laugh that quaked up through the center of him surprised no one so much as him. He laughed so loud squirrels took flight from the low branches of the nearest tree. He laughed so hard he could feel the porch shake.

He smiled now to remember it.

He'd told his son recently that life was luck. But life, he'd come to realize as he aged, was also memory. The recollection of moments often proved richer than the moments themselves.

Out of habit, he reached for his watch before he recalled that it was no longer in his pocket. He'd miss it, even if the truth of the watch was a bit more complicated than the legend that had arisen around it. It was a gift from Barrett W. Stanford Sr., that was true. And Thomas had, without question, risked his life to save Barrett W. Stanford II, the manager of First Boston in Codman Square. Also true was that Thomas had, in the performance of his duties, discharged his service revolver a single time into the brain of one Maurice Dobson, twenty-six, ending his life immediately.

But in the instant before he pulled that trigger, Thomas had seen something no one else had: the true nature of Maurice Dobson's intent. He would tell the hostage, Barrett

W. Stanford II, about it first, and then relate the same tale to Eddie McKenna, then to his watch commander, and then to the members of the BPD Shooting Board. With their permission, he told the same story to the members of the press and also to Barrett W. Stanford Sr., who was so overcome with gratitude that he gave Thomas a watch that had been presented to him in Zurich by Joseph Emile Philippe himself. Thomas attempted three times to refuse such an extravagant gift, but Barrett W. Stanford Sr. wouldn't hear of it.

So he carried the watch, not with the pride that so many presumed, but with a gravely intimate respect. In the legend, Maurice Dobson's intent was to kill Barrett W. Stanford II. And who could argue with that interpretation, given that he'd placed a pistol to Barrett's throat?

But the intent Thomas had read in Maurice Dobson's eyes in that final instant – and it was that quick: an instant – was surrender. Thomas had stood four feet away, service revolver drawn and steady in his hand, finger on the trigger, so ready to pull it – and you had to be, or else why draw the gun in the first place? – that when he saw an acceptance of his fate pass through Maurice Dobson's pebble-gray eyes, an acceptance that he was going to jail, that this was over now, Thomas felt unfairly denied. Denied of what, he couldn't rightly say at first. But as soon as he pulled the trigger, he knew.

The bullet entered the left eye of the unfortunate Maurice Dobson, the *late* Maurice Dobson before he even reached the floor, and the heat of it singed a stripe into the skin just below Barrett W. Stanford II's temple. When the finality of the bullet's purpose conjoined with finality of its usage,

Thomas understood what had been denied him and why he'd taken such permanent steps to rectify that denial.

When two men pointed theirs guns at each other, a contract was established under the eyes of God, the only acceptable fulfillment of which was that one of you send the other home to him.

Or so it had felt at the time.

Over the years, even in the deepest of his cups, even with Eddie McKenna, who knew most of his secrets, Thomas had never told another soul what kind of intent he'd actually seen in Maurice Dobson's eyes. And while he felt no pride in his actions that day and so took none in his possession of the pocket watch, he never left his house without it, because it bore witness to the profound responsibility that defined his profession – we don't enforce the laws of men; we enforce the will of nature. God was not some white-robed cloud king prone to sentimental meddling in human affairs. He was the iron that formed its core, and the fire in the belly of the blast furnaces that ran for a hundred years. God was the law of iron and the law of fire. God was nature and nature was God. There could not be one without the other.

And you, Joseph, my youngest, my wayward romantic, my prickly heart – it's now you who has to remind men of those laws. The worst men. Or die from weakness, from moral frailty, from lack of will.

I'll pray for you, because prayer is all that remains when power dies. And I have no power anymore. I can't reach behind those granite walls. I can't slow or stop time. Hell, at the moment, I can't even tell it.

He looked out at his garden, so close to harvest. He prayed for Joe. He prayed for a tide of his ancestors, most unknown to him, and yet he could see them so clearly, a diaspora of stooped souls stained by drink and famine and the dark impulse. He wished for their eternal rest to be peaceful, and he wished for a grandson.

Joe found Hippo Fasini on the yard and told him his father had undergone a change of heart.

'That'll happen,' Hippo said.

'He also gave me an address.'

'Yeah?' The fat man leaned back on his heels and looked out at nothing. 'Whose?'

'Albert White's.'

'Albert White lives in Ashmont Hill.'

'I hear he doesn't visit much lately.'

'So give me the address.'

'Fuck you.'

Hippo Fasini looked at the ground, all three chins dropping into his prison stripes. 'Excuse me?'

'Tell Maso I'll bring it to the wall with me tonight.'

'You ain't in a bargaining position, kid.'

Joe looked at him until Hippo met his eyes. He said, 'Sure I am,' and walked off across the yard.

An hour before his meeting with Pescatore, he threw up twice into the oak bucket. His arms shook. Occasionally so did his chin and his lips. His blood became a steady pounding of fists against his ears. He'd tied the shank to his wrist with a leather bootlace Emil Lawson had provided. Just before he left his cell, he was to move it from there to between his ass cheeks. Lawson had strongly suggested he shove it all the way up his ass, but he envisioned one of Maso's goons forcing him to sit for whatever reason and decided it was the cheeks or nothing at all. He figured he'd make the transfer with about ten minutes to go, get used to moving with it, but a guard came by his cell forty minutes early to tell him he had a visitor.

It was dusk. Visiting hours were long over.

'Who?' he asked as he followed the guard down the tier, only then realizing the shank remained tied to his wrist.

'Someone who knows how to grease the right palms.'

'Yeah' – Joe tried to keep up with the guard, a brisk walker – 'but who?'

The guard unlocked the ward gate and ushered Joe through. 'Said he was your brother.'

He entered the room removing his hat. Coming through the doorway, he had to duck, a man who stood a full head taller than most. His dark hair had receded some and was lightly salted over the ears. Joe did the math and realized he'd be thirty-five now. Still fiercely handsome, though his face was more weathered than Joe remembered.

He wore a dark, slightly battered three-piece suit with cloverleaf lapels. It was the suit of a manager in a grain warehouse or a man who spent a lot of time on the road – a salesman or union organizer. Danny wore a white shirt under it, no tie.

He placed his hat on the counter and looked through the mesh between them.

'Shit,' Danny said, 'you're not thirteen anymore, are you?'

Joe noticed how red his brother's eyes were. 'And you're not twenty-five.'

Danny lit a cigarette and the match quivered between his fingers. A large scar, puckered in the center, covered the back of his hand. 'Still whoop your ass.'

Joe shrugged. 'Maybe not. I'm learning to fight dirty.'

Danny gave that an arch of his eyebrows and exhaled a plume of smoke. 'He's gone, Joe.'

Joe knew who 'he' was. Some part of him had known the last time he'd laid eyes on him in this room. But another part of him couldn't accept it. Wouldn't.

'Who?'

His brother looked at the ceiling for a moment, then back at him. 'Dad, Joe. Dad's dead.'

'How?'

'My guess? Heart attack.'

'Did you . . . ?'

'Huh?'

'Were you there?'

Danny shook his head. 'I missed him by half an hour. He was still warm when I found him.'

Joe said, 'You're sure there was no . . .'

'What?'

'Foul play?'

'What the fuck are they doing to you in here?' Danny looked around the room. 'No, Joe, it was a heart attack or a stroke.'

'How do you know?'

Danny narrowed his eyes. 'He was smiling.'

'What?'

'Yeah.' Danny chuckled. 'That small one of his? One looked like he was hearing some private joke or remembering something from the way back, before any of us? You know that one?'

'Yeah, I do,' Joe said and was surprised to hear himself whisper again, 'I do.'

'No watch on him, though.'

'Huh?' Joe's head buzzed.

'His watch,' Danny said. 'He didn't have it. Never knew him to—'

'I got it,' Joe said. 'He gave it to me. In case I run into trouble. You know, in here.'

'So you've got it.'

'I got it,' he said, the lie burning his stomach. He saw Maso's hand closing over the watch and he wanted to beat his own head against concrete until he stove it in.

'Good,' Danny said. 'That's good.'

'It's not,' Joe said. 'It's shit. But it's about the size of things now.'

Neither of them spoke for a few moments. A factory whistle blew distantly from the other side of the walls.

Danny said, 'You know where I can find Con?'

Joe nodded. 'He's at the Abbotsford.'

'The blind school? What's he doing there?'

'Lives there,' Joe said. 'He just woke up one day and quit on everything.'

'Well,' Danny said, 'that kinda injury could make anyone bitter.'

'He was bitter long before the injury,' Joe said.

Danny shrugged in agreement and they sat in silence for a minute.

Joe said, 'Where was he when you found him?'

'Where do you think?' Danny dropped his cigarette to the floor and stepped on it, the smoke leaving his mouth from under the curl in his upper lip. 'Out back, sitting in that chair on the porch, you know? Looking out at his . . .' Danny lowered his head and waved at the air.

'Garden,' Joe said.

CHAPTER NINE

As the Old Man Goes

Even in prison, news of the outside world trickled in. That year all the sports talk concerned the New York Yankees and their Murderers' Row of Combs, Koenig, Ruth, Gehrig, Meusel, and Lazzeri. Ruth alone hit a mind-boggling sixty home runs, and the other five hitters were so dominant that the only question left was by how humiliating a margin they'd sweep the Pirates in the World Series.

Joe, a walking encyclopedia of baseball, would have loved to see this team play because he knew their like might never come around again. And yet his time in Charlestown had also instilled in him a reactionary contempt for anyone who would call a group of ballplayers Murderers' Row.

You want a Murderers' Row, he thought that evening just after dusk, I'm *walking* it. The entrance to the walkway along the top of the prison wall was on the other side of a door at the end of F Block on the uppermost tier of North Wing. It was impossible to reach that door unobserved. A man couldn't even reach the tier without going through three separate gates. Once he did, he faced an empty tier. Even in a prison as overcrowded as this, they kept the twelve cells there empty and cleaner than a church font before a baptism.

As Joe walked along the tier now, he saw how they kept it so clean – each cell was being mopped by a convict trustee. The high windows in the cells, identical to the window in his own, revealed a square of sky. The squares were all a blue so dark it was nearly black, which left Joe to wonder how much the moppers could see in those cells. All the light was on the corridor. Maybe the guards would provide lanterns when dusk became night in a matter of minutes.

But there were no guards. Just the one leading him down the tier, the one who'd led him to and from the visiting room, the one who walked too fast, which would get him into trouble someday because the objective was to keep the convict ahead of you. If you got ahead of the convict, he could get up to all sorts of nefarious things, which is how Joe had moved the shank from his wrist to his butt five minutes ago. He wished he'd practiced it, though. Trying to walk with clenched ass cheeks and appear natural was no easy thing.

But where were the other guards? On nights when Maso walked the wall, they kept their presence light up here; it wasn't like every guard was on the Pescatore payroll, though those who weren't would never go pigeon on those who were. But Joe glanced around as they continued along the tier and confirmed what he'd feared – there were no guards up here right now. And then he got a close look at the inmates cleaning the cells:

Murderers' Row, indeed.

Basil Chigis's pointy head tipped him off. Not even the prison-issue watch cap could disguise it. Basil pushed a mop in the seventh cell on the tier. The foul-smelling guy who'd put his shank to Joe's right ear mopped the eighth. Pushing a bucket around the tenth empty cell was Dom Pokaski, who'd burned his own family alive – wife, two daughters, mother-in-law, not to mention three cats he'd locked in the fruit cellar.

At the end of the tier, Hippo and Naldo Aliente stood by the stairwell door. If they thought there was anything odd about the higher-than-usual inmate presence and lower-than-ever guard presence, they were doing a first-class job of masking it. Nothing showed on their faces, really, except the smug entitlement of the ruling class.

Fellas, Joe thought, you might want to brace for change.

'Hands up,' Hippo told Joe. 'I gotta frisk you.'

Joe didn't hesitate, but he did regret not shoving the shank all the way up his ass. The handle, small as it was, rested against the base of his spine, but Hippo might feel an abnormal shape there, pull up his shirt and then use the shank on him. Joe kept his arms raised, surprised by how steady he seemed: no shakes, no sweat, no outward signs of fear. Hippo slapped his paws up Joe's legs and then along his ribs and ran one down his chest and the other down his back. The tip of Hippo's finger grazed the handle and Joe could feel it tilt back. He clenched harder, aware that his life depended on something as absurd as how tight he could clench his buttocks.

Hippo gripped Joe's shoulders and turned him to face him. 'Open your mouth.'

Joe did.

'Wider.'

Joe complied.

Hippo peered into his mouth. 'He's clean,' he said and stepped back.

As Joe went to pass, Naldo Aliente blocked the door. He looked into Joe's face like he knew all the lies behind it.

'Your life goes as that old man's goes,' he said. 'You understand?'

Joe nodded, knowing that whatever happened to him or Pescatore, Naldo was living the final minutes of his life right now. 'You bet.'

Naldo stepped aside, Hippo opened the door, and Joe stepped through. There was nothing on the other side but an iron spiral staircase. It rose from the concrete box to a trapdoor that had been left open to the night. Joe pulled the shank out of the back of his pants and placed it in the pocket of his coarse striped shirt. When he reached the top of the staircase, he made a fist of his right hand, then raised the index and middle fingers and thrust the hand out of the hole until the guard in the nearest tower could get a look. The light from the tower swung left, right, and left-right again in a quick zigzag – the all clear. Joe climbed through the opening and out onto the walkway and scanned his surroundings until he made out Maso about fifteen yards down the wall in front of the central watchtower.

He walked to him, feeling the shank bouncing lightly against his hip. The only blind spot to the central watchtower was the space directly below it. As long as Maso stayed where he was, they'd be invisible. When Joe reached him,

Maso was smoking one of the bitter French cigarettes he preferred, the yellow ones, and looking west across the blight.

He looked at Joe for a bit and said nothing, just inhaled and exhaled his cigarette smoke with a wet rattle.

And then he said, 'I'm sorry about your father.'

Joe stopped fishing for his own cigarette. The night sky dropped over his face like a cloak and the air around him evaporated until the lack of oxygen squeezed his head.

There was no way Maso could know. Even with all his power, all his sources. Danny had told Joe he'd reached out to no less than Superintendent Michael Crowley, who'd come up on foot patrol with their father and whose job their father had been expected to inherit before that night behind the Statler. Thomas Coughlin had been whisked out the back of his house into an unmarked police car and taken into the city morgue by the underground entrance.

I'm sorry about your father.

No, Joe told himself. No. He can't know. Impossible.

Joe found his cigarette and placed it between his lips. Maso struck a match off the parapet and lit it for him, the old man's eyes taking on the generous cast they were capable of when it suited.

Joe said, 'What're you sorry about?'

Maso shrugged. 'No man should ever be asked to do what's against his nature, Joseph, even if it's to help a loved one. What we asked of him, what we asked of you, it wasn't fair. But what's fucking fair in this world?'

Joe's heartbeat slid back out of his ears and throat.

He and Maso leaned their elbows on the parapet and

smoked. Lights from the barges along the Mystic scudded through the thick, distant gray like exiled stars. White snakes of foundry smoke pirouetted toward them. The air smelled of trapped heat and a rain that refused to fall.

'I won't ask anything so hard of you or your father again, Joseph.' Maso gave him a firm nod. 'I promise you that.'

Joe locked eyes with him. 'Sure you will, Maso.'

'Mr Pescatore, Joseph.'

Joe said, 'My apologies,' and his cigarette fell from his fingers. He bent to the walkway to pick it up.

Instead, he wrapped his arms around Maso's ankles and pulled up hard.

'Don't scream.' Joe straightened and the old man's head entered the space beyond the edge of the parapet. 'You scream, I drop you.'

The old man's breath came fast. His feet kicked against Joe's ribs.

'I'd stop struggling too, or I won't be able to hold on.'

It took a few moments, but Maso's feet stopped moving.

'Do you have any weapons on you? Don't lie.'

The voice floated back from the edge to him. 'Yes.'

'How many?'

'Just one.'

Joe let go of his ankles.

Maso waved his arms like he might, in that moment, learn to fly. He slid forward on his chest, and the dark swallowed his head and torso. He probably would have screamed, but Joe sank his hand into the waistband of Maso's prison uniform, dug a heel into the wall of the parapet, and leaned back.

Maso made a series of strange huffing sounds, very high-pitched, like a newborn abandoned in a field.

'How many?' Joe repeated.

Nothing but that huffing for a minute and then, 'Two.'

'Where are they?'

'Razor at my ankle, nails in my pocket.'

Nails? Joe had to see this. He patted the pockets with his free hand, found on odd lump. He reached in gingerly and came back with what he might have mistaken for a comb at first glance. Four short nails were soldered to a bar that was, in turn, soldered to four misshapen rings.

'This goes over your fist?' Joe said.

'Yes.'

'That's nasty.'

He placed it on the parapet and then found the straight razor in Maso's sock, a Wilkinson with a pearl handle. He placed it beside the nail knuckles.

'Getting light-headed yet?'

A muffled 'Yes.'

'Expect so.' Joe adjusted his grip on the waistband. 'Are we agreed, Maso, that if I open my fingers you're one dead guinea?'

'Yes.'

'I got a hole in my leg from a fucking *potato peeler* because of you.'

'I . . . I . . . you.'

'What? Speak clearly.'

It came out a hiss. 'I saved you.'

'So you could get to my father.' Joe pushed down between Maso's shoulders with his elbow. The old man let out a squeak.

'What do you want?' Maso's voice was starting to flutter from lack of oxygen.

'You ever hear of Emma Gould?'

'No.'

'Albert White killed her.'

'I never heard of her.'

Joe wrenched him back up and then flipped him on his back. He took one step back and let the old man catch his breath.

Joe held out his hand, snapped his fingers. 'Give me the watch.'

Maso didn't hesitate. He pulled it from his trouser pocket and handed it over. Joe held it tight in his fist, its ticking moving through his palm and into his blood.

'My father died today,' he said, aware he probably wasn't making much sense, jumping from his father to Emma and back again. But he didn't care. He needed to put words to something there weren't words for.

Maso's eyes skittered for a moment and then he went back to rubbing his throat.

Joe nodded. 'Heart attack. I blame myself.' He slapped Maso's shoe and that jolted the old man enough that he slammed both palms down on the parapet. Joe smiled. 'Blame you too, though. Blame you a whole fucking lot.'

'So kill me,' Maso said, but there wasn't much steel in his voice. He looked over his shoulder, then back at Joe.

'That's what I was ordered to do.'

'Who ordered you?'

'Lawson,' Joe said. 'He's got an army down there waiting for you – Basil Chigis, Pokaski, all of Emil's carny freaks.

Your guys? Naldo and Hippo?' Joe shook his head. 'They're definitely tits-up by now. You've got a whole hunting party at the bottom of that staircase there in case I fail.'

A bit of the old defiance returned to Maso's face. 'And you think they'll let you live?'

Joe had given that plenty of thought. 'Probably. This war of yours has put a lot of bodies in the earth. Ain't too many of us left who can spell *gum* and chew it at the same time. Plus, I know Albert. We used to have something in common. This was his peace offering, I think – kill Maso and rejoin the fold.'

'So why didn't you?'

'Because I don't want to kill you.'

'No?'

Joe shook his head. 'I want to destroy Albert.'

'Kill him?'

'Don't know about that,' Joe said. 'But destroy him definitely.'

Maso fished in his pocket for his French cigarettes. He removed one and lit it, still catching his breath. Eventually he met Joe's eyes and nodded. 'You have my blessing on that ambition.'

'Don't need your blessing,' Joe said.

'I won't try to talk you out of it,' Maso said, 'but I never saw much profit in revenge.'

'Ain't about profit.'

'Everything in a man's life is about profit. Profit, or succession.' Maso looked up at the sky and then back again. 'So how do we get back down there alive?'

'Any of the tower guards fully in your debt?'

'The one right above us,' Maso said. 'The other two are faithful to the money.'

'Could your guard contact guards inside, get them to flank Lawson's crew, raid them right now?'

Maso shook his head. 'If just one guard is close to Lawson, then word will get to the cons below and they'll storm up here.'

'Well, shit.' Joe exhaled a long slow breath and looked around. 'Let's just do it the dirty way.'

While Maso talked to the tower guard, Joe walked back down the wall to the trapdoor. If he was going to die, this was probably the moment. He couldn't shake the suspicion that every step he took was about to be interrupted by a bullet drilling through his brain or cracking through his spine.

He looked back down the way he'd come. Maso had left the pathway, so there was nothing to see but the gathering dark and the watchtowers. No stars, no moon, just the stone dark.

He opened the trapdoor and called down. 'He's done.'

'You hurt?' Basil Chigis called up.

'No. Gonna need clean clothes, though.'

Someone chuckled in the darkness.

'So, come on down.'

'Come on up. We got to get his body out of here.'

'We can—'

'The signal is your right hand, index and middle fingers raised and held together. You got anyone missing one of those digits, don't send him up.'

He rolled away from the doorway before anyone could argue.

After about a minute, he heard the first of them climb up. The man's hand extended out of the hole, two fingers raised as Joe had instructed. The tower light arced past the hand and then swung back over again. Joe said, 'All clear.'

It was Pokaski, the roaster of his family, who stuck his head carefully up and looked around.

'Hurry,' Joe said. 'And get the others up here. It'll take two more to drag him. He's deadweight and my ribs are busted up.'

Pokaski smiled. 'I thought you said you weren't hurt.'

'Not mortally,' Joe said. 'Come on.'

Pokaski leaned back into the hole. 'Two more guys.'

Basil Chigis followed Pokaski and then a small guy with a harelip came after him. Joe recalled someone pointing him out at chow once – Eldon Douglas – but couldn't remember his crime.

'Where's the body?' Basil Chigis asked.

Joe pointed.

'Well, let's—'

The light hit Basil Chigis just before the bullet entered the back of his head and exited the center of his face, taking his nose with it. As his final act on earth, Pokaski blinked. Then a door opened in his throat and the door flapped as a wash of red poured through it and Pokaski fell on his back, and his legs thrashed. Eldon Douglas leapt for the opening to the staircase, but the tower guard's third bullet collapsed his skull the way a sledgehammer would. He fell to the right of the door and lay there, missing the top of his head.

Joe looked into the light, the three dead men splattered all over him. Down below men shouted and ran off. He wished he could join them. It had been a naive plan. He could feel the gun sights on his chest as the light blinded him. The bullets would be the violent offspring his father had warned him about; not only was he about to meet his Maker, but he also was about to meet his children. The only consolation he could offer himself was that it would be a quick death. Fifteen minutes from now he'd be sharing a pint with his father and Uncle Eddie.

The light snapped off.

Something soft hit him in the face and then fell to his shoulder. He blinked into the darkness – a small towel.

'Wipe your face,' Maso said. 'It's a mess.'

When he finished, his eyes had adjusted enough to be able to make out Maso standing a few feet away, smoking one of his French cigarettes.

'You think I was going to kill you?'

'Crossed my mind.'

Maso shook his head. 'I'm a low-rent wop from Endicott Street. I go to a fancy joint, I still don't know what fork to use. So I might not have class or education, but I never double-cross. I come right at you. Just like you came at me.'

Joe nodded, looked at the three corpses at his feet. 'What about these guys? I'd say we double-crossed them pretty good.'

'Fuck them,' Maso said. 'They had it coming.' Stepping over Pokaski's corpse, he crossed to Joe. 'You'll be getting out of here sooner than you think. You ready to make some money when you do?'

'Sure.'

'Your duty will always be to the Pescatore Family first and yourself second. Can you abide that?'

Joe looked into the old man's eyes and was certain that they'd make a lot of money together and that he could never trust him.

'I can abide that.'

Maso extended his hand. 'Okay, then.'

Joe wiped the blood off his hand and shook Maso's. 'Okay.'

'Mr Pescatore,' someone called from below.

'Coming.' Maso walked to the trapdoor and Joe followed. 'Come, Joseph.'

'Call me Joe. Only my father called me Joseph.'

'Fair enough.' As he descended the spiral staircase in the dark, Maso said, 'Funny thing about fathers and sons – you can go forth and build an empire. Become king. Emperor of the United States. God. But you'll always do it in his shadow. And you can't escape it.'

Joe followed him down the dark staircase. 'Don't much want to.'

CHAPTER TEN

Visitations

After a morning funeral at Gate of Heaven in South Boston, Thomas Coughlin was laid to rest at Cedar Grove Cemetery in Dorchester. Joe was not allowed to attend the funeral but read about it in a copy of the *Traveler* that one of the guards on Maso's payroll brought to him that evening.

Two former mayors, Honey Fitz and Andrew Peters, attended, as well as the current one, James Michael Curley. So did two ex-governors, five former district attorneys, and two attorney generals.

The cops came from all over – city cops and state police, retired and active, from as far south as Delaware and as far north as Bangor, Maine. Every rank, every specialty. In the photo accompanying the article, the Neponset River snaked along the far edge of the cemetery, but Joe could barely see it because the blue hats and blue uniforms consumed the view.

This was power, he thought. This was a legacy.

And in nearly the same breath – So what?

So his father's funeral had brought a thousand men to a graveyard along the banks of the Neponset. And someday, possibly, cadets would study in the Thomas X. Coughlin Building at the Boston Police Academy or commuters would rattle over the Coughlin Bridge on their way to work in the morning.

Wonderful.

And yet dead was dead. Gone was gone. No edifice, no legacy, no bridge named after you could change that.

You were only guaranteed one life, so you'd better live it.

He placed the paper beside him on the bed. It was a new mattress and it had been waiting for him in the cell after work detail yesterday with a small side table, a chair, and a kerosene table lamp. He found the matches in the drawer of the side table beside a new comb.

He blew out the lamp now and sat in the dark, smoking. He listened to the sounds of the factories and the barges out on the river signaling one another in the narrow lanes. He flicked open the cover of his father's watch, then snapped it closed, then opened it again. Open-close, open-close, open-close as the chemical smell from the factories climbed over his high window.

His father was gone. He was no longer a son.

He was a man without history or expectation. A blank slate, beholden to none.

He felt like a pilgrim who'd pushed off from the shore of a homeland he'd never see again, crossed a black sea under a black sky, and landed in the new world, which waited, unformed, as if it had always been waiting.

For him.

To give the country a name, to remake it in his image so it could espouse his values and export them across the globe.

He closed the watch and closed his hand over it and closed his eyes until he saw the shore of his new country, saw the black sky above give way to a far-flung scatter of white stars that shone down on him and the small stretch of water left between them.

I will miss you. I will mourn you. But I am now newly born. And truly free.

Two days after the funeral, Danny made his last visit.

He leaned into the mesh and asked, 'How you doing, little brother?'

'Finding my way,' Joe said. 'You?'

'You know,' Danny said.

'No,' Joe said, 'I don't. I don't know anything. You went to Tulsa with Nora and Luther eight years ago and I haven't heard anything but rumors since.'

Danny acknowledged that with a nod. He fished for his cigarettes, lit one, and took his time before he spoke. 'Me and Luther started a business together out there. Construction. We built houses in the colored section. We were doing all right. Weren't booming, but okay. I was a sheriff's deputy too. You believe that?'

Joe smiled. 'You wear a cowboy hat?'

'Son,' Danny said with a twang, 'I wore six-guns. One on each hip.'

Joe laughed. 'String tie?'

Danny laughed too. 'Sure did. And boots.'

'Spurs?'

Danny narrowed his eyes and shook his head. 'Man's gotta draw the line somewhere.'

Joe was still chuckling when he asked, 'So what happened? We heard something about a riot?'

The light blew out inside Danny. 'They burned it to the ground.'

'Tulsa?'

'Black Tulsa, yeah. Section Luther lived in called Greenwood. One night at the jail, whites came to lynch a colored because he grabbed a white girl's pussy in an elevator? Truth was, though, she'd been dating the boy on the sly for months. The boy broke up with her, she didn't like it, so she filed her bullshit claim, and we had to arrest him. We were just about to turn him loose on lack of evidence when all the good white men of Tulsa showed up with their ropes. Then a bunch of coloreds, including Luther, they showed up too. The coloreds, well, they were armed. No one expected that. And that backed off the lynch mob. For the night.' Danny stubbed his cigarette out under his heel. 'Next morning, the whites crossed the tracks, showed the colored boys what happens when you raise a gun to one of them.'

'So that was the riot.'

Danny shook his head. 'Wasn't no *riot*. It was a massacre. They gunned down or lit on fire every colored they saw – kids, women, old men, didn't make a difference. These were the pillars of the community doing the shooting, mind you, the churchgoers and the Rotarians. In the end, the fuckers flew overhead in crop dusters, dropping grenades and homemade firebombs onto the buildings. The colored folk would run out of the burning buildings and the whites had machine gun nests set up. Just mowed 'em down in the fucking street. Hundreds of people killed. Hundreds, just lying in the streets. Looked like nothing more than piles of clothes gone red in the wash.' Danny laced his hands together behind his head and blew air through his lips. 'I walked around afterward, you know, loading the bodies onto flatbeds? I kept thinking, Where's my country? Where'd it go?'

Neither spoke for a long time until Joe said, 'Luther?'

Danny held up one hand. 'He survived. Last I saw him, him and his wife and kid were heading for Chicago.' He said, 'Thing about that kind of . . . event, Joe? You survive it and it's like you've got this shame. I can't even explain it. Just this shame, big as your whole body. And everyone else who survived? They have it too. And you can't look each other in the eye. You're all wearing the stink of it and trying to figure out how to live the rest of your life with the odor. So you sure as hell don't want anyone else who smells the same as you getting close enough to stink you up even more.'

Joe said, 'Nora?'

Danny nodded. 'We're still together.'

'Kids?'

Danny shook his head. 'You think you'd be walking around an uncle without me telling you?'

'I haven't seen you but once in eight years, Dan. I don't know what you'd do.'

Danny nodded, and Joe saw what until now he'd only suspected – something in his brother, something at the core, was broken.

But just as he thought it, a piece of the old Danny returned with a sly grin. 'Me and Nora have been in New York the last few years.'

'Doing what?'

'Making shows.'

'Shows?'

'Movies. That's what they call them there – shows. I mean, it's a little confusing because a lotta people call plays shows too. But anyway, yeah, movies, Joe. Flickers. Shows.'

'You work in movies?'

Danny nodded, animated now. 'Nora started it. She got a job with this company, Silver Frame? Jews, but good guys. She was handling all their bookkeeping and then they asked her to do some side work with publicity and even costumes. It was that kinda outfit back then, just everyone pitching in, the directors making coffee, the camera guys walking the lead actress's dog.'

'Movies?' Joe said.

Danny laughed. 'So, wait, it gets better. Her bosses meet me and one of them, Herm Silver, great guy, lot on the ball, he asks me – you ready? – he asks me if I ever did stunts.'

'Fuck are stunts?' Joe lit a cigarette.

'You see an actor fall off a horse? It ain't him. It's a stunt-man. A professional. Actor slips on a banana peel, trips over a curb, hell, runs down a street? Look close at the screen next time because it ain't him. It's me or someone like me.'

'Wait,' Joe said, 'how many movies have you been in?'

Danny thought about it for a minute. 'I'm guessing seventy-five?'

'Seventy-five?' Joe took the cigarette from his mouth.

'I mean, a lot of them were shorts. That's when—'

'Jesus, I know what shorts are.'

'You didn't know what stunts were, though, did you?'

Joe raised his middle finger.

'So, yeah, I've been in a bunch. Even wrote a few of the shorts.'

Joe's mouth opened wide. 'You wrote . . . ?'

Danny nodded. 'Little things. Kids on the Lower East Side try to wash a dog for a rich lady, they lose the dog, the rich lady calls the cops, high jinks ensue, that sort of thing.'

Joe dropped his cigarette to the floor before it could burn his fingers. 'How many have you written?'

'Five so far, but Herm thinks I got a knack for it, wants me to try for a full-length feature soon, become a scenarist.'

'What's a scenarist?'

'Guy who writes movies, genius,' Danny said and flipped his own middle finger back at Joe.

'So, wait, where's Nora in all this?'

'California.'

'I thought you were in New York.'

'We *were*. But Silver Frame made a couple of movies real cheap lately that turned out to be hits. Meanwhile, Edison's fucking suing everyone in New York over camera patents, but those patents don't mean shit in California. Plus the weather there is nice three hundred sixty days out of three sixty-five, so everyone's heading out there. The Silver brothers? They just figured now's the time. Nora headed out a week ago because she's become head of production – I mean, just flying up their ladder – and they've got me scheduled for stunts on a show called *The Lawmen of the Pecos* in three weeks. I just came back to tell Dad I was heading west again, tell him to come visit maybe, once he retired. I didn't know when I'd ever see him again. Hell, see you again.'

'I'm happy for you,' Joe said, still shaking his head at the absurdity of it. Danny's life – boxer, cop, union organizer, businessman, sheriff's deputy, stuntman, budding writer – was an American life, if ever there was one.

'Come,' his brother said.

'What?'

'When you get out of here. Come join us. I'm serious. Fall off a horse for money and pretend to get shot and fall through sugar windows made up to look like glass. Lie in the sun the rest of the time, meet a starlet by the pool.'

For a moment, Joe could see it – another life, a dream of blue water, honey-skinned women, palm trees.

'Only a brisk, two-week train ride away, little brother.'

Joe laughed some more, picturing it.

'It's good work,' Danny said. 'You ever want to come out and join me, I could train you.'

Joe, still smiling, shook his head.

'It's honest work,' Danny said.

'I know,' Joe said.

'You could stop living a life where you look over your shoulder all the time.'

'It's not about that.'

'What's it about?' Danny seemed authentically curious.

'The night. It's got its own set of rules.'

'Day's got rules too.'

'Oh, I know,' Joe said, 'but I don't like them.'

They stared through the mesh at each other for a long time.

'I don't understand,' Danny said softly.

'I know you don't,' Joe said. 'You, you buy into all this stuff about good guys and bad guys in the world. A loan shark breaks a guy's leg for not paying his debt, a banker throws a guy out of his home for the same reason, and you think there's a difference, like the banker's just doing his job but the loan shark's a criminal. I like the loan shark because he doesn't pretend to be anything else, and I think the banker should be sitting where I'm sitting right now. I'm not going to live some life where I pay my fucking taxes and fetch the boss a lemonade at the company picnic and buy life insurance. Get older, get fatter, so I can join a men's club in Back Bay, smoke cigars with a bunch of assholes in a back room somewhere, talk about my squash game and my kid's grades. Die at my desk, and they'll already have scraped my name off the office door before the dirt's hit the coffin.'

'But that's life,' Danny said.

'That's *a* life. You want to play by their rules? Go ahead. But I say their rules are bullshit. I say there are no rules but the ones a man makes for himself.'

Again, they considered each other through the mesh. His whole childhood, Danny had been Joe's hero. Hell, his god. And now god was just a man who fell off horses for a living, pretended to be shot for a living.

'Wow,' Danny said softly, 'did you ever grow up.'

'Yeah,' Joe said.

Danny placed his cigarettes in his pocket and put his hat on.

'Pity,' he said.

*

Within the prison, the White-Pescatore War was partially won the night three White soldiers were shot on the roof while 'trying to escape.'

Skirmishes continued to occur, however, and bad blood festered. Over the next six months, Joe learned that wars don't really end. Even as he and Maso and the rest of the Pescatore prison crew consolidated their power, it was impossible to tell if this guard or that guard had been paid to move against them or if this or that convict could be trusted.

Micky Baer was shanked in the yard by a guy who, it turned out, was married to the late Dom Pokaski's sister. Micky survived, but he'd have problems pissing for the rest of his life. They heard from the outside that Guard Colvin was laying off bets with Syd Mayo, a White associate. And Colvin was losing.

Then Holly Peletos, a White button man, rotated in to do five years for involuntary manslaughter and started running his mouth in the mess hall about regime change. So they had to throw him off the tier.

Some weeks Joe went two or three nights without sleep because of the fear, or because he was trying to figure out all the angles, or because his heart wouldn't stop banging inside his chest like it was trying to break free.

You told yourself it wouldn't get to you.

You told yourself this place wouldn't eat your soul.

But what you told yourself above all else was, *I will live. I will walk out of here.*

Whatever the cost.

Maso was released on a spring morning in 1928.

'Next time you see me,' he said to Joe, 'will be Visitors' Day. I'll be on the other side of that mesh.'

Joe shook his hand. 'Be safe.'

'I got my mouthpiece working on your case. You'll be out soon. Stay alert, kid, stay alive.'

Joe tried to take comfort in the words, but he knew that if that's all they were – words – then he was in for a sentence that would feel twice as long because he'd allowed hope in. As soon as Maso left this place behind, he could very easily leave Joe behind.

Or he could give him just enough of the carrot to keep Joe running his operation behind these walls for him with no intention of hiring him once he reached the outside.

Either way, Joe was powerless to do anything but sit and wait to see how things shook out.

When Maso hit the street, it was hard not to notice. What had been simmering on the inside got splashed with gasoline on the outside. Murderous May, as the rags dubbed it, left Boston looking for the first time like Detroit or Chicago. Maso's soldiers hit Albert White's bookies, distillers, trucks, and soldiers like it was open season. And it was. Within one month, Maso chased Albert White out of Boston, his few remaining soldiers scurrying after him.

In prison, it was as if harmony had been injected into the water supply. The stabbings stopped. For the rest of '28, no one got thrown off a tier or shanked in the chow line. Joe knew that peace had truly come to Charlestown Penitentiary when he was able to forge a deal with two of Albert White's best incarcerated distillers to ply their trade behind the walls. Soon, the guards were smuggling gin *out* of Charlestown

Penitentiary, the shit so good it even picked up a street name, Penal Code.

Joe slept soundly for the first time since he'd walked through the front gates in the summer of '27. It also gave him time to mourn his father and mourn Emma, a process he'd held at bay when it would have pulled his thoughts to places they shouldn't have gone while others plotted against him.

The cruelest trick God played on him through the second half of '28 was sending Emma to visit him while he slept. He'd feel her leg snake between his, smell the single drops of perfume she placed behind each ear, open his eyes to see hers an inch away, feel her breath on his lips. He'd raise his arms off the mattress so he could run his palms down her bare back. And his eyes would open for real.

No one.

Just the dark.

And he'd pray. He'd ask God to let her be alive, even if he never saw her again. Please let her be alive.

But, God, alive or dead, could you please, please stop sending her to my dreams? I can't lose her again and again. It's too much. It's too cruel. Lord, Joe asked, have mercy.

But he didn't.

The visitations continued – and would continue – for the rest of Joe's incarceration at Charlestown Penitentiary.

His father never visited. But Joe felt him in a way he never had while the man was alive. Sometimes he sat on his bunk, flicking the watch cover open and closed, open and closed, and he imagined conversations they might have had if all the stale sins and withered expectations hadn't stood in the way.

Tell me about Mom.

What do you want to know?

Who was she?

A frightened girl. A very frightened girl, Joseph.

What was she afraid of?

Out there.

What's out there?

Everything she didn't understand.

Did she love me?

In her own way.

That's not love.

For her it was. Don't look at it as if she left you.

How am I supposed to look at it?

That she hung on because of you. Otherwise, she would have left us all years ago.

I don't miss her.

Funny. I do.

Joe looked into the dark. *I miss you.*

You'll see me soon enough.

Once Joe had streamlined the prison's distillery and smuggling operations as well as its protection rackets, he had plenty of time to read. He read just about everything in the prison library, which was no small feat, thanks to Lancelot Hudson III.

Lancelot Hudson III had been the only rich man anyone could ever remember who'd been sentenced to hard time in Charlestown Pen'. But Lancelot's crime had been so outrageous and so public – he'd thrown his unfaithful wife, Catherine, from the roof of their four-story Beacon Street town house *into* the Independence Day Parade of 1919 as it flowed down Beacon Hill – that even the Brahmins had put down their bone china long enough to decide that if there was ever a time to feed one of their own to the natives, this was it. Lancelot Hudson III served seven years at Charlestown for involuntary manslaughter. If it wasn't exactly hard labor, it was hard time, mitigated only by the books he'd had shipped into the prison, a deal dependent on his leaving them behind when he left. Joe read at least a hundred books of the Hudson collection. You knew they were his because, in the top right corner of the title page, he'd written in tiny, cramped penmanship, 'Originally the Property of Lancelot Hudson III. Fuck you.' Joe read Dumas and Dickens and Twain. He read Malthus, Adam Smith, Marx and Engels, Machiavelli, *The Federalist Papers,* and Bastiat's *Economic Sophisms*. When he'd burned through the Hudson collection, he read whatever else was on hand – dime novels and Westerns mostly – as well as every magazine and newspaper they allowed in. He became something of an expert at figuring out what words or whole sentences they'd censored.

Browsing an issue of the *Boston Traveler*, he came across a story about a fire at the East Coast Bus Line Terminal on St James. A frayed electrical cord had sent sparks into the terminal Christmas tree. In short order, the building caught fire. The breath in Joe's body went small and trapped as he studied the photographs of the damage. The locker where he'd stashed his life's savings, including the $62,000 from the Pittsfield job, was in the corner of one shot. It lay on its side under a ceiling beam, the metal as black as soil.

Joe couldn't decide which felt worse – the sensation that

he'd never breathe again or the feeling that he was about to vomit fire through his windpipe.

The article claimed the building was a total loss. Nothing salvaged. Joe doubted that. Someday, when he had the time, he was going to track down which employee of the East Coast Bus Line had retired young and was rumored to be living abroad and in style.

Until then, he was going to need a job.

Maso offered it to him late that winter, the same day he told Joe his appeal was proceeding apace.

'You'll be out of here soon,' Maso told him through the mesh.

'All due respect,' Joe said, 'how soon?'

'By the summer.'

Joe smiled. 'Really?'

Maso nodded. 'Judges don't come cheap, though. You're going to have to work that off.'

'Why don't we call us even for me not killing you?'

Maso narrowed his eyes, a natty figure now in his cashmere topcoat and a wool suit complete with a white carnation in his lapel that matched his silk hatband. 'Sounds like a deal. Our friend, Mr White, is making a lot of noise in Tampa, by the way.'

'Tampa?'

Maso nodded. 'He still held on to a few places here. I can't get them all because New York owns a piece and they've made it clear I don't fuck with them right now. He runs the rum up on our routes and there's nothing I can do about that, either. But because he's infringing on my turf down there, the boys in New York gave us permission to push him out.'

'What level of permission?' Joe said.

'Short of killing him.'

'Okay. So what're you going to do?'

'Not what I'm going to do. It's what you're going to do, Joe. I want you to take over down there.'

'But Lou Ormino runs Tampa.'

'He's gonna decide he doesn't want the headache anymore.'

'When's he going to decide that?'

'About ten minutes before you get there.'

Joe gave it some thought. 'Tampa, huh?'

'It's hot.'

'I don't mind hot.'

'You ain't never felt hot like this hot.'

Joe shrugged. The old man had a penchant for exaggerating. 'I'm going to need somebody I can trust there.'

'I knew you'd say that.'

'Yeah?'

Maso nodded. 'It's already done. He's been there six months.'

'Where'd you find him?'

'Montreal.'

'Six months?' Joe said. 'How long you been planning this?'

'Since Lou Ormino started putting some of my cut in his pocket and Albert White showed up to grub up the rest.' He leaned forward. 'You go down there and make it right, Joe? Spend the rest of your life living like a king.'

'So if I take over, are we equal partners?'

'No,' Maso said.

'But Lou Ormino's an equal partner.'

'And look how that's going to end up.' Maso stared through the mesh at Joe with his true face.

'How much do I get then?'

'Twenty percent.'

'Twenty-five,' Joe said.

'Fine,' Maso said with a twinkle in his eye that said he'd have gone to thirty. 'But you better earn it.'

PART II

Ybor

1929–1933

CHAPTER ELEVEN

Best in the City

When Maso had first proposed that Joe take over his West Florida operations, he'd warned him about the heat. But Joe still wasn't prepared for the wall of it that met him when he stepped onto the platform at Tampa Union Station on an August morning in 1929. He wore a summer-weight glen plaid suit. He'd left the vest behind in his suitcase, but standing on the platform, waiting for the porter to bring his bags, jacket over his arm and tie loosened, he was soaked by the time he finished smoking a cigarette. He'd removed his Wilton when he stepped off the train, worried that the heat would leach the pomade from his hair and suck it into the silk lining, but he put it back on to protect his skull from the sun needles as more pores in his chest and arms sprang leaks.

It wasn't just the sun, which hung high and white in a sky swept so clear of clouds it was as if clouds had never existed (and maybe they didn't down here; Joe had no idea), it was the jungle humidity, like he was wrapped inside a ball of steel wool someone had dropped into a pot of oil. And every minute or so, the burner got turned up another notch.

The other men who'd exited the train had, like Joe, removed their suit jackets; some had removed their vests and ties and rolled up their sleeves. Some had donned their hats; others had removed them and waved them in front of their faces. The women travelers wore wide-brimmed velvet hats, felt cloches, or poke bonnets. Some poor souls had elected for even heavier material and ear treatments. They wore crepe dresses and silk scarves, but they didn't look very happy about it, their faces red, their carefully tended hair sprouting splits and curls, the chignons unraveling at the napes of a few necks.

You could tell the locals easily – the men wore skimmers, short-sleeved shirts, and gabardine trousers. Their shoes were two-toned like most men's these days but more brightly colored than those of the train passengers. If the women wore headgear, they wore straw gigolo hats. They wore very simple dresses, lots of white, like the one on the gal passing him now, absolutely nothing special about her white skirt and matching blouse and both a little threadbare. But, Jesus, Joe thought, the body under it – moving under the thin fabric like something outlawed that was hoping to slip out of town before the Puritans got word. Paradise, Joe thought, is dusky and lush and covers limbs that move like water.

The heat must have made him slower than usual because the woman caught him looking, something he'd never been nabbed for back home. But the woman – a mulatto or maybe even a Negress of some kind, he couldn't tell, but definitely dark, copper dark – gave him a damning flick of her eyes and kept walking. Maybe it was the heat, maybe it was the two years in prison, but Joe couldn't stop watching her move beneath the thin dress. Her hips rose and fell in the same languid motion as her ass, a music to it all as the bones and muscles in her back rose and fell in a concert of the body. Jesus, he thought, I have been in prison too long. Her dark wiry hair was tied into a chignon at the back of her head, but a single strand fell down her neck. She turned back to shoot him a glare. He looked down before it reached him, feeling like a nine-year-old who'd been caught pulling a girl's pigtails in the schoolyard. And then he wondered what he had to be ashamed of. She'd looked back, hadn't she?

When he looked up again, she was lost to the crowd down the other end of the platform. *You have nothing to fear from me,* he wanted to tell her. *You'll never break my heart and I'll never break yours. I'm out of the heartbreak business.*

Joe had spent the last two years accepting not only that Emma was dead but that, for him, there'd never be another love. Someday, he might marry, but it would be a sensible arrangement, certain to raise him up in his profession and give him heirs. He loved the idea of that word – *heirs*. (Working-class men had sons. Successful men had heirs.) In the meantime, he'd go to whores. Maybe the woman who'd shot him the dirty look was a whore playing the 'chaste' tip. If she was, he'd definitely try her out – a beautiful mulatto whore fit for a criminal prince.

When the porter deposited Joe's bags in front of him, Joe tipped him with bills grown as damp as everything else. He'd been told someone would meet his train, but he'd never thought to ask how they'd pick him out of the crowd. He turned in a slow pivot, looking for a man who appeared sufficiently disreputable, but instead he saw the mulatto woman walking back down the platform toward him. Another strand of hair fell from along her temple and she brushed it back off her cheekbone with her free hand. Her other arm was wrapped in the arm of a Latin guy in a straw skimmer and tan silk trousers with long, sharp pleats and a white collarless shirt buttoned to the top. In this heat, the man's face was dry, as was his shirt, even at the top, where the button was cinched tight below his Adam's apple. He moved with the same gentle sway as the woman; it was in his calves and his ankles, even as the steps themselves were so sharp his feet snapped off the platform.

They passed Joe speaking Spanish, the words coming fast and light, and the woman gave Joe the quickest of glances, so quick he might have imagined it, though he doubted it. The man pointed at something down the platform and said something in his rapid Spanish, and they both chuckled, and then they were past him.

He was turning to take another look for whoever was picking him up, when someone did just that – lifted him off the hot platform like he weighed no more than a sack of laundry. He looked down at the two beefy arms wrapped around his midsection and smelled a familiar reek of raw onions and Arabian Sheik cologne.

He was dropped back onto the platform and spun around and he faced his old friend for the first time since that awful day in Pittsfield.

'Dion,' he said.

Dion had traded chubbiness for corpulence. He wore a champagne-colored four-button suit, chalk-striped. His lavender shirt had a high white contrasting collar over a bloodred tie with black stripes. His black and white speculator shoes were laced up above the ankles. If you asked an old man gone poor of sight to identify the gangster on the platform from a hundred yards away, he'd point his shaking finger at Dion.

'Joseph,' he said with a starchy formality. Then his round face collapsed around a wide smile and he lifted Joe off the ground again, this time from the front and hugged him so tight Joe feared for his spine.

'Sorry about your father,' he whispered.

'Sorry about your brother.'

'Thank you,' Dion said with a strange brightness. 'All for canned ham.' He let Joe down and smiled. 'I would have bought him his own pigs.'

They walked down the platform in the heat.

Dion took one of Joe's suitcases from him. 'When Lefty Downer found me in Montreal and told me the Pescatores wanted me to come work for them, I thought it was a right bamboozle, I don't mind telling you. But then they said you were jailing with the old man and I thought, "If anyone could charm the devil himself, it's my old partner."' He slapped a thick arm against Joe's shoulders. 'It's just swell to have you back.'

Joe said, 'Good to be out in free air.'

'Was Charlestown . . . ?'

Joe nodded. 'Maybe worse than they say. But I figured out a way to make it livable.'

'Bet you did.'

The heat was even whiter in the parking lot. It bounced up off the crushed shell lot and off the cars, and Joe placed a hand above his eyebrows but it didn't help much.

'Christ,' he said to Dion, 'and you're wearing a three-piece.'

'Here's the secret,' Dion said as they reached a Marmon 34 and he dropped Joe's suitcase to the crushed shell pavement. 'Next time you're in a department store, clip every shirt in your size. I wear four in a day.'

Joe looked at his lavender shirt. 'You found four in that color?'

'Found eight.' He opened the back door of the car and put Joe's luggage inside. 'We're only going a few blocks, but in this heat . . . '

Joe reached for the passenger door but Dion beat him to it. Joe looked at him. 'You're having me on.'

'I work for you now,' Dion said. 'Boss Joe Coughlin.'

'Quit it.' Joe shook his head at the absurdity of it and climbed inside.

As they pulled out of the station lot, Dion said, 'Reach under your seat. You'll find a friend.'

Joe did and came back with a Savage .32 automatic. Indian Head grips and a three-and-a-half-inch barrel. Joe slid it into the right pocket of his trousers and told Dion he'd need a holster for it, feeling a mild irritation that Dion hadn't thought to bring one with him.

'You want mine?' Dion said.

'No,' Joe said. 'I'm fine.'

'Because I can give you mine.'

'No,' Joe said, thinking that being the boss was going to take some getting used to. 'I'll just need one soon.'

'End of the day,' Dion said. 'No later, I promise.'

Traffic moved as slow as everything else down here. Dion drove them into Ybor City. Here the sky lost its hard white and picked up a bronze smear from the factory smoke. Cigars, Dion explained, had built this neighborhood. He pointed at brick buildings and their tall smokestacks and the smaller buildings – some just shotgun shacks with front and back doors open – where workers sat hunched over tables rolling cigars.

He rattled off the names – El Reloj and Cuesta-Rey, Bustillo, Celestino Vega, El Paraiso, La Pila, La Trocha, El Naranjal, Perfecto Garcia. He told Joe the most esteemed position in any factory was that of the reader, a man who sat in a chair in the center of the work floor and read aloud from great novels as the workers toiled. He explained that a cigar maker was called a *tabaquero,* the small factories were *chinchals* or buckeyes, and the food he might be smelling through the smoke stench was probably *bolos* or *empanadas.*

'Listen to you.' Joe whistled. 'Speaking the language like the king of Spain.'

'You have to around here,' Dion said. 'Italian too. You better brush up.'

'You speak Italian, my brother did, but I never picked it up.'

'Well, I hope you're still as quick a learner as you used to be. Reason we get to do our business here in Ybor is because the rest of the city just leaves us alone. Far as they're concerned, we're just dirty spics and dirty wops and as long as we don't make too much noise or the cigar workers don't go on strike again, make the owners call in the cops and the head breakers, then we're left to do what we do.' He turned onto Seventh Avenue, apparently a main drag, people bustling along the clapboard sidewalks under two-story buildings with wide balconies and wrought iron trellises and brick or stucco facades that reminded Joe of the lost week-end he'd had in New Orleans a couple years ago. Tracks ran down the center of the avenue and Joe saw a trolley coming their way from several blocks off, its nose disappearing, then reappearing behind waves of heat.

'You'd think we'd all get along,' Dion said, 'but it doesn't always work out that way. The Italians and the Cubans keep to themselves. But the black Cubans hate the white Cubans, and the white Cubans look at the nigger Cubans like they're niggers, and they both high-hat everyone else. All Cubans hate the Spaniards. Spaniards think the Cubans are uppity coons who forgot their place since the US of A freed them back in '98. Then the Cubans *and* the Spanish look down on the Puerto Ricans, and everyone shits on the Dominicans. The Italians only respect you if you came off the boat from the Boot, and the *Americanos* actually think someone gives a shit what they think sometimes.'

'Did you actually call us *Americanos*?'

'I'm Italian,' Dion said, turning left and running them down another wide avenue, although this one wasn't paved. 'And around here? Proud of it.'

Joe saw the blue of the Gulf and the ships in port and the high cranes. He could smell salt, oil slicks, low tide.

'Port of Tampa,' Dion said with a flourish of his hand as

he drove them along redbrick streets where men crossed their path in forklifts that burped diesel smoke and the cranes swung two-ton pallets high over their heads, the shadows of the netting crisscrossing the windshield. A steam whistle blew.

Dion pulled over by a cargo pit and they got out, watched the men below take apart a bale of burlap sacks stamped ESCUINTIA, GUATEMALA. From the smell, Joe could tell some of the sacks held coffee and others chocolate. The half-dozen men off-loaded them in no time, and the crane swung the netting and the empty pallet back up, and the men in the hold disappeared through a doorway down there.

Dion led Joe to the ladder and descended.

'Where we going?'

'You'll see.'

At the bottom of the hold, the men had closed the door behind them. He and Dion stood on a dirt floor that smelled of everything ever off-loaded in the Tampa sun – bananas and pineapple and grain. Oil and potatoes and gas and vinegar. Gunpowder. Spoiled fruit and fresh coffee, the grounds crunching underfoot. Dion placed the flat of his hand to the cement wall opposite the ladder and moved his hand to the right and the wall went with it – just popped up and out of a seam Joe couldn't see from two feet away. Dion revealed a door and rapped on it twice, then waited, his lips moving as he counted. Then he rapped it another four times and a voice on the other side said, 'Who's it?'

'Fireplace,' Dion said, and the door opened.

A corridor faced them, as thin as the man on the other side of the door, who was dressed in a shirt that might have been white before the sweat tanned it for the ages. His trousers were a brown denim, and he wore a kerchief around his neck and a cowboy hat. A six-gun stuck out of the waistband of his denim trousers. The cowboy nodded at Dion and allowed them to pass before he pushed the wall back into place.

The corridor was so narrow Dion's shoulders brushed along the walls as he walked ahead of Joe. Dim lights hung from a pipe above them, one bare bulb for every twenty feet or so, half of them out. Joe was pretty sure he could make out a door down the far end of the corridor. He guessed it was about five hundred yards away, which meant he could easily be imagining it. They slogged through mud, water dripping from the ceiling and puddling the floor, and Dion explained that the tunnels commonly flooded; every now and then they'd find a dead drunk in the morning, the last of the stragglers from the night before who'd decided to take an ill-advised nap.

'Seriously?' Joe asked.

'Yeah. Know what makes it worse? Sometimes the rats get to them.'

Joe looked all around himself. 'That's just about the nastiest fucking thing I've heard all month.'

Dion shrugged and kept walking and Joe looked up and down the walls and then at the pathway ahead. No rats. Yet.

'The money from the Pittsfield bank,' Dion said as they walked.

Joe said, 'It's safe.' Above him, he could hear the clack of trolley wheels followed by the slow heavy clop of what he assumed was a horse.

'Safe where?' Dion looked back over his shoulder at him.

Joe said, 'How'd they know?'

Above them several horns beeped and an engine revved.

'Know what?' Dion said, and Joe noticed he'd grown closer to bald, his dark hair still thick and oily on the sides but ropey and hesitant up top.

'Where to ambush us.'

Dion looked back at him again. 'They just did.'

'There's no way they "just did." We scouted that location for weeks. The cops never came out that way because they had no reason to – nothing to protect and no one to serve.'

Dion nodded his big head. 'Well, they didn't hear anything from me.'

'Me, either,' Joe said.

Near the end of the tunnel now, the door revealed itself to be brushed steel with an iron dead bolt. The street sounds had given way to the distant clank of silverware and plates being stacked and waiters' footsteps rushing back and forth. Joe pulled his father's watch from his pocket and clicked it open: noon.

Dion produced a sizable key ring from somewhere in his wide trousers. He opened the locks on the door, threw back the bars, and unlocked the bolt. He removed the key from the ring and handed it to Joe. 'Take it. You'll use it, believe me.'

Joe pocketed the key.

'Who owns this place?'

'Ormino did.'

'Did?'

'Oh, you didn't read today's papers?'

Joe shook his head.

'Ormino sprung a few leaks last night.'

Dion opened the door, and they climbed a ladder to another door that was unlocked. They opened it and entered a vast, dank room with a cement floor and cement walls. Tables ran along the walls, and on top of the tables were what Joe would have expected to see – fermentors and extractors, retorts and Bunsen burners, beakers and vats and skimming utensils.

'Best money can buy,' Dion said, pointing out thermometers fixed to the walls and connected to the stills by rubber tubing. 'You want light rum, you got to remove the fraction at between one sixty-eight and one eighty-six Fahrenheit. That's really important to keep people from, you know, dying when they drink your hooch. These babies don't make a mistake, they—'

'I know how to make rum,' Joe said. 'In fact, you name the substance, D, after two years in prison, I know how to recondense it. I could probably distill your fucking shoes. What I don't see here, though, are two things that are pretty essential to making rum.'

'Oh?' Dion said. 'What's that?'

'Molasses and workers.'

'Shoulda mentioned,' Dion said, 'we got a problem there.'

They passed through an empty speakeasy and said 'Fireplace' through another closed door and entered the kitchen of an Italian restaurant on East Palm Avenue. They passed through the kitchen and into the dining room, where they found a table near the street and close to a tall black fan so heavy it looked like it would take three men and an ox to move it.

'Our distributor is coming up empty.' Dion unfolded his napkin and tucked it into his collar, smoothed it over his tie.

'I can see that,' Joe said. 'Why?'

'Boats have been sinking is what I hear.'

'Who's the distributor again?'

'Guy named Gary L. Smith.'

'Ellsmith?'

'No,' Dion said. '*L*. The middle initial. He insists you use it.'

'Why?'

'It's a Southern thing.'

'Not just an asshole thing?'

'Could be that too.'

The waiter brought their menus and Dion ordered them two lemonades, assuring Joe it would be the best he ever tasted.

'Why do we need a distributor?' Joe asked. 'Why aren't we dealing directly with the supplier?'

'Well, there's a lot of them. And they're all Cuban. Smith deals with Cubans so we don't have to. He also deals with the Dixies.'

'The runners.'

Dion nodded as the waiter brought their lemonades. 'Yeah, the local guns from here to Virginia. They run it across Florida and up the seaboard.'

'But you've been losing a lot of those loads too.'

'Yeah.'

'So how many boats can sink and how many trucks can get hit before it's more than bad luck?'

'Yeah,' Dion said again because apparently he couldn't think of anything else to say.

Joe sipped his lemonade. He wasn't sure it was the best he'd ever tasted, and even if it were, it was lemonade. Hard to get fucking excited about lemonade.

'You do what I suggested in my letter?'

Dion nodded. 'To a T.'

'How many ended up where I figured?'

'A high percentage.'

Joe scanned the menu for something he recognized.

'Try the osso buco,' Dion said. 'Best in the city.'

'Everything's the "best in the city" with you,' Joe said. 'The lemonade, the thermometers.'

Dion shrugged and opened his own menu. 'I have refined tastes.'

'That's it,' Joe said. He closed his menu and caught the waiter's eye. 'Let's eat and then drop in on Gary L. Smith.'

Dion studied his menu. 'A pleasure.'

The morning edition of the Tampa Tribune lay on a table in the waiting room of Gary L. Smith's office. Lou Ormino's corpse sat in a car with shattered windows and blood on the seats. In black-and-white, the death photo looked like they all did – undignified. The headline read:

REPUTED UNDERWORLD FIGURE SLAIN

'Did you know him well?'

Dion nodded. 'Yeah.'

'You like him?'

Dion shrugged. 'He wasn't a bad sort. Clipped his toenails in a couple meetings, but he gave me a goose last Christmas.'

'Live?'

Dion nodded. 'Till I got it home, yeah.'

'Why'd Maso want him out?'

'He never told you?'

Joe shook his head.

Dion shrugged. 'Never told me, either.'

For a minute Joe did nothing but listen to a clock tick and Gary L. Smith's secretary turning the stiff pages of an issue of *Photoplay*. The secretary's name was Miss Roe, and her dark hair was cut Eton-crop style into a finger-wave bob. She wore a silver short-sleeved vest blouse with a black silk necktie that fell over her breasts like an answered prayer. She had a way of barely moving in her chair – a kind of quarter-squirm – that had Joe folding up the paper and waving it in his face.

Good Lord, he thought, do I need to get laid.

He leaned forward again. 'He have family?'

'Who?'

'Who.'

'Lou? Yeah, he did.' Dion scowled. 'Why you got to ask that?'

'I'm just wondering.'

'He probably clipped his toenails in front of them too. They'll be glad not to have to sweep them into the dustpan anymore.'

The intercom buzzed on the secretary's desk and a thin voice said, 'Miss Roe, send the boys in.'

Joe and Dion stood.

'Boys,' Dion said.

'Boys,' Joe said and shot his cuffs and smoothed his hair.

Gary L. Smith had tiny teeth, like kernels of corn and almost as yellow. He smiled as they entered his office and Miss Roe closed the door behind them, but he didn't get up, and he didn't put too much into the smile, either. Behind his desk, plantation shutters blocked most of the West Tampa day, but enough creeped in to give the room a bourbon glow. Smith dressed the part of the Southern gentleman – white suit over white shirt and thin black tie. He watched them take their seats with an air of bemusement, which Joe read as fear.

'So you're Maso's new find.' Smith pushed a humidor across the desk at them. 'Help yourselves. Best cigars in the city.'

Dion grunted.

Joe waved off the humidor, but Dion helped himself to four cigars, placing three in his pocket and biting off the end of the fourth. He spit it into his hand and laid it on the edge of the desk.

'So what brings you by?'

'I've been asked to look over Lou Ormino's affairs for a little bit.'

'But it's not permanent,' Smith said, firing up his own cigar.

'What's not?'

'You as Lou's replacement. I just mention it because the

people 'round here like dealing with who they know, and no one knows you. No offense meant.'

'So who in the organization would you suggest?'

Smith gave it some thought. 'Rickie Pozzetta.'

Dion cocked his head at that. 'Pozzetta couldn't lead a dog to a hydrant.'

'Then Delmore Sears.'

'Another idiot.'

'Well, then, fine, I could do it.'

'That's not a bad idea,' Joe said.

Gary L. Smith spread his hands. 'Only if you think I could be right for the job.'

'It's possible, but we need to know why the last three supply runs have been hit.'

'You mean the ones heading north?'

Joe nodded.

'Bad luck,' he said. 'Best I can figure. It does happen.'

'Why don't you change the routes then?'

Smith produced a pen and scribbled on a piece of paper. 'That's a good idea, Mr Coughlin, is it?'

Joe nodded.

'A great idea. I'll definitely consider it.'

Joe watched the man for a bit, watched him smoke with the diffused light coming through the blinds and spreading over the top of his head, watched him until Smith started looking a little confused.

'Why have the boat runs been so erratic?'

'Oh,' Smith said easily, 'that's the Cubans. We don't have any control over that.'

'Two months ago,' Dion said, 'you got fourteen shipments

in one week, three weeks later it was five, last week it was none.'

'It's not cement mixing,' Gary L. Smith said. 'You don't add one-third water, get the same consistency every time. You've got various suppliers with various schedules, and they might be dealing with a sugar supplier over there had himself a strike? Or the guy who drives the boat gets sick.'

'Then you go to another supplier,' Joe said.

'Not that simple.'

'Why not?'

Smith sounded weary, as if he were being asked to explain airplane mechanics to a cat. 'Because they're all paying tribute to the same group.'

Joe removed a small notebook from his pocket and flipped it open. 'This would be the Suarez family we're talking about?'

Smith eyed the notebook. 'Yeah. Own the Tropicale up on Seventh.'

'So they're the only suppliers.'

'No, I just said.'

'Said what?' Joe narrowed his eyes at the man.

'I mean, they do supply some of what we sell but there are all these others too. This one guy I deal with, Ernesto? Old boy has a wooden hand. You believe it? He—'

'If all the other suppliers answer to one supplier, then that supplier is the only supplier. They set the prices and everyone else falls in line, I assume?'

Smith gave it all a sigh of exasperation. 'I guess.'

'You guess?'

'It's just not that simple.'

'Why isn't it?'

Joe waited. Dion waited. Smith relit his cigar. 'There are other suppliers. They have boats, they have—'

'They're subcontractors,' Joe said. 'That's all. I want to deal with the contractor. We'll need a meet with the Suarezes as soon as possible.'

Smith said, 'No.'

'No?'

'Mr Coughlin, you just don't understand how things are done in Ybor. I deal with Esteban Suarez and his sister. I deal with all the middlemen.'

Joe pushed the telephone across the desk to Smith's elbow. 'Call them.'

'You're not hearing me, Mr Coughlin.'

'No, I am,' Joe said softly. 'Pick up that phone and call the Suarezes and tell them my associate and I will have dinner tonight at the Tropicale, and we'd really appreciate the best table they have as well as a few minutes of their time once we've finished.'

Smith said, 'Why don't you take a couple of days to get to know the customs down here? Then, trust me, you'll come back and thank me for not calling. And we'll go meet them together. I promise.'

Joe reached into his pocket. He pulled out some change and placed it on the desk. Then his cigarettes, his father's watch, followed by his .32, which he left in front of the blotter pointed at Smith. He shook a cigarette from the pack, his eyes on Smith as Smith lifted the phone off the cradle and asked for an outside line.

Joe smoked while Smith spoke Spanish into the phone and Dion translated a bit of it, and then Smith hung up.

'He got us a table for nine o'clock,' Dion said.

'I got you a table for nine o'clock,' Smith said.

'Thank you.' Joe crossed his ankle over his knee. 'It's a brother and sister team, the Suarezes, right?'

Smith nodded. 'Esteban and Ivelia Suarez, yes.'

'Now, Gary,' Joe said and pulled a piece of string off his sock by the anklebone, 'are you working *directly* for Albert White?' He dangled the string, then let it drop to Gary L. Smith's rug. 'Or is there an intermediary we should know about?'

'What?'

'We marked your bottles, Smith.'

'You what?'

'If you distilled it, we marked it,' Dion said. 'A couple months back. Little dots on the upper-right corner.'

Gary smiled at Joe like he'd never heard such a thing.

'All those supply runs that didn't make it?' Joe said. 'Just about every bottle ended up in one of Albert White's speaks.' He flicked his ash on the desk. 'You explain that?'

'I don't understand.'

'You don't . . . ?' Joe put both feet back on the floor.

'No, I mean, I don't . . . What?'

Joe reached for his gun. 'Sure you do.'

Gary smiled. He stopped smiling. He smiled again. 'No, I don't. Hey. Hey.'

'You've been pointing Albert White to our northeastern supply runs.' Joe ejected the .32's magazine into his palm. He thumbed the top bullet.

Gary said it again. He said, 'Hey.'

Joe peered down the sight. He said to Dion, 'There's still one in the chamber.'

'You should always leave one there. In case.'

'In case of what?' Joe jacked the bullet out of the chamber and caught it. He placed it on the desk, the tip pointing at Gary L. Smith.

'I don't know,' Dion said. 'Things you can't see coming.'

Joe slammed the magazine back into the grip. He snapped a bullet into the chamber and placed the gun on his lap. 'I had Dion drive by your house on the way over. You've got a nice house. Dion said the neighborhood's called Hyde Park?'

'Yes, it is.'

'Funny.'

'What?'

'We've got a Hyde Park in Boston.'

'Oh. That is funny.'

'Well, it's not hilarious or anything. Just interesting, kind of.'

'Yes.'

'Stucco?'

'Sorry?'

'Stucco. It's made of stucco, right?'

'Well, it's a wood frame, but, yeah, stucco skin.'

'Oh. So I was wrong.'

'No, you weren't wrong.'

'You said wood.'

'The frame's wood, but the skin, the surface, that's, yeah, that's stucco. So you, yeah, that's what it is – a stucco house.'

'You like it?'

'Huh?'

'The wood-frame stucco house – do you like it?'

'It's a little big now that my kids are . . .'

'What?'

'Grown. They're gone.'

Joe scratched the back of his head with the barrel of the .32. 'You're going to have to pack it up.'

'I don't—'

'Or hire someone to pack it up for you.' He shot his eyebrows in the direction of the phone. 'They can send the stuff to wherever you end up.'

Smith tried to get back what had left the office fifteen minutes ago, the illusion that he was in control. 'End *up*? I'm not leaving.'

Joe stood and reached into the pocket of his suit jacket. 'You fucking her?'

'What? Who?'

Joe jerked his thumb at the door behind him. 'Miss Roe.'

Smith said, *'What?'*

Joe looked at Dion. 'He's fucking her.'

Dion stood. 'Without question.'

Joe pulled a pair of train tickets out of his jacket. 'She is a work of art, that one. Falling asleep inside of her must be like getting a glimpse of God. After that, you know everything's going to be all right.'

He placed the tickets on the desk between them.

'I don't care who you take – your wife, Miss Roe, hell, both of them or neither of them. But you will board the eleven o'clock Seaboard to do it. Tonight, Gary.'

He laughed. It was a short laugh. 'I don't think you under—'

Joe slapped Gary L. Smith across the face so hard he left his chair and banged his head on the radiator.

They waited for him to get off the floor. He righted his chair. He sat in it, all the blood gone from his face now, though some speckled his cheek and lip. Dion tossed a handkerchief at his chest.

'You either put yourself on that train, Gary' – Joe lifted his bullet off the desk – 'or we put you under it.'

Heading to the car, Dion said, 'You serious about that?'

'Yes.' Joe was irritated again, though not sure why. Sometimes a darkness just came over him. He'd like to say these sudden black moods had been happening only since prison, but the truth was they'd been descending on him since he could remember. Sometimes without reason or warning. But in this case, maybe because Smith had mentioned having children and Joe didn't like thinking about a man he'd just humiliated having any kind of life outside this job.

'So, if he doesn't get on that train, you're prepared to kill him?'

Or maybe simply because he was a dark guy given to dark moods.

'No.' Joe stopped at the car and waited. 'Men who work for us will.' He looked at Dion. 'What am I, a fucking field hand?'

Dion opened the door for him and Joe climbed inside.

CHAPTER TWELVE

Music and Guns

Joe had asked Maso to put him up in a hotel. His first month here, he didn't want to think about anything but business – that included where his next meal was coming from, how his sheets and clothes got washed, and how long the fella who'd gotten to the bathroom ahead of him was going to stay there. Maso said he'd put him up at the Tampa Bay Hotel, which sounded fine to Joe, if a little unimaginative. He assumed it was a middle-of-the-road place with decent beds, bland but serviceable food, and flat pillows.

Instead, Dion pulled up in front of a lakefront palace. When Joe spoke the thought aloud, Dion said, 'That's actually what they call it – Plant's Palace.' Henry Plant had built the place, much like he'd built most of Florida, to entice land speculators who'd come down over the past two decades in swarms.

Before Dion could pull up to the front door, a train crossed their path. Not a toy train, though he'd bet they had those here too, but a transcontinental locomotive, a quarter mile long. Joe and Dion sat just short of the parking lot and watched the train disgorge rich men and rich women and their rich children. While they waited, Joe counted more than a hundred windows in the building. At the top of the redbrick walls were several dormers Joe assumed housed the suites. Six minarets rose even higher than the dormers, pointing toward the hard white sky – a Russian winter palace in the middle of dredged Florida swampland.

A swank couple in starched whites left the train. Their three nannies and three swank children followed. Fast on their heels two Negro porters pushed luggage carts piled high with steamer trunks.

'Let's come back,' Joe said.

'What?' Dion said. 'We can park here and walk your bags over. Get you—'

'We'll come back.' Joe watched the couple stroll inside like they'd grown up in places twice this size. 'I don't want to wait in line.'

Dion looked like he was about to say more on the subject, but then he sighed softly, and they drove back down the road and over small wooden bridges and past a golf course. An older couple sat in a rickshaw pulled by a small Latin guy in a white long-sleeve shirt and white pants. Small wooden signs pointed to the shuffleboard courts, the hunting preserve, canoes, tennis courts, and a racetrack. They drove past the golf course, greener than Joe would have bet in all this heat, and most people they saw wore white and carried parasols, even the men, and their laughter was dry and distant on the air.

He and Dion drove onto Lafayette and into downtown. Dion told Joe the Suarezes went back and forth from Cuba and few knew much about them. Ivelia, it was rumored, had been married to a man who'd died during the sugar workers' rebellion back in '12. It was also rumored that the story was a front to disguise her lesbian tendencies.

'Esteban,' Dion said, 'owns a lot of companies, both here and over there. Young guy, way younger than his sister. But smart. His father was in business with Ybor himself when Ybor—'

'Wait a minute,' Joe said, 'this city's named after one guy?'

'Yeah,' Dion said, 'Vicente Ybor. He was a cigar guy.'

'Now, that,' Joe said, 'is power.' He looked out the window and saw Ybor City to the east, handsome from a distance, reminding Joe again of New Orleans, but a much smaller version.

'I dunno,' Dion said, 'Coughlin City?' He shook his head. 'Doesn't have a ring to it.'

'No,' Joe agreed, 'but Coughlin County?'

Dion chuckled. 'You know? That's not bad.'

'Sounds good, doesn't it?'

'How many sizes your hat go up when you were in prison?' Dion asked.

'Suit yourself,' Joe said, 'dream small.'

'How about Coughlin Country? No, hold it, Coughlin Conti-nent.'

Joe laughed and Dion roared and slapped the wheel and Joe was surprised to realize how much he'd missed his friend and how much it would break his heart if he had to order his murder by the end of the week.

Dion drove them down Jefferson toward the courthouses and government buildings. They ran into a snarl of traffic and the heat found the car again.

'Next on the agenda?' Joe asked.

'You want heroin? Morphine? Cocaine?'

Joe shook his head. 'Gave them all up for Lent.'

Dion said, 'Well, if you ever decide to get hooked, this is the place to come, sport. Tampa, Florida – illegal narcotics center of the South.'

'Chamber of commerce know that?'

'And they're plenty sore about it. Anyway, reason I bring it up is—'

'Oh, a *point*,' Joe said.

'I do have them now and again.'

'By all means then, proceed, sir.'

'One of Esteban's guys, Arturo Torres? He was pinched last week for cocaine. So normally he'd be out half an hour after he went in, but they got this Federal task force sniffing around right now. IRS guys came down beginning of the summer with a bunch of judges, and the furnace got turned on. Arturo is going to be deported.'

'Why do we care?'

'He's Esteban's best cooker. 'Round Ybor you see a bottle of rum with Torres's initials on the cork, it's gonna cost you double.'

'When's he supposed to be deported?'

'In about two hours.'

Joe placed his hat over his face and slouched in his seat. He felt exhausted suddenly from the long train ride, the heat, the thinking, that dizzying display of wealthy white people in their wealthy white clothes. 'Wake me when we get there.'

After meeting with the judge, they walked from the courthouse to pay a courtesy call on Chief Irving Figgis of the Tampa Police Department.

Headquarters sat on the corner of Florida and Jackson, Joe having oriented himself enough to realize he'd have to pass by it every day as he went from the hotel to work in Ybor. Cops were like nuns that way – always letting you know they were watching.

'He asked you to come to him,' Dion explained as they walked up the steps of headquarters, 'so he won't have to come to you.'

'What's he like?'

'He's a copper,' Dion said, 'so he's an asshole. Beyond that, he's okay.'

In his office, Figgis was surrounded by photographs of the same three people – a wife, a son, and a daughter. They were all apple-haired and startlingly attractive. The children had skin so unblemished it was as if angels had scrubbed them clean. The chief shook Joe's hand, looked him directly in the eye, and asked him to take a seat. Irving Figgis wasn't a tall man or one of great size or muscle. He was slim and ran small and kept his gray hair trimmed tight to his scalp. He looked like a man who'd give you a fair shake if you gave the same to him, but a man who'd give you twice the hell you'd come looking for if you played him for a fool.

'I won't insult you by asking the nature of your business,' he said, 'so you won't have to insult me by lying. Fair?'

Joe nodded.

'True you're a police captain's son?'

Joe nodded. 'Yes, sir.'

'So you understand.'

'What's that, sir?'

'That this' – he pointed back and forth between his chest and Joe's – 'is how we live. But everything else?' He gestured at all those photographs. 'Well, that's why we live.'

Joe nodded. 'And never the twain shall meet.'

Chief Figgis smiled. 'Heard you were educated too.' A small glance for Dion. 'Don't find much of that in your trade.'

'Or in yours,' Dion said.

Figgis smiled and tipped his head in acknowledgment. He fixed Joe in a mild gaze. 'Before I settled here, I was a soldier and then a U.S. marshal. I've killed seven men in my lifetime,' he said without a hint of pride.

Seven? Joe thought. Christ.

Chief Figgis's gaze remained mild, even. 'I killed them because it was my job. I take no pleasure from it and, truth be told, their faces haunt me most nights. But if I had to kill an eighth tomorrow to protect and serve this city? Mister, I would do so with a steady arm and a clear eye. You follow?'

'I do,' Joe said.

Chief Figgis stood by a city map on the wall behind his desk and used his finger to draw a slow circle around Ybor City. 'If you keep your business here – north of Second, south of Twenty-seventh, west of Thirty-fourth, and east of Nebraska – you and I will have little in the way of discord.' He gave Joe a small arch of his eyebrow. 'How's that sound?'

'Sounds good,' Joe said, wondering when he'd get around to naming his price.

Chief Figgis saw the question in Joe's eyes and his own darkened slightly. 'I don't take bribes. If I did, three of those seven dead I mentioned would still be among the living.' He came around to sit on the edge of the desk, spoke in a very low voice. 'I have no illusions, young Mr Coughlin, on how business is transacted in this town. If you were to ask me in private how I feel about Volstead, you'd see me do a pretty fair imitation of a kettle come to boil. I know plenty of my officers take money to look the other way. I know I serve a city swimming in corruption. I know we live in a fallen world. But just because I breathe corrupt air and rub elbows with corrupt people, never make the mistake of believing I am corruptible.'

Joe searched the man's face for signs of puffery, pride, or self-aggrandizement – the usual weaknesses he'd come to associate with 'self-made' men.

Nothing stared back at him but quiet fortitude.

Chief Figgis, he decided, was never to be underestimated.

'I won't make that mistake,' Joe said.

Chief Figgis held out his hand and Joe shook it.

'I thank you for coming by. Careful in the sun.' A flash of humor passed through Figgis's face. 'That skin of yours could catch fire, I suspect.'

'A pleasure meeting you, Chief.'

Joe went to the door. Dion opened it, and a teenage girl, all breathless energy, stood on the other side. It was the daughter in all the photographs, beautiful and apple-haired, rose gold skin so unblemished it achieved a soft-sun radiance. Joe guessed she was seventeen. Her beauty found his throat, stopped it for a moment, put a catch in the words about to leave his mouth, so all he could manage was a hesitant, 'Miss ...' Yet it wasn't a beauty that evoked anything carnal in him. It was somehow purer than that. The beauty of Chief Irving Figgis's daughter wasn't something you wanted to despoil, it was something you wanted to beatify.

'Father,' she said, 'I apologize. I thought you were alone.'

'That's all right, Loretta. These gentlemen were leaving. Your manners,' he said.

'Yes, Father, I'm sorry.' She turned and gave Joe and Dion a small curtsy. 'Miss Loretta Figgis, gentlemen.'

'Joe Coughlin, Miss Loretta. Pleased to meet you.'

When Joe lightly shook her hand, he felt the strangest urge to genuflect. It stayed with him all afternoon, how pristine she was, how delicate, and how hard it must be to parent something so fragile.

Later that evening, they ate dinner at Vedado Tropicale at a table off to the right of the stage, which gave them a perfect view of the dancers and the band. It was early so the band – a drummer, piano player, trumpeter, and slide trombonist – kept it peppy but didn't go full bore yet. The dancers wore little more than shifts, pale as ice, the color matching their headgear, which varied. A couple of them wore sequined bandeaux with aigrettes arching out from the center of their foreheads. Others wore silver hairnets with frosted bead rosettes and fringe. They danced with one hand on their hips and one raised to the air or pointing out at the audience.

They gave the dinner crowd just enough flesh and gyrations not to offend the missus but to guarantee the mister would return at a later hour.

Joe asked Dion if their dinner was the best in the city.

Dion smiled around a forkful of *lechon asado* and fried yucca. 'In the country.'

Joe smiled. 'It's not bad, I gotta say.' Joe had ordered *ropa vieja* with black beans and yellow rice. He wiped the plate clean and wished the plate was bigger.

The maître d' came over and informed them that their coffee was waiting with their hosts. Joe and Dion followed the man across the white tile floor, past the stage, and through a dark velvet curtain. They went down a corridor the cherry oak of rum casks, and Joe wondered if they'd brought a few hundred of them across the Gulf just to make this hallway. They would have had to bring more than a few hundred, actually, because the office was constructed of the same wood.

It was cool in there. The floor was dark stone, and iron ceiling fans hung from the crossbeams, clacking and creaking. The slats of the honey-colored plantation shutters were open to the evening and the infinite hum of dragonflies.

Esteban Suarez was a slim man with unblemished skin the color of weak tea. His eyes were the pale yellow of a cat's and his hair, slicked back off his forehead, was the color of the dark rum in the bottle on his coffee table. He wore a dinner jacket and black silk bow tie and he came to them with a bright smile and a vigorous handshake. He led them to high wingback armchairs that had been arranged around a copper coffee table. On the table were four tiny cups of Cuban coffee, four water glasses, and the bottle of Suarez Reserve Rum in a weave basket.

Esteban's sister, Ivelia, rose from her seat and extended her hand. Joe bowed, took her hand, and brushed it lightly with his lips. Her skin smelled of ginger and sawdust. She was much older than her brother, with tight skin over a long jaw and sharp cheekbones and brow. Her thick eyebrows rolled together like a silkworm and her wide eyes seemed trapped in her skull, bulging to escape but helpless to do so.

'How were your meals?' Esteban asked when they sat.

'Excellent,' Joe said. 'Thank you.'

Esteban poured them glasses of rum and raised his in toast. 'To a fruitful relationship.'

They drank. Joe was stunned by how smooth and rich it was. This is what liquor tasted like when you had more than an hour to distill it, more than a week to ferment it. Christ.

'This is exceptional.'

'It's the fifteen-year,' Esteban said. 'I never agreed with the Spanish mandate from the old days that lighter rum was superior.' He shook his head at the notion and crossed his legs at the ankles. 'Of course, we Cubans went along because of our belief that lighter is better in all things – hair, skin, eyes.'

The Suarezes were light-skinned themselves, descended from the Spanish strain, not the African.

'Yes,' Esteban said, reading Joe's thought. 'My sister and I aren't of the lesser classes. That doesn't mean we agree with the social order of our island.'

He took another sip of rum and Joe did the same.

Dion said, 'Be nice if we could sell this up north.'

Ivelia laughed. It was very sharp and very short. 'Someday. When your government treats you like adults again.'

'No rush,' Joe said. 'We'd all be out of a job.'

Esteban said, 'My sister and I would be fine. We have this restaurant and two in Havana and one in Key West. We have a sugar plantation in Cárdenas and a coffee plantation in Marianao.'

'So why do this at all?'

Esteban shrugged in his perfect dinner jacket. 'Money.'

'More money, you mean.'

He raised his glass to that. 'There are other things to spend money on besides' – he waved his arm at the room – 'things.'

'So says the man with a lot of things,' Dion said, and Joe shot him a look.

Joe noticed for the first time that the west wall of the office was given over entirely to black-and-white photographs – street scenes mostly, the facades of nightclubs, a few faces, a couple of villages so dilapidated they'd fall over in the next wind.

Ivelia followed his gaze. 'My brother takes them.'

Joe said, 'Yeah?'

Esteban nodded. 'On my trips home. It's a hobby.'

'A hobby,' his sister said with a scoff. 'My brother's photographs have been published in *Time* magazine.'

Esteban gave it all a diffident shrug.

'They're good,' Joe said.

'Someday maybe I'll photograph you, Mr Coughlin.'

Joe shook his head. 'I'm with the Indians on that one, I'm afraid.'

Esteban gave that a wry smile. 'Speaking of captured souls, I was sorry to hear of the passing of Senor Ormino last night.'

'Were you?' Dion asked.

Esteban gave that a chuckle so soft it was almost indistinguishable from an exhaled breath. 'And friends tell me Gary L. Smith was last seen on the Seaboard Limited with his wife in one Pullman and his *puta maestra* in another. They say his luggage looked hastily packed but there was a lot of it.'

'Sometimes a change of scenery gives a man a new lease on life,' Joe said.

'Is that the case with you?' Ivelia asked. 'Have you come to Ybor for a new life?'

'I've come to refine, distill, and distribute the demon rum. But I'm going to have trouble doing that successfully with an erratic import schedule.'

'We don't control every skiff, every tariff officer, every dock,' Esteban said.

'Sure you do.'

'We don't control the tides.'

'The tides haven't slowed the boats to Miami.'

'I don't have anything to do with boats to Miami.'

'I know.' Joe nodded. 'Nestor Famosa does. And he assured my associates that the seas this summer have been calm and predictable. I understand Nestor Famosa is a man of his word.'

'By which you imply I'm not.' Esteban poured them all another glass of rum. 'You also bring up Senor Famosa so that I will worry he could overtake my supply routes if you and I aren't in accord.'

Joe took his glass off the table and sipped the rum. 'I bring up Famosa – Jesus, this rum is flawless – to illustrate my point that the seas were calm this summer. Unseasonably calm, I've been told. I don't have a forked tongue, Senor Suarez, and I don't speak in riddles. Just ask Gary L. Smith. I want to cut out any middlemen and deal with you directly. For that, you can raise your price a bit. I'll buy all the molasses and sugar you've got. I further propose you and I cofinance a better distillery than the ones we've got fattening all the rodents along Seventh Avenue. I didn't just inherit the late Lou Ormino's responsibilities, I inherited the city councillors, cops, and judges in his pockets. Many of these men won't talk to you because you're Cuban, no matter how highly born. You can have access to them through me.'

'Mr Coughlin, the only reason Senor Ormino had access to those judges and police was because he had Senor Smith as his public face. Those men not only will refuse to do business with a Cuban, but they will also refuse to do business with an Italian. We are all Latin to them, all dark-skinned dogs, good for labor, but little else.'

'Good thing I'm Irish,' Joe said. 'I believe you know someone named Arturo Torres.'

A flick of the eyebrows from Esteban.

'I heard he got deported this afternoon,' Joe said.

Esteban said, 'I heard that too.'

Joe nodded. 'As a gesture of good faith, Arturo was released from jail half an hour ago and is probably downstairs as we speak.'

For one moment, Ivelia's long flat face grew longer with

surprise, even delight. She glanced over at Esteban and he nodded. Ivelia went around his desk to the telephone. While they waited, they sipped some rum.

Ivelia hung up the phone and returned to her seat. 'He's down at the bar.'

Esteban sat back in his chair and held out his hands, eyes on Joe. 'You would want exclusive rights to our molasses, I suppose.'

'Not exclusive,' Joe said. 'But you can't sell to the White organization or anyone affiliated with them. Any small operations not associated with them or us can still go about their business. We'll bring them into the fold eventually.'

'And for this I get access to your politicians and your police.'

Joe nodded. 'And my judges. Not just the ones we have now but the ones we'll get.'

'The judge you reached today was federally appointed.'

'And has three children with a Negro woman in Ocala that his wife and Herbert Hoover would be surprised to learn about.'

Esteban looked at his sister for a long time before turning back to Joe. 'Albert White is a good customer. Has been for some time.'

'Has been for two years,' Joe said. 'Ever since someone cut Clive Green's throat in a whorehouse on East Twenty-fourth.'

Esteban raised his eyebrows.

'I've been in prison since March of '27, Senor Suarez. I've had nothing to do but my homework. Can Albert White offer you what I'm offering?'

'No,' Esteban admitted. 'But to cut him out would bring me a war I can't afford. I simply can't. I would have liked to have met you two years ago.'

'Well, you're meeting me now,' Joe said. 'I've offered you judges, police, politicians, and a distilling model that's centralized so we both share all the profits evenly. I've weeded out the two weakest links in my organization and kept your prized liquor cook from being deported. I did all this so you would consider ending your embargo on the Pescatore operation in Ybor because I thought you were sending us a message. I'm here to tell you I heard the message. And if you tell me what you need, I'll get it. But you must give me what I need.'

Another look between Esteban and his sister.

'There's something you could get us,' she said.

'Okay.'

'But it's well guarded and won't be given up without a fight.'

'Fine, fine,' Joe said. 'We'll get it.'

'You don't even know what it is.'

'If we get it, will you cut all ties with Albert White and his associates?'

'Yes.'

'Even if it brings bloodshed.'

'It will most certainly bring bloodshed,' Esteban said.

'Yes,' Joe said, 'it will.'

Esteban mourned the thought for a moment, the sadness filling the room. Then he sucked it right back out of the room. 'If you do what I ask, Albert White will never see another drop of Suarez molasses or distilled rum. Not one.'

'Will he be able to buy sugar in bulk from you?'

'No.'

'Deal,' Joe said. 'What do you need?'

'Guns.'

'Okay. Name your model.'

Esteban reached behind him and took a piece of paper off his desk. He adjusted his glasses as he consulted it. 'Browning automatic rifles, automatic handguns, and fifty-caliber machine guns with mounting tripods.'

Joe looked at Dion and they both chuckled.

'Anything else?'

'Yes,' Esteban said. 'Grenades. And box mines.'

'What's a box mine?'

Esteban said, 'It's on the ship.'

'What ship?'

'The military transport ship,' Ivelia said. 'Pier Seven.' She tilted her head toward the rear wall. 'Nine blocks from here.'

'You want us to raid a navy ship,' Joe said.

'Yes.' Esteban looked at his watch. 'Within two days, please, or they leave port.' He handed Joe a folded piece of paper. As Joe opened it, he felt a hollowing of his center, and he remembered how he'd carried notes like these to his father. He'd spent two years telling himself the weight of those notes hadn't killed his father. Some nights he almost convinced himself.

Circulo Cubano, 8 A.M.

'You'll go there in the morning,' Esteban said. 'You'll meet a woman there, Graciela Corrales. You'll take your orders from her and her partner.'

Joe pocketed the paper. 'I don't take orders from a woman.'

'If you want Albert White out of Tampa,' Esteban said, 'you'll take orders from her.'

CHAPTER THIRTEEN

Hole of the Heart

Dion drove Joe to his hotel a second time, and Joe told him to stick around until he decided whether or not he was staying in tonight.

The bellman was dressed like a circus monkey in a red velvet tux and matching fez, and he swooped out from behind a potted palm on the veranda and took Joe's suitcases from Dion's hand and led Joe inside while Dion waited at the car. Joe checked in at a marble reception desk and signed the ledger with a gold fountain pen handed to him by a severe Frenchman with a brilliant smile and eyes as dead as a doll's. He was handed a brass key tied to a short length of red velvet rope. At the other end of the rope was a heavy gold square with this room number on it: 509.

It was a suite, actually, with a bed the size of South Boston and delicate French chairs and a delicate French desk overlooking the lake. He had his own bathroom, all right; it was bigger than his cell in Charlestown. The bellman showed him where the outlets were and how to turn on the lamps and the ceiling fans. He showed him the cedar closet where Joe could hang his clothes. He showed him the radio, complimentary in every room, and it made Joe think of Emma and the grand opening of the Hotel Statler. He tipped the bellman and shooed him out and sat in one of the delicate French chairs and smoked a cigarette and looked out at the dark lake and the massive hotel reflected in it, squares and squares of light tilted sideways on the black surface, and he wondered what his father could see right now and what Emma could see. Could they see him? Could they see the past and the future or vast worlds far beyond his imaginings? Or could they see nothing? Because they were nothing. They were dead, they were dust, bones in a box and Emma's not even attached.

He feared this was all there was. Didn't just fear it. Sitting in that ridiculous chair looking out the window at the yellow windows canted in the black water, he knew it. You didn't die and go to a better place; this was the better place because you weren't dead. Heaven wasn't in the clouds; it was the air in your lungs.

He looked around the room with its high ceilings and chandelier over the enormous bed and curtains as thick as his thigh and he wanted to come out of his skin.

'I'm sorry,' he whispered to his father, even though he knew he couldn't hear him, 'it wasn't supposed to be' – he looked around the room again – 'this.'

He stubbed out his cigarette and left.

Outside of Ybor, Tampa was strictly white. Dion showed him a few places above Twenty-fourth Street with wooden signs stating their position on the matter. A grocery store on Nineteenth Avenue wanted it known that NO DOGS OR LATINS were allowed and a druggist on Columbus had a NO LATINS on the left side of his door and NO DAGOS on the right.

Joe looked at Dion. 'You all right with that?'

'Of course not, but what're you going to do?'

Joe took a hit off Dion's flask and passed it back to him. 'Gotta be some rocks around here.'

It had started to rain, which did nothing to cool things off. Down here, rain felt like more sweat. It was close to midnight, and things just seemed hotter, the humidity a woolen embrace around everything you did. Joe got into the driver's seat and kept the engine idling while Dion shattered both of the druggist windows and then hopped into the car and they drove back into Ybor. Dion explained that the Italians lived around here, in the higher-numbered streets between Fifteenth and Twenty-third. The lighter spics were between Tenth and Fifteenth, the nigger spics below Tenth Street and west of Twelfth Avenue, where most of the cigar factories were.

They found a joint down there at the end of an almost-road that went past the Vayo Cigar Factory and vanished into a cowl of mangrove and cypress. It was nothing more than a shotgun shack on stilts overlooking a swamp. They'd strung netting from the trees along the banks, and the netting covered the shack and the cheap wood tables beside it and the porch out back.

They played some *music* in there. Joe had never heard anything quite like it – Cuban rumba, he guessed, but brassier and more dangerous, and the people on the dance floor were doing something that looked far more like fuck-ing than dancing. Most everyone in there was colored – some American black, mostly Cuban black, though – and those who were merely brown didn't have the Indian features of the highborn Cubans or the Spaniards. Their faces were rounder, their hair more wiry. Half the people knew Dion. The bartender, an older woman, gave him a jug of rum and two glasses without him asking.

'You the new boss?' she asked Joe.

'I guess I am,' Joe said. 'I'm Joe. And you are?'

'Phyllis.' She slipped a dry hand into his. 'This is my place.'

'It's nice. What's it called?'

'Phyllis's Place.'

'Of course.'

'What do you think of him?' Dion asked Phyllis.

'He too pretty,' she said and looked at Joe. 'Someone need to mess you up.'

'We'll get to work on that.'

'See you do,' she said and went to serve another customer.

They took the bottle out onto the back porch and set it on a small table and took residence in two rocking chairs. They looked out through the netting at the swamp as the rain stopped falling and the dragonflies returned. Joe heard something heavy moving through the brush. And something else, just as heavy, moved underneath the porch.

'Reptiles,' Dion said.

Joe lifted his feet off the porch. 'What?'

'Alligators,' Dion repeated.

'You're pulling my leg.'

'No,' Dion said, 'but they will.'

Joe raised his knees higher. 'What the fuck are we doing in a place with alligators?'

Dion shrugged. 'You can't escape 'em down here. They're everywhere. You see water, there's ten of 'em in there, big eyes watching.' He wiggled his fingers and bugged his eyes. 'Waiting for dumb Yankees to come take a dip.'

Joe heard the one below him slither away and then crash through the mangrove again. He didn't know what to say.

Dion chuckled. 'Just don't go in the water.'

'Or near it,' Joe said.

'That too.'

They sat on the porch and drank and the last of the rain clouds drifted off. The moon returned and Joe could see Dion as clearly as if they were inside. He found his old friend staring at him, so he stared back. For quite a while, neither of them said a word, but Joe felt a whole conversation pass between them nonetheless. He was relieved, and he knew Dion was too, to finally get on with it.

Dion took a swig of the rotgut rum, wiped his lips with the back of his hand. 'How'd you know it was me?'

Joe said, 'Because I knew it wasn't me.'

'Could've been my brother.'

'May he rest in peace,' Joe said, 'but your brother wasn't smart enough to double-cross a street.'

Dion nodded and looked down at his shoes for a bit. 'It'd be a blessing.'

'What's that?'

'Dying.' Dion looked at him. 'I got my brother killed, Joe. You know what living with that's like?'

'I have some idea.'

'How could you?'

'Trust me,' Joe said. 'I do.'

'He was older than me by two years,' Dion said, 'but I was the older brother, get me? I was supposed to look out for him. 'Member when we all first started palling around, knocking over newsstands, Paolo and me had that other little brother, called him Seppi?'

Joe nodded. Funny, he hadn't thought of the kid in years. 'Got the polio.'

Dion nodded. 'Died, he was eight? My mother was never right again after that. I said to Paolo at the time, you know, we couldn't do nothing to save Seppi; that was just God and God gets his way. But each other?' He twisted his thumbs together, raised his fists to his lips. 'We would protect each other.'

Behind them the shack thumped with bodies and bass. In front of them mosquitoes rose off the swamp like claps of dust and found the moonlight.

'So what now? You requested me from prison. You had them find me in Montreal and pull me all the way down here, give me a good living. And for what?'

'Why'd you do it?' Joe asked.

'Because he asked me to.'

'Albert?' Joe whispered.

'Who else?'

Joe closed his eyes for a moment. He reminded himself to breathe slowly. 'He asked you to rat us all out?'

'Yeah.'

'He pay you?'

'Fuck no. He offered, but I wouldn't take his fucking money. Fuck him.'

'You still work for him?'

'No.'

'Why would you tell the truth, D?'

Dion removed a switchblade from his boot. He placed it on the small table between them and followed it with two .38 long-barrels and one .32 snub-nose. He added a lead sap and brass knuckles, then wiped his hands clean of them and showed his palms to Joe.

'After I'm gone,' he said, 'ask around Ybor about a guy named Brucie Blum. You'll see him down around Sixth Avenue sometimes. He walks funny, talks funny, has no idea he used to be big noise. He used to work for Albert. Just six months ago. Big hit with the ladies, had himself some nice suits. Now he shuffles around with a cup, begging for change, pisses himself, can't tie his own fucking shoes. Last thing he did when he was still big noise? He come up to me in a blind pig over on Palm? He says, "Albert needs to talk to you. Or else, see." So I chose "or else" and beat his fucking head in. So, no, I don't work for Albert no more. It was a onetime job. Just ask Brucie Blum.'

Joe sipped the awful rum and said nothing.

'You going to do it yourself or get someone else to do it?'

Joe met his eyes. 'I'll kill you myself.'

'Okay.'

'If I kill you.'

'I'd appreciate you make up your mind about it, one way or the other.'

'Don't much give a shit what you'd appreciate, D.'

Now it was Dion's time to be silent. The thumps and the bass grew softer behind them. More and more cars left the grounds and headed back up the mud path toward the cigar factory.

'My father's gone,' Joe said eventually. 'Emma's dead. Your brother's dead. My brothers scattered. Shit, D, you're one of the only people I know anymore. I lose you, who the fuck am I?'

Dion stared at him, the tears rolling down his fat face like beads.

'So you didn't betray me for money,' Joe said. 'So why then?'

'You were gonna get us all killed,' he said eventually, sucking air up from the floor. 'The girl. You weren't yourself. Even that day at the bank. You were gonna get us into something we couldn't get out of. And my brother would have been the one to die, because he was slow, Joe. He wasn't us. I figured, I figured . . . ' He sucked in a few more breaths. 'I figured I'd get us all off the street for a year. That was the deal. Albert knew a judge. We were all going to get a year, that's why we never pulled guns during the job. One year. Long enough for Albert's girl to forget you and maybe you'd forget her.'

'Jesus,' Joe said. 'All this because I fell for the man's girlfriend?'

'You and Albert were both bugs when it came to her. You couldn't see it, but once she came into the picture, you were *gone*. And I'll never understand it. She was no different than a million dames.'

'No,' Joe said, 'she was.'

'*How?* What didn't I see?'

Joe finished the rest of his rum. 'Before I met her? I didn't realize there was this bullet hole right in the center of me.' He tapped his chest. 'Right here. Didn't realize it until she came along and filled it. Now she's dead and the hole's back. But it's grown to the size of a milk bottle. And it keeps growing. And I just want her to come back from the dead and fill it.'

Dion stared at him as the tears dried on his face. 'From the outside looking in, Joe? She *was* the hole.'

Back at the hotel, the night manager came from behind the desk and handed Joe a series of messages. They were all calls from Maso.

'Do you have a twenty-four operator?' Joe asked him.

'Of course, sir.'

When he got to his room, he called down and the operator patched him through. The phone rang on the North Shore of Boston and Maso answered it. Joe had a cigarette and told him all about the long day.

'A ship?' Maso said. 'They want you to hit a ship?'

'Navy ship,' Joe said. 'Yeah.'

'What about the other thing? You get your answer?'

'I got my answer.'

'And?'

'It wasn't Dion ratted me out.' Joe removed his shirt, dropped it to the floor. 'It was his brother.'

CHAPTER FOURTEEN

Boom

The Circulo Cubano was the most recent of Ybor's social clubs. The Spaniards had built the first, Centro Español, on Seventh Avenue back in the 1890s. At the turn of the century, a group of northern Spaniards had splintered from the Centro Español to form Centro Asturiano on the corner of Ninth and Nebraska.

The Italian Club was a couple blocks down Seventh from the Centro Español, both addresses prime Ybor real estate. The Cubans, though, in keeping with their lowly status in the community, had to settle for a far less fashionable block. The Circulo Cubano sat on the corner of Ninth Avenue and Fourteenth Street. Across the street was a seamstress and a pharmacist, both marginally respectable, but next door was Silvana Padilla's whorehouse, which catered to the cigar workers, not the managers, so knife fights were common and the whores were often sick and unkempt.

As Dion and Joe pulled to the curb, a whore in last night's wrinkled dress came out of an alley two doors up. She walked past them, smoothing her flounces and looking broken and very old and in need of a drink. Joe guessed she was about eighteen. The guy who came out of the alley after her wore a suit and a white skimmer and walked in the opposite direction, whistling, and Joe had the irrational urge to get out of the car, chase the guy down, and bang his head off one of the brick buildings lining Fourteenth. Bang it until blood rushed out of his ears.

'We own that?' Joe indicated the whorehouse with a tilt of his chin.

'We own a piece.'

'Then our piece says the girls don't do alley work.'

Dion looked at him to be sure he was serious. 'Fine. I'll look into it, Father Joe. Can we concentrate on the issue at hand?'

'I'm concentrating.' Joe checked his tie in the rearview mirror and got out of the car. They walked up a sidewalk already so hot at eight in the morning he felt it in the soles of his feet even though he wore good shoes. The heat made it harder to think. And Joe needed to think. Plenty of other guys were tougher, braver, and better with a gun, but he'd match wits with any man and feel he had a fighting chance. It would help, though, if someone dropped by to shut off the fucking heat.

Concentrate. Concentrate. You are about to be presented with a problem that you have to fix. How do you relieve the U.S. Navy of sixty crates of weaponry without them killing or maiming you?

As they walked up the steps of the Circulo Cubano a woman came out the front door to greet them.

The truth was, Joe did have an idea about how to remove the weapons, but now it went right out of his head because he was looking at the woman and she was looking at him, recognition blossoming. It was the woman he'd seen on the train platform yesterday, the one with skin the color of brass and long thick hair as black as anything Joe had ever seen except, perhaps, her eyes, which were just as dark and locked on him as he approached.

'Senor Coughlin?' She held out a hand.

'Yes.' He shook her hand.

'Graciela Corrales.' She slipped her hand out of his. 'You're late.'

She led them inside across a black and white tile floor to a white marble staircase. It was much cooler in here, the high ceilings and dark wood paneling and all the tile and marble managing to keep the heat at bay for a few hours longer.

Graciela Corrales spoke with her back to Joe and Dion. 'You are from Boston, yes?'

'Yes,' Joe said.

'Do all men from Boston leer at women on train platforms?'

'We try to stop short of making a career out of it.'

She looked back over her shoulder at them. 'It's very rude.'

Dion said, 'I'm originally from Italy.'

'Another rude place.' She led them through a ballroom at the top of the stairs, pictures on the wall of various groups of Cubans gathered in this very room. Some of the shots were posed, others catching the feel of the dance nights in full bloom, arms flung in the air, hips cocked, skirts twirling. They moved quickly, but Joe was pretty sure he saw Graciela in one of the photos. He couldn't be certain because the woman in the photo was laughing, with her head thrown back, and her hair down, and he couldn't imagine this woman with her hair down.

Past the ballroom was a billiards parlor, Joe starting to think some Cubans lived pretty well, and past the billiards parlor was a library with heavy white curtains and four wooden chairs. The man waiting for them approached with a broad smile and a vigorous handshake.

Esteban. He shook their hands as if they hadn't met last night.

'Esteban Suarez, gentlemen. Good of you to come. Sit, sit.'

They took their seats.

Dion said, 'Are there two of you?'

'I'm sorry?'

'We spent an hour with you last night. You shake our hands like we're strangers.'

'Well, last night you met the owner of El Vedado Tropicale. This morning you meet the recording secretary of Circulo Cubano.' He smiled as if he were a teacher humoring two schoolchildren who'd likely repeat the grade. 'Anyway,' he said, 'thank you for your help.'

Joe and Dion nodded but said nothing.

'I have thirty men,' Esteban said, 'but I estimate I'll need thirty more. How many can you—'

Joe said, 'We're not committing any men. We're not *committing* to anything.'

'No?' Graciela looked at Esteban. 'I'm confused.'

'We've come to hear you out,' Joe said. 'Whether we get involved from that point remains to be seen.'

Graciela took her seat beside Esteban. 'Please don't act like you have a choice. You're gangsters who depend on a product supplied by one man and one man only. If you refuse us, your supply dries up.'

'In which case,' Joe said, 'we go to war. And we'll win, because we've got numbers and, Esteban, you don't. I've looked into it. You want me to risk my life against the United States military? I'll take my chances against a few dozen Cubans on the streets of Tampa. At least I know what I'll be fighting for.'

'Profit,' Graciela said.

Joe said, 'A way to make a living.'

'A criminal way.'

'What do you do?' He leaned forward, his eyes scanning the room. 'Sit around here, counting your Oriental rugs?'

'I roll cigars, Mr Coughlin, at La Trocha. I sit in a wooden chair and do this from ten every morning until eight every evening. When you leered at me on the platform yesterday—'

'I didn't *leer* at you.'

'—that was my first day off in two weeks. And when I'm not working, I volunteer here.' She gave him a bitter smile. 'So don't let the pretty dress fool you.'

The dress was even more threadbare than the one she'd worn yesterday. It was cotton with a gypsy girdle straddling a flounced skirt, at least a year out of style, maybe two, washed and worn so many times it had traded its original color for something not-quite-white, not-quite-tan.

'Donations paid for this club,' Esteban said smoothly. 'Its doors are kept open the same way. When Cubans go out on a Friday night, they want to go to a place where they can dress up, a place that makes them feel like they are back in Havana, a place with style. Pizzazz, yes?' He snapped his fingers. 'In here, nobody calls us spics or mud men. We are free to speak our language and sing our songs and recite our poetry.'

'Well, that's nice. Why don't you tell me why I should poetically raid a navy transport ship on your behalf rather than just overthrow your whole organization?'

Graciela opened her mouth at that, eyes aflame, but Esteban stopped her with a hand to her knee. 'You're correct – you could probably overthrow my operation. But what would you get but a few buildings? My supply routes, my contacts in Havana, all the people I work with in Cuba – they would never work with you. So, do you really want to kill the golden goose for some buildings and a few old cases of rum?'

Joe met his smile with one of his own. They were starting to understand each other. They didn't respect each other yet, but the possibility was there.

Joe jerked his thumb behind him. 'You take those photos in the hallway?'

'Most of them.'

'What *don't* you do, Esteban?'

Esteban removed his hand from Graciela's knee and sat back. 'Do you know much about Cuban politics, Mr Coughlin?'

'No,' Joe said, 'and I don't need to. It won't help me get this job done.'

Esteban crossed his ankles. 'How about Nicaragua?'

'We put down a rebellion there a few years back, if I remember right.'

'That's where the weapons are going,' Graciela said. 'And there was no rebellion. Your country occupies theirs just like they occupy mine when they see fit.'

'Take it up with the Platt Amendment.'

That put a rise in one of her eyebrows. 'An educated gangster?'

'I'm not a gangster, I'm an outlaw,' he said, although he wasn't sure that was true anymore. 'And there's not much else to do where I've spent the last two years but read. So why's the navy running guns to Nicaragua?'

'They've opened a military training school there,' Esteban said. 'To train the armies and police of Nicaragua, Guatemala, and Panama, of course, how to best remind the peasants of their place.'

Joe said, 'So you're going to steal weapons from the U.S. Navy and reapportion them to Nicaraguan rebels?'

'Nicaragua is not my fight,' Esteban said.

'So you're going to arm Cuban rebels.'

A nod. 'Machado is no president. He is a common thief with a gun.'

'So you'll steal from our military to overthrow your military?'

Esteban gave that a small tip of his head.

Graciela said, 'Does it bother you?'

'Don't mean shit to me.' Joe looked over at Dion. 'Bother you?'

Dion asked Graciela, 'You ever think if you people could police yourselves, maybe pick a leader who didn't loot you six ways from Sunday five minutes after getting sworn in, we wouldn't have to keep occupying you?'

Graciela fixed him in a flat stare. 'I think if we didn't have a cash crop you wanted for yourselves, you'd have never heard of Cuba.'

Dion looked over at Joe. 'What do I care? Let's hear this plan.'

Joe turned to Esteban. 'You do *have* a plan, don't you?'

Esteban's eyes registered offense for the first time. 'We have a man who will be calling on the boat tonight. He'll cause a diversion in a forward compartment and—'

'What kind of diversion?' Dion asked.

'A fire. When they go to put it out, we'll go down to the hold and pull out the weapons.'

'The hold will be locked.'

Esteban gave them a confident smile. 'We have bolt cutters for that.'

'You've seen the lock?'

'It's been described to me.'

Dion leaned forward. 'But you don't know what kind of material it's made of. It could be stronger than your bolt cutters.'

'Then we will shoot it.'

'Which will alert the people fighting the fire,' Joe said. 'And probably get somebody killed by a ricochet.'

'We will move fast.'

'How fast can anyone move with sixty boxes of rifles and grenades?'

'We'll have thirty men. Thirty more men, if you provide them.'

'They'll have three hundred,' Joe said.

'But they won't be three hundred *Cubanos*. The American soldier fights for his own pride. The *Cubano* fights for his country.'

'Jesus,' Joe said.

Esteban's smile got even more smug. 'You doubt our bravery?'

'No,' Joe said. 'I doubt your intelligence.'

'I'm not afraid to die,' Esteban said.

'I am.' Joe lit a cigarette. 'And if I wasn't, I'd like to die for a better reason than this. It takes two guys to lift a crate of rifles. That means sixty guys would have to make two trips onto a burning naval ship. And you think this is possible?'

'We only learned about the ship two days ago,' Graciela said. 'If we had more time we could have more men and a better plan, but that ship leaves tomorrow.'

'Doesn't have to,' Joe said.

'What do you mean?'

'You said you can get a guy on the ship.'

'Yes.'

'That mean you already got an inside guy on there?'

'Why?'

'Jesus, because I fucking asked you, all right, Esteban? Do you have one of the sailors on your payroll or not?'

'We do,' Graciela said.

'What're his duties?'

'Engine room.'

'What was he going to do for you?'

'Cause an engine malfunction.'

'So your outside guy, he's a mechanic?'

A pair of nods.

'He comes in to fix the engine, starts the fire, you raid the weapons hold.'

Esteban said, 'Yes.'

'As plans go, it's not half bad,' Joe said.

'Thank you.'

'Don't thank me. If half a plan isn't bad, it means the other half is. When were you going to do this?'

'Tonight,' Esteban said. 'Ten o'clock. The moon's supposed to be quite weak.'

Joe said, 'Middle of the night, more like three in the morning, would be ideal. Most everyone will be asleep. No heroes to worry about, few witnesses. That's the only chance I see of your man making it back off that boat.' He laced his hands behind his head, gave it a bit more thought. 'Your mechanic, he Cuban?'

'Yes.'

'How dark?'

Esteban said, 'I don't see—'

'Does he look more like you or more like her?'

'He's very light-skinned.'

'So he could pass for Spanish.'

Esteban looked at Graciela, then back at Joe. 'Certainly.'

'Why is this important?' Graciela asked.

'Because after what we're about to do to the U.S. Navy, they're going to remember him. And they're going to hunt him.'

Graciela said, 'And what are we going to do to the U.S. Navy?'

'Blow a hole in that ship, for starters.'

The bomb wasn't a box of nails and steel washers they bought for short money off a street-corner anarchist. It was an object of much more refinement and precision. Or so they were told.

One of the bartenders at a Pescatore speakeasy on Central Avenue, over in St Petersburg, guy named Sheldon Boudre, had spent a fair portion of his thirties defusing bombs for the marines. Back in '15, he'd lost a leg in Haiti because of faulty communication equipment during the occupation of Port-au-Prince and he was still irate about it. He made them a honey of an explosive device – a steel square the size of a child's shoe box. He told Joe and Dion he'd packed it with ball bearings, brass doorknobs, and enough gunpowder to punch a tunnel through the Washington Monument.

'Make sure you put this directly under the engine.' Sheldon pushed the bomb, wrapped in brown paper, across the bar to them.

'We're not trying to just blow up an engine,' Joe said. 'We want to damage the hull.'

Sheldon sucked his top row of false teeth back and forth against his gums, his eyes on the bar, and Joe realized he'd insulted the man. He waited him out.

'What do you think's going to happen,' Sheldon said, 'when an engine the size of a fucking Studebaker blows through the hull and into Hillsborough Bay?'

'But we don't want to blow up the whole port,' Dion reminded him.

'That's the beauty of her.' Sheldon patted the package. 'She's focused. She ain't scattering all about on you. You just don't want to be in front of her when she goes.'

'How volatile is, um, she?' Joe asked.

Sheldon's eyes brimmed. 'Hit her with a hammer all day, she'll forgive you.' He stroked the brown paper wrapping like it was the spine of a cat. 'Throw her in the air, you don't even have to step out of the way when she lands.'

He nodded to himself several times, his lips still moving, and Joe and Dion exchanged a look. If this guy was less than sane, they were about to put a bomb of his making in their car and drive it across Tampa Bay.

Sheldon held up a finger. 'There is one small caveat.'

'One small what?'

'Detail you should know about.'

'And that is?'

He gave them an apologetic smile. 'Whoever lights her better be a runner.'

The drive from St Petersburg to Ybor was twenty-five miles, and Joe counted every yard of it. Every bump, every lurch of the car. Every rattle of the chassis became the sound of his immediate death. He and Dion never discussed the fear because they didn't have to. It filled their eyes, filled the car, turned their sweat metallic. They looked straight ahead mostly, occasionally off to the bay as they crossed the Gandy Bridge and the strip of shoreline on either side of them was sharp white against the dead blue water. Pelicans and egrets took flight from the rails. The pelicans often seized up in midflight and then fell from the sky as if they'd been shot. They'd plunge into the flat sea and swoop back out with contorting fish in their bills, open their mouths, and the fish, no matter what the size, vanished.

Dion hit a pothole, then a metal road bracket, then another pothole. Joe closed his eyes.

The sun flung itself against the windshield and breathed fire through the glass.

Dion reached the other side of the bridge, and the paved road gave way to a stretch of crushed shell and gravel, two lanes dropping to one, the pavement suddenly a patchwork of various grades and consistencies.

'I mean,' Dion said but said nothing else.

They bounced along for a block and then came to a standstill in the traffic and Joe had to fight the urge to bolt the car, abandon Dion, run away from this whole idea. Who in his right mind drove a fucking *bomb* from one point to another? Who?

An insane person. Guy with a death wish. Someone who thought happiness was a lie told to keep you docile. But Joe had seen happiness; he'd known it. And now he was risking any possibility of ever feeling it again to transport an explosive powerful enough to pitch a thirty-ton engine through a steel-plated hull.

There'd be nothing left of him to recover. No car, no clothes. His thirty teeth would sprinkle the bay like pennies flung into a fountain. Be lucky if they found a knuckle to mail back to the family plot in Cedar Grove.

The last mile was the worst. They left Gandy and drove

down a dirt road that ran parallel to some train tracks, the road sloughing to the right with the heat, creviced in all the wrong places. It smelled like mildew and things that had crawled and died in warm mud, and were left there until they fossilized. They entered a patch of high mangroves and soil pocked with puddles and sudden steep holes, and after another couple of minutes of bouncing through that terrain, they arrived at the shack of Daniel Desouza, one of the outfit's most reliable builders of concealment contraptions.

He'd fashioned them a toolbox with a false bottom. Per his instructions, he'd dirtied the toolbox down, gritted it to the point where it smelled not just of oil and grease and dirt but also of age. The tools he'd placed in it were top of the line, however, and well tended, some wrapped in oilskin, all recently cleaned and oiled.

As they stood by the kitchen table in his one-room shack, he showed them the release on the bottom of the box. His pregnant wife waddled around them, heading to the out-house, and his two kids played on the floor with a pair of dolls that weren't much more than rags stitched together with a butcher's finesse. Joe noted one mattress on the floor for the kids, one for the adults, neither with a sheet or pillow. A mongrel dog wandered in and out, sniffing, and flies buzzed everywhere, mosquitoes too, while Daniel Desouza checked Sheldon's work for himself out of idle curiosity or sheer insanity, Joe couldn't tell anymore, numb to it by this point, standing there waiting to meet his Maker as Desouza poked a screwdriver into the bomb and his wife came back in and swatted at the dog. The kids started fighting over one of the rag dolls, screeching all shrill until Desouza shot his wife a look. She left the dog alone and started clouting the kids, slapping them all over their faces and necks.

The kids wailed with shock and indignation.

'You boys got you a nice piece of craft right here, what it is,' Desouza said. 'Gonna make itself a statement.'

The younger of his two children, a boy of five or so, stopped crying. He'd been wailing his wail of stunned outrage, but when he stopped, he did so as if he'd snuffed out a match at the core of himself, and his face went blank. He picked one of his father's wrenches up off the floor and hit the dog in the side of the head with it. The dog snarled and looked like it might lunge for the boy, but then it thought better of it and scurried out of the shack.

'I'm a beat that dog or that boy to death,' Desouza said, his eyes never leaving the toolbox. 'One of the two.'

Joe met with their bomber, Manny Bustamente, in the library of the Circulo Cubano, where everyone but Joe smoked a cigar, even Graciela. Out on the streets, it was the same thing – nine- and ten-year-old kids walking around with stogies in their mouths the size of their legs. Every time Joe lit one of his puny Murads, he felt like the whole city laughed at him, but cigars gave him a headache. Looking around the library that night, though, at the brown blanket of smoke that hung above their heads, he assumed he was going to have to get used to headaches.

Manny Bustamente had been a civil engineer in Havana. Unfortunately his son had been part of the Student Federation at the University of Havana, which spoke out against the Machado regime. Machado closed the university and abolished the federation. One day several men in army uniforms came to Manny Bustamente's house a few minutes after sunup. They put his son on his knees in the kitchen and shot him in the face and then they shot Manny's wife when she called them animals. Manny was sent to prison. Upon his release, it was suggested to him that leaving the country would be an exceptional idea.

Manny told this to Joe in the library at ten o'clock that evening. It was, Joe assumed, a way to reassure him of Manny's devotion to his cause. Joe didn't question his devotion; he questioned his speed. Manny was five foot two and built like a bean pot. He breathed heavily after walking up a flight of stairs.

They were going over the layout of the ship. Manny had serviced the engine when it had first arrived in port.

Dion asked why the navy didn't have its own engineers.

'They do,' Manny said. 'But if they can get a *y . . . especialista* to look at these old engines, they do. This ship is twenty-five years old. It was built as a . . . ' He snapped his fingers and spoke quickly to Graciela in Spanish.

'A luxury liner,' she said to the room.

'Yes,' Manny said. He spoke to her again in rapid Spanish, a full paragraph of it. When he finished, she explained to them that the ship had been sold to the navy during the Great War and then turned into a hospital ship afterward. Recently it had been recommissioned as a transport ship with a crew of three hundred.

'Where's the engine room?' Joe asked.

Again Manny spoke to Graciela and she translated. It actually made things move a lot faster.

'Bottom of the ship, at the stern.'

He asked Manny, 'If you're called to the ship in the middle of the night, who will greet you?'

He started to speak to Joe but then turned to Graciela and asked her a question.

'The police?' she said, frowning.

He shook his head, spoke again to her.

'Ah,' she said, '*veo, veo, sí.*' She turned to Joe. 'He means the naval police.'

'The Shore Patrol,' Joe said, looking over at Dion. 'You on top of that?'

Dion nodded. 'On top of it? I'm ahead of you.'

'So you get past the Shore Patrol,' Joe said to Manny, 'you get into the engine room. Where's the nearest sleeping berth?'

'One deck up and down the other end,' Manny said.

'So the only personnel near you are the two engineers?'

'Yes.'

'And how do you get them out of there?'

From over by the window, Esteban said, 'We have it on good authority that the chief engineer is a drunk. If he even goes to the engine room to double-check our man's assessment, he won't stay.'

'What if he does, though?' Dion said.

Esteban shrugged. 'They improvise.'

Joe shook his head. 'We don't improvise.'

Manny surprised them all when he reached into his boot and came back with a one-shot derringer with a pearl handle. 'I will take care of this man if he does not leave.'

Joe rolled his eyes at Dion, who was closer to Manny.

Dion said, 'Give me that,' and snatched the derringer from Manny's hand.

'You ever shot anybody?' Joe said. 'Ever kill a man?'

Manny sat back. 'No.'

'Good. Because you're not starting tonight.'

Dion tossed the gun to Joe. He caught it and held it up before Manny. 'I don't care who you kill,' he said and wondered if that were true, 'but if they frisked you, they would have found this. Then they would have taken an extra hard look at your toolbox and found the bomb. Your primary job tonight, Manny? Is to not fuck this up. Think you can handle that?'

'Yes,' Manny said. 'Yes.'

'If the chief engineer stays in that room, you repair the engine and walk away.'

Esteban came off the window. 'No!'

'Yes,' Joe said. 'Yes. This is an act of treason against the United States government. Do you comprehend that? I'm not doing it just so I can get caught and strung up at Leavenworth. If anything goes south, Manny, you walk the fuck back off that boat and we figure out another way. Do not – look at me, Manny – do *not* improvise. *¿Comprende?*'

Manny nodded eventually.

Joe indicated the bomb in the canvas bag at his feet. 'This has a short, short fuse.'

'I understand this.' Manny blinked at a drop of sweat that fell from his eyebrow and then wiped the brow with the back of his hand. 'I am fully committed to this event.'

Great, Joe thought, he's overweight *and* overheated.

'I appreciate that,' Joe said, catching Graciela's eyes for a moment, seeing the same concern in hers that probably lived in his. 'But, Manny? You have to be committed to doing it *and* getting off that boat alive. I'm not saying this because I'm so swell and I care about you. I'm not and I don't. But if you're killed and they identify you as a Cuban national, the plan falls apart right there and then.'

Manny leaned forward, his cigar as thick as a hammer grip between his fingers. 'I want freedom for my country and I want Machado dead and the United States to leave my lands. I have remarried, Mr Coughlin. I have three niños, all under six years old. I have a wife I love, God forgive me, more than my wife who died. I'm old enough that I would rather live as a weak man than die a brave one.'

Joe gave him a grateful smile. 'Then you're the guy I want delivering this bomb.'

The USS *Mercy* weighed ten thousand tons. It was a four-hundred-foot-long, fifty-two-foot-wide, plumb-bow displacement ship with two smokestacks and two masts. The mainmast sported a crow's nest that seemed to Joe like it belonged on a ship from another time, when brigands roamed the high seas. Two faded crosses were painted on the smokestacks, which confirmed her history as a hospital ship, as did the white of her paint. She looked worked over, creaky, but the white of her gleamed against the black water and the night sky.

They were up on the catwalk above a grain silo at the end of McKay Street – Joe, Dion, Graciela, and Esteban, looking out at the ship moored at Pier 7. A dozen silos clustered there, sixty feet high, the last of the grain having been stored there this afternoon by a Cargill ship. The night watchman had been paid off, told to make sure he told the police tomorrow that it was Spaniards who tied him up, and then Dion knocked him out with two swings of a lead sap to make it look authentic.

Graciela asked Joe what he thought.

'Of what?'

'Our chances.' Graciela's cigar was long and thin. She blew rings over the rail of the catwalk and watched them float over the water.

'Honestly?' Joe said. 'Slim to none.'

'Yet it's your plan.'

'And it's the best one I could think of.'

'It seems quite good.'

'Is that a compliment?'

She shook her head, though he thought he saw the smallest twitch of her lips. 'It's a statement. If you played good guitar, I would tell you and still not like you.'

'Because I leered?'

'Because you are arrogant.'

'Oh.'

'Like all Americans.'

'And all Cubans are what?'

'Proud.'

He smiled. 'According to the papers I've been reading, you're also lazy, quick to anger, incapable of saving money, and childish.'

'You think this is true?'

'No,' he said. 'I think assumptions about an entire country or an entire people are pretty fucking stupid in general.'

She drew on her cigar and looked at him for a bit. Eventually, she turned to look out at the ship again.

The lights of the waterfront turned the lower edges of the sky a pale, chalky red. Beyond the channel, the city lay sleeping in the haze. Far off at the horizon line, thin bolts of lightning carved jagged white veins in the skin of the world. Their faint and sudden light would reveal swollen clouds as dark as plums massed out there like an enemy army. At one point, a small plane passed directly overhead, four lights in the sky, one small engine, a hundred yards above, possibly for a legitimate purpose, though it was hard to imagine what that could be at three in the morning. Not to mention, in the short time he'd been in Tampa, Joe had come across very little activity he'd describe as legitimate.

'Did you mean what you told Manny tonight, that it makes no difference to you whether he lives or dies?'

They could see him now, walking along the pier toward the ship, toolbox in hand.

Joe leaned his elbows on the rail. 'Pretty much.'

'How does anyone become so callous?'

'Takes less practice than you'd think,' Joe said.

Manny stopped at the gangplank where two sailors of the Shore Patrol met him. He raised his arms while one of the SPs patted him down and the other opened the toolbox. He rifled through the top tray and then removed it and placed it on the pier.

'If this goes well,' Graciela said, 'you'll take over rum distribution in Tampa.'

'In half of Florida, actually,' Joe said.

'You'll be powerful.'

'I guess.'

'Your arrogance will reach new heights then.'

'Well,' Joe said, 'one can hope.'

The SP stopped frisking Manny and he lowered his hands, but then that sailor joined his partner and they both looked at something in the toolbox, started conferring, their heads lowered, one with his hand on the butt of his .45.

Joe looked down the parapet at Dion and Esteban. They were frozen, necks extended, eyes locked on that toolbox.

Now the SPs were ordering Manny to join them. He stepped in between them and looked down too. One of them pointed, and Manny reached down into the toolbox and came back with two pints of rum.

'Shit,' Graciela said. 'Who told him to bribe them?'

'I didn't,' Esteban said.

'He's making up things on the fly,' Joe said. 'This is fucking great. This is wonderful.'

Dion slapped the parapet.

'I didn't tell him to do this,' Esteban said.

'I specifically told him not to do this,' Joe said. '"Don't improvise," I said. You were wit—'

'They're taking it,' Graciela said.

Joe narrowed his eyes, saw each of the SPs put a bottle inside his tunic and step aside.

Manny closed his toolbox and walked up the gangplank.

For a moment, they were very quiet on the roof.

Then Dion said, 'I think I just coughed up my own asshole.'

'It's working,' Graciela said.

'He got on,' Joe said. 'He's still got to do his job and get back off.' He looked at his father's watch: 3 A.M. on the nose.

He looked over at Dion, who read his thoughts. 'I'd figure they started busting up that joint ten minutes ago.'

They waited. The metal of the catwalk was still warm from a day of baking in the August sun.

Five minutes later one of the SPs walked to a ringing phone on the deck. A few moments later, he came running back down the gangplank and slapped his partner's arm. The SPs ran a few yards along the pier to a scout car. They drove down the pier and turned left, headed into Ybor, to the club on Seventeenth where ten of Dion's guys were, at this moment, beating the shit out of about twenty sailors.

'So far' – Dion smiled at Joe – 'admit it.'

'Admit what?'

'Everything's going like clockwork.'

'So far,' Joe said.

Beside him, Graciela drew on her cigar.

The sound reached them, the echo of a surprisingly dull thud. Didn't sound like much, but the catwalk swayed for a moment, and they all held out their arms as if they stood atop the same bicycle. The USS *Mercy* shuddered. The water around it rippled and small waves broke against the pier. Smoke as thick and gray as steel wool billowed from a hole in the hull the size of a piano.

The smoke grew thicker, darker, and after a few moments of staring at it, Joe could see a yellow ball blooming behind it, pulsing like a beating heart. He kept looking until he saw red flames mixed in with the yellow, but then both colors vanished behind the plumes of smoke, which was now the black of fresh tar. It filled the channel and blotted out the city beyond, blotted out the sky.

Dion laughed and Joe met his eyes and Dion kept laughing, shaking his head, and nodding at Joe.

Joe knew what the nod meant – *this* was why they became outlaws. To live moments the insurance salesmen of the world, the truck drivers and lawyers and bank tellers and carpenters and Realtors would never know. Moments in a world without nets – none to catch you and none to envelop you. Joe looked at Dion and recalled what he'd felt after the first time they'd knocked over that newsstand on Bowdoin Street when they were thirteen years old: *We will probably die young.*

But how many men, as they stepped into the night country of their own final hour and crossed dark fields toward the fog bank of whatever world lay beyond this one, could take one last look over their shoulders and say, *I once sabotaged a ten-thousand-ton transport ship*?

Joe met Dion's eyes again and chuckled.

'He never came back out.' Graciela stood beside him, looking at the ship, which was now almost completely obscured by the smoke.

Joe said nothing.

'Manny,' she said, though she didn't have to.

Joe nodded.

'Is he dead?'

'I don't know,' Joe said, but what he thought was: I certainly hope so.

CHAPTER FIFTEEN

His Daughter's Eyes

At dawn, the sailors off-loaded the weapons and placed them on the pier. The crates sat in the rising sun, beaded with dew that turned to steam as it evaporated. Several smaller boats arrived, and sailors got off them followed by officers, and they all took a look at the hole in the hull. Joe, Esteban, and Dion wandered among the crowd behind the cordons set up by the Tampa Police and heard that the ship had settled at the bottom of the bay and there was some question as to whether she could be salvaged. The navy was purportedly sending a crane on a barge down from Jacksonville to answer that question. As for the weapons, they were looking into getting a ship to Tampa that could handle the load. In the meantime, they'd have to stow them someplace.

Joe walked back off the pier. He met Graciela at a café on Ninth. They sat outdoors under a stone portico and watched a streetcar clack along the tracks in the center of the avenue and come to a stop in front of them. A few passengers got on, a few got off, and the streetcar rattled away again.

'Did you see any sign of him?' Graciela asked.

Joe shook his head. 'But Dion's watching. And he put a couple of his guys in the crowd, so ...' He shrugged and sipped his Cuban coffee. He'd been up all night and hadn't slept much the previous night, but as long as the Cuban coffee kept coming, he assumed he could stay awake for a week.

'What do they put in this stuff? Cocaine?'

Graciela said, 'It's just coffee.'

'That's like saying vodka is just potato juice.' He finished it and returned the cup to the saucer. 'Do you miss it?'

'Cuba?'

'Yeah.'

She nodded. 'Very much.'

'Then why are you here?'

She looked off at the street as if she could see Havana on the other side of it. 'You don't like the heat.'

'What?'

'You,' she said. 'You are always waving your hand at the air, your hat. I see you make faces and look up at the sun, as if you want to tell it to set faster.'

'I didn't realize it was that obvious.'

'You're doing it now.'

She was right. He'd been waving his hat by the side of his head. 'This kinda heat? Some people would say it's like living on the sun. I say it's like living *in* the sun. Christ. How do you people function down here?'

She leaned back in her chair, lovely brown neck arching

against the wrought iron. 'It can never get too warm for me.'

'Then you're insane.'

She laughed and he watched the laugh run up her throat. She closed her eyes. 'So you hate the heat but you are here.'

'Yes.'

She opened her eyes, tilted her head, looked at him. 'Why?'

He suspected – no, he knew – that what he'd felt for Emma was love. It was love. So the feeling Graciela Corrales stirred in him had to be lust. But a lust unlike any he'd ever encountered. Had he ever seen eyes that dark? There was something so languid in everything she did – from walking, to smoking her cigars, to picking up a pencil – that it was easy to imagine that languid motion in play as her body draped over his, took him inside her while she exhaled a long breath into his ear. The languor in her didn't resemble laziness but precision. Time didn't bend it; it bent time to uncoil as she desired.

No wonder the nuns had railed so vehemently against the sins of lust and covetousness. They could possess you surer than a cancer. Kill you twice as quick.

'Why?' he said, not even sure where he was in the conversation for a moment.

She was looking at him curiously. 'Yes, why?'

'A job,' he said.

'I come for the same reason.'

'To roll cigars?'

She straightened in her chair and nodded. 'The pay is much better than anything in Havana. I send it home to family, most of it. When my husband is released, we will decide where to live.'

'Oh,' Joe said, 'you're married.'

'Yes.'

He saw a flash of triumph in her eyes, or did he imagine it?

'But your husband's in prison.'

Another nod. 'But not for what you do.'

'What do I do?'

She waved at the air. 'Little dirty crimes.'

'Oh, that's what I do.' He nodded. 'I'd been wondering.'

'Adan fights for something bigger than himself.'

'What kinda sentence they hand out for that?'

Her face darkened, the joking over. 'He was tortured to tell them who his accomplices were – myself and Esteban. But he did not tell them. No matter what they did to him.' Her jaw was extended, her eyes flashing in a way that reminded Joe of the slim bolts of lightning they'd seen last night. 'I don't send money home to my family because I don't have a family. I send it to Adan's family so they can get him out of that shithole prison and home to me.'

Was it just lust he felt or something he hadn't been able to define yet? Maybe it was his exhaustion and two years in prison and the heat. Maybe so. Probably so. Still, he couldn't shake the feeling that he was drawn to a part of her he suspected was deeply broken, something frightened and angry and hopeful all at the same time. Something at her core that struck at something at his.

'He's a lucky man,' Joe said.

Her mouth opened before she realized there was nothing to retort to.

'A very lucky man.' Joe stood and placed some coins on the table. 'Time to make that phone call.'

They made the call from a phone in the back of a bankrupt cigar factory on the east side of Ybor. They sat on a dusty floor in the empty office and Joe dialed while Graciela took one last glance over the message he'd typed up last night around midnight.

'City desk,' the guy on the other end said, and Joe handed the phone to Graciela.

Graciela said, 'I take responsibility for last night's triumph over American imperialism. You know of the bombing of the USS *Mercy*?'

Joe could hear the guy's voice. 'Yes, yes, I do.'

'The United Peoples of Andalusia claim responsibility. We further pledge a direct attack on the sailors themselves and all American armed forces until Cuba is returned to its rightful owners, the people of España. Good-bye.'

'Wait, wait. The sailors. Tell me about the attack on the—'

'By the time I hang up this phone, they will already be dead.'

She hung up, looked at Joe.

'That should get things moving,' he said.

Joe got back there in time to see them run the convoy trucks down the pier. The crew came off in groups of about fifty, moving fast, eyes scanning the rooftops.

The convoy trucks barreled off the pier one after another and then immediately split up, each truck carrying about twenty sailors, the first one heading east, the next heading southwest, the next north, and so on.

'You see any sign of Manny?' Joe asked Dion.

Dion gave him a grim nod and pointed, and Joe looked through the crowd and past the crates of weapons. There, on the edge of the pier, lay a canvas body bag tied off at the legs, the chest, and the neck. After a while, a white van arrived and picked up the corpse and drove it off the pier with a Shore Patrol escort.

Not long after that, the last convoy truck on the pier rumbled to life. It made a U-turn, then stopped, its gears grinding with the high pitch of gulls, and then it backed up to the crates. A sailor hopped out and opened its rear gate. The few sailors left on the USS *Mercy* started filing off then, all carrying BARs and most wearing sidearms. A chief warrant officer waited on the pier for them as they mustered by the gangplank.

Sal Urso, who worked in the central office of the Pescatore sports book in South Tampa, sidled up and handed Dion some keys.

Dion introduced him to Joe, and they shook hands.

Sal said, 'She's about twenty yards behind us. Full tank of gas, uniforms on the seat.' He looked Dion up and down. 'You weren't an easy fit, mister.'

Dion slapped the side of his head but not too hard. 'What's it like out there?'

'The laws are everywhere. They're looking for Spaniards, though.'

'Not Cubans?'

Sal shook his head. 'You got this city riled up, son.'

The last of the sailors had mustered and the chief was giving them orders, pointing at the crates.

'Time to move,' Joe said. 'Good to meet you, Sal.'

'You too, sir. I'll see you there.'

They left the edge of the crowd and found the truck where Sal had said it would be. It was a two-ton flatbed with a steel bed and steel roll bars covered by a canvas tarp. They hopped up front, and Joe ground the shifter into first and they lurched out onto Nineteenth Street.

Twenty minutes later, they pulled over along the side of Route 41. There was a forest here, longleaf pines taller than Joe had imagined a tree could get and smaller slash and pond pines, all rising from a thick warren of overgrown palmetto and briars and scrub oak. By the smell of it, he guessed a swamp lay somewhere just east of them. Graciela was waiting for them by a tree that had snapped in half during a recent storm. She'd changed the dress she'd been wearing for a gaudy black net evening gown with zigzag hem. Imitation gold seed beads, black sequins, and a low neckline that exposed her cleavage and the edges of her brassiere cups completed the impression of a party girl who'd stayed out well past the end of the party and drifted, in the light of day, into a much crueler place.

Joe looked at her through the windshield and didn't get out of the truck. He could hear his own breathing.

'I can do it for you,' Dion said.

'No,' Joe said. 'My plan, my responsibility.'

'You got no problem delegating other things.'

He turned and looked at Dion. 'You saying I *want to* do this?'

'I seen the way you look at each other.' Dion shrugged. 'Maybe she likes it rough. Maybe you do too.'

'What the fuck are you talking about – the way we look at each other? You keep your eyes on your work, not on her.'

'All due respect,' Dion said, 'you too.'

Shit, Joe thought, as soon as a guy felt sure you weren't going to kill him, he sassed you.

Joe got out of the truck and Graciela watched him come. She'd already done some of the work herself – there was a tear in her dress by her left shoulder blade and light scratches on her left breast and she'd bit her lower lip hard enough to draw blood. As he approached, she dabbed at it with a handkerchief.

Dion got out of the truck on his side and they both looked over at him. He held up the uniform Sal Urso had left on the seat for him.

'Go about your business,' Dion said. 'I'm gonna change.' He chuckled and walked to the back of the truck.

Graciela held out her right arm. 'You don't have much time.'

Suddenly Joe didn't know how to take someone's hand. It seemed unnatural.

'You don't,' she said.

He reached out, took her hand in his. It was harder than any woman's hand he'd ever touched. The heels of the palm were rocks from rolling cigars all day, the slim fingers as strong as ivory.

'Now?' he asked her.

'Now would be best,' she said.

He gripped her wrist with his left hand and curled the fingers of his right into the flesh by her shoulder. He pulled his nails down her arm. At the elbow he broke off and took a breath because his head felt like it was filled with wet newspaper.

She snatched her wrist out of his grip and looked at the scratches on her arm. 'You have to make them look real.'

'They look plenty real.'

She pointed at her biceps. 'They're pink. And they stop at the elbow. They need to bleed, *bobo niño,* and go down to my hand. Yes? You remember?'

'Of course I remember,' Joe said. 'It's *my* plan.'

'Then act like it.' She thrust her arm at him. 'Dig and pull.'

Joe wasn't sure, but he thought he heard laughter coming from the back of the truck. He wrapped his hand firmly around her bicep this time and his fingernails sank into the faint tracks he'd already laid. Graciela wasn't quite as brave as her talk. Her eyes wiggled in their sockets and her flesh quivered.

'Shit. I'm sorry.'

'Hurry, hurry.'

She locked eyes with him and he pulled his hand down the inside of her arm, stripping the skin as he went, opening the seams in her flesh. As he continued on past her elbow, she hissed and turned her arm so that his nails plowed along her forearm and ended at her wrist.

When he dropped her hand, she slapped him with it.

'Christ,' he said, 'I'm not doing it because I like it.'

'So you claim.' She slapped him again, this time across the lower jaw and the top of his neck.

'Hey! I can't pull up to a fucking guard shack with welts all over my face.'

'Then you better stop me,' she said and swung for him again.

He sidestepped this one because she'd telegraphed it for him and then he did what they'd agreed on – what had certainly seemed easier to discuss than to do until she'd hit him twice to get his blood up. The back of his hand connected with her cheek, all knuckle. Her upper body snapped to the side and her hair covered her face and she stayed that way for a moment, breathing hard. When she righted herself, her face had turned red and the skin around her right eye twitched. She spit into the palmetto bush on the side of the road.

She wouldn't look at him. 'I have it from here.'

He wanted to say something but he couldn't think of what, so he walked around the front of the truck, Dion watching him from the passenger seat. He stopped as he opened the door and looked back at her. 'I hated doing that.'

'And yet,' she said and spit onto the road, 'it was your plan.'

On the road, Dion said, 'Hey, I don't like hitting 'em either but sometimes it's all a dame respects.'

'I didn't hit her because she had it coming,' Joe said.

'No, you hit her to help her get her hands on a bunch of BARs and Thompsons to send back to all her little friends on Sin Island.' Dion shrugged. 'It's a shitty business, so we do shitty things. She asked you to get the guns. You came up with a way to get them.'

'Ain't got 'em yet,' Joe said.

*

They pulled to the side of the road one last time for Joe to change into his uniform. Dion rapped his hand on the wall between the cab and the back of the truck and said, 'Everybody be as quiet as cats when the dogs are around. *¿Comprende?*'

From the back of the truck came a chorus of '*Sí,*' and then the only thing they could hear were the ever-present insects in the trees.

'You ready?' Joe said.

Dion slapped the side of the door. 'Why I get up every morning, chum.'

The National Guard Armory was way up in unincorporated Tampa, at the northern edge of Hillsborough County, a harsh landscape of citrus groves and cypress swamps and broom sage fields gone dry and brittle in the sun, waiting for the chance to burn and turn the whole county black with the smoke.

Two guards manned the gate, one armed with a Colt .45, the other with a Browning automatic rifle, the very items they'd come to steal. The guard with the sidearm was tall and lanky with dark spiky hair and the sunken cheeks of a very old man or a very young man with bad teeth. The boy with the BAR was barely out of diapers; he had burnt orange hair and dull eyes. Black pimples covered his face like pepper.

He was no problem, but the lanky one worried Joe. Something about him was too coiled and too keen. He took his time when he looked at you and he didn't care what you thought about it.

'You the ones got blowed up?' His teeth, as Joe had

guessed, were gray and slanted, several tipping back into his mouth like old headstones in a flooded graveyard.

Dion nodded. 'Put a hole in our hull.'

The lanky boy looked past Joe at Dion. 'Shit, tubby, how much you pay to pass your last FITREP?'

The short one left the shack with his BAR cradled lazily in his arm, the barrel slanting across his hip. He started down the side of the truck, his mouth half open like he was hoping it would rain.

The one by the door said, 'I asked you a question, tubby.'

Dion smiled pleasantly. 'Fifty bucks.'

'That what you paid?'

'Yep,' Dion said.

'Got yourself a bargain. And who was that you paid, exactly?'

'What's that?'

'Name and rank of the man you paid,' the boy said.

'Chief Petty Officer Brogan,' Dion said. 'Why, you thinking of joining?'

The guy blinked and gave them both a cold smile but said nothing, just stood there while the smile evaporated. 'Don't accept bribes myself.'

'All right,' Joe said, his nerves getting the better of him.

'All right?'

Joe nodded and resisted the urge to smile like a fool, show the guy how nice he was.

'I know it's all right. I know.'

Joe waited.

'I know it's all right,' the guy repeated. 'Gave you the impression I needed your counsel on the matter?'

Joe said nothing.

'I did not,' the boy said.

Something thumped in the back of the truck and the boy looked back there for his partner and when he looked at Joe again Joe placed his Savage .32 against the boy's nose.

The kid's eyes crossed to stare at the gun barrel and his breathing came heavy and long through his mouth. Dion came out of the truck and around to the boy and relieved him of his sidearm.

'Man with teeth like yours,' Dion said, 'should not be remarking on the flaws of others. Man with teeth like yours should just keep his mouth shut.'

'Yes, sir,' the boy whispered.

'What's your name?'

'Perkin, sir.'

'Well, Perkinsir,' Dion said, 'me and my partner will at some point discuss whether we let you live today. If we decide in your favor, you'll know 'cause you ain't dead. If we don't, it'll be to teach you you should have been nicer to people. Now put your fucking hands behind your back.'

Pescatore gangsters came out of the back of the truck first – four of them in summer suits and florid ties. They pushed the orange-haired boy ahead of them, Sal Urso pointing the kid's own rifle at his back, the boy blubbering that he didn't want to die today, not today. The Cubans, about thirty of them, came out after them, most of them dressed in the white drawstring pants and white shirts with the bell-hemlines that reminded Joe of pajamas. They all carried rifles or pistols. One carried a machete and another carried two large knives at the ready. Esteban led them. He wore a dark green tunic and matching trousers, the field outfit of choice, Joe assumed, for banana republic revolutionaries. He nodded at Joe as he and his men entered the grounds and then spread out around the back of the building.

'How many men inside?' Joe asked Perkin.

'Fourteen.'

'How come so few?'

'Middle of the week. You come here on a weekend?' A little bit of mean returned to his eyes. 'You'd have met some men.'

'I'm sure I would have.' Joe climbed out of the truck. 'Right now though, Perkin, I'll have to settle for you.'

The only guy to put up a fight when he saw thirty armed Cubans flood the halls of the armory was a giant. Six and a half feet tall, Joe guessed. Maybe taller. A huge head and a long jaw and shoulders like crossbeams. He rushed three Cubans who were under orders not to shoot. They shot anyway. Didn't hit the giant. Missed him clean from twenty feet away. Hit another Cuban instead. A guy who'd been rushing up behind the giant.

Joe and Dion were right behind the Cuban when he got shot. He spun and toppled in front of them like a bowling pin and Joe shouted, 'Stop shooting!'

Dion screamed, '¡Dejar de disparar! ¡Dejar de disparar!'

They stopped, but Joe couldn't be sure if they were just reloading their creaky bolt-action rifles or not. He grabbed the rifle from the one who'd been shot, grabbed it by the barrel and cocked his arm as the giant rose from the defensive crouch he'd adopted when they started shooting at him.

Joe swung the rifle into the side of his head, and the giant bounced off the wall and came for him, arms flailing. Joe changed his grip and drove the butt of the rifle through the flurry of the guy's arms and into his nose. He heard it break, heard his cheekbone break with it as the butt slid off his face. Joe dropped the rifle when the big man hit the ground. He pulled handcuffs from his pocket and Dion got one of the guy's wrists and Joe got the other and they cuffed them behind his back as he took a lot of huffing breaths, his blood pooling on the floor.

'You gonna live?' Joe asked him.

'Gonna kill you.'

'Sounds like you're gonna live.' Joe turned to the three trigger-happy Cubans. 'Get another guy and take this one to the cells.'

He looked at the one they'd shot. He was curled on the floor, mouth open and gasping. He didn't sound good and he didn't look good – marble white, way too much blood flowing from his midsection. Joe knelt by him, but in the moment it took to do so, the boy died. His eyes were open and tilted up and to the right, as if he were trying to remember his wife's birthday or where he'd left his wallet. He lay on his side, one arm pinned awkwardly beneath him, the other splayed up and behind his head. His shirt had bunched up at his ribs and left his abdomen exposed.

The three men who'd killed him blessed themselves as they dragged the giant past him and Joe.

When Joe closed the boy's eyelids, he looked quite young. He might have been twenty, or he could have been as young as sixteen. Joe rolled him onto his back and crossed his arms over his chest. Below his hands, just below the steeple where his lowest ribs met, dark blood climbed from a hole in him the size of a dime.

Dion and his men lined the National Guardsmen up against the wall and Dion told them to strip to their skivvies.

The dead boy had a wedding ring on his finger. Looked to be made of tin. Probably had a picture of her on him somewhere, but Joe wasn't going to look for it.

He was also missing one of his shoes. It must have come off when he was shot, but damned if Joe could see it near the corpse. As they marched the Guardsmen past him in their underwear, he searched the corridor for the shoe.

No luck. It might have been under the boy. Joe thought of rolling the body again to check – it seemed important to find it – but he was due back at the gate and he needed to change into another uniform.

He felt watched by bored or indifferent gods as he pulled the boy's shirt back over his abdomen and left him lying there, one shoe on, one shoe off, in his own blood.

The guns arrived five minutes later when the truck pulled up to the gate. The driver was a seaman no older than the boy Joe had just watched die, but riding shotgun was a petty officer in his midthirties with a permanently windburned face. He had a '17 Colt .45 riding his hip, the butt weathered from use. One look in his pale eyes and Joe knew that if those three Cubans had charged him in that corridor, they'd be the ones lying on the ground with sheets over them.

The IDs they handed over identified them as Seaman

Apprentice Orwitt Pluff and Petty Officer Walter Craddick. Joe handed the IDs back with the signed orders Craddick had given him.

Craddick gave that a cock of his head, left Joe's hand hanging in the space between them. 'That's for your CO's files.'

'Right.' Joe withdrew his hand. He gave them an apologetic smile, not putting much into it. 'A little too much fun last night in Ybor. You know how that is.'

'No, I don't.' Craddick shook his head. 'I don't drink. It's against the law.' He looked out the windshield. 'We backing up to that ramp?'

'Yes,' Joe said. 'You want, you can off-load it and we'll take it all inside.'

Craddick took note of the chevrons on Joe's shoulder. 'Our orders are to deliver and secure the weapons, Corporal. We'll be walking them all the way into the hold.'

'Outstanding,' Joe said. 'Just back it up to the ramp.' He raised the gate, catching Dion's eyes as he did so. Dion said something to Lefty Downer, the smartest of the four guys he'd brought along, and then walked off toward the armory.

Joe, Lefty, and the other three Pescatore men, all four dressed as corporals, followed the truck to the loading ramp. Lefty had been chosen because he was smart and didn't lose his cool. The other three – Cormarto, Fasani, and Parone – had been picked because they spoke English without an accent. For the most part, they looked like weekend soldiers, although Joe noted as they crossed the lot that Parone's hair was too long, even for a Guardsman.

He hadn't slept properly, if at all, in two days and he could feel it now in every step he took, every thought he tried to formulate.

As the truck backed up to the ramp, he saw Craddick watching him, and he wondered if the older man was just naturally suspicious or if Joe had given him a reason to be. And then Joe realized something that nauseated him.

He'd abandoned his post.

He'd left the gate unmanned. No soldier would do that, not even a hungover National Guardsman.

He glanced back, expecting to see it empty, expecting a shot in the back from Craddick's .45 and the peal of alarms, but instead he saw Esteban Suarez standing erect in the guard shack, wearing a corporal's uniform, looking to all but the most curious eyes every inch the soldier.

Esteban, Joe thought, I barely know you but I could kiss your head.

Joe glanced back at the truck, saw that Craddick wasn't looking at him any longer. He was turned on the seat, saying something to the seaman apprentice as the boy applied the brake and then shut off the engine.

Craddick hopped from the cab and shouted orders to the back of the truck, and by the time Joe got there, the sailors were out on the ramp and the tailgate was down.

Craddick handed Joe a clipboard. 'Initial the first and third pages, sign the second. Clearly states that we are leaving these weapons in your charge for no less than three and no more than thirty-six hours.'

Joe signed 'Albert White, SSG, USANG,' initialed where appropriate, and handed it back.

Craddick looked at Lefty, Cormarto, Fasani, and Parone, then back at Joe. 'Five men? That's all you got?'

'We were told you were bringing the muscle.' Joe gestured at the dozen sailors on the ramp.

'Just like the army,' Craddick said, 'putting its feet up when the work gets tough.'

Joe blinked in the sun. 'That why you guys were late – you were working hard?'

''Scuse me?'

Joe squared off, not just because his blood was up, but because not to do so would look suspicious. 'You were supposed to be here half an hour ago.'

'Fifteen minutes,' Craddick said, 'and we were delayed.'

'By?'

'Fail to see how any of this is your business, Corporal.' Craddick stepped up close. 'But, in truth, we were delayed by a woman.'

Joe looked back at Lefty and his men and laughed. 'Women can be hard work.'

Lefty chuckled and the others followed suit.

'All right, all right.' Craddick held up a hand and smiled to show he was in on the joke. 'Well, this one, boys, was a beauty. Ain't that right, Seaman Pluff?'

'Aye, sir. She was a looker. Bet she's a real biscuit too.'

'Little dark for my tastes,' Craddick said. 'But she come out the middle of the road, been all roughed up by her spic boyfriend, lucky he didn't cut her, fond as they are of their knives.'

'You leave her where you found her?'

'Left a sailor with her. Pick him up on the way back if you ever give us a chance to unload these weapons.'

'Fair enough,' Joe said and stepped back.

Craddick may have eased up a notch, but he was still a man on the alert. His eyes soaked up everything. Joe stuck with him, taking one end of a crate while Craddick took the other, lifting by the rope handles built into the ends. As they walked the loading bay corridor to the hold, they could see through the windows to the next corridor over and the offices beyond. Dion had placed all the fair-skinned Cubans in the offices with their backs to the windows, all of them typing gibberish on their Underwoods or crooking receivers to their ears with thumbs pressed down on the cradles. Even so, on their second trip down the corridor it occurred to Joe that every head they saw over there had black hair. Not a blond or a sandy dome in the bunch.

Craddick's eyes were on the windows as they walked, so far unaware that the corridor between theirs and those offices had just played host to an armed assault and the death of one man.

'Where'd you serve overseas?' Joe asked.

Craddick kept his eyes on the window. 'How'd you know I was overseas?'

Bullet holes, Joe thought. Those fucking itchy-fingered Cubans would have left bullet holes behind in the walls. 'You have the look of a man seen some action.'

Craddick looked over at Joe. 'You recognize men who've been in battle?'

'I do today,' Joe said. 'With you, anyway.'

'Almost shot that spic woman by the side of the road,' Craddick said mildly.

'Really?'

He nodded. 'It was spics tried to blow us up last night. And these boys with me don't know it yet, but spics called in a threat against the whole crew, said we were all going to die today.'

'I hadn't heard that.'

'That's 'cause it ain't for hearing yet,' Craddick said. 'So I see a spic girl waving us down in the middle of Highway 41? I think, Walter? Shoot that bitch between the tits.'

They reached the hold and stacked the crate on top of the first stack to the left. They stepped aside and Craddick took a handkerchief to his forehead in the hot hallway and they watched the last of the crates come to them as the sailors filed down the corridor.

'Woulda done it too but that she had my daughter's eyes.'

'Who?'

'The spic girl. Got me a daughter from my time in the DR. Don't see her or nothing, but her mama sends me pictures every now and then. She got them big dark eyes most Carib' women have? I see those eyes in this gal today, I holstered my weapon.'

'It was already out?'

'Halfway.' He nodded. 'I already had it in my head, you know? Why take chances? Put the bitch down. White men don't get much more'n a tongue-lashing for that around here. But . . .' He shrugged. 'My daughter's eyes.'

Joe said nothing, his blood loud in his ears.

'Sent a boy to do it.'

'What?'

He nodded. 'One of the boys we got, Cyrus, I believe. Looking for a war but he can't find one right now. Spic woman saw the look in his eyes, she took off running. Cyrus is part coon hound though, grew up in swampland near the Alabama border. Should find her without breaking him a sweat.'

'Where will you take her?'

'There's no taking her anywhere. She attacked us, boy. Her people did anyway. Cyrus will do what he will with her, leave the rest for the reptiles.' He put the stub of a cigar in his mouth and struck a match off his boot. He squinted over the flame at Joe. 'Confirm your assumption – I seen battle, son, yeah. Killed me one Dominican, killed me Haitians by the bushel, point of fact. Few years later, I took out three Panamanians with one Thompson burst on account they were all bunched together, praying I wouldn't. The truth of it all and don't let no one ever tell you different?' He got the cigar going and flicked the match over his shoulder. 'It was some fun.'

CHAPTER SIXTEEN

Gangster

As soon as the sailors left, Esteban ran to the motor pool to grab a vehicle. Joe changed out of his uniform as Dion backed the truck over to the ramp and the Cubans began pulling the crates right back out of the hold.

'You got this?' Joe asked Dion.

Dion beamed. 'Got it? We *own* it. You go get her. We'll see you at the spot in an hour.'

Esteban pulled up in a scout car and Joe hopped in and they took off down Highway 41. Within five minutes they saw the transport truck about a half mile ahead rumbling down a road so straight and flat you could practically see Alabama at the other end.

'If we can see them,' Joe said, 'they can see us.'

'Not for long,' Esteban said.

The road appeared to their left. It cut through the palmettos and across the crushed-shell highway and back into the scrub and palmettos on the other side. Esteban turned left, and they bounced onto it. It was gravel and dirt and half the dirt was mud. Esteban drove like Joe felt – harried and reckless.

'What was his name?' Joe said. 'The boy who died?'

'Guillermo.'

Joe could see the boy's eyes as they'd closed, and he didn't want to find Graciela's looking the same.

'We shouldn't have left her out there,' Esteban said.

'I know.'

'We should have assumed they'd have left someone behind with her.'

'I *know*.'

'We should have had somebody waiting with her, hiding.'

'I fucking *know*,' Joe said. 'How is this helping us now?'

Esteban goosed the gas and they soared over a dip in the road and hit the ground on the other side so hard Joe feared the scout would rise onto its front wheels, flip them onto their fucking heads.

But he didn't tell Esteban to slow down.

'I've known her since we were no taller than the dogs on my family farm.'

Joe didn't say anything. A swamp lay off to their left through the pines. Cypress and sweet gum trees and plants Joe couldn't begin to identify raced by on either side of them, blurring until the greens and yellows were the greens and yellows of a painting.

'Her family were migrant farmers. You should see the village she called "home" a few months every year. America has not seen poverty until it's seen that village. My father realized how bright she was and asked her family if he could hire her as a maid-in-training, yes? What he was really doing was hiring me a friend. I had none, just the horses and the cattle.'

Another bump in the road.

'Strange time to be telling me this,' Joe said.

'I loved her,' Esteban said, speaking loudly over the engine. 'Now, I love somebody else, but for many years, I thought I was in love with Graciela.'

He turned to look at Joe and Joe shook his head and pointed. 'Eyes on the road, Esteban.'

Another bump, this one lifting them both out of their seats and then back down again.

'She says she's doing all this for her husband?' Talking helped put the fear in a manageable place, made Joe feel less helpless.

'Ach,' Esteban said. 'He's no husband. He's no man.'

'I thought he was a revolutionary?'

This time Esteban spat. 'He is a thief, a . . . a . . . *estafador*. You call them con men. Yes? He dresses the part of the revolutionary, he recites the poetry, and she fell for him. She lost everything for this man – her family, all her money and she never had much, most of her friends but me.' He shook his head. 'She doesn't even know where he is.'

'I thought he was in jail.'

'He's been out for two years.'

Another bump. This time they went sideways and the rear quarter panel on Joe's side slapped a pine sapling before they bounced back into the road.

'But she still pays his family.'

'They lie to her. They tell her he escaped, that he's hiding in the hills and a gang of *los chacales* from Nieves Morejón

288

prison are hunting him and Machado's men are hunting him. They tell her she cannot return to Cuba to see him or they will both be in danger. No one, Joseph, is hunting this man, except for those he owes money. But you cannot tell Graciela that; she does not hear when it comes to him.'

'Why? She's a smart woman.'

He gave Joe a quick glance and shrugged. 'We all believe lies that bring us more comfort than the truth. She's no different. Her lie is just bigger.'

They missed the turnoff, but Joe caught it out of the corner of his eye and told Esteban to stop. He braked and they slid twenty yards before they finally stopped. He backed up and they turned onto the road.

'How many men have you killed?' Esteban asked.

'None,' Joe said.

'But you're a gangster.'

Joe didn't see the point in arguing the distinction between gangster and outlaw because he wasn't sure there was one anymore. 'Not all gangsters kill people.'

'But you must be willing to.'

Joe nodded. 'Just like you.'

'I'm a businessman. I provide a product people want. I kill no one.'

'You're arming Cuban revolutionaries.'

'That's a cause.'

'In which people will die.'

'There's a difference,' Esteban said. 'I kill *for* something.'

'What? A fucking ideal?' Joe said.

'Exactly.'

'And what ideal is that, Esteban?'

289

'That no man should rule another's life.'

'Funny,' Joe said, 'outlaws kill for the same reason.'

She wasn't there.

They came out of the pine forest and approached Route 41, and there was no sign of Graciela or the sailor who'd been left behind to hunt her. Nothing but the heat and the hum of dragonflies and the white road.

They drove down the road half a mile and then back up to the dirt road and then north another half mile. When they drove back again, Joe heard something he thought was a crow or a hawk.

'Kill the engine, kill the engine.'

Esteban did, and they both stood in the scout car and looked out at the road and the pines and the cypress swamp beyond and the hard white sky that matched the road.

Nothing. Nothing but the dragonfly buzz Joe now suspected never stopped – morning, noon, or night, like living with your ear to a train track just after the train had passed over it.

Esteban sat back down and Joe went to but stopped.

He thought he saw something just to the east, back the way they'd come, something that—

'There.' He pointed, and as he did she ran out from behind a stand of pines. She didn't run in their direction and Joe realized she was too smart for that. If she had, she would have been running full out for fifty yards through low palmettos and pine saplings.

Esteban gunned the engine and they dropped down the shoulder and through a ditch and then back out again, Joe holding on to the top of the windshield and hearing the shots now – hard cracks strangely muted even out here with nothing around them. From his vantage point, he still couldn't see the shooter, but he could see the swamp and he knew she was headed for it. He nudged Esteban with his foot and waved his arm to the left, a little farther southwest than the line they were on.

Esteban turned the wheel and Joe got a sudden glimpse of dark blue, just a flash of it, and saw the man's head and heard his rifle. Up ahead, Graciela fell to her knees in the swamp and Joe couldn't tell whether she'd fallen because she'd tripped or because she'd been shot. They ran out of firm land, the shooter just off to their right. Esteban slowed as he entered the swamp and Joe jumped out of the scout.

It was like jumping out onto the moon if the moon was green. The bald cypress rose like great eggs from the milky green water, and prehistoric banyan trees with a dozen or more trunks stood watch like palace guards. Esteban drove to his right just as Joe saw Graciela dart between two of the bald cypress trees to his left. Something uncomfortably heavy crawled over his feet just as he heard a rifle report, the shot much closer now. The bullet tore a chunk from the cypress tree where Graciela was hiding.

The young seaman stepped out from behind a cypress ten feet away. He was about Joe's height and build, his hair quite red, his face very lean. His Springfield was raised to his shoulder, the sight raised to his eye, the barrel pointed at the cypress. Joe extended his .32 automatic and exhaled a long breath as he shot the man from ten feet. The rifle jerked and spun in the air so erratically Joe assumed it was all he'd hit.

But as it fell to the tea-colored water, the young man fell with it, and the blood spilled from under his left armpit and darkened the water as he landed with a splash.

'Graciela,' he called, 'it's Joe. Are you okay?'

She peeked out from behind the tree and Joe nodded. Esteban came around behind her in the scout car and she climbed in it and they drove over to Joe.

He picked up the rifle and looked down at the sailor. He sat in the water with his arms draped over his knees and his head down, like a man trying to catch his breath.

Graciela climbed out of the scout. Actually, she half fell out, half reeled into Joe. He put his arm around her to right her and felt the adrenaline racking her body as if she'd been hit with a cattle prod.

Behind the sailor, something moved through the mangroves. Something long and so dark green it was almost black.

The sailor looked up at Joe, his mouth open as he drew shallow breaths. 'You're white.'

'Yeah,' Joe said.

'Fuck you shoot me for then?'

Joe looked at Esteban and then at Graciela. 'If we leave him here, something's gonna eat him within a couple minutes. So we either take him with us or ...'

He could hear more of them out there as the sailor's blood continued to spill into the green swamp.

Joe said, 'So we either take him with us ...'

Esteban said, 'He's gotten too good a look at her.'

'I know it,' Joe said.

Graciela said, 'He turned it into a game.'

'What?'

'Hunting me. He kept laughing like a girl.'

Joe looked at the sailor and the kid looked back at him. The fear lived far back in the young man's eyes, but the rest of him was pure defiance and backwoods grit.

'You want me to beg, you barking up the wrong—'

Joe shot him in the face and the exit hole splattered pink all over the ferns, and the alligators thrashed in anticipation.

Graciela let out a small involuntary cry and Joe might have as well. Esteban caught his eye and nodded, thanks, Joe realized, for doing what they all knew had to be done but which none had been willing to do. Hell, Joe – standing in the sound of the gunshot, the cordite smell of it, a wisp of smoke trailing from the barrel of the .32 no more substantial than the smoke from one of his cigarettes – couldn't believe he'd actually done it.

A man lay dead at his feet. Dead, on some fundamental level, only because Joe had been born.

They climbed into the scout without another word. As if they'd been waiting for permission, two alligators came at the body at once – one walking out of the mangroves with the steady waddle of an overweight dog and the other gliding up through the water and the lily pads beside the scout's tires.

Esteban drove away as both reptiles reached the body at the same time. One took an arm, the other went for a leg.

Back in the pines, Esteban drove southeast along the edge of the swamp, running parallel to the road, but not turning toward it yet.

Joe and Graciela sat in the backseat. Alligators and humans weren't the only predators in the swamp that day:

a panther stood at the edge of the waterline, lapping up the copper water. It was the same tan color as some of the trees, and Joe might have missed it altogether if it didn't look up as they passed from twenty yards away. It was at least five feet long, wet limbs all grace and muscle. Its underbelly and throat were creamy white, and steam rose off its wet fur as it considered the car. Actually, it wasn't considering the car, it was considering him. Joe met its liquid eyes, as ancient, yellow, and pitiless as the sun. For a moment, in his jagged exhaustion he thought he heard its voice in his head.

You can't outrun this.

What's *this*? he wanted to ask, but Esteban turned the wheel and they left the edge of the swamp and bounced violently over the roots of a fallen tree, and when Joe looked again the panther was gone. He scanned the trees to catch another glimpse but he never saw it again.

'You see that cat?'

Graciela stared at him.

'The panther,' he said, holding his arms wide.

Her eyes narrowed like she worried he might have sunstroke. She shook her head. She was a mess – more scratches on her body than skin it seemed. Her face was swollen from where he'd hit her, of course, and the mosquitoes and deerflies had feasted on her – and not just them but the fire ants as well, leaving behind their white welts with red rings all over her feet and calves. Her dress was torn at the shoulder and over her left hip and the hem was shredded. Her shoes were gone.

'You can put it away,' she said.

Joe followed her gaze, saw that he still held the gun in his right hand. He thumbed the safety on and placed it in the holster behind his back.

Esteban pulled out onto 41 and stomped the gas so hard the scout shuddered in place before streaking down the road. Joe looked out at the crushed-shell pavement racing away from them, at the merciless sun in the merciless sky.

'He would have killed me.' Her wet hair blew across her face and neck.

'I know.'

'He hunted me like a squirrel for his lunch. He kept saying, "Honey, honey, I will put one in your leg, honey, and then have at you." Does "have at you" mean ...?'

Joe nodded.

'And if you'd let him live,' she said, 'I would have been arrested. And then you would have been arrested.'

He nodded. He considered the insect bites on her ankles and then raised his eyes up her calves, across her dress, and into her eyes. She held his gaze just long enough to slide hers off his face. She looked out at an orange grove as they raced past it. After a while, she looked back at him.

'Do you think I feel bad?' he asked.

'I can't tell.'

'I don't,' he said.

'You shouldn't.'

'I don't feel good.'

'You shouldn't feel that, either.'

'But I don't feel bad.'

That pretty much summed it up.

I'm not an outlaw anymore, he thought. I'm a gangster. And this is my gang.

In the back of the scout car with the sharp smell of citrus giving way, once again, to the stench of swamp gas, she held his gaze for a full mile, and neither of them said another word until they reached West Tampa.

CHAPTER SEVENTEEN

About Today

When they got back to Ybor, Esteban dropped Graciela and Joe at the building where Graciela kept a room above a café. Joe walked her up while Esteban and Sal Urso went to dump the scout car in South Tampa.

Graciela's room was very small and very neat. The wrought iron bed was painted the same white as the porcelain washbasin under a matching oval mirror. Her clothes hung in a battered pine wardrobe that looked to predate the building, but she kept it clear of dust or mold, which Joe would have guessed impossible in this climate. The one window overlooked Eleventh Avenue, and she'd left the shade down to keep the room cool. She had a dressing screen made of the same raised-grain wood as the wardrobe, and she pointed Joe to face the window as she went behind it.

'So you are a king now,' she said as he raised the shade and looked out at the avenue.

'I'm sorry?'

'You have cornered the rum market. You will be a king.'

'A prince, maybe,' he admitted. 'Still gotta deal with Albert White.'

'Why do I think you've already figured out how to do that?'

He lit a cigarette and sat on the edge of the windowsill. 'Plans are just dreams until they're executed.'

'Is this what you always wanted?'

'Yes,' he said.

'Well, then, congratulations.'

He looked back at her. The filthy evening gown hung over the screen and her shoulders were bare. 'You don't sound like you mean it.'

She pointed for him to turn back around. 'I do. It's what you wanted. You achieved it. That's admirable in some way.'

He chuckled. 'In some way.'

'But how will you hold the power now that you have it? That's an interesting question, I think.'

'You think I'm not strong enough?' He looked back at her again and she allowed him to because she'd covered her upper body with a white blouse.

'I don't know if you're cruel enough.' Her dark eyes were very clear. 'And if you are, then that will be sad.'

'Powerful men don't have to be cruel.'

'But they usually are.' Her head ducked below the screen as she stepped into her skirt. 'Now that you've seen me dress and I've seen you shoot a man, can I ask you a personal question?'

'Sure.'

'Who is she?'

'Who?'

Her head appeared above the screen again. 'The one you love.'

'Who says I'm in love with anyone?'

'I say so.' She shrugged. 'A woman knows these things. Is she in Florida?'

He smiled, shook his head. 'She's gone.'

'She left you?'

'She died.'

She blinked and then stared at him to see if he was putting her on. When she realized he wasn't, she said, 'I'm sorry.'

He changed the subject. 'Are you happy about the guns?'

She leaned her arms on the top of the screen. 'Very. When the day comes to end Machado's rule – and that day *will* come – we will have a . . . ' She snapped her fingers, looked at him. 'Help me.'

'An arsenal,' he said.

'Arsenal, yes.'

'So these aren't the only weapons.'

She shook her head. 'Not the first and they will not be the last. When the time comes, we will be ready.' She came out from behind the screen in the standard clothes of a female cigar worker – white blouse with string tie over tan skirt. 'You think what I'm doing is foolish.'

'Not at all. I think it's noble. It's just not my cause.'

'What is?'

'Rum.'

'You do not want to be a noble person?' She held her thumb and index finger close together. 'A little bit?'

He shook his head. 'I've got nothing against noble people, I've just noticed they rarely live past forty.'

'Neither do gangsters.'

'True,' he said, 'but we eat in better restaurants.'

From the wardrobe, she selected a pair of flats the same color as her shirt, sat on the bed to put them on.

He stayed at the window. 'Let's say someday you have this revolution.'

'Yes.'

'Will anything change?'

'People can change.' She put one shoe on.

He shook his head. 'The world can change, but people, no, people stay pretty much the same. So even if you replace Machado, there's a good chance you'll replace him with a worse version. Meanwhile, you could be maimed or you could—'

'I could die.' She twisted her torso to put on the other shoe. 'I know how this probably ends, Joseph.'

'Joe.'

'Joseph,' she said. 'I could die because a comrade betrays me for money. I could get captured by damaged men, as damaged as the one today or even worse, and they will torture me until my body can no longer endure it. And there won't be anything *noble* in my death because death is never noble. You weep and beg and the shit flows out of your ass as you die. And those who kill you laugh and spit on your corpse. And I will be quickly forgotten. As if' – she snapped her fingers – 'I was never here. I know all that.'

'So why do it?'

She stood and smoothed the skirt. 'I love my country.'

'I love mine but—'

'There is no but,' she said. 'That's the difference between us. Your country is something you see out that window. Yes?'

He nodded. 'Pretty much.'

'My country is something in here.' She tapped the center of her chest and then her temple. 'And I *know* she won't thank me for my efforts. She's not going to return my love. That would be impossible, because I don't just love the people and the buildings and the smell of her. I love the idea of her. And that's something I made up, so I love what isn't there. Like you love that dead girl.'

He couldn't think of anything to say to that so he just watched her cross the room and pull the dress she'd worn in the swamp off the screen. She handed it to him as they left the room.

'Burn that, will you?'

The guns were bound for the Pinar del Río province, west of Havana. They left St Petersburg on five grouper boats out of Boca Ciega Bay at three in the afternoon. Dion, Joe, Esteban, and Graciela saw them off. Joe had changed from the suit he'd ruined in the swamp to the lightest one he owned. Graciela had watched as he'd burned it along with her dress, but she was fading now from her time as prey in a cypress swamp. She kept nodding off on the bench that sat under the dock lamp yet refused all offers to sit in one of the cars or let someone drive her back to Ybor.

When the last of the grouper captains had shaken their hands and shoved off, they stood looking at one another. Joe realized they had no idea what to do next. How could you

301

top the last two days? The sky had grown red. Somewhere down the jagged shoreline, past a clump of mangroves, a canvas sail or tarp fluttered in the hot breeze. Joe looked at Esteban. He looked at Graciela, who leaned against the lamppost with her eyes closed. He looked at Dion. A pelican swooped over his head, its bill bigger than its belly. Joe looked at the boats, way out there now, the size of dunce caps from this distance, and he started laughing. He couldn't help himself. Dion and Esteban were right behind him, all three of them roaring in no time. Graciela covered her face for a moment and then she started laughing too, laughing and crying actually, Joe noticed, peeking out from between her fingers like a small girl until she dropped her hands entirely. She laughed and cried and ran both hands through her hair repeatedly and then wiped her face with the collar of her blouse. They walked to the edge of the dock and the laughs became chuckles and then echoes of chuckles and they looked out at the water as it grew purple under the red sky. The boats found the horizon and slipped past it, one by one.

Joe didn't remember much about the rest of that day. They went to one of Maso's speaks behind a veterinarian on the corner of Fifteenth and Nebraska. Esteban arranged to have a case of dark rum aged in cherry casks sent over, and word got around to everyone involved in the heist. Soon Pescatore gunsels mingled with Esteban's revolutionaries. Then the women arrived in their silk dresses and sequined hats. A band took the stage. In no time, the joint was hopping enough to crack the masonry.

Dion danced with three women simultaneously, swinging

them behind his broad back and under his stubby legs with surprising dexterity. When it came to dance, however, Esteban proved to be the artist of the group. He moved on his feet as lightly as a cat on a high branch, but with a command so total that the band soon began to fashion songs to his tempo, not the other way around. He reminded Joe of Valentino in that flicker where he played a bullfighter – it was that degree of masculine grace. Soon half the women in the speak were trying to match his steps or land him for the night.

'I never saw a guy move like that,' Joe said to Graciela.

She was sitting in the corner of a booth, while he sat on the floor in front of it. She leaned over to speak in his ear. 'It's what he did when he first came here.'

'What do you mean?'

'It was his job,' she said. 'He was a taxi dancer downtown.'

'You're putting me on.' He tilted his head, looked up at her. 'What *doesn't* this guy do well?'

She said, 'He was a professional dancer in Havana. Very good. Never the lead in any productions but always in high demand. It's how he supported himself during law school.'

Joe almost spit up his drink. 'He's a lawyer?'

'In Havana, yes.'

'He told me he grew up on a farm.'

'He did. My family worked for his. We were, uh—' She looked at him.

'Migrant farmers?'

'Is that the word?' She scrunched her face at him, at least as drunk as he was. 'No, no, we were *tenant* farmers.'

'Your father rented land from his father and paid his rent in crops?'

'No.'

'That's tenant farming. It's what my grandfather did in Ireland.' He tried to appear sober, learned, but it was work under the circumstances. 'Migrant farming is when you go from farm to farm with the seasons, depending on the crop.'

'Ah,' she said, unhappy with the clarification. 'So smart, Joseph. You know *everything*.'

'You asked, *chica*.'

'Did you just call me "*chica*"?'

'I believe I did.'

'Your accent is horrible.'

'So's your Gaelic.'

'What?'

He waved it off. 'I'm a work in progress.'

'His father was a great man.' Her eyes shone. 'He took me into the home, gave me my own bedroom with clean sheets. I learned English from a private tutor. Me, a village girl.'

'And his father asked for what in return?'

She read his eyes. 'You're disgusting.'

'It's a fair question.'

'He asked nothing. Maybe his head, it swelled a bit for all he did for this little village girl, but that was all.'

He held up a hand. 'Sorry, sorry.'

'You see the worst in the best of people,' she said, shaking her head, 'and the best in the worst of people.'

He couldn't think of a reply to that, so he shrugged and let the silence and the liquor return the mood to a softer place.

'Come.' She slid out of the booth. 'Dance.' She pulled at his hands.

'I don't dance.'

'Tonight,' she said, 'everyone dances.'

He allowed her to pull him to his feet even though it was a fucking abomination to share the same dance floor as Esteban or, to a lesser extent, Dion, and call what he did the same thing.

Sure enough, Dion laughed openly at him, but he was too drunk to care. He let Graciela lead and he followed and soon he found a beat he could keep a kind of pace with. They stayed out on the floor for quite some time, passing a bottle of Suarez dark rum back and forth. At one point he found himself lost in cross-images of her; in one she ran through the cypress swamp like desperate prey and in the other she danced a few feet away from him, hips twitching, shoulders and head swaying as she tipped the bottle to her lips.

He'd killed for this woman. Killed for himself too. But if there was one question he hadn't been able to answer all day, it was why he'd shot the sailor in the face. You didn't do that to a man unless you were angry. You shot him in the chest. But Joe had blown his face up. That was personal. And that, he realized as he lost himself in the sway of her, was because he'd seen clearly in the sailor's eyes that the man held Graciela in contempt. Because she was brown, raping her wasn't a sin; it was just indulging in the spoils of war. Whether she'd been alive or dead when he did it would have made little difference to Cyrus.

Graciela raised her arms above her head, the bottle up there with her, her wrists crossing, forearms snaking around each other, crooked smile on her bruised face, eyes at half-mast.

'What are you thinking?' she said.

'About today.'

'What about today?' she asked but then saw it in his eyes. She lowered her arms and handed him the bottle and they moved out of the center and stood by the table again and drank the rum.

'I don't care about him,' Joe said. 'I guess I just wish there had been another way.'

'There wasn't.'

He nodded. 'Which is why I don't regret what I did. I just regret that it happened.'

She took the bottle from him. 'How do you thank the man who saved your life after he dangered it?'

'Dangered it?'

She wiped at her mouth with her knuckles. 'Yes. How?'

He cocked his head at her.

She read his eyes and laughed. 'Some other way, *chico*.'

'You just say thanks.' He took the bottle from her and had a sip.

'Thanks.'

He gave her a flourish and a bow and fell into her. She shrieked and swatted at his head and helped him right himself. They were both laughing and out of breath when they staggered to a table.

'We will never be lovers,' she said.

'Why's that?'

'We love other people.'

'Well, mine's dead.'

'Mine may as well be.'

'Oh.'

She shook her head several times, a reaction to the alcohol. 'So we love ghosts.'

'Yes.'

'Which makes us ghosts.'

'You're drunk,' he said.

She laughed and pointed across the table. '*You're* drunk.'

'No argument.'

'We will not be lovers.'

'You said that.'

The first time they made love in her room above the café it was like a car crash. They mashed each other's bones and fell off the bed and toppled a chair and when he entered her, she sank her teeth into his shoulder so hard she drew blood. It was over in the time it took to dry a dish.

The second time, half an hour later, she poured rum onto his chest and licked it off and he returned the favor and they took their time and learned each other's rhythms. She had said no kissing, but that went the way of their not being lovers in the first place. They tested slow ones and hard ones, kisses with nips of the lips, kisses in which only their tongues touched.

What surprised him was how much fun they had. Joe had had sex with seven women in his life, but he'd only made love, as he understood the definition, with Emma. And while their sex had been reckless and occasionally inspired, Emma had always held a part of herself in reserve. He would catch her watching them have sex while they were having it. And afterward, she always withdrew even further into the locked box of herself.

Graciela reserved nothing. This left a high likelihood for injury – she pulled at his hair, she gripped his neck so hard with her cigar roller hands he half-worried she was going to snap it, she sank her teeth into skin and muscle and bone. But it was all part of her enveloping him, pushing the act to the edge of something that, to Joe, resembled vanishing, as if he'd wake up in the morning alone with her dissolved into his body or vice versa.

When he did wake that morning, he smiled at the foolishness of the notion. She slept on her side, with her back to him, her hair gone wild and overflowing on the pillow and headboard. He wondered if he should slide out of bed, grab his clothes, and get gone before the inevitable discussion of too much alcohol and muddy thinking. Before the regret cemented. Instead, he kissed her shoulder very lightly, and she rolled his way in a rush. She covered him. And regret, he decided, would have to wait for another day.

'It will be a professional arrangement,' she explained to him over breakfast in the café downstairs.

'How's that?' He ate a piece of toast. He couldn't stop smiling like an idiot.

'We will fill this' – she was smiling too as she searched for the word – 'need for each other until such time as—'

'"Such time"?' he said. 'That tutor taught you well.'

She leaned back in her chair. 'My English is very good.'

'I agree, I agree. Outside of using *dangered* when you meant *endangered,* it's pretty flawless.'

She grew an inch in her chair. 'Thank you.'

He continued to smile like an idiot. 'My pleasure. So we fill each other's, um, need until when?'

'Until I return to Cuba to be with my husband.'

'And me?'

'You?' She speared a piece of fried egg.

'Yeah. You get to return to a husband. What do I get?'

'You get to become king of Tampa.'

'Prince,' he said.

'Prince Joseph,' she said. 'It's not bad, but I'm afraid it doesn't quite fit you. And shouldn't a prince be benevolent?'

'As opposed to?'

'A gangster who is only out for himself.'

'And his gang.'

'And his gang.'

'Which is a type of benevolence.'

She gave him a look somewhere between frustration and disgust. 'Are you a prince or a gangster?'

'I don't know. I like to think of myself as an outlaw, but I'm not sure that's any more than a fantasy now.'

'Well, you be my outlaw prince until I return home. How is that?'

'I would love to be your outlaw prince. What are my duties?'

'You must give back.'

'Okay.' She could have asked for his pancreas at this point and he would have said, 'Fine.' He looked across the table at her. 'Where do we start?'

'Manny.' She held him in dark eyes that were suddenly serious.

'He had a family,' Joe said. 'Wife and three daughters.'

'You remember.'

'Of course I remember.'

'You said you didn't care whether he lived or died.'

'I was exaggerating a little bit.'

'Will you take care of his family?'

'For how long?'

'For life,' she said, as if it were a perfectly logical answer. 'He gave his life for you.'

He shook his head. 'With all due respect, he gave his life for you. You and your cause.'

'So ...' She held a piece of toast just below her chin.

'So,' he said, 'on behalf of your cause, I would be happy to send a bag of money over to the Bustamente family just as soon as I have a bag of money. Does that please you?'

She smiled at him as she bit into her toast. 'It pleases me.'

'Then consider it done. By the way, anyone ever call you anything but Graciela?'

'What would they call me?'

'I dunno. Gracie?'

She made a face like she'd sat on a hot coal.

'Grazi?'

Another face.

'Ella?' he tried.

'Why would anyone do such a thing? Graciela is the name my parents gave me.'

'My parents gave me a name too.'

'But you cut it in half.'

'It's Joe,' he said. 'Like José.'

'I know what it means,' she said as she finished her meal. 'But José means Joseph. It does not mean Joe. You should be called Joseph.'

'You sound like my father. He would only call me Joseph.'

'Because that's your name,' she said. 'You eat very slowly, like a bird.'

'I've heard that.'

Her eyes rose at something behind him and he turned in his chair to see Albert White walk through the back door. He hadn't aged a day, though he was softer than Joe remembered, a banker's paunch beginning to form over his belt. He still favored white suits and white hats and white spats. Still had that saunter that suggested the world was a playground built to amuse him. He walked in with Bones and Brenny Loomis and picked up a chair as he came. His boys followed suit, and they put the chairs down at Joe's table and sat in them – Albert beside Joe, Loomis and Bones flanking Graciela, their impassive faces fixed on Joe.

'What's it been?' Albert said. 'A little over two years?'

'Two and a half,' Joe said and sipped his coffee.

'If you say so,' Albert said. 'You're the one who went to prison, and if there's one thing I know about convicts it's that they count days real keen.' He reached over Joe's arm and plucked a sausage off his plate, started eating it like it was a chicken leg. 'Why didn't you go for your heater?'

'Maybe I'm not carrying.'

Albert said, 'No, truly.'

'I figure you're a businessman, Albert, and this place is a bit public for a gunfight.'

'I disagree.' Albert gave the place the once-over. 'Looks

perfectly acceptable to me. Good lighting, nice sight lines, not too much clutter.'

The café owner, a nervous Cuban woman in her fifties, looked even more nervous. She could read the energy between the men and she wanted that energy to leave through the windows or leave through the door but leave soon. An older couple sat at the counter by her and they were oblivious, arguing over whether to see a flicker tonight at Tampa Theatre or catch Tito Broca's set at the Tropicale.

Otherwise, the place was empty.

Joe checked on Graciela. Her eyes were a fair bit wider than usual, and a vein he'd never seen before had appeared, throbbing, in the center of her throat, but otherwise she seemed calm, hands as steady as her breathing.

Albert took another bite of sausage and leaned toward her. 'What's your name, hon'?'

'Graciela.'

'You a light nigger or a dark spic? I can't tell.'

She smiled at him. 'I'm from Austria. Isn't it obvious?'

Albert roared. He slapped his thigh and slapped the table and even the oblivious old couple looked over.

'Oh, that's a good one.' He said to Loomis and Bones, 'Austria.'

They didn't get it.

'Austria!' he said, thrusting both hands out at them, the sausage still dangling from one. He sighed. 'Forget it.' He turned back. 'So Graciela from Austria, what's your full name?'

'Graciela Dominga Maela Corrales.'

Albert whistled. 'That's quite a mouthful, but I bet you have plenty of experience with mouthfuls, don't you, hon'?'

'Don't,' Joe said. 'Just ... Albert? Don't. Leave her out of this.'

Albert turned back to Joe as he chewed the last of the sausage. 'Past experience would suggest I'm not good at that, Joe.'

Joe nodded. 'What do you want here?'

'I want to know why you didn't learn anything in prison. Too busy taking it up the ass? You get out, come down here, and in two days you try to muscle me? How fucking stupid they make you in there, Joe?'

'Maybe I was just trying to get your attention,' Joe said.

'Then you were a smashing success,' Albert said. 'Today we started hearing back from my bars, my restaurants, my pool halls, every speak I got tucked away from here to Sarasota that they don't pay me anymore. They pay you. So naturally I went to talk to Esteban Suarez, and he's suddenly got more armed guards than the U.S. Mint. Can't be bothered to meet with me. You think you and a gang of wops and, what, niggers I hear?'

'Cubans.'

Albert helped himself to a piece of Joe's toast. 'You think you're going to push me out?'

Joe nodded. 'I think I did, Albert.'

Albert shook his head. 'Soon as you're dead, the Suarezes will fall in line and you can be damn sure the dealers will.'

'If you wanted me dead, you would have done it. You came to negotiate.'

Albert shook his head. 'I do want you dead and there's no

negotiation. I just wanted you to see that I've changed. I've mellowed. We're going to walk out the back door and leave the girl behind. Won't touch a hair on her head, though, Lord knows, she could spare it.' Albert stood. He buttoned his suit coat over his softening belly. He straightened the brim of his hat. 'You make a fuss, we take her with us, kill you both.'

'That's the proposition?'

'That's it.'

Joe nodded. He pulled a piece of paper from his jacket pocket and placed it on the table. He smoothed it. He looked up at Albert and began reading the names listed there. 'Pete McCafferty, Dave Kerrigan, Gerard Mueler, Dick Kipper, Fergus Dempsey, Archibald—'

Albert pulled the list from Joe's fingers, read the rest of it.

'You can't find them, can you, Albert? All your best soldiers, and they're not answering their phones or their doorbells. You keep telling yourself it's a coincidence, but you know that's bullshit. We got to them. Every one of them. And, Albert, I hate to tell you this, but they're not coming back to you.'

Albert chuckled, but his normally ruddy face was now the white of an elephant tusk. He looked at Bones and Loomis and chuckled some more. Bones chuckled along with him, but Loomis looked sick.

'While we're on the subject of people in your organization,' Joe said, 'how'd you know where to find me?'

Albert glanced at Graciela, a little bit of color returning to his face. 'You're simple, Joe – just follow the pussy.'

Graciela's jaw tightened but she said nothing.

'It's a good line, I guess,' Joe said, 'but unless you knew where to find me last night – and you didn't, because nobody did – then you wouldn't have been able to tail me here.'

'You got me.' Albert held up his hands. 'I guess I have other methods.'

'Like a guy inside my organization?'

The smile slid through Albert's eyes before he blinked it away.

'Same guy who told you to take me in the café, not on the street?'

No smile in Albert's eyes anymore. They turned flatter than pennies.

'He tell you if you took me in the café, I wouldn't put up a fight because of the girl? Tell you I'd even take you to a bag of cash I stashed in a flop over in Hyde Park?'

Brendan Loomis said, 'Shoot him, boss. Shoot him now.'

Joe said, 'You should have shot me coming through the door.'

'Who says I won't?'

'I do,' Dion said, coming up behind Loomis and Bones, a long-barrel .38 pointed at each of them. Sal Urso entered through the front door and Lefty Downer came in behind Sal, both of them wearing trench coats on a cloudless day.

The café owner and the couple at the counter were officially rattled now. The old man kept patting his chest. The café owner thumbed her rosary beads, her lips moving frantically.

Joe asked Graciela, 'Could you go tell them we won't hurt them?'

She nodded and got up from the table.

Albert said to Dion, 'So betrayal's your defining personality trait, eh, fat boy?'

'Only once, you dandy fuck,' Dion said. 'Shoulda thought long and hard about what I did to your boy Blum last year before you bought my bullshit this time around.'

'How many more we got on the street?' Joe asked.

'Four cars full,' Dion said.

Joe stood. 'Albert, I don't want to kill anybody in this café but that doesn't mean I won't if you give me half a reason.'

Albert smiled, smug as always, even outnumbered and outgunned. 'We won't give you a *quarter* of a reason. How's that for cooperation?'

Joe spit in his face.

Albert's eyes went as small as peppercorns.

For a very long moment, no one in the café moved.

'I'm going to reach for my handkerchief,' Albert said.

'You reach for anything, we plug you where you stand,' Joe said. 'Use your fucking sleeve.'

As he did, Albert's smile returned but his eyes remained filled with murder. 'So you're either killing me or running me out of town.'

'That's right.'

'Which?'

Joe looked at the café owner and her rosary, at Graciela standing beside her, her hand on the woman's shoulder.

'Don't think I feel like killing you today, Albert. You don't have the guns or the funds to start a war, and you'd need years of building new alliances to make me look over my shoulder.'

Albert took a seat. Just as easy as you please. Like he was visiting old friends. Joe remained standing.

'You planned this since the alley,' he said.

'Sure did.'

'At least tell me some of this was just business,' he said.

Joe shook his head. 'This was completely personal.'

Albert took that in and nodded. 'You want to ask about her?'

Joe felt Graciela's eyes on him. And Dion's.

He said, 'Not particularly, no. You fucked her, I loved her, and then you killed her. What's left to discuss?'

Albert shrugged. 'I did love her. More than you could imagine.'

'I got a hell of an imagination.'

'Not this good,' he said.

Joe tried to read the face behind Albert's face, and he got the same feeling he'd gotten in the basement service corridor of the Hotel Statler – that Albert's feelings for Emma matched his own.

'So why'd you kill her?'

'I didn't kill her,' Albert said. 'You did. The moment you put your dick in her. Thousands of other girls in that city and you a pretty boy to boot, but you take mine. You give a man horns, he has two choices – gore himself or gore you.'

'But you didn't gore me. You gored her.'

Albert shrugged and Joe could see clearly that it pained him still. Christ, he thought, she owns a piece of both of us.

Albert looked around the café. 'Your master ran me out of Boston. Now you're running me out of Tampa. That the play?'

317

'Pretty much.'

Albert pointed at Dion. 'You know he sold you out in Pittsfield? That he's the reason you did two years in jail?'

'Yeah, I do. Hey, D.'

Dion never took his eyes off Bones and Loomis. 'Yeah?'

'Put a couple bullets in Albert's brain.'

Albert's eyes popped wide and the café owner let out a yelp and Dion crossed the floor with his arm extended. Sal and Lefty revealed Thompsons under their raincoats to cover Loomis and Bones, and Dion put the gun to Albert's temple. Albert scrunched his eyes closed and held up his hands.

Joe said, 'Hold it.'

Dion stopped.

Joe fixed his trousers and squatted in front of Albert. 'Look in my friend's eyes.'

Albert looked up at Dion.

'You see any love for you in them, Albert?'

'No.' Albert blinked. 'No, I don't.'

Joe nodded at Dion, and Dion removed the gun from Albert's head.

'You drive here?'

'What?'

'Did you drive here?'

'Yes.'

'Good. You're gonna go to your car and drive north out of the state. I suggest Georgia because as of now I control Alabama, the Mississippi coast, and every town between here and New Orleans.' He smiled at Albert. 'And I've got a meeting about New Orleans next week.'

'How do I know you won't have men waiting on the road for me?'

'Hell, Albert, I *will* have men on the road. In fact, they're going to follow you out of the state. Ain't that right, Sal?'

'Car's all gassed up, Mr Coughlin.'

Albert got a look at Sal's tommy gun. 'How do I know they won't kill us on the road?'

'You don't,' Joe said. 'But if you don't leave Tampa right now and leave for good, I'll give you the A & P fucking guarantee you won't see tomorrow. And I know you want to see tomorrow because that's when you'll start planning your revenge.'

'Then why leave me alive?'

'So everyone knows I took everything you had, and you weren't man enough to stop me.' Joe straightened from his crouch. 'I'm letting you keep your life, Albert, because I can't think of a soul who would fucking want it.'

CHAPTER EIGHTEEN

Nobody's Son

During the good years, Dion said to Joe, 'Luck ends.'

He said it more than once.

Joe would reply, 'Good luck *and* bad.'

'It's just your luck has been good so long,' Dion said, 'no one remembers your bad.'

He built a house for himself and Graciela on the corner of Ninth and Nineteenth. He used Spanish labor, Cuban labor, Italians for the marble work, and brought in architects from New Orleans to ensure that a multitude of styles coalesced into a Latin Vieux Carré. He and Graciela made several trips to New Orleans to tour the French Quarter for inspiration and took long walking trips around Ybor as well. They came up with a design that married Greek Revival with Spanish Colonial. The house sported a facade of redbrick and pale concrete balconies with wrought iron rails. The windows were green and kept shuttered so the house looked almost plain from the street, and it was difficult to tell when it was occupied.

But in the back, wide rooms with high copper ceilings and tall archways looked onto a courtyard, a wading pool, and gardens where spotted horsemint, violets, and tickseeds grew alongside European fan palms. The stucco walls were covered in Algerian ivy. In the winter the bougainvillea flowered alongside a riot of yellow Carolina jessamine, both fading in the spring to be replaced by trumpet creepers as dark as blood oranges. The stone paths snaked around a fountain in the courtyard, then passed through the loggia archways to a staircase that curled up into the house past walls of eggshell brick.

All the doors in the home were at least six inches thick and sported ram's horn hinges and door latches of black iron. Joe had helped design the third-floor salon with the domed ceiling and an *azotea* overlooking the alley that ran behind the house. It was a frivolous porch, given the second-story balcony that wrapped around the rest of the house and the cast-iron third-story gallery with a veranda as wide as the street, and he often forgot it was there.

Once Joe got started, though, he couldn't stop himself. Guests lucky enough to be invited to one of Graciela's charity fund-raisers couldn't help noticing the salon or the grand center hall with the double-wide staircase or the imported silk draperies, Italian bishop's chairs, Napoléon III cheval mirror with attached candelabras, marble mantels from Florence, or gilt-framed paintings from a gallery in Paris Esteban had recommended. Exposed Augusta Block brick walls met walls covered in satin paper or stenciled patterns or fashionably cracked stucco. Parquet floors at the front of the house yielded to stone floors at the back to keep the rooms cool. In the summer, the furniture was slip-covered in white cotton, and gauze dripped from chandeliers to keep them safe from insects. Mosquito netting hung from Joe and Graciela's bed and over the claw-foot tub in the bathroom where they often gathered at the end of a day with a bottle of wine, the sounds of the streets rising to them.

Graciela lost friends over the opulence. These were mostly her friends from the factory and those who'd volunteered with her during the early days of the Circulo Cubano. It wasn't that they begrudged Graciela her newfound wealth and good fortune (though a few did), it was more that they feared they'd bump into something valuable and knock it to the stone floors. They couldn't sit without fidgeting, and soon they ran out of things they had in common with Graciela and so had nothing left to discuss.

In Ybor, they called the house El Alcalde de la Mansión – The Mayor's Mansion – but Joe wouldn't learn of the nickname for at least a year because the voices in the street never rose high enough for him to hear them distinctly.

Meanwhile, the Coughlin-Suarez partnership created enviable stability in a business not known for it. Joe and Esteban established a distillery in the Landmark Theater on Seventh and then another behind the kitchen of the Romero Hotel, and they kept them clean and in constant production. They brought all the mom-and-pop operations into the fold, even the ones who'd worked for Albert White, by giving them a healthier cut and a better product. They bought faster boats and replaced all the engines in their trucks and transport cars. They bought a two-seater seaplane to fly cover for the Gulf runs. The seaplane was piloted by Farruco

Diaz, a former Mexican revolutionary as talented as he was insane. Farruco, a notable mess of ancient pockmarks as deep as fingertips and long hair as pale and stringy as wet pasta, lobbied to install a machine gun in the passenger seat 'just in case.' When Joe pointed out to him that since he flew solo, there would be nobody to man the gun on those times that 'just in case' occurred, Farruco agreed to a compromise, by which they allowed him to install the mount but not the gun.

On the ground, they bought into routes all over the South and along the Eastern Seaboard, Joe's logic being that if they paid the various Dixie gangs tribute to use their roads, the gangs would pay off the local laws, and the number of arrests and lost loads would drop by 30 to 35 percent.

They dropped by seventy.

In no time at all, Joe and Esteban had turned a one-million-dollars-a-year operation into a six-million-dollars-a-year juggernaut.

And this during a global financial crisis that kept worsening, each shock wave followed by a bigger one, day after day, month after month. People needed jobs and they needed shelter and they needed hope. When none of those proved forthcoming, they settled for a drink.

Vice, he realized, was Depression-proof.

Just about nothing else was, though. Even insulated from it, Joe was still as bewildered as everyone else by the elevator drop the country had taken in the last few years. Since the '29 crash, ten thousand banks had gone belly-up and thirteen million people had lost their jobs. Hoover, facing a reelection fight, kept talking about a light at the end of the tunnel, but most people decided that light came from the train barreling up to run them over. So Hoover made a last-ditch scramble to raise the tax rate for the richest of the rich from 25 to 63 percent and lost the only people left who supported him.

In Greater Tampa, oddly, the economy surged – ship-building and canneries thrived. But no one got the word in Ybor. The cigar factories started sinking faster than the banks. Rolling machines replaced people; radios supplanted the readers on the floor. Cigarettes, so cheap, became the nation's new legal vice, and sales of cigars plummeted by more than 50 percent. The workers of a dozen factories went out on strike, only to see their efforts crushed by management goons, police, and the Ku Klux Klan. The Italians left Ybor in droves. The Spaniards started to move out too.

Graciela lost her job to a machine. This was fine with Joe – he'd been wanting to get her out of La Trocha for months. She was too valuable to his organization. She met the Cubans who came off the boats and brought them to the social club or the hospitals or the Cuban hotels, depending on what they needed. If she saw one she believed was suited for Joe's line of work, she spoke to him of an even more unique job opportunity.

In addition, it was her instinct for philanthropy, coupled with Joe and Esteban's need to clean their money, that led to Joe's buying up roughly 5 percent of Ybor City. He bought two failed cigar factories and reemployed all the workers, turned a failed department store into a school and a bankrupt plumbing supplier into a free clinic. He turned eight empty buildings into speakeasies, though from the street they all looked like their fronts: a haberdasher, a tobacconist, two florists, three butchers, and a Greek lunch counter that much to everyone's shock – none more so than Joe's own – became so successful they had to import the rest of the cook's family from Athens and open a sister lunch counter seven blocks east.

Graciela missed the factory, though. Missed the jokes and tales the other rollers would tell, missed hearing the readers narrate her favorite novels in Spanish, missed speaking in her mother tongue all day.

Even though she spent every night at the house Joe had built for them, she kept her room above the café, although as far as Joe knew, all she ever did there was change her clothes. And not very often, either. Joe had filled a closet in his home with clothes he'd bought her.

'Clothes *you* bought me,' she'd say when he'd ask her why she didn't wear them more often. 'I like to buy my own things.'

Which she never had the money for because she sent all her money back to Cuba, either to the family of her deadbeat husband or to friends in the anti-Machado movement. Esteban made trips back to Cuba on her behalf sometimes too, fund-raising trips that coincided with the opening of this nightclub or that. He'd come back with news of fresh hope in the movement that, experience had taught Joe, would be dashed on his next trip. He'd also come back with his photographs – his eye getting sharper and sharper, wielding that camera like a great violinist wielded his bow. He'd become a name in the insurgency circles of Latin America, a reputation built, in no small part, on the sabotage of the USS *Mercy*.

'You've got a very confused woman on your hands,' he told Joe after his last trip over.

'This I know,' Joe said.

'Do you understand why she is confused?'

Joe poured them each a glass of Suarez Reserve. 'No, I don't. We can buy or do anything we want. She can have the finest clothes, get her hair done at the nicest shops, go to the nicest restaurants—'

'That allow Latins.'

'That goes without saying.'

'Does it?' Esteban leaned forward in his chair, put his feet on the floor.

'The point I'm trying to make,' Joe said, 'is that we won. We can relax, she and I. Grow old together.'

'And you think that's what she wants – to be a rich man's wife?'

'Isn't that what most women want?'

Esteban gave that a strange smile. 'You told me once you did not grow up poor like most gangsters.'

Joe nodded. 'We weren't rich but ...'

'But you had a nice house, food in your bellies, could afford to go to school.'

'Yes.'

'And was your mother happy?'

Joe said nothing for a long time.

'I'll assume that's a no,' Esteban said.

Eventually Joe said, 'My parents seemed more like distant cousins. Graciela and me? We're not those people. We talk all the time. We' – he lowered his voice – 'fuck all the time. We truly enjoy each other's company.'

'So?'

'So why won't she love me?'

Esteban laughed. 'Of course she loves you.'

'She won't say it.'

'Who cares if she says it?'

'I do,' Joe said. 'And she won't divorce Shithead.'

'I can't speak to that,' Esteban said. 'I could live a thousand years and never understand the hold that *pendejo* has over her.'

'Have you seen him?'

'Every time I walk down the worst block in Old Havana he sits there in one of the bars, drinking her money.'

My money, Joe thought. Mine.

'Is anyone still looking for her over there?'

'Her name's on a list,' Esteban said.

Joe thought about it. 'But I could get her false papers in a fortnight. Couldn't I?'

Esteban nodded. 'Of course. Maybe sooner.'

'So I could send her back there, she could see this asshole sitting on his barstool, and she'd ... She'd what, Esteban? You think it would be enough for her to leave him?'

He shrugged. 'Joseph, listen to me. She loves you. I have known her all my life and I have seen her in love before. But you? Whoosh.' He widened his eyes, fanned his face with his hat. 'It's something different than she's ever felt. But you must remember, she's spent the last ten years defining herself as a revolutionary, and now she wakes up to discover that what she *really* wants is to throw all that off her shoulders – her beliefs, her country, her calling, and, yes, her stupid old husband – to be with an American gangster. You think she's just going to admit that to herself?'

'Why not?'

'Because then she has to admit she's a café rebel, a fake. She's not going to admit that. She's going to redouble her commitment to the cause and hold you at arm's length.' He shook his head and grew thoughtful, staring up at the ceiling. 'When you say it out loud, it's quite mad actually.'

Joe rubbed his face. 'You got that right.'

Everything hummed along smoothly for a couple years – a hell of a run in their business – until Robert Drew Pruitt came to town.

The Monday after Joe's talk with Esteban, Dion came in to tell him that RD had stuck up another of their clubs. Robert Drew Pruitt was called RD, and he'd been a concern to everyone in Ybor since he'd gotten out of prison eight weeks ago and showed up here to make his way in the world.

'Why can't we just find this asshole and put him down?'

'The Klavern ain't going to like that.'

The KKK had gained a lot of power in Tampa recently. They'd always been fanatic drys, not because they didn't drink themselves – they did, and constantly – but because they believed alcohol gave delusions of power to the mud people and led to fornication between the races and was also part of a papist plot to sow weakness in the practitioners of true religion so Catholics could eventually take over the world.

The Klan had left Ybor alone until the crash. Once the economy went in the tank, their message of white power began to find desperate believers, the same way the fire-and-brimstone preachers had seen attendance in their tents swell. People were lost and people were scared and their lynch ropes couldn't reach bankers or stockbrokers, so they looked for targets closer to home.

They found it in the cigar workers, who had a long history of labor battles and radical thought. The Klan ended the last strike. Every time the strikers gathered, the KKK would bust into the meetings firing rifles and pistol-whipping whoever was in reach. They burned a cross on one striker's lawn, fire-bombed the house of another on Seventeenth, and raped two female cigar workers walking home from the Celestino Vega factory.

The strike was called off.

RD Pruitt had been Klan before he left to do a two-year bid at the State Prison Farm at Raiford, so there was little reason to believe he hadn't joined right back up when he got out. The first speak he stuck up, a hole-in-the-wall in the back of a bodega on Twenty-seventh, was directly across the train tracks from an old shotgun shack rumored to be the headquarters for the local Klavern run by Kelvin Beauregard. As RD was helping himself to the night's till, he gestured at the wall closest to the tracks and said, 'We all be watching so we best not see no laws.'

When Joe heard that, he knew he was dealing with a moron – who the fuck would call the police when a speakeasy was robbed? But the 'we' gave him pause because the Klan were just waiting for someone like Joe to stick his head up. A Catholic Yankee who worked with the Latins, Italians, and Negroes, shacked up with a Cuban, and made his money selling the demon rum – what wasn't there to hate about him?

In fact, he realized pretty quickly, that's exactly what they were doing. They were calling him out. The foot soldiers of the Klan might have been a collection of inbred idiots with fourth-grade educations at third-rate schools, but their leaders tended to be a bit smarter. Besides Kelvin Beauregard, a local cannery owner and city councilman, the group was rumored to include Judge Franklin of the 13th Judicial Court, a dozen cops, and even Hopper Hewitt, publisher of the *Tampa Examiner.*

The other, far more meaningful complication, in Joe's view, was that RD's brother-in-law was Irving Figgis, also known as Eagle Eye Irv, but more formally as Tampa's chief of police.

Since their first meeting back in '29, Chief Figgis had brought Joe in for questioning a few times, just to keep clear the adversarial nature of their relationship. Joe would sit in his office and sometimes Irv would have his secretary bring them lemonade, and Joe would look at the pictures on his desk – the beautiful wife, and the two apple-haired children, the boy, Caleb, a dead ringer for his daddy, and the girl, Loretta, still so beautiful it muddied Joe's brain whenever he looked at her. She'd been homecoming queen at Hillsborough High School and had been winning all sorts of awards in local theater since she was a pup. So no one was surprised when she headed west for Hollywood upon graduation. Like everyone else, Joe expected to see her up on the big screen any day now. She had that light about her that turned people around her into moths.

Surrounded by the images of his perfect life, Irv had warned Joe on more than one occasion that if his department ever found anything to tie him to the *Mercy* job, they'd damn well rope Joe up for the rest of his life. And who knew what the Feds would do from there – maybe tie that rope around his neck, drop him through the gallows. But otherwise, Irv let Joe and Esteban and their people be, as long as they all stayed the hell out of white Tampa.

But now here came RD Pruitt sticking up the fourth Pescatore speakeasy in a single month and fairly begging Joe to retaliate.

'All four bartenders have said the same thing about this kid,' Dion told Joe, 'said he's sick-mean. You can see it in him. He's gonna kill somebody next time or the time after.'

Joe had known plenty of guys in prison who fit that description and they normally left you with only three choices – get them to work for you, get them to ignore you, or kill them. There was no way Joe wanted RD to work for him and no way RD would take orders from a Catholic or a Cuban, so that left options two and three.

One morning in February, he met with Chief Figgis at the Tropicale, the day warm and dry, Joe having learned by now that from late October to the end of April, the climate here was hard to beat. They sipped their coffees with a boost of Suarez Reserve added to it, and Chief Figgis looked out onto Seventh with an itch in his stare and fidgeted in his chair.

Lately there was something tucked just behind the corner of him that was trying not to drown. Some second heart beating in his ears, beating in his throat, beating behind his eyes enough to make them bulge sometimes.

Joe didn't have a clue what had gone wrong in the man's life – maybe his wife had run off, maybe someone he loved had died – but it was clear something ate at him lately, took the vigor from him, took the certainty too.

He said, 'You hear the Perez factory is closing?'

'Shit,' Joe said. 'That's got, what, four hundred workers?'

'Five hundred. Five hundred more people without jobs, five hundred pairs of idle hands waiting to do the devil's handiwork. But, shit, even the devil ain't hiring these days. So they ain't going to get up to much of anything but drinking and fighting and robbing and making my job all the harder, but at least I got one.'

Joe said, 'I heard Jeb Paul's closing his dry goods store.'

'Heard that too. Been in his family since before this city had a name.'

'A shame.'

'Damn shame, what it is.'

They drank, and RD Pruitt sauntered in off the street. Wore himself a tan knicker suit with wide lapels, a white golf cap, and two-toned Oxfords like he was heading out to the back nine. Rolled a toothpick across his lower lip.

Soon as he sat down, Joe saw it in his face clear as a stream – fear. It lived back behind his eyes, leaked out of his pores. Most people didn't see it because they mistook its public faces – hatred and ill temper – for rage. But Joe had studied it for two years in Charlestown, and he'd discovered that the worst of the men in there were also the most terrified – terrified of being found out as cowards or, worse, victims, themselves, of other terrible and terrified men. Terrified someone was going to infect them with more poison and terrified someone might come and take their poison away. This terror moved through their eyes like quicksilver; you had to catch it on your first meeting, in the first minute, or you'd never see it again. But in that moment of original contact, they were still assembling themselves for you, so you could spy the fear animal as it dashed back into its cave, and Joe was sad to see that RD Pruitt's animal was as big as a boar, which meant he'd be twice as mean and twice as unreasonable because he was twice as scared.

As RD sat, Joe offered his hand.

RD shook his head. 'Don't shake hands with papists.' He smiled and showed Joe his palms. 'I mean no offense.'

'None taken.' Joe left the hand out there. 'Help if I said I haven't been in church for half my life?'

RD chuckled and shook his head some more.

Joe took his hand back and settled into his seat.

Chief Figgis said, 'RD, word around the fire is you've taken to your old ways down here in Ybor.'

RD looked at his brother-in-law, eyes wide and innocent. 'And how's that?'

'We hear you're sticking up places,' Figgis said.

'What kind of places?'

'Speakeasies.'

'Oh,' RD said, his eyes suddenly dark and small. 'Mean them places don't exist in a law-abiding town?'

'Yes.'

'Mean them places that are *illegal* and should therefore be shuttered?'

'That would be them,' Figgis said, 'yes.'

RD shook his small head and his face returned to its cherubic innocence. 'I just don't know anything about that.'

Joe and Figgis exchanged a look, and Joe got the impression both of them were trying hard not to sigh.

'Ha-ha,' RD said. 'Ha-ha.' He pointed at the two of them. 'I'm just playing with you all. And you know that.'

Chief Figgis indicated Joe with a tilt of his head. 'RD, this is a businessman who's come to do business. I'm here to suggest you do it with him.'

'You do know that, right?' RD asked Joe.

'Sure.'

'What am I playing at?' RD said.

'You're just joking around,' Joe said.

'I am. You know. You know.' He smiled at Chief Figgis. 'He knows.'

'Okay, then,' Figgis said. 'So we're all friends.'

RD gave them a vaudevillian roll of the eyes. 'I didn't say *that*.'

Figgis blinked a few times. 'Either case, we all understand one another.'

'This man' – RD pointed his finger in Joe's face – 'is a bootlegger and a fornicator with niggers. He needs to be tarred and feathered, not done business with.'

Joe smiled at the finger and considered snatching it out of the air, slamming it on the table, and snapping it at the knuckle.

Before he could, RD removed it and said, 'I'm just josh-ing!' very loudly. 'You take a joke, right?'

Joe said nothing.

RD reached across the table and chucked his fist off Joe's shoulder. 'You take a joke? Huh? Huh?'

Joe looked across at possibly the friendliest face he'd ever come across. A face that wished only the best of things for you. Kept looking until he saw the fear animal make a dash through RD's sick and friendly eyes.

'I can take a joke.'

'Long as you don't become one, right?' RD said.

Joe nodded. 'My friends tell me you frequent the Parisian.'

RD narrowed his eyes like he was trying to recall the place.

Joe said, 'I hear you're fond of the French seventy-five they serve.'

RD hitched his trouser leg. 'And if I was?'

'I'd say you should become more than a regular.'

'What's more than a regular?'

'A partner.'

'What's the stake?'

'Cut you in for ten percent of the house take.'

'You'd do that?'

'Sure.'

'Why?'

'Let's say I respect ambition.'

'That all?'

'And I recognize talent.'

'Well, that ought to be worth more than ten percent.'

'What were you thinking?'

RD's face went as blandly beautiful as a wheat field. 'I was thinking sixty.'

'You want sixty percent of the take of one of the most successful clubs in the city?'

RD nodded, blithe and bland.

'For doing what, exactly?'

'You give me my sixty percent, my friends might look on you less unkindly.'

'Who are your friends?' Joe asked.

'Sixty percent,' RD said, as if for the first time.

'Son,' Joe said, 'I'm not giving you sixty percent.'

'Ain't your son,' RD said mildly. 'Ain't nobody's son.'

'Much to your father's relief.'

'What's that?'

'Fifteen percent,' Joe said.

'Beat you to death,' RD whispered.

At least that's what Joe thought he whispered. He said, 'What?'

RD rubbed his jaw hard enough Joe could hear the stubble bristle. He fixed Joe with eyes that were blank and too bright at the same time. 'You know, that sounds like a right fair arrangement.'

'What does?'

'Fifteen percent. You wouldn't go to twenty?'

Joe looked at Chief Figgis, then back at RD. 'I'm thinking fifteen is about as generous as it gets for a job I'm not even asking you to show up to.'

RD scratched his stubble some more and looked down at the table for a bit. He looked up eventually, gave them his most boyish smile.

'You're right, Mr Coughlin. That is a fair deal, sir. And I'm just pleased as corn on the cob to agree to it.'

Chief Figgis leaned back in his chair, hands on his flat belly. 'That's great to hear, Robert Drew. I just knew we could come to an accord.'

'And we did,' RD said. 'How will I pick up my cut?'

'Just drop by the bar every second Tuesday around seven at night,' Joe said. 'Ask for the manager, Sian McAlpin.'

'Schwan?'

'Close enough,' Joe said.

'He a papist too?'

'He's a she, and I never asked her.'

'Sian McAlpin. The Parisian. Tuesday nights.' RD slapped the table with his palms and stood up. 'Well, that's just great, I tell ya. A pleasure, Mr Coughlin. Irv.' He tipped his hat to them both and gave them a half-wave, half-salute as he left.

For a full minute, no one said anything.

Eventually Joe turned in his chair a bit and asked Chief Figgis, 'How soft is that kid's head?'

'As a grape.'

'That's what I'm afraid of. Do you think he'll really take the deal?'

Figgis shrugged. 'Time will tell.'

When RD showed up at the Parisian for his cut, he thanked Sian McAlpin when she handed it to him. He asked her to spell her name for him and told her it was right pretty when she did. He said he looked forward to their long association and had a drink at the bar. He was pleasant to all he encountered. Then he walked out, got in his car, and drove out past the Vayo Cigar Factory to Phyllis's Place, the first speak where Joe had a drink in Ybor.

The bomb RD Pruitt threw into Phyllis's Place wasn't much of a bomb, but it didn't have to be. The main room was so small a tall man couldn't clap his hands without his elbows hitting the wall.

No one was killed, but a drummer named Cooey Cole lost his left thumb and never played again, and a seventeen-year-old girl who'd come in to pick up her daddy and drive him home lost a foot.

Joe sent three two-man teams to find the bugsy fuck, but RD Pruitt went hard to ground. They scoured the whole of Ybor, then the whole of West Tampa, then the whole of Tampa itself. Nobody could find him.

A week later, RD walked into another of Joe's speaks on the east side, a place frequented almost exclusively by black Cubans. Walked in while the band was in full swing and the place was jumping. Ambled up to the stage and shot the bass trombonist in the knee and shot the singer in the stomach. He flipped an envelope onto the stage and walked out the back door.

The envelope was addressed to Sir Joseph Coughlin Nigger Fucker. Inside was a two-word note:

Sixty percent.

Joe went to see Kelvin Beauregard at his cannery. He took Dion and Sal Urso with him, and they met in Beauregard's office at the back of the building. It looked down on the sealing floor. Several dozen women dressed in frocks and aprons with matching headbands stood on the sweltering floor around a serpentine system of conveyor belts. Beauregard watched them through a floor-to-ceiling window. He didn't get up when Joe and his men entered. He didn't look at them for a full minute. Then he turned in his chair and smiled and jerked his thumb at the glass.

'Got my eye on a new one,' he said. 'What do you think of that?'

Dion said, 'New becomes old the second you drive it off the lot.'

Kelvin Beauregard raised an eyebrow. 'Good point, good point. Gentlemen, what can I do for you?'

He took a cigar from a humidor on his desk but didn't offer anyone else one.

Joe crossed his right leg over his left and hitched the crease in the ankle cuff. 'We'd like to see if you could talk some sense into RD Pruitt.'

Beauregard said, 'Ain't too many people had success doing that in their lives.'

'Be that as it may,' Joe said, 'we'd like you to try.'

Beauregard bit the end off his cigar and spit it into a wastebasket. 'RD's a grown man. He's not requested my counsel, so it would be disrespectful to give it. Even if I agreed with the reason. And tell me, because I'm confused, what the reason would be?'

Joe waited until Beauregard had lit his cigar, waited while he stared through the flame at him and then stared through the smoke at him.

'In the interest of his own self-preservation,' Joe said, 'RD needs to quit shooting up my clubs and meet with me so we can come to an accommodation.'

339

'Clubs? What kind of clubs?'

Joe looked over at Dion and Sal and said nothing.

'Bridge clubs?' Beauregard said. 'Rotary clubs? I belong to the Greater Tampa Rotary Club, myself, and I don't recall seeing you—'

'I come to you as an adult to discuss a piece of business,' Joe said, 'and you want to play fucking games.'

Kelvin Beauregard put his feet up on his desk. 'Is that what I want to do?'

'You sent this boy up against us. You knew he was crazy enough to do it. But all you're going to do is get him killed.'

'I sent who?'

Joe took a long breath through his nostrils. 'You're the grand wizard of the Klan around here. Great, good for you. But you think we got where we got allowing a bunch of inbred shit packers like you and your friends to muscle us?'

'Ho, boy,' Beauregard said with a weary chuckle, 'if you think that's all we are, you are making a fatal miscalculation. We're town clerks and bailiffs, jail guards and bankers. Police officers, deputies, even a judge. And we've decided something, Mr Coughlin.' He lowered his feet from the desk. 'We've decided we're going to squeeze you and your spics and your dagos or we're going to run you right out of town. If you're dim enough to fight us, we'll rain holy hellfire down on you and all you love.'

Joe said, 'So what you're threatening me with is a whole bunch of people who are more powerful than you?'

'Exactly.'

'Then why am I talking to you?' Joe said and nodded at Dion.

Kelvin Beauregard had time to say 'What?' before Dion crossed the office and blew his brains all over his enormous window.

Dion lifted the cigar off Kelvin Beauregard's chest and popped it in his mouth. He unscrewed the Maxim silencer from his pistol and hissed as he dropped it into the pocket of his raincoat.

'Thing's hot.'

Sal Urso said, 'You're becoming such a little gal lately.'

They left the office and walked down the metal stairs to the cannery floor. Coming in, they'd worn fedoras pulled down over their foreheads and light-colored raincoats over flashy suits so that all the workers could see them for what they were – gangsters – and not look too long. They walked out the same way. If anyone recognized them from around Ybor, they'd know their reputation, and that would be enough to ensure a consensus of faulty vision on the sealing floor of the late Kelvin Beauregard's cannery.

Joe sat on Chief Figgis's front porch in Hyde Park, absently flicking the cover of his father's watch open and closed, open and closed. The house was a classic bungalow with Arts and Crafts flourishes. Brown with eggshell trim. The chief had built the porch from wide planks of hickory, and he'd placed rattan furniture out there and a swing painted the same eggshell as the trim.

Chief Figgis pulled up in his car and got out and walked up the redbrick path between the perfectly manicured lawn.

'Come to my house?' he said to Joe.

'Save you the trouble of hauling me in.'

'Why would I haul you in?'

'Some of my men tell me you were looking for me.'

'Oh, right, right.' Figgis reached the porch and put his foot on the steps for a moment. 'You shoot Kelvin Beauregard in the head?'

Joe squinted up at him. 'Who's Kelvin Beauregard?'

'There endeth my questions,' Figgis said. 'Want a beer? It's near beer but it's not bad.'

'Much obliged,' Joe said.

Figgis went into the house and came back out with two near beers and a dog. The beers were cold and the dog was old, a gray bloodhound with soft ears the size of banana leaves. He lay on the porch between Joe and the door and snored with both eyes open.

'I need to get to RD,' Joe said after thanking Figgis for the beer.

'I expect you would feel that way.'

'You know how this ends if you don't help me,' Joe said.

'No,' Chief Figgis said, 'I don't.'

'It ends with more bodies, more bloodshed, more newspapers writing about "Cigar City Slaughter" and the like. It ends with you getting pushed out.'

'You too.'

Joe shrugged. 'Maybe.'

'Difference is, when you get pushed out, someone does it with a bullet to the back of your ear.'

'If he goes away,' Joe says, 'the war ends. Peace returns.'

Figgis shook his head. 'I'm not selling my wife's brother down the river.'

Joe looked out on the street. It was a lovely brick street

with several tidy bungalows cheerfully painted and some old Southern homes with farmers' porches and even a couple of bowfront brownstones at the head of the street. The oaks were all stately and tall and the air smelled of gardenias.

'I don't want to do this,' Joe said.

'Do what?'

'What you're about to make me do.'

'I'm not making you do anything, Coughlin.'

'Yeah,' Joe said softly, 'you are.'

He removed the first of the photos from his inside jacket pocket and placed it on the porch beside Chief Figgis. Figgis knew he shouldn't look at it. He just knew it. And for a moment, he kept his chin tilted hard toward his right shoulder. But then he turned his head back and looked down at what Joe had laid on his porch, two steps from the front door to his home, and his face was stricken white.

He looked up at Joe, then down at the photo and quickly away, and Joe went in for the kill.

He placed a second photo beside the first. 'She didn't make it to Hollywood, Irv. She just made it to Los Angeles.'

Irving Figgis took a quick glance at the second photo, enough that it burned his eyes. He shut them tight and whispered, 'That's not right, that's not right,' over and over.

He wept. Sobbed, actually. Hands over his face, head down, back heaving.

When he stopped, he left his face in his hands, and the dog came over and lay beside him on the porch and pressed its head against Figgis's outer thigh and shuddered, its lips flapping.

'We've got her with a special doctor,' Joe said.

Figgis lowered his hands, looked at Joe with hate in his red eyes. 'What kind of doctor?'

'Kind gets people off heroin, Irv.'

Figgis held up one finger. 'Do not ever call me by my Christian name again. You will call me Chief Figgis and Chief Figgis only for whatever days or years remain in our acquaintance. Are we clear?'

'We didn't *do* this to her,' Joe said. 'We just found her. And pulled her out of where she was, which was a pretty bad spot.'

'And then figured out how to profit from it.' Figgis pointed at the picture of his daughter with the three men and the metal collar and chain. 'You people peddle in that. Whether it's my daughter or someone else's.'

'I don't,' Joe said, knowing how feeble it sounded. 'I just run rum.'

Figgis wiped his eyes with the heels of his hands and then the backs of them. 'The profit from the rum buys the organization the other things. Don't you sit there, sir, and pretend it don't. Name your price.'

'What?'

'Your price. For telling me where my daughter is.' He turned and looked at Joe. 'You tell me. Tell me where she is.'

'She's with a good doctor.'

Figgis thumped his fist off his porch.

'In a clean facility,' Joe said.

Figgis punched the floorboard.

'I can't tell you,' Joe said.

'Until?'

Joe looked at him for a long time.

Eventually Figgis rose and the dog rose with him. He went through his screen door and Joe heard him dialing. When he spoke into the phone his voice was higher and hoarser than normal. 'RD, you're gonna meet this boy again and there ain't another discussion to be had on that matter.'

On the porch, Joe lit a cigarette. A few blocks away, horns beeped distantly on Howard.

'Yeah,' Figgis said into the phone, 'I'll come too.'

Joe plucked a piece of tobacco off his tongue and gave it to the small breeze.

'You'll be safe. I swear.'

He hung up and stood at the screen for some time before pushing the door open, and he and the dog came back out on the porch.

'He'll meet you on Longboat Key, where they built that Ritz, at ten tonight. He said you come alone.'

'Okay.'

'When do I get her location?'

'When I walk out of my meeting with RD alive.'

Joe walked to his car.

'Do it yourself.'

He looked back at Figgis. 'What?'

'If you're going to kill him, be man enough to pull the trigger yourself. Ain't no pride in having other people do what you're too weak to do yourself.'

'Ain't no pride in most things,' Joe said.

'You're wrong. I wake up every morning, look myself in the mirror, and know I walk a righteous path. You?' Figgis let the question hang in the air.

Joe opened his car door, started to get in.

'Wait.'

Joe looked back at the man on the porch, who was now less of a man because Joe had stolen a crucial part of him and was going to drive off with it.

Figgis flashed his torn eyes at Joe's suit jacket. His voice was shaky. 'You got any more in there?'

Joe could feel them sitting in the pocket, as repugnant as abscessed gums.

'No.' He got into his car and drove off.

CHAPTER NINETEEN

No Better Days

John Ringling, the circus impresario and great benefactor to Sarasota, had built the Ritz-Carlton on Longboat Key back in '26, whereupon he'd promptly run into money problems and left it sitting there on a cove, its back to the Gulf, rooms with no furniture, walls with no crown molding.

Back when he'd first moved to Tampa, Joe had taken a dozen trips along the coastline, looking for spots to off-load contraband. He and Esteban had some boats running molasses into the Port of Tampa, and they had the town so locked up they only lost one in ten loads. But they also paid boats to run bottled rum, Spanish *anís*, and *orujo* straight from Havana to West Central Florida. This allowed them to skip the distilling process on U.S. soil, which removed a time-consuming step, but it left the boats open to a wider array of Volstead enforcers, including T-men, G-men, and the Coast Guard. And no matter how crazy and how talented a pilot Farruco Diaz was, all he could do was spot the laws coming, not stop them. (Which is why he continued to lobby for a machine gun and gunner to go with his machine gun mount.)

Until such a day as Joe and Esteban decided to declare open war on the Coast Guard and J. Edgar's men, however, the small barrier islands that dotted this stretch of Gulf coastline – Longboat Key, Casey Key, Siesta Key, among others – were perfect places to duck and hide or temporarily stow a load.

They were also perfect places to get boxed in, because those same keys had only two ways on and off – one, the boat you'd sailed in on, and two, a bridge. One bridge. So if the laws were closing in, megaphones blaring, searchlights scouring, and you didn't have a way to fly off the island, then you, sir, were going to jail.

Over the years, they'd temporarily dumped a dozen or so loads at the Ritz. Not Joe, personally, but he'd heard the stories about the place. Ringling had gotten the skeleton up, even installed the plumbing and subflooring, but then he'd walked away. Just left it sitting there, this three-hundred-room Spanish Mediterranean, so big that if they'd lit the rooms, you could probably see it from Havana.

Joe got there an hour early. He'd brought a flashlight with him, had asked Dion to pick him up a good one, and this one wasn't bad, but it still needed frequent rests. The beam would gradually dim, begin to flicker, and then it would vanish entirely. Joe would have to shut it off for a few minutes and then turn it back on and go through the same process all over again. It occurred to him as he waited in the dark of what he believed had been meant to be a third-floor restaurant, that people were flashlights – they beamed, they dimmed, they flickered and died. It was a morbid and childish observation, but on the drive down he'd grown morbid and maybe a bit childish in his pique at RD Pruitt because he knew that RD was just one in a line. He wasn't the exception, he was the rule. And if Joe succeeded in erasing him as a problem tonight, another RD Pruitt would come along soon after.

Because the business was illegal, it was, by necessity, dirty. And dirty businesses attracted dirty people. People of small minds and big cruelty.

Joe walked out onto the white limestone veranda and listened to the surf and Ringling's imported royal palm fronds rustling in the warm night breeze.

The drys were losing; the country was pushing back against the Eighteenth. Prohibition would end. Maybe not for ten years, but it could be as soon as two. Either way, its obituary was written, it just hadn't been published. Joe and Esteban had bought into importing companies up and down the Gulf Coast and along the Eastern Seaboard. They were cash poor right now, but the first morning alcohol became legal again, they could flip a switch and their operation would arise, gleaming, into the bright new day. The distilleries were all in place, the shipping companies currently specializing in glassware, the bottling plants servicing soda pop companies. By the afternoon of that first morning, they'd be up and running, ready to take over what they estimated to be well within their reach – 16 to 18 percent of the U.S. rum market.

Joe closed his eyes and sucked in the sea air and wondered

how many more RD Pruitts he'd have to deal with before he achieved that goal. Truth was, he didn't understand an RD, a guy who came at the world wanting to beat it at some competition that existed only in his head, a battle to the death, no question, because death was the only blessing and the only peace he'd ever find on this earth. And maybe it wasn't only RD and his ilk who bothered Joe; maybe it was what you had to do to put an end to them. You had to kneel down in the grime with them. You had to show a good man like Irving Figgis pictures of his firstborn with a cock in her ass and a chain around her neck, track marks running down her arm like garter snakes baked crisp by the sun.

He hadn't needed to put the second picture down in front of Irving Figgis, but he'd done so because it made things go quicker. What concerned him more and more about this business to which he'd hitched his star was that every time you sold off another piece of yourself in the name of expediency, the easier it got.

The other night, he and Graciela had gone out for drinks at the Riviera and dinner at the Columbia and then caught a show at the Satin Sky. They'd been accompanied by Sal Urso, who was Joe's full-time driver now, and their car was shadowed by Lefty Downer, who watched them when Dion was dealing with other matters. The bartender at the Riviera had tripped and fallen to one knee trying to get Graciela's chair pulled out for her before she arrived at the table. When the waitress at the Columbia spilled a drink on the table and some of it leaked onto Joe's pants, the maître d', the manager, and eventually the owner had come to the table to apologize. Joe then had to convince them not to fire the waitress. He argued that her mistake was honest, and that her service was, in all other respects, impeccable and had been every time they'd been lucky to have her service their table. (*Service.* Joe hated that word.) The men had relented, of course, but as Graciela reminded him on their way to Satin Sky, what else would they say to Joe's face? See if she still has a job next week, Graciela said. At the Satin Sky, the tables were all taken, but then before Joe and Graciela could turn back to the car where Sal waited, the manager, Pepe, rushed over to them and assured them that four patrons had just paid their check. Joe and Graciela watched two men approach a table of four, whisper in the ears of the couples sitting there, and hasten their exit with hands on their elbows.

At the table, neither Joe nor Graciela spoke for some time. They drank their drinks, they watched the band. Graciela looked around the room and then out at Sal standing by the car, his eyes never leaving them. She looked at the patrons and the waiters who pretended not to watch them.

She said, 'I've become the people my parents worked for.'

Joe said nothing because every response he thought of would be a lie.

Something was getting lost in them, something that was starting to live by day, where the swells lived, where the insurance salesmen and the bankers lived, where the civic meetings were held and the little flags were waved at the Main Street parades, where you sold out the truth of yourself for the story of yourself.

But along the sidewalks lit by dim, yellow lamps and in the alleys and abandoned lots, people begged for food and blankets. And if you got past them, their children worked the next corner.

The reality was, he liked the story of himself. Liked it better than the truth of himself. In the truth of himself, he was second-class and grubby and always out of step. He still had his Boston accent and didn't know how to dress right, and he thought too many thoughts that most people would find 'funny.' The truth of himself was a scared little boy, mislaid by his parents like reading glasses on a Sunday afternoon, treated to random kindnesses by older brothers who came without notice and departed without warning. The truth of himself was a lonely boy in an empty house, waiting for someone to knock on his bedroom door and ask if he was okay.

The story of himself, on the other hand, was of a gangster prince. A man who had a full-time driver and bodyguard. A man of wealth and stature. A man for whom people abandoned their seats simply because he coveted them.

Graciela *was* right – they had become the people her parents worked for. But they were better versions. And her parents, hungry as they were, would have expected no less. You couldn't fight the Haves. The only thing you could do was become them to such a degree that they came to you for what they had not.

He left the veranda and reentered the hotel. He turned his flashlight back on, saw the great wide room where high society had been poised to drink and eat and dance and do whatever else it was that high society did.

What else *did* high society do?

He couldn't think of an answer right off.

What else did people do?

They worked. When they could find it. Even when they couldn't, they raised families, drove their cars if they could afford the upkeep and gas. They went to movies or listened to the radio or caught a show. They smoked.

And the rich . . . ?

They gambled.

Joe could see it in a great smash of light. While the rest of the country lined up for soup and begged for spare change, the rich remained rich. And idle. And bored.

This restaurant he walked through, this restaurant that never was, wasn't a restaurant at all. It was a casino floor. He could see the roulette wheel in the center, the craps tables over by the south wall, the card tables along the north wall. He saw a Persian carpet and crystal chandeliers with ruby and diamond pendants.

He left the room and moved down the main corridor. The conference rooms he passed became music halls – big band in one, vaudeville in another, Cuban jazz in the third, maybe even a movie theater in the fourth.

The rooms. He ran up to the fourth floor and looked at the ones overlooking the Gulf. Jesus, they were breathtaking. Every floor would have its own butler, standing at the ready when you got off the lifts. He'd be at the service of all guests on that floor twenty-four hours a day. Every room would, of course, have a radio. And a ceiling fan. And maybe those French toilets he'd heard about, ones shot water up your ass. They'd have masseuses on call, twelve hours of room service, two, no three, concierges. He walked back down to the second floor. The flashlight needed another rest, so he shut it off, because he knew the staircase now. On the second floor, he found the ballroom. It was in the center of the floor with a large viewing rotunda above it, a place to stroll on warm spring nights and watch others of bottomless wealth dance under the stars painted on the domed roof.

What he saw, clearer than any clear he'd ever known, was that the rich would come in here for the dazzle and the elegance and the chance to risk it all against a rigged game, as rigged as the one they'd been running on the poor for centuries.

And he'd indulge it. He'd encourage it. And he'd profit from it.

Nobody – not Rockefeller, not Du Pont or Carnegie or J. P. Morgan – beat the house. Unless they were the house. And in this casino, the only house was him.

He shook his flashlight several times and turned it on.

For some reason, he was surprised to find them waiting for him – RD Pruitt and two other men. RD, in a stiff tan suit and a black string tie. The cuffs of his trousers stopped just short of his black shoes, exposing the white socks underneath. He had two boys with him – 'shine runners by the look of them, smelling of corn, sour mash, and methanol. No suits on these boys—just short ties on short collar shirts, wool trousers held up by suspenders.

They turned their flashlights on Joe, and it was all he could do not to blink into them.

RD said, 'You came.'

'I came.'

'Where's my brother-in-law?'

'He didn't come.'

'Just as well.' He pointed at the boy to his right. 'This here is Carver Pruitt, my cousin.' He pointed at the boy on his left. 'And *his* cousin on his mama's side? Harold LaBute.' He turned to them. 'Boys, this here is the one killed Kelvin. Careful now, he might decide to kill you all.'

Carver Pruitt raised his rifle to his shoulder. 'Not likely.'

'This one?' RD sidestepped along the ballroom, pointing at Joe. 'He's rat tricky. You take your eye off that pea shooter, I promise it'll be in his hands.'

'Aww,' Joe said, 'shucks.'

'You a man of your word?' RD asked Joe.

'Depends on who I give it to.'

'So you ain't come alone like I ordered.'

'No,' Joe said, 'I ain't come alone.'

'Well, where they at?'

'Shit, RD, I tell you that, I spoil the fun.'

'We watched you come in,' RD said. 'We been sitting out there three hours. You show up an hour early, think you get the drop on us?' He chuckled. 'So we know you came alone. How you like that?'

'Trust me,' Joe said, 'I'm not alone.'

RD crossed the ballroom, and his guns followed him until they were all standing in the center.

The switchblade Joe had brought with him was already open, the base of the handle tucked lightly under the band of the wristwatch he wore solely for this occasion. All he had to do was flex his wrist and the blade would drop into his palm.

'I don't want no sixty percent.'

'I know that,' Joe said.

'What you think I want then?'

'Don't know,' Joe said. 'I suspect? I suspect a return to, I dunno, the way things *used to be*? Am I warm?'

'You about on the griddle.'

'But there wasn't no way things used to be,' Joe said. 'That's our problem, RD. I spent two years in prison doing nothing but reading. Know what I found out?'

'No. You tell me, though, won't ya?'

'Found out we were always fucked. Always killing each other and raping and stealing and laying waste. It's who we are, RD. Ain't no Used to Be. Ain't no better days.'

RD said, 'Uh-huh.'

'You know what this place could be?' Joe said. 'You realize what we could do with this spot?'

'I do not.'

'Build the biggest casino in the United States.'

'Ain't nobody going to allow gambling.'

'Gotta disagree with you, RD. Whole country's in the tank, banks going under, cities going bankrupt, people out of work.'

''Cause we got us a Communist for a president.'

'No,' Joe said, 'not even close, actually. But I'm not here to debate politics with you, RD. I'm here to tell you that the reason Prohibition will end is because—'

'Prohibition ain't gonna end in a God-fearing country.'

'Yes, it will. Because the country needs all the millions it didn't get the past ten years on tariffs and import taxes and distribution taxes and interstate transport levies and, shit, you name it – could be billions they gave away. And they're going to ask me and people like me – you, for example – to make millions of dollars selling legal booze so we can save the country for them. And that's exactly why, in the spirit of the moment, they'll allow this state to legalize gambling. Long as we buy off the right county commissioners, the right city councillors and state senators. We could do that. And you could be part of it, RD.'

'I don't want to be part of nothing with you.'

'Then why are you here?'

'To tell you to your face, mister, that you're a cancer. You're the pestilence that gonna bring this country to its knees. You and your nigger whore girlfriend and your dirty spic friends and your dirty dago friends. I'm a take the Parisian. Not sixty percent – the whole place. Then? I'm a *take* all your clubs. I'm a take everything you got. Might even go by your fancy house and tear me off a piece that nigger girl 'fore I cut her throat.' He looked back at his boys and laughed. He turned to Joe again. 'You ain't got this yet, but you leaving town, boy. You just forgot to pack your bags.'

Joe looked into RD's bright, mean eyes. Stared deep into them until he got all the way past anything bright and was left with nothing but the mean. It was like staring into the eyes of a dog beat so much and starved so much and uglied so much that all it had to give back to the world was its teeth.

In that moment, he pitied him.

RD Pruitt saw that pity in Joe's eyes. And what surged up in his own was a howl of outrage. And a knife. Joe saw the knife coming in his eyes and by the time he glanced down at RD's hand, he'd already buried it in Joe's abdomen.

Joe gripped RD's wrist, gripped it fiercely, so RD couldn't move that knife right, left, up, or down. Joe's own knife clattered to the floor. RD struggled against Joe's grip, both their teeth gritted now.

'I got you,' RD said. 'I got you.'

Joe removed his hands from RD's wrist and punched the heels of his palms into the center of RD and chucked him back. The knife slid back out and Joe fell on the floor and RD laughed and the two boys with him laughed.

'Got you!' RD said and walked toward Joe.

Joe watched his own blood drip from the blade. He held up a hand. 'Wait.'

RD stopped. 'That's what everyone says.'

'I wasn't talking to you.' Joe looked up into the darkness, saw the stars on the dome above the rotunda. 'Okay. Now.'

'Then who you talking to?' RD said, a step too slow, always a step too slow, which was probably what made him so ass-dumb mean.

Dion and Sal Urso turned on the searchlights they'd lugged up to the rotunda this afternoon. It was like a harvest moon popping out from behind a bank of storm clouds. The ballroom turned white.

When the bullets rained down, RD Pruitt, his cousin, Carver, and Carver's cousin, Harold, did the bone-yard foxtrot, like they were having terrible coughing fits while running across hot coals. Dion, of late, had turned into an artist with the Thompson, and he stitched an *X* up one side and down the other of RD Pruitt's body. By the time they stopped firing, scraps of the three men were flung all over the ballroom.

Joe heard their footsteps on the stairs as they ran down to him.

Dion called to Sal when they entered the ballroom, 'Get the doc', get the doc'.'

Sal's footsteps ran the other way as Dion ran over to Joe and ripped open his shirt.

'Oooh, Nellie.'

'What? Bad?'

Dion shrugged off his coat and then tore off his own shirt. He wadded it up and pressed it to the wound. 'Hold it there.'

'Bad?' Joe repeated.

'Ain't good,' Dion said. 'How do you feel?'

'Feet are cold. Stomach's on fire. I want to scream actually.'

'Scream, then,' Dion said. 'Ain't no one else around.'

Joe did. The force of it shocked him. It echoed all over the hotel.

'Feel better?'

'You know what?' Joe said. 'No.'

'Then don't do it again. Well, he's on his way. The doc'.'

'You bring him with you?'

Dion nodded. 'He's on the boat. Sal's already hit the signal light by now. He'll be motoring up to the dock lickety-split.'

'That's good.'

'Why didn't you make some kind of noise when he put it in? We couldn't fucking see you up there. We just kept waiting for the signal.'

'I don't know,' Joe said. 'It seemed important not to give him the satisfaction. Oh, Jesus, this hurts.'

Dion gave him his hand and Joe clenched it.

'Why'd you let him get so close if you weren't going to stab him?'

'So what?'

'So close? With the knife? You were supposed to stab *him*.'

'I shouldn't have shown him those pictures, D.'

'You showed him pictures?'

'No. What? No. I mean Figgis. I shouldn't have done it.'

'Christ. That's what we had to do to put this fucking mad dog down.'

'It's not the right price.'

'But it's the price. You don't go letting this piece of shit stab you because the price is the price.'

'Okay.'

'Hey. Stay awake.'

'Stop slapping my face.'

'Stop closing your eyes.'

'It's going to make a nice casino.'

'What?'

'Trust me,' Joe said.

CHAPTER TWENTY

Mi Gran Amor

Five weeks.

That's how long he spent in a hospital bed. First in the Gonzalez Clinic on Fourteenth, just up the block from the Circulo Cubano, and then, under the alias Rodriguo Martinez, at the Centro Asturiano Hospital twelve blocks east. The Cubans might have fought with the Spaniards and the southern Spaniards might have fought with the northern Spaniards, and all of them had their beefs with the Italians and the American Negroes, but when it came to medical care, Ybor was a mutual aid collective. Everyone down there knew that no one in white Tampa would lift a finger to stop up a hole in their hearts if there was a Caucasian nearby who needed treatment for a fucking hangnail.

Joe was worked on by a team that Graciela and Esteban assembled – a Cuban surgeon who performed the original laparotomy, a Spanish specialist in thoracic medicine who oversaw the abdominal wall reconstruction during the second, third, and fourth surgeries, and an American doctor on the forefront of pharmacology who had access to the tetanus toxoid vaccine and regulated the administering of the morphine.

All the initial work done on Joe – the irrigation, cleansing, exploration, debridement, and suturing – had been done at the Gonzalez Clinic, but word slipped out he was there. Midnight riders of the KKK showed up the second night, galloping their horses up and down Ninth, the oily stench of their torches climbing through the window grates. Joe wasn't awake for any of this – he would never have more than scant recollection of the first two weeks after the stabbing – but Graciela would tell him all about it during the months of his recovery.

When the riders departed, thundering out of Ybor along Seventh and firing their rifles in the air, Dion sent men to follow them – two men per horse. Just before dawn, unknown assailants entered the homes of eight local men across the Greater Tampa/St Petersburg area and beat those men nearly to death, some in front of their families. When a wife intervened in Temple Terrace, they broke her arms with a bat. When a son in Egypt Lake tried to impede them, they tied the boy to a tree and let the ants and mosquitoes have at him. The most prominent of the victims, the dentist Victor Toll, was rumored to have replaced Kelvin Beauregard as the head of the town Klavern. Dr Toll was tied to the hood of his car. He was forced to lie there in a soup of his blood and smell his own house burn to the ground.

This effectively ended the power of the Ku Klux Klan in

Tampa for three years, but the Pescatore Family and the Coughlin-Suarez Gang had no way of knowing that, so they took no chances and moved Joe to the Centro Asturiano Hospital. There a surgical drain was inserted to offset the internal bleeding, the source of which mystified the original doctor, which is why they sent for the second doctor, a gentle Spaniard with the most beautiful fingers Graciela had ever seen.

By this point, Joe was mostly out of danger for hemorrhagic shock, the main killer of abdominal knifing victims. Second to that was liver damage, and his liver had been given a clean bill of health. This, the doctors told him much later, was thanks to his father's watch, which bore a new scrape on the dust cover. The point of the knife had glanced off the cover first, altering its path, however slightly.

The first doctor had done his best to check for damage to the duodenum, the rectum, the colon, the gallbladder, the spleen, and the terminal ileum, but the conditions had not been ideal. Joe had been stabilized on the dirty floor of an abandoned building and then moved across the bay on a boat. By the time they got him into an operating room, more than an hour had passed.

The second doctor who examined Joe suspected, due to the angle the blade had traveled during its peritoneal penetration, that there was damage to the spleen, and they cut Joe open again. The Spanish doctor was on the money. He repaired the nick in Joe's spleen and removed the toxic bile that had begun to ulcerate his abdominal wall, though some damage was already done. Joe would require two more surgeries before the month was out.

After the second surgery, he woke to someone sitting at the foot of his bed. His vision was blurred to the point that it turned the air to gauze. But he could make out a thick head and a long jaw. And a tail. The tail thumped against the sheet over his leg and the panther came into focus. It stared at him with its hungry yellow eyes. Joe's throat constricted and the flesh that covered it was slick with sweat.

The panther licked its upper lip and nose.

It yawned, and Joe wanted to close his eyes in the face of those magnificent teeth, the white of every bone they'd ever cracked in half and torn the meat from.

The mouth closed and the yellow eyes found him again and the cat placed its front paws on his stomach and walked up his body to his head.

Graciela said, 'What cat?'

He stared up into her face, blinking at the sweat. It was morning; the air coming through the windows was cool and bore the scent of camellias.

After the surgeries, he was also prohibited from having sex for three months. Alcohol, Cuban food, shellfish, nuts, and corn were forbidden. If he feared that the lack of love-making would drive him and Graciela apart (and he did; so did she), it actually had the opposite effect. By the second month, he learned a different way to satisfy her, using his mouth, a way he'd stumbled upon by accident a few times over the years, but which now became his sole method of giving her pleasure. Kneeling before her, her ass cupped in his hands, his mouth covering the gateway to her womb, a gateway he'd come to think of as sacred and sinful and lux-uriously slippery all at the same time, he felt he'd finally found something worth taking a knee for. If surrendering all preconceived notions of what a man was expected to give and receive from a woman was what it took to feel as pure and useful as he felt with his head between Graciela's thighs, then he wished he'd lost those notions years ago. Her initial protestations – *no, you can't; a man does not do that; I must bathe; you cannot possibly like the taste* – gave way to something bordering on addiction. For the final month before she could return the favor, Joe realized they were averaging five acts of oral gratification a day.

When the doctors finally cleared him, he and Graciela closed the shutters of their home on Ninth and filled the icebox on the second floor with food and champagne and confined themselves to the canopy bed or the claw-foot tub for two days. Near the end of the second day, lying in the red dusk, the shutters reopened to the street, the ceiling fan drying their bodies, Graciela said, 'There will never be another.'

'What's that?'

'Man.' She ran her palm over his patchwork abdomen. 'You are my man until death.'

'Yeah?'

She pressed her open mouth to his neck and exhaled. 'Yes, yes, yes.'

'What about Adan?'

For the first time he saw contempt enter her eyes at the mention of her husband.

'Adan is no man. You, *mi gran amor,* are a man.'

'You're certainly all woman,' he said. 'Christ, I get so lost in you.'

'I get lost in you.'

'Well, then . . .' He looked around the room. He'd waited so long for this day, he wasn't sure how to treat it now that it had arrived. 'You'll never get a divorce in Cuba, right?'

She shook her head. 'Even if I could return under my own name, the Church does not allow it.'

'So you'll always be married to him.'

'In name,' she said.

'But what's a name?' he said.

She laughed. 'Agreed.'

He moved her on top of him and looked up her brown body into her brown eyes. *'Tú eres mi esposa.'*

She wiped at her eyes with both hands, a small wet laugh escaping her. 'And you are my husband.'

'Para siempre.'

She placed her warm palms on his chest and nodded. 'Forever.'

CHAPTER TWENTY-ONE

Light My Way

Business continued to boom.

Joe began greasing the skids on the Ritz deal. John Ringling was open to selling the building but not the land. So Joe had his lawyers work with Ringling's to see if they could reach an accommodation that would suit both. Lately the two sides had investigated a ninety-nine-year lease but had gotten hung up on air rights with the county. Joe had one set of bagmen buying the inspectors in Sarasota County, another set up in Tallahassee working on state politicians, and a third group in Washington targeting members of the IRS and senators who frequented whorehouses, gambling parlors, and opium dens the Pescatore Family had stakes in.

His earliest success was to get bingo decriminalized in Pinellas County. He then got a statewide bingo decriminalization bill on the docket, to be heard by the state legislature in the autumn session and possibly put on the ballot as early as 1932. His friends in Miami, a much easier town to buy, helped soften the state even further when Dade and Broward Counties legalized pari-mutuel betting. Joe and Esteban had crawled out on a limb to buy up land for their Miami friends, and now that land was being turned into racetracks.

Maso had flown down to take a look at the Ritz. He'd survived a bout with cancer recently, though no one but Maso and his doctors knew what kind. He claimed to have come through it with flying colors, though it had left him bald and frail. Some even whispered that his thinking had grown muddy, though Joe saw no evidence of it. He'd loved the property and he'd liked Joe's logic – if there was ever a time to strike at the gambling taboos, it was now, as Prohibition tragically collapsed before their eyes. The money they'd lose on the legalization of booze would go right into the government's pocket, but the money they'd lose on legal casino and racetrack taxation would be offset by the profit they'd make from people dumb enough to bet against the house on a mass scale.

The bagmen also began to report back that Joe's hunch was looking good. The country was soft enough for this. You had cash-strapped municipalities from one end of Florida to the other and one end of the country to the other. Joe had sent his men out with pledges of infinite dividends – a casino tax, a hotel tax, a food and beverage tax, an entertainment tax, a room tax, a liquor license tax, plus – and all the pols loved this one – an excess revenue tax. If, on any given day, the casino cleared more than eight hundred thousand dollars, the casino would kick 2 percent of it back to the state. Truth was, any time the casino came close to clearing eight hundred large, they'd skim the take blind. But the politicians with their small plates and their big eyes didn't need to know that.

By late '31, he had two junior senators, nine members of the U.S. House of Representatives, four senior senators, thirteen county representatives, eleven city councillors, and two judges in his pocket. He'd also bought off his old KKK rival, Hopper Hewitt, editor of the *Tampa Examiner,* who'd begun running editorials and hard news stories that questioned the logic of allowing so many people to starve when a first-class casino on Florida's Gulf Coast could put them all to work, which would give them the money to buy up all those foreclosed houses, which would need lawyers to come off the breadlines to do the closings proper, who would need clerical staff to make sure it was written up nice.

As Joe drove him to his train for the return journey, Maso said, 'Whatever you need to do on this, you do.'

'Thanks,' Joe said, 'I will.'

'You've done some real good work down here.' Maso patted his knee. 'Don't think it won't be taken into consideration.'

Joe didn't know what his work could be 'taken into consideration' for. He'd built something down here out of the mud, and Maso was talking to him like he'd found him a new grocer to shake down. Maybe there was something to those rumors about the old man's thinking of late.

'Oh,' Maso said as they neared Union Station, 'I heard you still got a rogue out there. That true?'

It took Joe a few seconds. 'You mean that 'shiner won't pay his dues?'

'That's the one,' Maso said.

369

The 'shiner was Turner John Belkin. He and his three sons sold white lightning out of their stills in unincorporated Palmetto. Turner John Belkin meant no harm to anyone; he just wanted to sell to the people he'd been selling to for a generation, run some games out of his back parlor, run some girls out of a house down the street. But he wouldn't come into the fold, no matter what. Wouldn't pay tribute, wouldn't sell Pescatore product, wouldn't do anything but go about his business as he'd always run it, and his father and grand-fathers had run it before him, going back to when Tampa was still called Fort Brooke and yellow fever killed three times more people than old age.

'I'm working on him,' Joe said.

'I hear you been working on him for six months now.'

'Three,' Joe admitted.

'Then get rid of him.'

The car pulled to a stop. Seppe Carbone, Maso's personal bodyguard, opened the door for him and stood waiting in the sun.

'I've got guys working on it,' Joe said.

'I don't want you to have guys working on it. I want you to end it. Personally, if you have to.'

Maso got out of the car, and Joe followed him to the train to see him off even though Maso said he didn't need to. But the truth was, Joe wanted to see Maso leave, needed to, so he could confirm that it was okay to breathe again, to relax. Having Maso around was like having an uncle move in with you for a couple of days and never leave. And worse, the uncle thought he was doing you a favor.

*

A few days after Maso left, Joe sent a couple guys to put a little scare into Turner John, but he put a scare into them instead, beat one into a hospital, and this without his sons or a weapon.

Joe met with Turner John a week later.

He told Sal to stay behind in the car and stood on the dirt road out front of the man's copper-roof shack, the porch collapsed on one end, just a Coca-Cola icebox sitting on the other end, so red and shiny Joe suspected it was polished every day.

Turner John's sons, three beefy boys in cotton long johns and not much else, not even shoes (though one wore a red wool sweater with snowflakes on it for some ungodly reason), frisked Joe and took his Savage .32 and then frisked him again.

After that, Joe went inside the shack and sat across from Turner John at a wood table with uneven legs. He tried adjusting the table, gave up, and then asked Turner John why he'd beaten his men. Turner John, a tall, skinny, and severe-looking man with eyes and hair the same brown as his suit, said because they'd come upon him with a threat in their eyes so clear wasn't no point waiting for it to leave their mouths.

Joe asked if he knew this meant Joe would have to kill him to save face. Turner John said he suspected as much.

'So,' Joe said, 'why you doing it? Why not just pay a bit of tribute?'

'Mister,' Turner John said, 'your father still with us?'

'No, he passed.'

'But you still his son, am I right?'

'I am.'

'You have twenty great-grandkids, you still be that man's son.'

Joe was unprepared for the flood of emotion that found him in that moment. He had to look away from Turner John before that flood found his eyes. 'Yes, I will.'

'You want to make him proud, right? Make him see you for a man?'

'Yeah,' Joe said. 'Of course I do.'

'Well, I'm the same way. I had me a fine daddy. Only beat me hard when I had it coming and never when he'd taken to drink. Mostly, he'd just whack my head when I snored. I'm a champeen in the snoring, sir, and my daddy just couldn't abide it when he was dog tired. Other than that, he was the finest of men. And a son wants his father to be able to look down and see his teachings took root. Right about now, Daddy's watching me and saying, "Turner John, I ain't raised you to pay tribute to another man didn't get down in the muck with you to earn his keep."' He showed Joe his big scarred palms. 'You want my money, Mr Coughlin? Well then you best set to working with me and my boys on the mash and helping us work our farm, till the soil, rotate the crops, milk the cows. You follow?'

'I follow.'

'Else, ain't nothing to discuss.'

Joe looked at Turner John, then up at the ceiling. 'You really think he's looking?'

Turner John revealed a mouth full of silver teeth. 'Mister, I know he is.'

Joe unzipped his fly and withdrew the derringer he'd

taken off Manny Bustamente a few years ago. He pointed it at Turner John's chest.

Turner John unleashed a long, slow breath.

Joe said, 'Man sets to a job, he's supposed to complete it. Right?'

Turner John licked his lower lip and never took his eyes off the gun.

'You know what kind of gun this is?' Joe asked.

'It's a woman's derringer.'

'No,' Joe said, 'it's a What Coulda Been.' He stood. 'You do whatever you want out here in Palmetto. You get me?'

Turner John blinked an affirmative.

'But don't you let me see your label or taste your product in Hillsborough or Pinellas County. Or Sarasota neither, Turner John. We clear on that?'

Turner John blinked again.

'I need to hear you say it,' Joe said.

'We clear,' Turner John said. 'You have my word.'

Joe nodded. 'What's your father thinking now?'

Turner John stared past the gun barrel, up Joe's arm and into his eyes. 'Thinking he came a damn sight close to having to put up with my snoring again.'

As Joe maneuvered to legalize gambling and buy the hotel, Graciela opened lodging of her own. Whereas Joe was after the Waldorf salad crowd, Graciela built accommodations for the fatherless and the husbandless. It was a national shame that men these days were leaving their families like armies during wartime. They left Hoovervilles and tenement apartments or, in the case of Tampa, the shotgun shacks locals

called *casitas,* went up the road to get milk or cadge a cigarette or because they'd heard a rumor of work, and they
never came back. Without men to protect them, the women
were sometimes victims of rape or forced into the basement
levels of prostitution. The children, suddenly fatherless and
possibly motherless, entered the streets and the back roads,
and the news that returned of them was rarely good.

Graciela came to Joe one night as he sat in the tub. She
brought them two cups of coffee laced with rum. She
removed her clothes and slipped under the water across
from him and asked him if she could take his name.

'You want to marry me?'

'Not in the Church. I can't.'

'Okay ...'

'But we are married, are we not?'

'Yes.'

'So I would like to call myself by your surname.'

'Graciela Dominga Maela Rosario Maria Concetta
Corrales Coughlin?'

She slapped his arm. 'I don't have that many names.'

He leaned in for a kiss, then leaned back. 'Graciela
Coughlin?'

'*Sí.*'

He said, 'I'd be honored.'

'Ah,' she said, 'good. I've bought some buildings.'

'You've bought *some* buildings?'

She looked at him, those brown eyes as innocent as a
deer's. 'Three. That, um, cluster? Yes. That cluster by the old
Perez factory?'

'On Palm?'

She nodded. 'And I would like to give shelter there to abandoned wives and their children.'

Joe wasn't surprised. Lately Graciela had talked about little else but these women.

'What happened to Latin American politics for a cause?'

'I fell in love with you.'

'So?'

'So you restrict my mobility.'

He laughed. 'I do, huh?'

'Terribly.' She smiled. 'It can work. Maybe someday we could even profit from it and it could stand as a model for the rest of the world.'

Graciela dreamed of land reform and farmers' rights and a fair distribution of wealth. She believed in fairness, essentially, a concept Joe was certain had left the earth about the time the earth left diapers.

'I don't know about a model for the rest of the world.'

'Why can't it work?' she said to him. 'A just world.' She splashed bubbles at him to show she was only half serious, but there was no 'half' about it really.

'You mean one where everyone lives on what they need and sits around singing songs and, shit, smiling all the time?'

She flicked suds into his face. 'You know what I mean. A good world. Why can't it be so?'

'Greed,' he said. He raised his arms to their bathroom. 'Look how we live.'

'But you give back. You gave a quarter of our money last year to the Gonzalez Clinic.'

'They saved my life.'

'The year before you built the library.'

'So they'd get books I like to read.'

'But all the books are in Spanish.'

'How do you think I learned the language?'

She propped her foot on his shoulder and used his hair to scratch an itch along the outside of her arch. She left it there and he gave it a kiss and found himself, as he often did at times like these, experiencing a peace so total he couldn't imagine a heaven that could compare. Compare to her voice in his eardrums, her friendship in his pocket, her foot on his shoulder.

'We can do good,' she said, looking down.

'We do,' he said.

'After so much bad,' she said softly.

She was looking into the suds below her breasts, disappearing into herself, loosing herself from this tub. Any moment, she'd reach for a towel.

'Hey,' he said.

Her eyelids rose.

'We're not bad. Maybe we're not good. I dunno. I just know we're all scared.'

'Who's scared?' she said.

'Who isn't? The whole world. We tell ourselves we believe in this god or that god, this afterlife or that one, and maybe we do, but what we're all thinking at the same time is, "What if we're *wrong*? What if this *is* it? Well if it is, shit, I better get me a real big house and a real big car and a whole bunch of nice tie pins and a pearl-handled walking stick and a—"'

She was laughing now.

'"—a toilet that washes my ass *and* my armpits. Because I

376

need one of those."' He'd been chuckling too, but the chuckles trailed off into the suds. '"But, wait, I believe in God. Just to be safe. But I believe in greed too. Just to be safe."'

'And that's all it is – we're scared?'

'I don't know if that's all it is,' he said. 'I just know we're scared.'

She pulled the suds around her neck like a scarf and nodded. 'I want it to matter that we were here.'

'I know you do. Look, you want to rescue these women and their kids? Good. I love you for that. But some bad people are going to want to stop some of those women from leaving their grips.'

'I know that,' she said in a singsong that told him he was naive to think she didn't. 'That's why I'll need a couple of your men.'

'A couple?'

'Well, four for starters. But, *mi amado*?' She smiled at him. 'I want the toughest ones you've got.'

That was also the year Chief Irving Figgis's daughter, Loretta, returned to Tampa.

She got off the train accompanied by her father, their arms entwined. Loretta was dressed from head to toe in black, as if she were in mourning, and the way Irv held so tight to her arm, maybe she was.

Irv locked her up in his house in Hyde Park, and no one saw either of them for the whole of the season. Irv had taken a leave of absence after he'd gone to L.A. to retrieve her and he extended it through the fall when he got back. His wife moved out, taking his son with her, and neighbors said the only sound they ever heard from over there was the sound of praying. Or chanting. There was some argument over the particulars.

When they emerged from the house at the end of October, Loretta wore white. At a Pentecostal tent meeting later that evening, she declared that her decision to wear white hadn't been hers at all; it had been Jesus Christ's, to whose teachings she would now be wed. Loretta took the stage at the tent in Fiddlers Cove Field that night and she spoke of her descent into the world of vice, of the demons alcohol and heroin and marijuana that had led her there, of wanton fornication that led to prostitution that led to more heroin and nights of such sinful debauchery she knew Jesus had blocked them from her memory in order to keep her from taking her own life. And why was he so interested in keeping her alive? Because he wanted her to speak his truth to the sinners of Tampa, St Petersburg, Sarasota, and Bradenton. And if he saw fit, she was to carry that message across Florida and even across these here United States.

What differentiated Loretta from so many speakers who stood before worshippers in the revival tents was that Loretta spoke with no fire and no brimstone. She never raised her voice. She spoke so softly, in fact, that many a listener had to lean forward. Occasionally glancing sideways at her father, who'd grown quite stern and unapproachable since her return, she gave plaintive testimony to a fallen world. She didn't claim to know the will of God so much as she claimed to hear the crestfallen dismay of Christ at what his children had gotten up to. So much good could be salvaged from this world, so much virtue could be reaped, if it were virtue that was sown in the first place.

'They are saying this country will soon return to the despair of wanton alcohol consumption, of husbands beating their wives because of the rum, of carrying home venereal disease because of the rye, of falling to sloth and losing their jobs and the banks putting even more little ones out in the street because of the gin. Don't blame the banks. Don't blame the banks,' she whispered. 'Blame those who profit from sin, from the peddling of flesh and the weakening of it through spirits. Blame the bootleggers and the bordello owners and those who allow them to spread their filth through our fair city and in God's sight. Pray for them. And then ask God for guidance.'

God apparently guided some of the good citizens of Tampa to raid a couple of Coughlin-Suarez clubs and take axes to the rum and beer barrels. When Joe heard, he had Dion contact a guy in Valrico who made steel barrels and they put them in all the speaks, lifted the wooden casks into them, and waited to see who would come through their doors and take a swing now, snap their holy elbows off their holy fucking arms.

Joe was sitting in the front office of his cigar export company – a fully legitimate corporation; they lost a small fortune every year exporting superior tobacco to countries like Ireland and Sweden and France, where cigars had never really caught on – when Irv and his daughter walked through the front door.

Irv gave Joe a quick nod but wouldn't meet his eyes. In the years since Joe had shown him those pictures of his daughter, he hadn't met Joe's eyes once and Joe estimated they'd passed each other on the street at least thirty times.

'My Loretta has some words for you.'

Joe looked up at the pretty young woman in her white dress and bright, wet eyes. 'Yes, ma'am. Do take a seat if you'd like.'

'I'd prefer to stand, sir.'

'As you wish.'

'Mr Coughlin,' she said, clasping her hands over her thighs, 'my father said there was once a good man in you.'

'I wasn't aware that man had departed.'

Loretta cleared her throat. 'We know of your philanthropy. And that of the woman with whom you choose to cohabitate.'

'The woman with whom I choose to cohabitate,' Joe said, just to try it out.

'Yes, yes. We understand she is quite active in charitable work within the Ybor community and even in Greater Tampa.'

'She has a name.'

'But her good works are strictly temporal in nature. She refuses all religious affiliation and rebuffs all attempts to embrace the one true Lord.'

'She is named Graciela. And she is a Catholic,' Joe said.

'But until she publicly embraces the Lord's hand moving through her work, she is – however well intentioned – aiding the devil.'

'Wow,' Joe said, 'you completely lost me on that one.'

She said, 'Luckily, you have not lost me. For all your good works, Mr Coughlin, we both know they are unmitigated by your evil deeds and your distance from the Lord.'

'How so?'

'You profit from the illegal addictions of others. You profit off people's weakness and their need for sloth and gluttony and libidinous behavior.' She gave him a sad and kindly smile. 'But you can free yourself of that.'

Joe said, 'I don't want to.'

'Of course you do.'

'Miss Loretta,' Joe said, 'you seem like a lovely person. And I understand Preacher Ingalls has seen his flock triple since you've begun preaching before them.'

Irv held up five fingers, his eyes on the floor.

'Oh,' Joe said, 'I'm sorry. So attendance has quintupled. My.'

Loretta's smile never left her face. It was soft and sad. It knew what you were going to say before you said it and it judged those words pointless before they left your mouth.

'Loretta,' Joe said, 'I sell a product people enjoy so much that the Eighteenth Amendment will be overturned within the year.'

'That's not true,' Irv said, his jaw set.

'Or,' Joe said, 'it is. Either way, Prohibition is dead. They used it to keep the poor in line and it failed. They used it to make the middle class more industrious, and instead the middle class got curious. More booze was drunk in the last ten years than ever before, and that's because people wanted it and didn't want to be told they couldn't have it.'

'But, Mr Coughlin,' Loretta said reasonably, 'the same could be said of fornication. People want it and they don't want to be told they can't have it.'

'Nor should they.'

'I'm sorry?'

'Nor should they,' Joe said. 'If people wish to fornicate, I see no pressing reason to stop them, Miss Figgis.'

'And if they wish to lie down with animals?'

'Do they?'

'I'm sorry.'

'Do people wish to lie down with animals?'

'Some do. And their sickness will spread if you have your way.'

'I'm afraid I don't see a correlation between drinking and fornication with animals.'

'But that isn't to say there isn't a correlation.'

Now she sat, hands still clasped in her lap.

'Sure it is,' Joe said. 'That's exactly what I said.'

'But that's just your opinion.'

'As some would call your belief in God.'

'So you do not believe in God?'

'No, Loretta, I just don't believe in your God.'

Joe looked over at Irv because he could feel the man seething, but, as always, Irv wouldn't meet his eyes, just stared at his hands, which were clasped into fists.

'Well, he believes in you,' she said. 'Mr Coughlin, you will renounce your evil path. I just know it. I can see it in you. You will repent and become baptized in Jesus Christ. And you will make a great prophet. I see this as clearly as I see a sinless city on a hill, here in Tampa. And, yes, Mr Coughlin, before you can make fun, I realize there are no hills in Tampa.'

'Well, none you'd notice, even if you were driving fast.'

She smiled a real smile, and it was the one he remembered

from a few years ago, coming across her at the soda fountain or in the magazine section of Morin Drugstore.

Then it transformed into the sad, frozen one again, and her eyes brightened and she extended a gloved hand across the desk to him, and he shook it, thinking of the track scars it covered, as Loretta Figgis said, 'I will one day spirit you off your path, Mr Coughlin. Of that, you can be sure. I feel this to my bones.'

'Just because you feel it,' Joe said, 'doesn't make it so.'

'But that doesn't mean it isn't so.'

'I'll grant you that.' Joe looked up at her. 'Now why can't you grant my opinions the same benefit of the doubt?'

Loretta's sad smile brightened. 'Because they're wrong.'

Unfortunately for Joe, Esteban, and the Pescatore Family, as Loretta's popularity rose, so did her legitimacy. After a few months, her proselytizing began to endanger the casino deal. Those who'd initially brought her up in public company had done so mostly to ridicule her or marvel at the circumstances that had brought her to her current state – all-American police chief's daughter goes to Hollywood, comes back a raving loon with track marks in her arms that yokels mistake for stigmata. But the tone of the conversation began to shift not only as the roads clogged with both cars and foot traffic on nights it was rumored Loretta would appear at a revival, but also as regular townsfolk were exposed to her. Loretta, far from hiding from the public eye, engaged it. Not just in Hyde Park but also in West Tampa, Port of Tampa, and Ybor as well, where she liked to come to purchase coffee, her one vice.

She didn't talk religion much during daylight hours. She was unfailingly polite, always quick to ask after someone's health or the health of their loved ones. She never forgot a name. And she remained, even as the hard year of her 'trials,' as she called them, had aged her, a strikingly beautiful woman. And beautiful in a conspicuously American way – full lips the same color as her burgundy hair, eyes honest and blue, skin as smooth and white as the sweet cream at the top of the morning milk bottle.

The fainting spells began to occur late in '31 after the European banking crisis sucked the rest of the world into its vortex and killed all remaining hope for financial recovery. The spells came without warning or theatrics. She would be speaking of the ills of liquor or lust or (more and more lately) gambling – always in a quiet, slightly tremulous voice – and the visions God had sent her of a Tampa burned black by its own sins, a smoke-wisped wasteland of charred soil and smoldering piles of wood where homes had once stood, and she would remind them all of Lot's wife and implore them not to look back, never to look back, but to look ahead to a shining city of white homes and white clothing and white people united in love of Christ and prayer and earnest desire to leave behind a world their children could be proud of. Somewhere in this sermon, her eyes would roll left and then right, her body swaying with them, and then she would drop. Sometimes she convulsed, sometimes a small amount of spittle leaked over her beautiful lips, but mostly she just appeared to be asleep. It was suggested (but only in the lowest circles) that part of the surge in her popularity stemmed from how lovely she looked when she lay prone on a stage, dressed in thin white crepe, thin enough so you could see her small, perfectly formed breasts and her slim, unblemished legs.

When Loretta lay on the stage like that, she was proof of God because only God could make something that beautiful, that fragile, and that powerful.

And so her swelling ranks of followers took her causes quite personally and none more so than the attempts of a local gangster to ravage their communities with the scourge of gambling. Soon the congressmen and the councilmen returned to Joe's bagmen with 'No,' or 'We'll need more time to consider all the variables,' though Joe noted the one thing they didn't return with was his money.

The window was closing fast.

If Loretta Figgis were to meet with an untimely end – but in such a way as to be plausibly considered an 'accident' – then after a respectful period of mourning, the casino idea would reach full flower. She loved Jesus so much, Joe told himself, he'd be doing her a service by bringing them together.

So he knew what he had to do, but he had yet to give the order.

He went to see her preach. He stopped shaving for a day and dressed the part of a man who sold farming equipment or possibly owned a feed store – clean dungarees, white shirt, string tie, a dark canvas sport coat and a straw cowboy hat pulled low over his eyes. He had Sal drive him to the edge of the campgrounds the Reverend Ingalls was using that night, and he made his way down a thin dirt road between a small stand of pines until he reached the back of the crowd.

Along the shore of a pond, someone had built a small

stage out of crate board, and Loretta stood on it with her father on the left and the reverend on the right, heads bowed. Loretta was speaking of a recent vision or dream (Joe came too late to hear which). With her back to the dark pond, in her white dress and white bonnet, she stood out against the black night like a midnight moon in a sky swept of stars. A family of three, she said – mother, father, tiny baby – had arrived in a strange land. The father, a business-man sent by his company to this strange land, had been instructed to wait for their driver inside the railway station and not venture outside. But it was hot inside the terminal and they had traveled far and wished to see their new land. They stepped outside and were instantly beset upon by a leopard as black as the inside of a coal bucket. And before the family had so much as its wits about them, the leopard had torn open their throats with its teeth. The man lay dying, watching the leopard slake itself on the blood of his wife, when another man appeared and shot that black leopard dead. This man told the dying businessman that he was the driver who had been hired by the company and all they'd had to do was wait for him.

But they hadn't waited. Why hadn't they waited?

And so it is with Jesus, Loretta said. Can you wait? Can you not give yourselves over to the earthly temptations that will tear your families asunder? Can you find a way to keep your loved ones safe from the beasts of prey until our Lord God and Savior returns?

'Or are you too weak?' Loretta asked.

'No!'

'Because I know that in my darkest hours, *I'm* too weak.'

'No!'

'I am,' Loretta cried. 'But he gives me strength.' She pointed at the sky. 'He fills my heart. But I need you to help me complete his wishes. I need your strength to continue preaching his word and doing his works and keeping the black leopards from eating our children and staining our hearts with endless sin. Will you help me?'

The crowd said *Yes* and *Amen* and *Oh, yes.* When Loretta closed her eyes and began to sway, the crowd opened its eyes and surged forward. When Loretta sighed, they moaned. When she fell to her knees, they gasped. And when she lay on her side, they exhaled as one. They reached for her without stepping any closer to the stage, as if some invisible barrier lay between them. They reached for something that wasn't Loretta. Cried out to it. Promised all to it.

Loretta was its gateway, the portal by which they entered a world without sin, without dark, without fear. One where you were never alone. Because you had God. And you had Loretta.

'Tonight,' Dion said to him on the third-floor gallery of Joe's home. 'She's gotta go.'

'You don't think I've thought about it?' Joe said.

'Thinking about it ain't the issue,' Dion said. 'Acting on it is, boss.'

Joe pictured the Ritz, light pouring from its windows onto the dark sea, music flowing through its porticos and out across the Gulf as the dice rattled on the tables and the crowds cheered a winner, and he presided over all of it in tux and tails.

He asked himself, as he had so often over the past few weeks, What is one life?

People always died during building construction or laying steel tracks in the sun. They died from electrocution and other industrial accidents every single day, the world over. And for what? For the building of something good, something that would employ their fellow countrymen, put food on the table of the human race.

How would Loretta's death be any different?

'It just would,' he said.

'What?' Dion peered at him.

Joe held up a hand in apology. 'I can't do it.'

'I *can*,' Dion said.

Joe said, 'If you buy a ticket to the dance, then you know the consequences or you damn well should. But these people who sleep while the rest of us stay up? Work their jobs, mow their lawns? They didn't buy a ticket. Which means they don't suffer the same penalties for their mistakes.'

Dion sighed. 'She's jeopardizing the entire fucking deal.'

'I know that.' Joe was thankful for the sunset, for the darkness that had found them on the gallery. If Dion could see his eyes clearly, he'd know how shaky Joe was with the decision, how close he was to crossing the line and never looking back. Christ, she was *one* woman. 'But my mind's made up. No one touches a hair on her head.'

'You'll regret this,' Dion said.

Joe said, 'No shit.'

A week later, when John Ringling's minions asked for a meeting, Joe knew it was over. If not completely, certainly tabled for a while. The entire country was going wet again, wet with abandon, wet with fervor and joy, but Tampa, under Loretta Figgis's influence, was swinging the other way. If they couldn't trump her when it came to the acceptance of booze, which was a signature away from being legalized, they were sunk when it came to gambling. John Ringling's men told Joe and Esteban that their boss had decided to hold on to the Ritz a little longer, wait out the dip in the economy, and revisit his options at a later time.

The meeting was held in Sarasota. When Joe and Esteban left, they drove over to Longboat Key and stood looking at the gleaming Mediterranean Almost Was on the Gulf of Mexico.

'It would have been a great casino,' Joe said.

'You'll have another chance. Things swing back around.'

Joe shook his head. 'Not all things.'

CHAPTER TWENTY-TWO

Quench Not the Spirit

The last time Loretta Figgis and Joe saw each other alive was early in 1933. It had rained heavily for a week. That morning, the first cloudless day in some time, the ground fog rose so thick off the streets of Ybor it was as if the earth had turned itself upside down. Joe walked the boardwalk along Palm Avenue, distracted, Sal Urso pacing him from the opposite boardwalk, and Lefty Downer pacing both of them in a car inching along the center. Joe had just confirmed a rumor that Maso was considering another trip down here, his second in a year, and the fact that Maso hadn't told him himself didn't sit right. On top of that, stories in this morning's papers said that President-elect Roosevelt planned to sign the Cullen-Harrison Act as soon as someone put a pen in his hand, effectively ending Prohibition. Joe had known it could never last, but he still hadn't been prepared somehow. And if he was unprepared, he could only imagine how poorly all the mugs in the bootleg boomtowns like KC, Cincy, Chicago,

New York, and Detroit were going to take the news. He'd sat on his bed this morning and tried to read the article so he could identify the exact week or month Roosevelt was going to wield that most popular of pens, but he was distracted because Graciela was puking up last night's paella to beat the band. Normally, she had a cast-iron stomach, but lately the stress of running three shelters and eight different fund-raising groups was shredding her digestive system.

'Joseph.' She stood in the doorway and wiped her mouth with the back of her hand. 'We may need to face something.'

'What's that, doll?'

'I think I'm with child.'

For a few moments Joe thought she'd smuggled one of the street urchins back from the shelter with her. He actually glanced past her left hip before it dawned on him.

'You're . . . ?'

She smiled. 'Pregnant.'

He got off the bed and stood before her and wasn't sure if he should touch her because he was afraid she'd break.

She put her arms around his neck. 'It's okay. You're going to be a father.' She kissed him, her hands finding the back of his head where his scalp tingled. Actually everything tingled, as if he'd woken to find himself encased in fresh skin.

'Say something.' She looked at him, curious.

'Thanks,' he said because nothing else occurred to him.

'Thanks?' She laughed and kissed him again, mashing his lips with her own. 'Thanks?'

'You're going to be an amazing mother.'

She pressed her forehead to his. 'And you'll be a great father.'

If I live, he thought.

And knew she was thinking it too.

So he was a little off his feed that morning when he entered Nino's Coffee Shop without looking through the windows first.

There were only three tables in the coffee shop, a crime for a place that served coffee this good, and two of them were occupied by Klan. Not that an outsider would have recognized them as such, but Joe had no trouble seeing hoods even if they weren't wearing them – Clement Dover and Drew Altman and Brewster Engals, at one table, the older, smart guard; at the other, Julius Stanton, Haley Lewis, Carl Joe Crewson, and Charlie Bailey, morons all, more likely to set themselves on fire than any cross they were trying to burn. But, like a lot of dumb people who didn't have the sense to know how dumb they were, mean and merciless.

As soon as he stepped over the threshold, Joe knew it wasn't an ambush. He could see in their eyes that they hadn't expected to see him. They'd just come here for the coffee, maybe to intimidate the owners into paying some protection. Sal was right outside, but that wasn't the same thing as inside. Joe pushed his suit jacket back and left his hand there, one inch from his gun as he looked at Engals, the leader of this particular pack, a fireman with Engine 9 at Lutz Junction.

Engals nodded, a small smile growing on his lips, and he flicked his eyes at something behind Joe, at the third table by the window. Joe glanced over, saw Loretta Figgis sitting there, watching the whole thing happen. Joe removed his hand from his hip, let his suit jacket fall free. No one was getting into a gun battle with the Madonna of Tampa Bay sitting five feet away.

Joe nodded back and Engals said, 'Another time then.'

Joe tipped his hat and turned to exit when Loretta said, 'Mr Coughlin, sit. Please.'

Joe said, 'No, no, Miss Loretta. You look like you're having a peaceful morning without me disrupting it.'

'I insist,' she said as Carmen Arenas, the owner's wife, came to the table.

Joe shrugged and removed his hat. 'The usual, Carmen.'

'Yes, Mr Coughlin. Miss Figgis?'

'I will have another, yes.'

Joe sat and placed his hat on his knee.

'Do those gentlemen not like you?' Loretta asked.

Joe noticed she wasn't wearing white today. Her dress was more a light peach. In most people, you wouldn't notice, but pure white had become so identified with Loretta Figgis that seeing her in anything else was a bit like seeing her naked.

'They aren't going to invite me for Sunday dinner anytime soon,' Joe told her.

'Why?' She leaned into the table as Carmen brought their coffees.

'I lie down with mud people, work with mud people, fraternize with mud people.' He looked over his shoulder. 'I leave anything out, Engals?'

''Sides you killed four of our number?'

Joe nodded his thanks and turned back to Loretta. 'Oh, and they think I killed four friends of theirs.'

'Did you?'

'You're not wearing white,' he said.

'It's almost white,' she said.

'How will that go over with your' – he searched for the word but couldn't come up with anything better than – 'followers?'

'I don't know, Mr Coughlin,' she said, and there was no false brightness in her voice, no desperate serenity in her eyes.

The Klavern boys got up from their tables and filed past, each of them managing either to bump Joe's chair or hit his foot with his own.

'Be seeing *you*,' Dover said to him and then tipped his hat to Loretta. 'Ma'am.'

They filed out and then it was just Joe and Loretta and the sound of last night's rain ticking off the balcony gutter and down onto the boardwalk. Joe studied Loretta as he sipped his coffee. She'd lost the sharp light that had lived in her eyes since the day she walked back out of her father's house two years ago, having traded the black mourning dress of her death for the white dress of her rebirth.

'Why does my father hate you so much?'

'I'm a criminal. He used to be chief of police.'

'But he liked you then. He even pointed you out to me once when I was still in high school and said, "That's the mayor of Ybor. He keeps the peace."'

'He said that, huh?'

'He did.'

Joe drank some more coffee. 'Those were more innocent days, I guess.'

She sipped her own coffee. 'So what did you do to deserve his rancor?'

Joe shook his head.

Now it was her turn to study him for a long, uncomfortable minute. He held her eyes as she searched his. Searched until the realization dawned.

'You were how he knew where to find me.'

Joe said nothing, his jaw clenching and unclenching.

'It was you.' She nodded and looked down at the table. 'What did you have?'

She stared at him for another uncomfortable period of time before he answered.

'Photographs.'

'And you showed them to him.'

'I showed him two.'

'How many did you have?'

'Dozens.'

She looked down at the table again, turned her cup on its saucer. 'We're all going to hell.'

'I don't think so.'

'No?' She twirled the coffee cup again. 'Do you know what truth I've learned these last two years of preaching and fainting and thrusting my soul out to God?'

He shook his head.

'That *this* is heaven.' She indicated the street, the roof above their heads. 'We're in it now.'

'How come it feels so much like hell?'

'Because we fucked it all up.' Her sweet and serene smile returned. 'This is paradise. And it's lost.'

Joe was surprised by the depths of his own mourning for her loss of belief. For reasons he couldn't explain, he had hoped that if anyone did have a direct line to the Almighty, it was Loretta.

'When you started,' he asked her, 'you *did* believe, though, didn't you?'

She stared back at him with clear eyes. 'With such a certainty, it just had to be divinely inspired. It felt like my blood had been replaced with fire. Not burning fire, just a constant warmth that never ebbed. I'd felt that way as a child, I think. I felt safe and loved and *so sure* this is how life would always be. I would always have my daddy and my mommy and the world would look just like Tampa and everyone would know my name and wish good things for me. But I grew up, and I went west. And when all those beliefs turned out to be lies? When I realized I wasn't special, I wasn't safe?' She turned her arms to show him the track marks. 'I took the news poorly.'

'But after you came back here, after your ...'

'Trials?' she said.

'Yes.'

'I came back and my father chased my mother from the house and beat the devil from me and taught me to pray again on my knees and without wishing for personal gain. To pray as a supplicant. To pray as a sinner. And the flame returned. On my knees, by the bed I'd slept in as a child. I'd been on my knees all day. I'd been awake most of the week. And the flame found my blood, found my heart, and I felt *certain* again. Do you know how much I'd missed it? I'd missed it more than any drug, any love, any food, maybe more even than the God who supposedly bequeathed it to me. Certainty, Mr Coughlin. Certainty. It's the most gorgeous lie of them all.'

Neither said anything for a bit, long enough for Carmen

to return with fresh cups of coffee to replace the ones they'd emptied.

'My mother passed away last week. Did you know that?'

'I hadn't heard, Loretta, I'm sorry.'

She waved off his apology and drank some coffee. 'My father's beliefs and my beliefs drove her from our home. She would say at him, "You don't love God. You love the idea of being special to him. You want to believe he sees you." When I learned of her passing, I understood what she meant. I took no comfort in God. I don't *know* God. I just wanted my mommy back.' She nodded several times to herself.

A couple walked into the shop, the bell tinkling over the door as Carmen came out from behind the counter to seat them.

'I don't know if there's a God.' She fingered her coffee cup handle. 'I certainly hope there is. And I hope he is kind. Wouldn't that be swell, Mr Coughlin?'

'It would,' Joe said.

'I don't believe he casts people into eternal flame for fornication, as you pointed out. Or for believing in a version of him that is a little off the mark. I believe – or, I *want* to believe – he considers the worst sins to be those we commit in his name.'

He looked at her very carefully. 'Or those we commit against ourselves in despair.'

'Oh,' she said brightly, 'I'm not in despair. Are you?'

He shook his head. 'Not even close.'

'What's your secret?'

He chuckled. 'This is a little intimate for coffee shop chat.'

'I want to know. You seem ...' She looked around the café, and for a fleeting moment a wild abandonment slid through her eyes. 'You seem whole.'

He smiled and shook his head repeatedly.

'You do,' she said.

'No.'

'You *do*. What's the secret?'

He fingered his saucer for a moment, said nothing.

'Come now, Mr Cough—'

'Her.'

'I'm sorry?'

'Her,' Joe said. 'Graciela. My wife.' He looked across the table at her. 'I hope there's a God too. I so deeply hope that. But if there isn't? Then Graciela is enough.'

'But what if you lose her?'

'I don't intend to lose her.'

'But what if you do?' She leaned into the table.

'Then I would be all head, no heart.'

They sat in silence. Carmen came over and warmed their cups and Joe added a bit more sugar to his and looked at Loretta and felt the most powerful and inexplicable urge to hug her to him and tell her it would be okay.

'What are you going to do now?' he asked.

'How do you mean?'

'You're a pillar of this city. Hell, you came up against me at the height of my power and you won. The Klan couldn't do that. The law couldn't. But you did.'

'I didn't get rid of alcohol.'

'But you killed gambling. And until you came along? It was a lock.'

She smiled, then covered the smile with her hands. 'I did do that, didn't I?'

Joe smiled with her. 'Yes, you did. You've got thousands of people who will follow you right off a cliff, Loretta.'

She laughed a wet laugh and looked up at the tin ceiling. 'I don't want anyone to follow *me* anywhere.'

'Have you told them that?'

'He doesn't listen.'

'Irv?'

She nodded.

'Give him time.'

'He used to love my mother so much I remember him trembling sometimes when he got too close to her. Because he wanted to touch her so badly? But he couldn't because we children were around and it wasn't proper. Now she's died, and he didn't even go to her funeral. Because the God he imagines would have disapproved. The God he imagines doesn't share. My father sits in his chair every night, reading his Bible, blind with rage because men were allowed to touch his daughter the way he used to touch his wife. And worse.' She leaned into the table and rubbed at a stray grain of sugar with her index finger. 'He walks around the house in the dark whispering one word over and over.'

'What word?'

'*Repent.*' She looked up at him. 'Repent, repent, repent.'

'Give him time,' Joe said again, because he couldn't think of anything else to say.

Within a few weeks, Loretta went back to wearing white. Her preaching continued to pack them in. She'd added a few new wrinkles, though – tricks, some people scoffed – speaking in tongues, frothing at the mouth. And she spoke with twice the thunder and twice the volume.

Joe saw a picture of her in the paper one morning, preaching to a gathering of the General Council of the Assemblies of God in Lee County, and he didn't recognize her at first, even though she looked exactly the same.

President Roosevelt signed the Cullen-Harrison Act on the morning of March 23, 1933, legalizing the manufacture and sale of beer and wine with an alcohol content no greater than 3.2 percent. By the end of the year, FDR promised, the Eighteenth Amendment to the Constitution would be a memory.

Joe met with Esteban at the Tropicale. Joe was uncharacteristically late, something that had been happening a lot lately because his father's watch had started to run behind. Last week it consistently lost five minutes a day. Now it was averaging ten, sometimes fifteen. Joe kept meaning to get it fixed, but that would mean releasing it from his possession for however long the repair took and, even though he knew it was an irrational reaction, he couldn't bear the thought of that.

When Joe entered the back office, Esteban was framing yet another photograph he'd taken on his last trip to Havana, this one of the opening night of Zoot, his new club in the Old City. He showed the photo to Joe – pretty much like all the others, drunk, well-dressed swells and their well-dressed wives or girlfriends or escorts, a dancing girl or two over by the band, everyone glassy-eyed and joyous. Joe barely glanced at it before giving the requisite whistle of appreciation and Esteban turned it facedown on the mat that awaited it on the glass. He poured them drinks and set them on the desk amid the frame pieces and set to work joining the pieces, the smell of the glue so strong it even overpowered the smell of tobacco in his study, something Joe would have assumed impossible.

'Smile,' he said at one point and raised his glass. 'We are about to become extremely wealthy men.'

Joe said, 'If Pescatore lets me go.'

'If he is reluctant,' Esteban said, 'we will let him buy his way into a legitimate business.'

'He'll never come back out again.'

'He's old.'

'He has partners. Hell, he has sons.'

'I know all about his sons – one's a pederast, one's an opium addict, and one beats his wife and all his girlfriends because he secretly likes men.'

'Yeah, but I don't think blackmail works on Maso. And his train gets in tomorrow.'

'That soon?'

'From what I hear.'

'Eh. I've been in business with his kind all my life. We'll manage him.' Esteban raised his glass again. 'You're worth it.'

'Thank you,' Joe said, and this time he drank.

Esteban went back to work on the frame. 'So smile.'

'I'm trying.'

'It's Graciela then.'

'Yes.'

'What about her?'

They'd decided not to tell anyone until she started to show. This morning, before she left for work, she pointed at the small cannonball protruding from under her dress and told him she was pretty sure the secret was going to get out today, one way or the other.

So it was with a surprisingly large relinquishing of a hidden weight that he said to Esteban, 'She's pregnant.'

Esteban's eyes filled and he clapped his hands together and then came around the desk and hugged Joe. He slapped Joe's back several times and much harder than Joe would have guessed he could.

'Now,' he said, 'you are a man.'

'Oh,' Joe said, 'that's what it takes?'

'Not always, but in your case . . . ' Esteban made a back-and-forth gesture with his hand and Joe threw a mock punch at him and Esteban stepped inside it and hugged him again. 'I'm very happy for you, my friend.'

'Thank you.'

'Is she glowing?'

'You know what? She is. It's strange. I can't describe it. But, yeah, this *energy* comes off her in a different way.'

They drank a toast to fatherhood, an Ybor Friday night kicking up outside Esteban's shutters, past his lush green garden and tree lights and stone wall.

'Do you like it here?'

'What?' Joe said.

'When you arrived, you were so pale. You had that terrible prison haircut, and you talked so *fast*.'

Joe laughed, and Esteban laughed with him.

'Do you miss Boston?'

'I do,' Joe said because sometimes he missed it terribly.

'But this is your home now.'

Joe nodded, even though it surprised him to realize it. 'I think so.'

'I know how you feel. I do not know the rest of Tampa. Even after all these years. But I know Ybor like I know Habana, and I'm not sure what I would do if I had to choose.'

'You think Machado will—?'

'Machado's done. It may take some time. But he is finished. The Communists think they can replace him, but America would never allow it. My friends and I have a wonderful solution, a very moderate man, but I'm not sure anyone's ready for moderation these days.' He made a face. 'Makes them think too much. Gives them headaches. People like sides, not subtleties.'

He lay the picture glass on the frame and placed the cork square on the back and applied more glue. He wiped off the excess with a small towel and stepped back to appraise his work. When he was satisfied, he took their empty glasses over to the bar and poured them each another drink.

He brought Joe his glass. 'You heard about Loretta Figgis.'

Joe took the glass. 'Someone see her walking on the Hillsborough River?'

Esteban stared at him, his head very still. 'She killed herself.'

That stopped the drink halfway to Joe's mouth. 'When?'

'Last night.'

'How?'

Esteban shook his head several times and moved behind his desk.

'Esteban, how?'

He looked out at his garden. 'We have to assume she had returned to using heroin.'

'Okay . . .'

'Else, it would have been impossible.'

'Esteban,' Joe said.

'She cut off her genitalia, Joseph. Then—'

'Fuck,' Joe said. 'Fuck no.'

'Then she cut her own windpipe.'

Joe put his face in his hands. He could see her in the coffee shop a month ago, could see her as a girl walking up the stairs of police headquarters in her plaid skirt and her little white socks and her saddle shoes, books under her arm. And then the one he only imagined but which was twice as vivid – mutilating herself as a bathtub filled with her blood, her mouth open in a permanent scream.

'Was it a bathtub?'

Esteban gave him a curious frown. 'Was what a bathtub?'

'Where she killed herself.'

'No.' He shook his head. 'She did it in bed. Her father's bed.'

Joe put his hands over his face again and kept them there.

'Please tell me you're not blaming yourself,' Esteban said after a while.

Joe said nothing.

'Joseph, look at me.'

Joe lowered his hands and exhaled a long breath.

'She went west, and like so many girls who do that, she was preyed upon. You didn't prey on her.'

'But men in our profession did.' Joe placed his drink on the corner of the desk and paced the length of the rug and back again, trying to find the words. 'Each compartment in this thing we do? Feeds the other compartments. The booze profits pay for the girls and the girls pay for the narcotics needed to hook other girls into fucking strangers for our profit. Those girls try to get off the shit or forget how to be docile? They get beaten, Esteban, you know that. They try to get clean, then they make themselves vulnerable to a smart cop. So someone cuts their throats and throws them in a river. And we've spent the last ten years raining bullets on the competition and on one another. And for what? For fucking money.'

'This is the ugly side of living life outside the law.'

'Aw, shit,' Joe said. 'We're not outlaws. We're gangsters.'

Esteban held his gaze for a bit and then said, 'There's no talking to you when you're like this.' He flipped the framed photo over on his desk and gazed at it. 'We're not our brother's keeper, Joseph. In fact, it's an insult to our brother to presume he can't take care of himself.'

Loretta, Joe thought. Loretta, Loretta. We took and took from you and expected you to somehow soldier on without the parts we stole.

Esteban was pointing at the photograph. 'Look at these people. They are dancing and drinking and *living*. Because they could be dead tomorrow. We could be dead tomorrow, you and I. If one of these revelers, say this man—'

Esteban pointed at a bulldog-faced gent in a white dinner jacket, a group of women arrayed behind him, like they were about to lift the chunky bastard onto their shoulders, the women all aglitter in sequins and lamé.

'—were to die on his drive home because he was too drunk on Suarez Reserve to see straight, is that our fault?'

Joe looked past the bulldog man to all those lovely women, most of them Cuban with hair and eyes the color of Graciela's.

'Is that our fault?' Esteban said.

Except one woman. A smaller woman, looking away from the camera, at something out of the frame, as if someone had come into the room and called her name as the camera flashed. A woman with hair the color of sand and eyes as pale as winter.

'What?' Joe said.

'Is it our fault?' Esteban said. 'If some *mamón* decides to—'

'When was this taken?' Joe said.

'When?'

'Yes, yes. When?'

'That's the opening night of Zoot.'

'And when did it open?'

'Last month.'

Joe looked across the desk at him. 'You're sure?'

Esteban laughed. 'It's my restaurant. Of course I'm sure.'

Joe gulped his drink down. 'There's no way this photo could have been taken at another time and gotten mixed up with the one taken last month?'

'What? No. What other time?'

'Say six years ago.'

Esteban shook his head, still chuckling, but his eyes darkening with concern. 'No, no, no, Joseph. No. This was taken a month ago. Why?'

'Because this woman right here?' Joe put his finger on Emma Gould. 'She's been dead since 1927.'

PART III

All the Violent Children

1933–1935

CHAPTER TWENTY-THREE

The Haircut

'You're sure it's her?' Dion said the next morning in Joe's office.

From his inside pocket, Joe removed the photograph Esteban had pulled back out of the frame last night. He placed it on the desk in front of Dion. 'You tell me.'

Dion's eyes drifted and then locked and finally widened. 'Oh, yeah, that's her all right.' He looked sideways at Joe. 'You tell Graciela?'

'No.'

'Why not?'

'You tell your women everything?'

'I don't tell 'em shit, but you're more of a nance than me. And she's carrying your child.'

'That's true.' He looked up at the copper ceiling. 'I didn't tell her yet because I don't know how.'

'It's easy,' Dion said. 'You just say "Honey, sweetie, dearest, you remember that filly I was sweet on before you? One

I told you went tits-up? Well, she's alive and living in your hometown and still quite the dish. Speaking of dishes, what's for dinner?"'

Sal, standing by the door, looked down to hide a chuckle.

'You enjoying yourself?' Joe asked Dion.

'Time of my life,' Dion said, his girth shaking the chair.

'D,' Joe said, 'we're talking about six years of rage here, six years of . . .' Joe threw his hands up at it, unable to put it into words. 'I survived Charlestown because of that rage, I hung Maso off a fucking roof because of it, chased Albert White out of Tampa, hell, I—'

'Built an empire because of it.'

'Yeah.'

'So when you see her?' Dion said. 'Tell her thanks from me.'

Joe's mouth was open, but he couldn't think of anything to say.

'Look,' Dion said, 'I never liked the cooze. You know that. But she sure found a way to inspire you, boss. Reason I ask if you told Graciela is because I *do* like her. I like her a lot.'

'I like her a lot too,' Sal said, and they both looked over at him. He held up his right hand, the Thompson in his left. 'Sorry.'

'We talk a certain way,' Dion said to him, 'because we used to beat each other up when we were kids. To you, he's always the boss.'

'Won't happen again.'

Dion turned back to Joe.

'We didn't beat each other up when we were kids,' Joe said.

'Sure we did.'

'No,' Joe said. 'You beat the shit out of me.'

'You hit me with a brick.'

'So you'd stop beating the shit out of me.'

'Oh.' Dion was quiet for a moment. 'I had a point.'

'When?'

'When I came through the door. Oh, we gotta talk about Maso's visit. And you hear about Irv Figgis?'

'I heard about Loretta, yeah.'

Dion shook his head. 'We all heard about Loretta. But last night? Irv walked into Arturo's place? Apparently that's where Loretta scored her last vial of junk the night before last?'

'Okay ...'

'Yeah, well, Irv beat Arturo near to death.'

'No.'

Dion nodded. 'Kept saying "Repent, repent," and just driving his fists down like fucking pistons. Arturo could lose an eye.'

'Shit. And Irv?'

Dion whirled his index finger beside his temple. 'They got him on a sixty-day observation bit at the bughouse in Temple Terrace.'

'Christ,' Joe said, 'what did we do to these people?'

Dion's face darkened to scarlet. He turned and pointed at Sal Urso. 'You never fucking saw this, get me?'

Sal said, 'Saw what?' and Dion slapped Joe across the face.

Slapped him so hard Joe hit the desk. He bounced off it and came back with his .32 already pointed into the folds under Dion's chin.

Dion said, 'I'm not watching you walk into another life-or-death meeting knowing you're half-hoping to die over something you had nothing to do with. You want to shoot me here and now?' He flung his arms wide. 'Pull the fucking trigger.'

'Don't think I will?'

'I don't care if you *do*,' Dion said. 'Because I'm not going to watch you try to kill yourself a second time. You're my brother. You get me, you stupid fucking mick? You. More than Seppi or Paolo, God rest 'em. You. And I can't lose another fucking brother. Can't do it.'

Dion grabbed Joe's wrist, curled his finger over Joe's trigger finger, and dug the gun even deeper into the folds of his neck. He closed his eyes and tightened his lips against his teeth.

'By the way,' he said, 'when you going over there?'

'Where?'

'Cuba.'

'Who said I'm going over there?'

Dion frowned. 'You just found out this dead girl you used to be bugs for is alive and breathing about three hundred miles south of here, and you're going to just *sit* with that information?'

Joe removed his gun and placed it back in its holster. He noticed Sal looking white as ash and moist as a hot towel. 'I'm going as soon as this meeting with Maso's over. You know how the old man can talk.'

'Which is what I come here to discuss.' Dion opened the moleskin notebook he carried with him everywhere, thumbed the pages. 'There's a lot of things I don't like about this.'

'Such as?'

'Him and his guys took over half a train to come down here. That's an awful big entourage.'

'He's old – he got the nurse with him everywhere, maybe a doctor, and he keeps four gunners around him at all times.'

Dion nodded. 'Well, he's got at least twenty guys with him. That's not twenty nurses. He took over the Romero Hotel on Eighth. The whole hotel. Why?'

'Security.'

'But he always stays at the Tampa Bay Hotel. Just takes over a floor. His security's guaranteed that way. Why commandeer a whole hotel in the middle of Ybor?'

'I think he's getting more paranoid,' Joe said.

He wondered what he'd say to her when he saw her. *Remember me?*

Or was that too corny?

'Boss,' Dion said, 'listen to me for a second. He didn't take the Seaboard out here direct. He started on the Illinois Central. He stopped in Detroit, KC, Cincinnati, and Chicago.'

'Right. Where all his whiskey partners are.'

'It's also where all the bosses are. All the ones who matter outside of New York and Providence, and guess where he went two weeks ago?'

Joe looked across the desk at his friend. 'New York and Providence.'

'Yup.'

'So you think what?'

'I don't know.'

'You think he's barnstorming the country asking permission to take us out?'

'Maybe.'

Joe shook his head. 'Makes no sense, D. In five years, we've quadrupled the profits of this organization. This was a fucking cow town when we got here. Last year we netted – what? – eleven million from rum alone?'

'Eleven-five,' Dion said. 'And we've more than quadrupled.'

'So why fuck up a good thing? I don't buy Maso's "Joseph, you're like a son to me" bullshit any more than you do. But he respects the numbers. And our numbers are first-rate.'

Dion nodded. 'I agree it makes no sense to take us out. But I don't like these signs. I don't like how they make my stomach feel.'

'That's the paella you ate last night.'

Dion gave him a weak smile. 'Sure. Maybe that's it.'

Joe stood. He parted the blinds and looked out on the factory floor. Dion was worried, but Dion was paid to worry. So he was doing his job. In the end, Joe knew, everyone in this business did what they did to make the most money they could make. Simple as that. And Joe made money. Bags and bags of it that went up the seaboard with the bottles of rum and filled the safe in Maso's mansion in Nahant. Every year Joe made more than he had the year before. Maso was ruthless and he'd grown a bit less predictable as his health declined. But he was, above all else, greedy. And Joe fed that greed. He kept its stomach warm and full. There was no logical reason Maso would risk going hungry again to replace

Joe. And why replace Joe? He'd committed no transgressions. He didn't skim off the top. He posed no threat to Maso's power.

Joe turned from the window. 'Do whatever you have to do to guarantee my safety at that meeting.'

'I can't guarantee your safety at the meeting,' Dion said. 'That's my problem with it. He's got you walking into a building where he's bought up every room. They're probably sweeping the place right now, so I can't get any soldiers in there, I can't tuck any weapons anywhere, nothing. You're going in blind. And we'll be on the outside just as blind. If they decide you're not walking out of that building?' Dion tapped the desktop with his index finger several times. 'Then you are not walking out of that building.'

Joe considered his friend for a long time. 'What's gotten into you?'

'A feeling.'

'A feeling ain't a fact,' Joe said. 'And the facts are there's no percentage in killing me. It benefits no one.'

'As far as you know.'

The Romero Hotel was a ten-story redbrick building on the corner of Eighth Avenue and Seventeenth Street. It catered to commercial travelers who weren't quite important enough for their companies to put them up at the Tampa Hotel. It was a perfectly fine hotel – every room had a toilet and washbasin, and the sheets were changed every second day; room service was available in the morning and on Friday and Saturday evenings – but it wasn't palatial by any means.

Joe, Sal, and Lefty were met at the front door by Adamo and Gino Valocco, brothers from Calabria. Joe had known Gino in Charlestown Pen', and they chatted as they walked through the lobby.

'Where you living now?' Joe said.

'Salem,' Gino said. 'It's not so bad.'

'You settled down?'

Gino nodded. 'Found a nice Italian girl. Two kids now.'

'Two?' Joe said. 'You work fast.'

'I like a big family. You?'

Joe wasn't telling a fucking gun monkey, pleasant as he could be to chat with, about his impending fatherhood. 'Still thinking about it.'

'Don't wait too long,' Gino said. 'You need the energy for when they're young.'

It was one of the things about the business Joe always found charming and absurd at the same time – five men walking to an elevator, four of them carrying machine guns, all of them packing handguns, two of them asking each other about the wife and kids.

At the elevator, Joe kept Gino talking about his kids a bit more as he tried to catch a whiff of ambush odor. Once they climbed in that elevator, any illusions they had of an exit route ended.

But that's all they were – illusions. The moment they'd walked through the front door, they'd given up their freedom. Given up their lives if Maso, for some demented motive Joe couldn't fathom, wanted to end them. The elevator was just the smaller box within the bigger box. But the fact that they were in a box was impossible to argue.

Maybe Dion was right.

And maybe Dion was wrong.

Only one way to find out.

They left the Valocco brothers and got in the elevator. The operator was Ilario Nobile, permanently gaunt and yellowed by hep', but a magician with a gun. They said he could put a rifle shot through a flea's ass during a solar eclipse and could sign his name on a windowsill with a Thompson and not chip a pane of glass.

As they rode up to the top floor, Joe chatted with Ilario as easily as he had with Gino Valocco. In Ilario's case, the trick was to talk about the man's dogs. He bred beagles out of his home in Revere and was known to produce dogs of gentle temperament and the softest ears.

But as they rose in the car, Joe wondered again if maybe Dion had been onto something. The Valocco brothers and Ilario Nobile were all known gunners. They weren't muscle and they weren't brains. They were killers.

In the tenth-floor hallway, though, the only other person waiting for them was Fausto Scarfone, another artisan with a weapon to be sure, but it was him and only him, which left an even match to wait in the corridor – two of Maso's guys, two of Joe's.

Maso himself opened the doors to the Gasparilla Suite, the nicest suite in the hotel. He hugged Joe and took both sides of his face in his hands when he kissed his forehead. He hugged him again and patted him hard on the back.

'How are you, my son?'

'I'm very good, Mr Pescatore. Thanks for asking.'

'Fausto, see if his men need anything.'

'Take their rods, Mr Pescatore?'

Maso frowned. 'Of course not. You gentlemen make your-selves comfortable. We shouldn't be too long.' Maso pointed at Fausto. 'Anyone wants a sandwich or something, you call room service. Anything these boys want.'

He led Joe into the suite and closed the doors behind them. One set of windows looked out on an alley and the yellow brick building next door, a piano manufacturer who'd gone belly-up in '29. All that remained was his name, HORACE R. PORTER, fading on the brick, and a bunch of boarded-up windows. The other windows, though, looked out on nothing that would remind guests of the Depression. They overlooked Ybor and the channels that led out to Hillsborough Bay.

In the center of the living area four armchairs were arranged around an oak coffee table. A sterling silver cof-feepot and matching creamer and sugar bowl sat in the center. So did a bottle of anisette and three small glasses of it, already poured. Maso's middle son, Santo, sat waiting for them, looking up at Joe as he poured himself a cup of coffee and placed the cup down beside an orange.

Santo Pescatore was thirty-one and everyone called him Digger, though no one could remember why, not even Santo himself.

'You remember Joe, Santo.'

'I dunno. Maybe.' He half rose from his chair and gave Joe a limp, damp handshake. 'Call me Digger.'

'Good to see you again.' Joe took a seat across from him, and Maso came around, took the seat beside his son.

Digger peeled the orange, tossing the peels onto the coffee

table. He wore a permanent scowl of confused suspicion on his long face, like he'd just heard a joke he didn't get. He had curly dark hair that was thinning up front, a fleshy chin and neck, and his father's eyes, dark and small as sharpened pencil points. There was something dulled about him, though. He didn't have his father's charm or cunning because he'd never needed to.

Maso poured Joe a cup of coffee and handed it across the table. 'How've you been?'

'Very good, sir. You?'

Maso tipped a hand back and forth. 'Good days and bad.'

'I hope more good than bad.'

Maso raised a glass of the anisette to that. 'So far, so far. *Salud.*'

Joe raised a glass. *'Salud.'*

Maso and Joe drank. Digger popped an orange slice in his mouth and chewed with his mouth open.

Joe was reminded, not for the first time, that for such a violent business, it was filled with a surprising number of regular guys – men who loved their wives, who took their children on Saturday-afternoon outings, men who worked on their automobiles and told jokes at the neighborhood lunch counter and worried what their mothers thought of them and went to church to ask God's forgiveness for all the terrible things they had to render unto Caesar in order to put food on the table.

But it was also a business that was populated by an equal number of pigs. Vicious oafs whose primary talent was that they felt no more for their fellow man than they did for a fly sputtering on the windowsill at summer's end.

Digger Pescatore was one of the latter. And like so many of the breed Joe had come across, he was the son of a founding father of this thing they all found themselves entwined with, grafted to, subjects of.

Over the years Joe had met all three of Maso's sons. He'd met Tim Hickey's only boy, Buddy. He'd met the sons of Cianci in Miami, Barrone in Chicago, and DiGiacomo in New Orleans. The fathers were fearsomely self-made creatures, one and all. Men of iron will and some vision and not even a passing acquaintance with sympathy. But men, unquestionably men.

And every one of their sons, Joe thought as the sound of Digger's chewing filled the room, was a fucking embarrassment to the human race.

As Digger ate his orange and then a second one, Maso and Joe discussed Maso's trip down, the heat, Graciela, and the baby on the way.

After those topics had been exhausted, Maso produced a newspaper that had been tucked into the seat beside him. He took the bottle around the table and sat beside Joe. He poured two more drinks and opened the *Tampa Tribune*. Loretta Figgis's face stared back at them under the headline:

DEATH OF A MADONNA

He said to Joe, 'This the filly who caused us all the trouble on the casino?'

'That's her.'

'Why didn't you clip her then?'

'Would've been too much blowback. The whole state was watching.'

Maso tore an orange slice free of the peel. 'That's true but that's not why.'

'No?'

Maso shook his head. 'Why didn't you kill the 'shiner like I told you back in '32?'

'Turner John?'

Maso nodded.

'Because we came to an accommodation.'

Maso shook his head. 'You weren't ordered to accommodate. You were ordered to kill the son of a bitch. And the reason you didn't was the same reason you didn't kill this *puttana pazzo* – because you're not a killer, Joseph. Which is a problem.'

'It is? Since when?'

'Since now. You're not a gangster.'

'Trying to hurt my feelings, Maso?'

'You're an outlaw, a bandit in a suit. And now I hear you're thinking of going legitimate?'

'Thinking about it.'

'So you won't mind if I replace you down here?'

Joe smiled for some reason. Chuckled. He found his cigarettes and lit one.

'When I got here, Maso? This outfit grossed a million a year.'

'I know.'

'*Since* I got here? We've averaged almost eleven million.'

'Mostly because of the rum, though. Those days are ending. You've neglected the girls and the narcotics.'

'Bullshit,' Joe said.

'Excuse me?'

'I concentrated on the rum because, yeah, it was most profitable. But our narcotic sales are up sixty-five percent. As for the girls, we added four houses in my time here.'

'But you could have added more. And the whores claim they're rarely beaten.'

Joe found himself looking down at the table into Loretta's face, then looking up, then looking back down again. It was his turn to exhale a loud breath. 'Maso, I—'

'Mr Pescatore,' Maso said.

Joe said nothing.

'Joseph,' Maso said, 'our friend Charlie wants to make some changes to the way we run our thing.'

'Our friend Charlie' was Lucky Luciano out of New York. King, essentially. Emperor for Life.

'What changes?'

'Considering Lucky's right hand is a kike, the changes are a bit ironic, even unfair. I won't lie to you.'

Joe gave Maso a tight smile and waited for the old man to get to it.

'Charlie wants Italians, and only Italians, in the top slots.'

Maso wasn't kidding – it was the height of irony. Everyone knew that no matter how smart Lucky was – and he was smart as hell – he was nothing without Meyer Lansky. Lansky, a Jew from the Lower East Side, had done more than anyone in this thing of theirs to turn a collection of mom-and-pop shops into a corporation.

The thing was, though, Joe had no desire to reach the top. He was happy with his small local operation.

He said as much now to Maso.

'You're far too modest,' Maso said.

'I'm not. I run Ybor. And the rum, yeah, but that's over, like you said.'

'You run a lot more than Ybor and a lot more than Tampa, Joseph. Everyone knows that. You run the Gulf Coast from here to Biloxi. You run the out routes from here to Jacksonville and half the ones that head north. I've been through the books. You've made us a force down here.'

Instead of saying *And this is how you thank me?* Joe said, 'So if I can't be in charge because Charlie says "No Irish need apply," what can I be?'

'What I tell you to.' This from Digger, finished with his second orange, wiping his sticky palms on the sides of the armchair.

Maso gave Joe a don't-mind-him look and said, '*Consigliere*. You stay with Digger and teach him the ropes, introduce him to people around town, maybe teach him how to golf or fish.'

Digger fixed Joe in his tiny eyes. 'I know how to shave and tie my shoes.'

Joe wanted to say, *But you have to think about it, don't you?*

Maso patted Joe's knee once. 'You'll have to take a little haircut, financially speaking. But don't worry, we're going to muscle the port this summer, take the whole fucking thing over, and there'll be plenty of work, I promise.'

Joe nodded. 'What kind of haircut?'

Maso said, 'Digger takes over your cut. You assemble a crew and keep whatever you make, less tribute.'

Joe looked at the windows. He looked out at the ones overlooking the alley for a moment. Then the ones over-looking the bay. He counted down slowly from ten. 'You're demoting me to crew boss?'

Maso patted his knee again. 'It's a realignment, Joseph. On Charlie Luciano's orders.'

'Charlie said, "Replace Joe Coughlin in Tampa."'

'Charlie said, "No non-Italians at the top."' Maso's voice was still smooth, kindly even, but Joe could hear a bit of frustration creeping in.

Joe took a moment to keep his own voice in check because he knew how fast Maso could drop the courtly old gentleman mask and reveal the savage cannibal behind it.

'Maso, I think Digger wearing the crown is a great idea. The two of us together? We'll take over the state, take over Cuba while we're at it. I have the connections to do that. But my cut needs to stay *close* to what it is now. I step down to crew boss? I'll make maybe a tenth of what I'm making now. And I gotta make my monthly nut on – what? – shaking down longshoremen unions and cigar factory owners? There's no power there.'

'Maybe that's the point.' Digger smiled for the first time, a piece of orange stuck in his upper teeth. 'You ever think of that, smart guy?'

Joe looked at Maso.

Maso stared back at him.

Joe said, 'I built this.'

Maso nodded.

Joe said, 'I pulled ten-eleven times out of this city what Lou Ormino was fucking making for you.'

'Because I let you,' Maso said.

'Because you needed me.'

'Hey, smart guy,' Digger said, 'nobody *needs* you.'

Maso patted the air between him and his son, the kind of calming gesture you used on a dog. Digger sat back in his chair, and Maso turned to Joe. 'We could use you, Joseph. We could. But I am sensing a lack of gratitude.'

'So am I.'

This time Maso's hand settled on his knee and squeezed. 'You work for me. Not for yourself, not for the spics or the niggers you surround yourself with. If I tell you to go clean the shit out of my toilet, guess what you're going to do?' He smiled, his voice as soft as ever. 'I'll kill your cunt girlfriend and burn your house to embers if I feel like it. You know this, Joseph. Your eyes got a little big for your head down here, that's all. I've seen it happen before.' He raised the hand from Joe's knee and patted Joe's face with it. 'So, do you want to be a crew boss? Or do you want to clean the shit out of my toilets on diarrhea day? I'm accepting applications for both.'

If Joe played ball, he'd have a few days' head start to talk to all his contacts, marshal his forces, and align the chess pieces correctly. While Maso and his guns were back on the train heading north, Joe would fly up to New York, talk to Luciano directly, put a balance sheet on his desk and show him what Joe would make him versus what a retard like Digger Pescatore would lose him. There was an excellent chance Lucky would see the light and they could move past this with minimal bloodshed.

'Crew boss,' Joe said.

'Ah,' Maso said with a broad smile, 'my boy.' He pinched Joe's cheeks. 'My boy.'

When Maso got out of his chair, Joe did too. They shook hands. They hugged. Maso kissed both his cheeks in the same spots where he'd pinched them.

Joe shook hands with Digger and told him how much he looked forward to working with him.

'*For*,' Digger reminded him.

'Right,' Joe said. 'For you.'

He headed for the door.

'Dinner tonight?' Maso said.

Joe stopped at the door. 'Sure. Tropicale at nine sound good?'

'Sounds great.'

'Okay. I'll get us the best table.'

'Wonderful,' Maso said. 'And make sure he's dead by then.'

'What?' Joe took his hand off the knob. 'Who?'

'Your friend.' Maso poured himself a cup of coffee. 'The large one.'

'Dion?'

Maso nodded.

'He hasn't done anything,' Joe said.

Maso looked up at him.

'What am I missing?' Joe said. 'He's been a great earner and a great gun.'

'He's a rat,' Maso said. 'Six years ago, he ratted on you. Means six minutes from now, six days, six months, he'll do it again. I can't have a rat working for my son.'

'No,' Joe said.

'No?'

'No, he didn't sell me out. That was his brother. I told you.'

'I know what you told me, Joseph. I also know you lied. Now, I allow you one lie.' He held up his index finger while he added cream to his coffee. 'You've had yours. Kill that hunk of shit before dinner.'

'Maso,' Joe said. 'Listen. It was his brother. I know it for a fact.'

'You do?'

'I do.'

'You're not lying to me?'

'I'm not lying to you.'

'Because you know what it means if you are.'

Jesus, Joe thought, you came down here to steal my operation for your useless fucking son. Just steal it already.

'I know what it means,' Joe said.

'You're sticking to your story.' Maso dropped a cube of sugar into his cup.

'I'm sticking to it because it's not a story. It's the truth.'

'The whole truth and nothing but, uh?'

Joe nodded. 'The whole truth and nothing but.'

Maso shook his head slowly, sadly, and the door behind Joe opened and Albert White walked into the room.

CHAPTER TWENTY-FOUR

How You Meet Your End

The first thing Joe noticed about Albert White was how much he'd aged in three years. Gone were the white- and cream-colored suits and fifty-dollar spats. His shoes were one step above the cardboard worn by the people who lived in the streets and the tents all over the country now. The lapels of his brown suit were frayed and the elbows thin. His haircut was the kind you got at home from a distracted wife or daughter.

The second thing Joe noticed was that he held Sal Urso's Thompson in his right hand. Joe knew it was Sal's because of the markings along the breech. Sal had a habit of rubbing the breech with his left hand when he was sitting with the Thompson on his lap. He still wore his wedding ring, even though his wife had caught the typhus in '23, not long before he came to work for Lou Ormino in Tampa. When Sal rubbed the Thompson, the ring scratched the metal. Now, after years of cradling that gun, there was almost no bluing left.

Albert raised it to his shoulder as he crossed to Joe. He appraised Joe's three-piece suit.

'Anderson and Sheppard?' he asked.

Joe said, 'H. Huntsman.'

Albert nodded. He opened the left side of his own jacket so Joe could admire the label – Kresge's. 'My fortunes have changed a bit since the last time I was here.'

Joe said nothing. There was nothing to say.

'I'm back in Boston. I was close to getting a tin cup, you know? Selling fucking pencils, Joe. But then I run into Beppe Nunnaro in this little basement place in the North End. Beppe and I used to be friends. A long time ago, before all this unfortunate series of misunderstandings with Mr Pescatore. And Beppe and me, Joe, we got to talking. Your name didn't come up immediately but Dion's did. See, Beppe used to be a newsie with Dion and Dion's dumb brother, Paolo. Did you know that?'

Joe nodded.

'So you can probably see where this is going. Beppe said he'd known Paolo most of his life and had a hard time believing Paolo would double-cross anyone, never mind his own brother and a police captain's son, on a bank job.' Albert slung his arm around Joe's neck. 'To which *I* said, "Paolo didn't double-cross anyone. Dion did. I know because I'm the guy he ratted *to*."' Albert walked toward the window that faced the alley and Horace Porter's defunct piano warehouse. Joe had no choice but to walk with him. 'At this point, Beppe thought it might be a good idea if I talked to Mr Pescatore.' They stopped at the window. 'Which leads us to now. Raise your hands.'

Joe did and Albert frisked him as Maso and Digger wandered over and stood by the windows. He removed the Savage .32 from behind Joe's back and the derringer single-shot above his right ankle and the switchblade in his left shoe.

'Anything else?' Albert said.

'Usually that suffices,' Joe said.

'Cracking wise to the end.' Albert put his arm around Joe's shoulders.

Maso said, 'The thing about Mr White, Joe, that you should probably have grasped—'

'And what's that, Maso?'

'It's that he knows Tampa.' Maso raised a thick eyebrow at Joe.

'Which makes you a lot less "needed,"' Digger said. 'Dumb fuck.'

'The language,' Maso said. 'Is that really necessary?'

They all turned back to the window, like kids waiting for the curtain to part at a puppet show.

Albert raised the tommy gun in front of their faces. 'Nice piece. I understand you know the owner.'

'I do.' Joe heard the sadness in his own voice. 'I do.'

They stood facing the window for about a minute before Joe heard the scream and the shadow plummeted down the yellow brick wall across from him. Sal's face flew past the window, his arms flapping wildly at the air. And then he stopped falling. His head snapped up straight and his feet jerked up toward his chin as the noose snapped his neck. The body swung into the building twice and then twirled on the rope. The idea, Joe assumed, had been for Sal to end up hanging directly in front of their eyes, but someone had mis-judged the length of rope or maybe the effect of a man's weight at the end of it. So they stood looking down at the top of his head as his body hung between the tenth and ninth floors.

They'd cut Lefty's rope correctly, however. He arrived without a scream, his hands free and clasped to the noose. He looked resigned, as if someone had just told him a secret he'd never wanted to hear but had always expected to. Because he'd relieved the weight of the rope with his hands, his neck didn't break. He arrived in front of their faces like something conjured by magicians. He bounced up and down a few times and then dangled. He kicked at the windows. His movements were not desperate or frantic. They were strangely precise and athletic and the look on his face never changed, even when he saw them watching. He tugged at the rope even as the tracheal cartilage pressed over the edges of it and his tongue flopped over his lower lip.

Joe watched it ebb out of him, slowly, and then all at once. The light left Lefty like a hesitant bird. But once it left, it flew high and fast. The only solace Joe took from it was that Lefty's eyes, at the very end, fluttered to a close.

He looked at Lefty's sleeping face and the top of Sal's head and begged their forgiveness.

I will see you both soon. I will see my father soon. I will see Paolo Bartolo. I will see my mother.

And then:

I am not brave enough for this. I am not.

And then:

Please. God. Please, God. I do not want to meet the dark.

I will do anything. I beg your mercy. I cannot die today. I'm not supposed to die today. I'm to be a father soon. She's to be a mother. We will be good parents. We will raise a fine child.

I am not ready.

He could hear his own breathing as they walked him to the windows that looked down on Eighth Avenue and the streets of Ybor and the bay beyond, and he heard the gunfire before he got there. From this height, the men on the street looked two inches tall as they fired Thompsons and handguns and BARs. They wore hats and raincoats and suits. Some wore police uniforms.

The police were aligned with the Pescatore men. Some of Joe's men lay in the streets or half out of cars and others kept firing, but they were in retreat. Eduardo Arnaz took a burst straight through his chest and fell against the window of a dress shop. Noel Kenwood was shot in the back and lay in the street, clawing at it. The rest Joe couldn't identify from up here as the battle moved west, first one block, then two. One of his men crashed a Plymouth Phaeton into the lamppost at the corner of Sixteenth. Before he could get out, the police and a couple Pescatore men surrounded the car and unloaded their Thompsons into it. Giuseppe Esposito had owned a Phaeton, but Joe couldn't tell from here if he'd been the one driving it.

Run, boys. Just run.

As if they'd heard him, his men stopped firing back and scattered.

Maso placed a hand to the back of Joe's neck. 'It's over, son.'

Joe said nothing.

'I wished it could have been different.'

'Do you?' Joe said.

Pescatore cars and Tampa PD cars raced down Eighth, and Joe saw several heading north or south along Seventeenth and then east along Ninth or Sixth to outflank his men.

But his men disappeared.

One second a man ran along the street, and the next he was gone. The Pescatore cars would meet at the corners, the gunners pointing desperately, and go back on the hunt.

They gunned down someone on the porch of a *casita* on Sixteenth, but that seemed to be the only Coughlin-Suarez man they could find at the moment.

One by one, they'd slipped away. Into the air. One by one, they simply weren't there anymore. The police and the Pescatore men milled in the streets now, pointing fingers, shouting at one another.

Maso said to Albert, 'The fuck did they all go?'

Albert held up his hands and shook his head.

'Joseph,' Maso said, 'you tell me.'

'Don't call me Joseph,' Joe said.

Maso slapped him across the face. 'What happened to them?'

'They vanished.' Joe looked into the old man's double-zero eyes. 'Poof.'

'Yeah?'

'Yeah,' Joe said.

And now Maso raised his voice. Raised it to a roar. And it was a terrifying sound. 'Where the fuck *are they*?'

'Shit.' Albert snapped his fingers. 'It's the tunnels. They dropped into the tunnels.'

Maso turned to him. 'What tunnels?'

'The ones running underneath this fucking neighborhood. It's how they get the booze in.'

'So put men in the tunnels,' Digger said.

'No one knows where most of them are.' Albert jerked a thumb at Joe. 'That's this asshole's genius. Ain't that right, Joe?'

Joe nodded, first at Albert and then at Maso. 'This is our town.'

'Yeah, well, not anymore,' Albert said and drove the butt of the Thompson into the back of Joe's head.

CHAPTER TWENTY-FIVE

Higher Ground

Joe woke to blackness.

He couldn't see and he couldn't speak. At first he feared somebody had gone so far as to stitch his lips together, but after a minute or so, he suspected something that pressed up against the base of his nose might be tape. The more he accepted this, the more the tacky sensation around his lips, as if the skin were smeared with bubble gum, made sense.

His eyes weren't taped, though. What had initially presented itself as total dark began to give way to the occasional shape on the other side of a dense shroud of wool or rope.

It's a hood, something in his chest told him. They've got a hood over you.

His hands were cuffed behind his back. Definitely not rope binding them; metal all the way. His legs felt tied, and not terribly tight judging by how much he could move them – what felt like a full inch before he met resistance.

He lay on his right side, his face pressed to warm wood.

He could smell low tide. He could smell fish and fish blood. He realized he'd been hearing the engine for some time before he recognized it as such. He'd been on enough boats in his life to recognize what it powered. And then the other sensations coalesced and made sense – the slap of waves against the hull, the rise and fall of the wood on which he lay. He could hardly be sure of this but he didn't hear any other engines, no matter how hard he concentrated on isolating the various sounds around him. He heard men's voices and footsteps passing back and forth on the deck and, after a while, he discerned the sharp inhale and fluttering exhale of someone close by smoking a cigarette. But no other engines, and the boat wasn't going terribly fast. Didn't feel like it anyway. Didn't sound like something in flight. Which meant it was fair to assume no one was coming after them.

'Someone get Albert. He's awake.'

Then they were lifting him – one hand sinking through the hood and into his hair, two more hands under his armpits. He was dragged back along the deck and dropped into a chair, could feel the hard wooden seat under him and the hard wood slats at his back. Hands slid over his wrists and then the cuffs were unlocked. They'd barely had time to pop open before his arms were pulled around the back of the chair and the cuffs were snapped back on. Someone tied his arms and chest to the chair, tied them just short of too tight to breathe. Then someone – maybe the same someone, maybe someone else – did the same to his legs, tying them so tight to the chair legs that movement was out of the question.

They tilted the chair back and he screamed against the tape, the sound of it in his ears, because they were pushing him over the side of the boat. Even with the hood covering his head, he clenched his eyes shut, and he could hear his breath exit his nostrils so desperate and ragged. If breath could beg, his did.

The chair stopped tipping when it met a wall. Joe sat there at a forty-degree angle or so. He guessed his feet and the front chair legs were a foot and a half to two feet off the deck.

Someone removed his shoes. Then his socks. Then the hood.

He batted his eyelids rapid-time at the sudden return of light. And not any light – Florida light, immeasurably strong even though it was diffused by banks of roiling gray clouds. He couldn't see any sun, but the light managed to bounce off a nickel-plated sea. Somehow the brightness lived in the gray, lived in the clouds, lived in the sea, not strong enough to point to, just strong enough for him to feel its effect.

When he could see clearly again, the first thing that came into focus was his father's watch. It dangled in front of his eyes. Then Albert's face came into focus behind it. He let Joe see as he opened the pocket of his cheap vest and dropped the watch in. 'I was making do with an Elgin, myself,' he said and leaned forward, hands on his knees. He smiled his small smile at Joe. Behind him, two men dragged something heavy across the deck toward them. Black metal of some kind. With silver handles. The men neared them. Albert stepped back with a bow and a flourish, and they slid the object just below Joe's bare feet.

439

It was a tub. The kind one saw at summer cocktail parties. The hosts would have it filled with ice and bottles of white wine and good beer. There wasn't any ice in it now, though. Or wine. Or good beer.

Just cement.

Joe bucked against his ropes but it was like bucking against a brick house as it fell on top of him.

Albert stepped behind him and slapped the back of the chair and the chair dropped forward and Joe's legs sank into the cement.

Albert watched him struggle – or try to – with the distant curiosity of a scientist. About the only thing Joe could move was his head. As soon as his feet entered the bucket, they were there to stay. His legs were already bound fast, ankles to knees, not a twitch of mobility available. The cement had been mixed a little earlier judging by the feel of it. It wasn't soupy. His feet sank into it like they were sinking into slits in a sponge.

Albert sat on the deck in front of him and watched Joe's eyes as the cement began to set. The sponge sensation gave way to something firmer under the soles of his feet that proceeded to snake around his ankles.

'Takes a while to harden,' Albert said. 'Longer than some would think.'

Joe got his bearings when he saw a small barrier island off to his left that looked an awful lot like Egmont Key. Otherwise, nothing around them but water and sky.

Ilario Nobile brought Albert a canvas folding chair and wouldn't meet Joe's eyes. Albert rose from the deck. He adjusted the chair so the glare off the sea was off his face. He leaned forward and clasped his hands between his knees. They were on a tugboat. Joe and his chair leaned against the rear wall of the wheelhouse, looking out at the back of the boat. It was a great choice in crafts, Joe had to admit; you wouldn't know it to look at one, but tugs were fast and they could turn on a fucking dime.

Albert spun Thomas Coughlin's watch on its chain for a minute, like a boy with his yo-yo, sending it out into the air and then back into his palm with a snap. He said to Joe, 'It's running slow. You know that?'

Even if he could have spoken, Joe doubted he would have.

'Big, expensive watch like this, and it can't even keep the fucking time right.' He shrugged. 'All the money in the world, am I right, Joe? All the money in the world, and some things are just meant to run their course.' Albert looked up at the gray sky and out at the gray sea. 'This isn't a race we enter to place second. We all know the stakes. Fuck up, you die. Trust the wrong person? Stake the wrong horse?' He snapped his fingers. 'Lights-out. Have a wife? Kids? That's unfortunate. Planning a trip to Merry Olde England next summer? The plan just changed. Thought you'd be breathing tomorrow? Fucking, eating, taking a bath? You won't.' He leaned forward and stabbed his finger into Joe's chest. 'You will be sitting at the bottom of the Gulf of Mexico. And the world will be shut to you. Hell, if two fish go up your nose and a few nibble your eyes? You won't mind. You'll be with God. Or the devil. Or no place. Where you won't be, Joe?' He raised his hands to the clouds. 'Is here. So take a good last look. Take some deep breaths. Really suck that oxygen in.' He slipped the watch back into his vest, leaned in, grasped Joe's face in his hands, and kissed the top of his head. 'Because you die now.'

The cement had hardened. It squeezed Joe's toes, heels, ankles. It squeezed everything so hard he could only assume some of the bones in his feet were broken. Maybe all of them.

He met Albert's eyes and flicked his own at his left inside pocket.

'Stand him up.'

'No,' Joe tried to say, 'look in my pocket.'

'Mmmm! Mmmm! Mmmm!' Albert mimicked, his eyes bulging. 'Coughlin, show a little class. Don't beg.'

They slashed the rope over Joe's chest. Gino Valocco walked over with a hacksaw and dropped to his knees and sawed away at the front chair legs, cutting them free of the chair bottom.

'Albert,' he said through the tape, 'look in this pocket. This pocket. This pocket. This one.'

Every time he said 'this,' he jerked his head and his eyes toward the pocket.

Albert laughed and continued to mimic him and some of the other men joined in, Fausto Scarfone going so far as to imitate an ape. He made 'hoo hoo hoo' sounds and scratched his armpits. Over and over, he jerked his head to the left.

The left chair leg came free of the seat, and Gino went to work on the right.

'Those are good cuffs,' Albert said to Ilario Nobile. 'Take 'em off. He ain't going anywhere.'

Joe could see he'd hooked him. He wanted to see in Joe's

pocket, but he had to find a way to do it without appearing to give in to his victim's wishes.

Ilario removed the cuffs and tossed them to Albert's feet because apparently Albert hadn't earned enough respect to have them handed to him.

The right chair leg broke free of the seat and they pulled the chair off Joe and he stood upright in the tub of cement.

Albert said, 'You get to use your hand once. You either rip the tape off your mouth or you show me what you're trying to buy your pathetic fucking life with. You can't do both.'

Joe didn't hesitate. He reached into his pocket. He removed the photograph and flung it at Albert's feet.

Albert picked it up off the deck as a dot appeared over his left shoulder, just beyond Egmont Key. Albert looked at the photo with a cocked eyebrow and that small, smug fucking smile of his, and he saw nothing special about it. His eyes flicked all the way to the left again and he began to move them slowly to the right and then his head went very still.

The dot became a dark triangle, moving fast over the glassy gray sea – a hell of a lot faster than the tug, fast as it was, could move.

Albert looked at Joe. It was a sharp and furious look. Joe saw clearly that he wasn't furious because Joe had stumbled upon his secret. He was furious because he'd been kept as deep in the dark as Joe.

All this time, he'd thought she was dead too.

Christ, Albert, he wanted to say, in this we're both her sons.

Even with six inches of electrical tape across his mouth, Joe knew Albert could see him smile.

The dark triangle was now, quite clearly, a boat. A classic runabout modified to accommodate extra passengers or bottles in the stern. Cut its speed by a third but that still made it faster than anything on the water. Several of the men on deck pointed and nudged one another.

Albert ripped the tape off Joe's mouth.

The sound of the boat reached them. A buzz, like a distant wasp swarm.

Albert held the photograph in Joe's face. 'She's dead.'

'Look dead to you, does she?'

'Where is she?' Albert's voice was ragged enough for several men to look over at him.

'In the fucking picture, Albert.'

'Tell me where it was taken.'

'Sure,' Joe said, 'and I'm sure nothing will happen to me then.'

Albert slammed both his fists into Joe's ears and the sky pinwheeled overhead.

Gino Valocco shouted something in Italian. He pointed starboard.

A second boat had appeared, another modified runabout, with four men in it, coming out from behind a spoil bank about four hundred yards away.

'Where is she?'

The ringing in Joe's ears was like a cymbal symphony. He shook his head repeatedly.

'Love to tell you,' he said, 'but I'd love not to fucking drown more.'

Albert pointed at first one boat, then the other. 'They won't stop us. Are you a fucking idiot? Where is she?'

'Oh, let me think,' Joe said.

'*Where?*'

'In the photograph.'

'It's an old one. You just folded up an old—'

'Yeah, I thought that too at first. But look at that asshole in the tux. The tall one, all the way to the right, leaning against the piano? Look at the newspaper. The one by his elbow, Albert. Look at the fucking headline.'

PRESIDENT-ELECT ROOSEVELT SURVIVES MIAMI ASSASSINATION ATTEMPT

'That was last month, Albert.'

Now both boats were within 350 yards.

Albert looked at the boats, looked at Maso's men, looked back at Joe. He let out a long breath through pursed lips. 'You think they're going to rescue you? They're half our size and we have the high ground. You could send six boats our way and we'll turn every last one of them into fucking matchsticks.' He turned to the men. 'Kill them.'

They lined up along the gunwales. They knelt. Joe counted an even dozen of them. Five to starboard, five to port, Ilario and Fausto heading into the cabin for something. Most of the men on deck carried tommy guns and a few handguns but none had the rifles necessary for long-range shooting.

Ilario and Fausto made that point moot when they dragged a crate back out of the cabin. Joe noticed for the first time that there was a bronze tripod bolted to the deck at the gunwale and a toolbox sitting beside it. Then he realized it wasn't a tripod exactly; it was a deck mount. For a gun. A big fucking gun. Ilario reached into the crate and removed two ammunition belts of .30-06 rounds that he lay beside the tripod. He and Fausto then reached into the crate and came back out with a 1903 ten-barrel Gatling. They placed it on top of the deck mount and went to work securing it.

The approaching runabouts grew louder. They were maybe 250 yards away now, which put them about a hundred yards out of range for anything but the Gatling. But once that fucker got locked onto the deck mount, it was capable of firing up to nine hundred rounds a minute. One sustained burst into either of the boats and the only thing left would be meat for the sharks.

Albert said, 'Tell me where she is, and I'll make it fast. One shot. You'll never feel it. If you make me force it out of you, I'll tear the pieces off you long after you've told me. I'll stack them on the deck until the stack falls over.'

The men shouted at one another, changing their positions as the runabouts began to move erratically, the one on the port side adopting a serpentine pattern while the starboard assault boat jerked right-left, right-left, the engines ratcheting up in pitch.

Albert said, 'Just tell me.'

Joe shook his head.

'Please,' Albert said so quietly no one else could hear. With the boat engines and the Gatling assembly, Joe could barely hear. 'I love her.'

'I loved her too.'

'No,' Albert said. 'I *love* her.'

They finished securing the Gatling to the deck mount. Ilario inserted the ammunition belt into the feed guide and blew at any dust that might be in the hopper.

Albert leaned into Joe. He looked around them. 'I don't want this. Who wants *this*? I just want to feel like I felt when I made her laugh or when she threw an ashtray at my head. I don't even care about the fucking. I just want to watch her drink coffee in a hotel bathrobe. You *have* that, I hear. With the spic woman?'

'Yeah,' Joe said, 'I do.'

'What is she by the way? Nigger or spic?'

'Both,' Joe said.

'And that doesn't bother you?'

'Albert,' Joe said, 'why on earth would it bother me?'

Ilario Nobile, a veteran of the Spanish-American War, manned the crank handle of the Gatling while Fausto took a seat below the gun, the first of the ammunition belts lying across his lap like a grandmother's blanket.

Albert drew his long-barrel .38 and placed it to Joe's forehead. 'Tell me.'

No one heard the fourth engine until it was too late.

Joe looked as deep into Albert as he ever had and what he saw there was someone as shit-scared-terrified as everyone else he'd ever known.

'No.'

Farruco Diaz's plane appeared out of the western clouds. It came in high but dove fast. Dion stood tall in the rear seat, his machine gun secured to the mount Farruco Diaz had busted Joe's balls about for months until he let him install it. Dion wore thick goggles and seemed to be laughing.

The first thing Dion and his machine gun aimed at was the Gatling.

Ilario turned to his left and Dion's bullets blew off his ear and moved through his neck like a scythe and the ricochets bounced off the gun and bounced off the deck mount and the deck cleats, and collided with Fausto Scarfone. Fausto's arms danced in the air by his head and then he tipped over, spitting red everywhere.

The deck was spitting too – wood and metal and sparks. The men ducked, crouched, and curled into balls. They screamed and fumbled with their weapons. Two fell off the boat.

Farruco Diaz's plane banked and surged toward the clouds and the gunners recovered. They got to their feet and fired away. The steeper the plane climbed, the more vertical they fired.

And some of the bullets came back down.

Albert took one in the shoulder. Another guy grabbed the back of his neck and fell to the deck.

The smaller boats were now close enough to be fired upon. But all of Albert's gunners had turned their backs to shoot at Farruco's plane. Joe's gunners weren't the best shots – they were in boats and boats that were moving wildly – but they didn't have to be. They managed to hit hips and knees and abdomens and a third of the men on the boat flopped to the deck and made the noises men made when they were shot in the hip and the knees and the abdomen.

The plane came back for a second pass. Men were firing from the boats and Dion was working that machine gun like it was a fireman's hose and he was the fire chief. Albert righted himself and pointed his .32 long-barrel at Joe as the back of the boat turned into a tornado of dust and chips of wood and men failing to escape a fusillade of lead and Joe lost sight of Albert.

Joe was hit in the arm by a bullet fragment and once in the head by a wood chip the size of a bottle cap. It ripped off a piece of his left eyebrow and nicked the top of his left ear on its way into the Gulf. A Colt .45 landed at the base of the tub, and Joe picked it up and dropped the magazine into his hand long enough to confirm there were at least six bullets left in it before he slammed it back home.

By the time Carmine Parone reached him, the blood flowing out of the left side of his face looked a lot worse than it was. Carmine gave Joe a towel, and he and one of the new kids, Peter Wallace, set to work on the cement with axes. While Joe had assumed it had already set, it hadn't, and after fifteen or sixteen swings of the axes and a shovel Carmine had found in the galley, they got him out of there.

Farruco Diaz set his plane down on the water and cut the engine. The plane glided over to them. Dion climbed aboard and the men went about killing the wounded.

'How you doing?' Dion asked Joe.

Ricardo Cormarto tracked a young man who was dragging himself toward the stern, his legs a mess, but the rest of him looking ready for a night out in a beige suit and cream-colored shirt, mango-red tie flipped over his shoulder, like he was preparing to eat a lobster bisque. Cormarto put a burst into his spine and the young man exhaled an outraged sigh, so Cormarto put another burst into his head.

Joe looked at the bodies piled on the deck and said to Wallace, 'If he's alive in all that, bring him to me.'

'Yes, sir. Yes, sir,' Wallace said.

He tried flexing his ankles but it hurt too much. He placed a hand to the ladder under the wheelhouse and said to Dion, 'What was the question again?'

'How you doing?'

'Oh,' Joe said, 'you know.'

A guy by the gunwale begged for his life in Italian, but Carmine Parone shot him in the chest and kicked him overboard.

Fasani flipped Gino Valocco over onto his back next. Gino held his hands in front of his face, the blood coming from his side. Joe remembered their conversation about parenting, about there never being a good time to have a kid.

Gino said what everyone said. He said, 'Wait.' He said, 'Hold—'

But Fasani shot him through the heart and kicked him into the Gulf.

Joe looked away only to find Dion looking at him steadily, carefully. 'They would have killed every last one of us. Hunted us down. You know that.'

Joe blinked an affirmative.

'And why?'

Joe didn't answer.

'No, Joe. Why?'

Joe still didn't answer.

'Greed,' Dion said. 'Not sensible greed, not fucking *sane* greed. Endless greed. Because it's never enough for them.' Dion's face was purple with rage when he leaned in so close to Joe their noses touched. 'It's never fucking *enough*.'

Dion leaned back and Joe stared at his friend a long time and in that time he heard someone say there was no one left to kill.

'It's never enough for any of us,' Joe said. 'You, me, Pescatore. Tastes too good.'

'What?'

'The night,' Joe said. 'Tastes too good. You live by day, you play by their rules. So we live by night and play by ours. But, D? We don't really have any rules.'

Dion gave that some thought. 'Not too many, no.'

'Starting to wear me out.'

'I know it,' Dion said. 'I can see it.'

Fasani and Wallace dragged Albert White across the deck and dropped him in front of Joe.

He was missing the back of his head and there was a black gout of blood where his heart should have been. Joe squatted by the corpse and fished his father's watch from Albert's vest pocket. He checked it quickly for damage, found none, and pocketed it. He sat back on the deck.

'I was supposed to look him in the eye.'

'How's that?' Dion said.

'I was supposed to look him in the eye and say, "You thought you got me, but I fucking got you."'

'You had that chance four years ago.' Dion lowered his hand to Joe.

'I wanted it again.' Joe took the hand.

'Shit,' Dion said as he lifted him to his feet, 'ain't no one gets that kinda chance twice.'

CHAPTER TWENTY-SIX

Back to Black

The tunnel that led to the Romero Hotel began at Pier 12. From there it ran eight blocks under Ybor City and took fifteen minutes to traverse if the tunnel wasn't flooded by high tide or overrun with night rats. Luckily for Joe and his crew, it was midday and low tide when they arrived at the pier. They covered the distance in ten minutes. They were sunburned, they were dehydrated, and in Joe's case they were wounded, but Joe had impressed upon everyone during the ride in from Egmont Key that if Maso was half as smart as Joe knew he was, he'd have put a limit on when he was supposed to hear back from Albert. If he assumed it had all gone to hell, he'd waste no time making tracks.

The tunnel ended at a ladder. The ladder rose to the door of the furnace room. Beyond the furnace room was the kitchen. Past the kitchen was the manager's office and beyond that was the front desk. In each of the latter three positions, they could see and hear if anything was waiting for them beyond the doors, but between the top of the ladder and the furnace room lay one hell of a question mark. The steel door was always locked because it was, during normal operation, opened only upon hearing a password. The Romero had never been raided because Esteban and Joe paid the owners to pay the proper people to look the other way and also because it brought no attention to itself. It didn't run an active speakeasy; it merely distilled and distributed.

After several arguments about how to get through a steel door with three bolts and the wrong end of the lock cylinder on their side, they decided that the best shot among them – in this case, Carmine Parone – would cover from the top of the ladder while Dion solved the lock with a shotgun.

'If there's anyone on the other side of that door, we're all fish in a barrel,' Joe said.

'No,' Dion said. 'Me and Carmine are fish in a barrel. Hell, I'm not even sure we'll survive the ricochets. Rest of you nancy boys? Shit.' He smiled at Joe. 'Fire in the hole.'

Joe and the other men went back down the ladder and stood in the tunnel and they heard Dion say, 'Last chance,' to Carmine and then he fired the first shot into the hinge. The blast was loud – metal meeting metal in a concrete and metal enclosure. Dion didn't pause, either. With the sound of the fragments still pinging around up there, he fired a second and third blast and Joe assumed that if anyone was left in the hotel, they were coming for them now. Hell, if all that was left was people on the tenth floor, they damn sure knew they were here.

'Let's go, let's go,' Dion shouted.

Carmine hadn't made it. Dion lifted his body out of the way and sat him against the wall as they came up the ladder. A piece of metal – who knew from what – had entered Carmine's brain through his eye, and he stared back at them with his good one, an unlit cigarette still drooping from his lips.

They wrenched the door off its hinges and went into the boiler room and through the boiler room into the distillery and the kitchen beyond. The door between the kitchen and the manager's office had a circular window in the center that looked out onto a small access way with a rubber floor. The manager's door was ajar, and the office beyond showed evidence of a recent war party – wax paper with crumbs on top, coffee cups, an empty bottle of rye, overflowing ashtrays.

Dion took a look and said to Joe, 'Never expected to see old age, myself.'

Joe exhaled through his mouth and went through the door. They went through the manager's office and came out behind the front desk and by that point they knew the hotel was empty. It didn't feel ambush-empty, it felt empty-empty. The place for an ambush had been the boiler room. If they'd wanted to draw them in a little farther just to be sure they caught any stragglers, the kitchen would have been the spot. The lobby, though, was a logistical nightmare – too many places to hide, too easy to scatter, and ten steps from the street.

They sent some men up to the tenth in the elevator and a few more by way of the stairs, just in case Maso had come up with an ambush plan Joe simply couldn't fathom. The men came back and reported that the tenth was cleaned out, though they had found both Sal and Lefty laid out on the beds in 1009 and 1010.

'Bring 'em down,' Joe said.

'Yes, sir.'

'And have someone bring Carmine in from the ladder too.'

Dion lit a cigar. 'I can't believe I shot Carmine in the face.'

'You didn't shoot him,' Joe said. 'Ricochets.'

'Splitting hairs,' Dion said.

Joe lit a cigarette and allowed Pozzetta, who'd been an army medic in Panama, to take another look at his arm.

Pozzetta said, 'You need to get that treated, boss. Get you some drugs.'

'We got drugs,' Dion said.

'The right drugs,' Pozzetta said.

'Go out the back,' Joe said. 'Go get me what I need or find the doc'.'

'Yes, sir,' Pozzetta said.

Half a dozen members of the Tampa PD on their payroll were called and came down. One of them brought a meat wagon and Joe said good-bye to Sal and Lefty and Carmine Parone, who just ninety minutes ago had dug Joe out of a cement bucket. It was Sal who got to him the most, though; only in retrospect did the full measure of their five years together hit him. He'd had him into the house for dinner countless times, sometimes brought sandwiches to him in the car at night. He'd entrusted him with his life, with Graciela's life.

Dion put a hand on his back. 'This is a tough one.'

'We gave him a hard time.'

'What?'

'This morning in my office. You and me. We gave him a hard time, D.'

'Yeah.' Dion nodded a couple of times and then blessed himself. 'Why'd we do that again?'

'I don't even know,' Joe said.

'There had to be a reason.'

'I wish it meant something,' Joe said and stepped back so his men could load them into the meat wagon.

'It means something,' Dion said. 'Means we should settle up with the fucks who killed him.'

The doctor was waiting at the front desk when they got back from the loading dock and he cleaned Joe's wound and sutured it while Joe got his reports from the police officers he'd sent for.

'The men he had working for him today,' Joe said to Sergeant Bick of the Third District, 'they on his permanent payroll?'

'No, Mr Coughlin.'

'Did they know they were going after *my* men in the streets?'

Sergeant Bick looked at the floor. 'I gotta assume so.'

'I gotta too,' Joe said.

'We can't kill cops,' Dion said.

Joe was looking into Bick's eyes when he said, 'Why not?'

'It's frowned upon,' Dion said.

Joe said to Bick, 'You know of any cops who are with Pescatore now?'

'Everyone who shot it out today, sir? They're writing

reports right now. The mayor's not happy. The chamber of commerce is livid.'

'The mayor's not happy?' Joe said. 'The chamber of fucking commerce?' He slapped Bick's hat off the top of his head. '*I'm* not happy! Fuck everyone else! *I'm* not happy!'

There was an odd silence in the room, and no one knew where to put their eyes. To the best of anyone's recollection, even Dion's, no one had ever heard Joe raise his voice before.

When he spoke to Bick again, his voice had returned to its normal pitch. 'Pescatore doesn't fly. He doesn't like boats, either. That means he's got only two ways out of this city. So he's either part of a convoy heading north on Forty-one. Or he's on the train. So, Sergeant Bick? Pick up your fucking hat and find him.'

A few minutes later, in the manager's office, Joe called Graciela.

'How you feeling?'

'Your child is a brute,' she said.

'*My* child, uh?'

'He kick, kick, kick. All the time.'

'On the bright side,' Joe said, 'only four more months to go.'

'You,' she said, 'are so very funny. I would like to get you pregnant next time. I would like you to feel your stomach in your windpipe. And have to pee more times than you blink.'

'We'll give that a try.' Joe finished his cigarette and lit another.

'I heard about a gunfight on Eighth Avenue today,' she said, and her voice was much smaller and much harder.

'Yes.'

'Is it over?'

'No,' Joe said.

'You are at war?'

'We are at war,' Joe said. 'Yes.'

'When will you be finished?'

'I don't know.'

'Ever?'

'I don't know.'

For a minute they said nothing. He heard her smoking from her end and she could hear him smoking from his. He checked his father's watch and saw that it was now running a full half an hour behind, even though he'd reset it on the boat.

'You don't see it,' she said eventually.

'See what?'

'That you have been at war since the day we met. And why?'

'To make a living.'

'Is dying a living?'

'I'm not dead,' he said.

'By the end of the day you could be, Joseph. You could. Even if you win today's battle and the next one and the one after that, there is so much violence in what you do, that it must – it *must* – come back for you. It will find you.'

Just what his father had told him.

Joe smoked and blew it up toward the ceiling and watched it evaporate. He couldn't say there wasn't truth in her words, just as there may have been some in his father's. But he didn't have the time for the truth right now.

He said, 'I don't know what I'm supposed to say here.'

'I don't either,' she said.

'Hey,' he said.

'What?'

'How do you know it's a boy?'

'Because he's kicking at things all the time,' she said. 'Just like you.'

'Ah.'

'Joseph?' She inhaled on her cigarette. 'Don't leave me to raise him on my own.'

The only train scheduled to leave Tampa that afternoon was the Orange Blossom Special. Seaboard's two standard trains had already left and no more were scheduled until tomorrow. The Orange Blossom Special was a deluxe passenger train that ran to and from Tampa in the winter months only. The problem for Maso, Digger, and their men was that it was booked solid.

While they were working on bribing the conductor, the police showed up. And not the ones on their payroll.

Maso and Digger were sitting in the back of an Auburn sedan in a field just west of Union Station, where they had a clear view of the redbrick building and its cake-icing white trim and the five tracks that ran from the back of it, gunmetal rails of hot rolled steel that stretched from this small brick building and endlessly flat land to points north and east and west, splaying like veins across the country.

'Should've gotten into railroads,' Maso said. 'When there was still a chance back in the teens.'

'We got trucks,' Digger said. 'That's better.'

'Trucks ain't getting us out of this.'

'Let's just drive,' Digger said.

'You don't think they'll notice a bunch of wops in swell cars and black hats driving through the fucking orange groves?'

'We drive at night.'

Maso shook his head. 'Roadblocks. By now? That Irish cocksucker has them set up on every road from here to Jacksonville.'

'Well, a train ain't the way to go, Pop.'

'Yes,' Maso said, 'it is.'

'I can get us a plane out of Jacksonville in—'

'You fly on one of those fucking deathtraps. Don't ask me to.'

'Pop, they're safe. They're safer than ... than—'

'Than trains?' Maso pointed. As he did, the air popped with a percussive echo and smoke rose from a field about a mile away.

'Duck hunting?' Digger said.

Maso looked over at his son and thought how sad it was that a man this stupid was the smartest of his three offspring.

'You seen any ducks around here?'

'So then ...?' Digger's eyes narrowed. He actually couldn't figure it out.

'He just blew up the tracks,' Maso said and looked across at his son. 'You get your retard from your mother, by the way. Woman couldn't win a game of checkers against a bowl of fucking soup.'

*

Maso and his men waited by a pay phone on Platt while Anthony Servidone went on ahead with a suitcase full of money to the Tampa Bay Hotel. He called an hour later to report that the rooms were taken care of. There was no police presence and no local hoods as far as he could see. Send in the security detail.

They did. Not that there was much of one left after whatever had happened on that tugboat. They'd sent twelve guys out on that boat, thirteen if you counted that Slick Sammy fuck, Albert White. That left a security detail of seven men plus Maso's personal bodyguard, Seppe Carbone. Seppe was from the same town Maso had grown up in, Alcamo, on the northwest coast of Sicily, though Seppe was much younger, so he and Maso had grown up there in different times. Still, Seppe was a man from that town – merciless, fearless, and loyal to the death.

After Anthony Servidone called back to confirm that the security detail had cleared the floor and the lobby, Seppe drove Maso and Digger to the back of the Tampa Bay Hotel, and they took the service elevator to the seventh floor.

'How long?' Digger said.

'Day after tomorrow,' Maso said. 'We keep our heads down until then. Even that mick son of a bitch doesn't have the pull to keep roadblocks up that long. We drive down to Miami, catch the train from there.'

'I want a girl,' Digger said.

Maso slapped his son hard in the back of the head. 'What part of lying low don't you understand? A girl? A fucking *girl*? Why don't you ask her to bring some friends, maybe a couple of guns, you dumb fuck.'

Digger rubbed his head. 'A man has needs.'

'You see a man around here,' Maso said, 'you point him out to me.'

They arrived at the seventh floor and Anthony Servidone met the lift. He handed Maso his room key and Digger his.

'You clear the room?'

Anthony nodded. 'They're clean. Every one. Whole floor.'

Maso had met Anthony in Charlestown, where everyone was loyal to Maso because it was death if you weren't. Seppe, on the other hand, had come from Alcamo with a letter from Todo Bassina, the local boss, and had distinguished himself more times than Maso could count.

'Seppe,' he said now, 'give the room another look.'

'*Subito, capo. Subito.*' Seppe's Thompson cleared his rain-coat and he walked through the men gathered outside Maso's suite and let himself inside.

Anthony Servidone stepped in close. 'They were seen at the Romero.'

'Who?'

'Coughlin, Bartolo, a bunch of Cubans and Italians on their side.'

'Coughlin, definitely?'

Anthony nodded. 'No question.'

Maso closed his eyes for just a moment. 'He even get a scratch?'

'Yeah,' Anthony said quickly, excited to deliver some good news. 'Big cut on his head and took a slug to his right arm.'

Maso said, 'Well, I guess we should wait for him to die of fucking blood poisoning.'

Digger said, 'I don't think we got that kind of time.'

And Maso closed his eyes again.

Digger walked down to his room with a man on either side of him as Seppe came back out of Maso's suite.

'It's all clear, boss.'

Maso said, 'I want you and Servidone on the door. Everyone else better act like centurions on the Hun border. *Capice?*'

'*Capice.*'

Maso entered the room and removed his raincoat and his hat. He poured himself a drink but from the bottle of anisette they'd sent up. Booze was legal again. Most of it, anyway. And what wasn't, would be. The country had found sanity again.

A fucking shame, what it was.

'Pour me one, would ya?'

Maso turned, saw Joe sitting on the couch by the window. He had his Savage .32 sitting on his knee with a Maxim silencer screwed onto the muzzle.

Maso wasn't surprised. Not even a little bit. Just curious about one thing.

'Where were you hiding?' He poured Joe a glass and brought it to him.

'Hiding?' Joe took the glass.

'When Seppe cleared the room?'

Joe used his .32 to point Maso to a chair. 'I wasn't hiding. I was sitting on the bed over there. He walked in and I asked him if he wanted to work for someone who'd be alive tomorrow.'

'That's all it took?' Maso said.

'It took you wanting to place a fucking dunce like Digger

463

in a position of power. We had a great thing here. A great thing. And you come in and fuck it all up in one day.'

'That's human nature, isn't it?'

'Fixing what ain't broke?' Joe said.

Maso nodded.

'Well, shit,' Joe said, 'it doesn't have to be.'

'No,' Maso said, 'but it usually is.'

'You know how many people died today because of you and your fucking greed? You, the "simple Wop from Endicott Street"? Well, you ain't that.'

'Someday, maybe you'll have a son and then you'll understand.'

'Will I?' Joe said. 'And what will I understand?'

Maso shrugged, as if to put it into words would sully it. 'How is my son?'

'By now?' Joe shook his head. 'Gone.'

Maso pictured Digger lying facedown on a floor in the next room over, a bullet in the back of his head, the blood pooling on the carpet. He was surprised by how deep and suddenly the grief overtook him. It was so black, so black and hopeless and horrific.

'I'd always wanted you for a son,' he said to Joe and heard his voice break. He looked down at his drink.

'Funny,' Joe said, 'I never wanted you for a father.'

The bullet entered Maso's throat. The last thing he ever saw was a drop of his blood landing in his glass of anisette.

Then it all went back to black.

When Maso fell, he dropped the glass and landed on his knees and his head hit the coffee table. It lay on the right cheek, empty eye staring at the wall to his left. Joe stood and looked at the silencer he'd picked up at the hardware store for three bucks that afternoon. Rumor was Congress was going to raise the price to $200 and then outlaw them entirely.

Pity.

Joe shot Maso through the top of the head just to be sure.

Out in the hall, they'd disarmed the Pescatore guns without a fight as Joe suspected they might. Men didn't like to fight for a man who thought so little of their lives he'd put an idiot like Digger in charge. Joe exited Maso's suite and closed the doors behind him and looked at everyone standing around, unsure what would happen next. Dion exited Digger's room, and they stood in the hallway for a moment, thirteen men and a few machine guns.

'I don't want to kill anyone,' Joe said. He looked at Anthony Servidone. 'You want to die?'

'No, Mr Coughlin, I do not want to die.'

'Anyone?' Joe looked around the hallway and got a bunch of solemn head shakes. 'If you want to go back to Boston, head back with my blessing. You want to stay down here, get some sun, meet some pretty ladies, we got jobs for you. Ain't too many people offering those these days, so let us know if you're interested.'

Joe couldn't think of anything else to say. He shrugged, and he and Dion got on the lift and took it down to the lobby.

A week later, in New York, Joe and Dion walked into an office at the back of an actuarial firm in Midtown Manhattan and sat across from Lucky Luciano.

Joe's theory that the most terrifying men were also the most terrified went right out the window. There was no fear in Luciano. There was very little that resembled emotion, in fact, except a hint of black and endless rage in the furthest depths of his dead sea gaze.

The only thing this man knew about terror was how to infect other people with it.

He was dressed impeccably and would have been a handsome man if his skin didn't look like veal that had been pounded with a meat tenderizer. His right eye drooped from a failed hit on him back in '29 and his hands were large and looked like they could squeeze a skull until it popped like a tomato.

'You two hoping to walk back out that door?' he said when they took their seats.

'Yes, sir.'

'Then tell me why I gotta replace my Boston management group.'

They did, and as they talked, Joe kept looking for some indication in those dark eyes that he saw their point or didn't, but it was like talking to a marble floor – the only thing you got back, if you caught the light right, was your own reflection.

When they finished, Lucky stood and looked out the window at Sixth Avenue. 'You've made a lot of noise down there. What happened to that Holy Roller who died? Wasn't her father police chief?'

'They forced him into retirement,' Joe said. 'Last I heard he was at some kind of sanitarium. He can't hurt us.'

'But his daughter did. And you let her. That's why the

word on you is that you're soft. Not a coward. I didn't say that. Everyone knows how close you got to take care of that yokel back in '30 and that ship heist took brass ones. But you didn't take care of that 'shiner back in '31 and you let a dame – a fucking dame, Coughlin – block your casino play.'

'That's true,' Joe said. 'I got no excuse.'

'No, you don't,' Luciano said. He looked across the desk at Dion. 'What would you have done with the 'shiner?'

Dion looked uncertainly at Joe.

'Don't you look at him,' Luciano said. 'You look at me and you tell me straight.'

But Dion continued to look at Joe until Joe said, 'Tell him the truth, D.'

Dion turned to Lucky. 'I would have turned out his fucking lights, Mr Luciano. His sons' too.' He snapped his fingers. 'Taken out the whole family.'

'And the Holy Roller dame?'

'Her I would have disappeared-like.'

'Why?'

'Give her people the option of turning her into a saint. They can tell themselves she's immaculately concepted up to heaven, whatever. Meanwhile, they'd damn well know we chopped her up and fed her to the reptiles, so they'd never fuck with us again, but the rest of the time, they'd gather in her name and sing her praises.'

Luciano said, 'You're the one Pescatore said was a rat.'

'Yup.'

'Never made sense to us.' He said to Joe, 'Why would you knowingly trust a rat who sent you up the river for two years?'

467

Joe said, 'I wouldn't.'

Luciano nodded. 'That's what we thought when we tried to talk the old man out of the hit.'

'But you sanctioned it.'

'We sanctioned it *if* you refused to use our trucks and our unions in your new liquor business.'

'Maso never brought that up to me.'

'No?'

'No, sir. He just said I was going to take orders from his son and I had to kill my friend.'

Luciano stared at him for a long time.

'All right,' he said eventually, 'make your proposal.'

'Make him boss.' Joe jerked his thumb at Dion.

Dion said, *'What?'*

Luciano smiled for the first time. 'And you'll stay on as *consigliere*?'

'Yes.'

Dion said, 'Hold on a second. Just hold on.'

Luciano looked at him and the smile died on his face.

Dion read the tea leaves fast. 'I'd be honored.'

Luciano said, 'Where you from?'

'Town called Manganaro in Sicily.'

Luciano's eyebrows rose. 'I'm from Lercara Friddi.'

'Oh,' Dion said. 'The big town.'

Luciano came around the desk. 'You gotta be from a real shithole like Manganaro to call Lercara Friddi the "big town."'

Dion nodded. 'That's why we left.'

'When was that? Stand up.'

Dion stood. 'I was eight.'

'Been back?'

'Why would I go *back*?' Dion said.

'It'll remind you of who you are. Not who you pretend to be. Who you *are*.' He put an arm around Dion's shoulders. 'And you're a boss.' He pointed at Joe. 'And he's a brain. Let's go have some lunch. I know a great place a few blocks from here. Best gravy in the city.'

They left the office, and four men fell in around them as they headed for the elevator.

'Joe,' Lucky said, 'I need to introduce you to my friend, Meyer. He's got some great ideas about casinos in Florida and in Cuba.' Now Luciano put his arm around Joe. 'You know much about Cuba?'

CHAPTER TWENTY-SEVEN

A Gentleman Farmer
in Pinar del Río

When Joe Coughlin met up with Emma Gould in Havana in the late spring of 1935, it had been nine years since the speakeasy robbery in South Boston. He remembered how cool she'd been that morning, how unflappable, and how those qualities had unnerved him. He'd then mistaken being unnerved for being smitten and mistook being smitten for being in love.

He and Graciela had been in Cuba almost a year, staying at first in the guesthouse of one of Esteban's coffee plantations high in the hills of Las Terrazas, about fifty miles west of Havana. In the morning they woke to the smell of coffee beans and cocoa leaves while mist ticked and dripped off the trees. In the evenings, they walked the foothills while rags of fading sunlight clung to the thick treetops.

Graciela's mother and sister visited one weekend and never left. Tomas, not even crawling when they'd arrived, took his first step late in his tenth month. The women spoiled him shamelessly and fed him to the point he turned into a ball with thick, wrinkly thighs. But once he began to walk, he quickly began to run. He would run through the fields and up and down the slopes, and the women would chase him so that very soon he was not a ball but a slim boy with his father's light hair but his mother's dark eyes and skin that was a cocoa-butter combination of them both.

Joe made a few trips back to Tampa on the tin goose, a Ford Trimotor 5-AT that rattled in the wind and lurched and dipped without warning. He exited a couple of times with his ears so blocked he couldn't hear the rest of the day. The air nurses gave him gum to chew and cotton to stuff in there, but it was still a primitive way to travel and Graciela wanted no part of it. So he would make the trip without her and find that he missed her and Tomas at a physical level. He would wake in the middle of the night at their house in Ybor with stomach pain so sharp it stole his breath.

As soon as his business was concluded he'd take the first plane he could get down to Miami. Take the next available one out of there.

It wasn't that Graciela didn't want to return to Tampa — she did. She just didn't want to fly there. And she didn't want to return *right* now. (Which, Joe suspected, meant she really didn't want to go back.) So they stayed in the hills of Las Terrazas, and her mother and sister, Benita, were joined by a third sister, Ines. Whatever bad blood had existed between Graciela, her mother, Benita, and Ines looked to have been healed by time and the presence of Tomas. On a couple of unfortunate occasions, Joe followed the sound of their laughter to catch them dressing Tomas like a girl.

One morning Graciela asked if they could buy a place here.

'Here?'

'Well, it doesn't have to be right here. But in Cuba,' she said. 'Just a place we could visit.'

'We'd be "visiting"?' Joe smiled.

'Yes,' she said. 'I must get back to work soon.'

She didn't really. On his trips back, Joe had checked in on the people in whose care she'd left her various charities, and they were all trustworthy men and women. She could stay away from Ybor for a decade and all her organizations would still be standing, hell, flourishing, when she returned.

'Sure, doll. Whatever you want.'

'It wouldn't have to be a big place. Or a fancy place. Or a—'

'Graciela,' Joe said, 'pick whatever you want. You see something and it's not for sale? Offer them double.'

Not unheard of in those days. Cuba, hit by the Depression worse than most countries, was taking tentative steps toward recovery. The abuses of the Machado regime had been replaced by the hope of Colonel Fulgencio Batista, leader of the Sergeants Revolt that had sent Machado packing. The official president of the Republic was Carlos Mendieta, but everyone knew Batista and his army ran the show. So favored was this arrangement, the American government had started pouring money into the island five minutes after the revolt that put Machado on a plane to Miami. Money for hospitals and roads and museums and schools and a new commercial district along the Malecón. Colonel Batista not only loved the American government, but he also loved the American gambler, so Joe, Dion, Meyer Lansky, and Esteban Suarez, among others, had full access to the highest offices in government. They'd already purchased ninety-nine-year leases on some of the best land along the Parque Central and in the Tacon Market district.

There was no end to the money they'd make.

Graciela said Mendieta was Batista's puppet and Batista was the puppet of United Fruit and the United States; he'd raid the coffers and rape the land, while the United States kept him propped in place because America believed good deeds could somehow follow bad money.

Joe didn't argue. He also didn't point out that they, themselves, had followed bad money with good deeds. Instead he asked her about this house she'd found.

It was a bankrupt tobacco plantation, actually, just outside the village of Arcenas, fifty miles farther west in the Pinar del Río province. It came with a guesthouse for her family and endless fields of black soil for Tomas to run in. The day Joe and Graciela purchased it from the widow, Domenica Gomez, she introduced them to Ilario Bacigalupi outside the attorney's office. Ilario, she explained, would teach them everything there was to know about farming tobacco, if they were interested.

Joe looked at the small round man with the bandit's mustache as the widow's driver whisked her away in a two-toned Detroit Electric. He'd noticed Ilario with the Widow Gomez a few times, always in the background, and had assumed he was a bodyguard in a region where kidnapping wasn't unheard of. But now he noticed the scarred, oversize hands, the prominence of their bones.

He'd never thought about what he'd do with all those fields.

Ilario Bacigalupi, on the other hand, had given it plenty of thought.

First, he explained to Joe and Graciela, no one called him Ilario; they called him Ciggy, which had nothing to do with tobacco. As a child he'd been incapable of pronouncing his own last name, always getting hung up on the second syllable.

Ciggy told them that 20 percent of the village of Arcenas had, until very recently, depended on the Gomez plantation for work. Since Senor Farmer Gomez had fallen to drink and then fallen off his horse and then fallen into insanity and sickness, there had been no work. For three harvests, Ciggy said, no work. It was why many of the children in the village wore no pants. Shirts, carefully tended to, could last a lifetime, but pants always gave way at some point in the seat or the knees.

Joe had noticed a prevalence of bare-assed children on his drives through Arcenas. Hell, if they weren't bare-assed, they were naked. Arcenas, in the foothills of Pinar del Río, was more the hope of a village than an actual one. It was a collection of sagging huts with roofs and walls constructed of dried palm fronds. Human waste exited through a trio of ditches that flowed into the same river from which the villagers drank. There was no mayor or town leader to speak of. The streets were cuts of mud.

'We don't know anything about farming,' Graciela said.

By this point, they were in a cantina in Pinar del Río City.

'I do,' Ciggy said. 'I know so much, senorita, that whatever I've forgotten is not worth teaching.'

Joe looked into Ciggy's cagey, knowing eyes and reevaluated the relationship between the foreman and the widow. He'd thought the widow had kept Ciggy for protection, but he now realized Ciggy had spent the sales process watching after his livelihood and making sure the Widow Gomez knew what was expected of her.

'How would you start?' Joe asked him, pouring them all another glass of rum.

'You will need to prepare the seed beds and plow the fields. First thing, *patrón*. First thing. The season starts next month.'

'Can you stay out of my wife's way while she fixes up the house?'

He nodded at Graciela several times. 'Of course, of course.'

'How many men will you need for this?' she asked.

Ciggy explained that they would need men and children to seed and men to build the seedbeds. They would need men or children to monitor the soil for fungus and disease and mold. They would need men and children to plant and hoe and plow some more and kill the cut worms and mole crickets and stinkbugs. They would need a pilot who didn't drink too much to dust the crops.

'Jesus Christ,' Joe said. 'How much work does this take?'

'We haven't even discussed topping, suckering, or harvesting,' Ciggy said. 'Then there is the stringing, the hanging, the curing, having someone tend the fire in the barn.' He waved his big hand at the breadth of the labor.

Graciela asked, 'How much would we make?'

Ciggy pushed the figures across the table to them.

Joe sipped his rum as he looked them over. 'So, a good year, if there's no blue mold or locusts or hailstorms and God shines his light down on Pinar del Río without stop, we make four percent back on our investment.' He looked across the table at Ciggy. 'That right?'

'Yes. Because you are only using a quarter of your land. But if you invest in your other fields, bring them back to the state they were in fifteen years ago? In five years, you will be rich.'

'We're already rich,' Graciela said.

'You will be richer.'

'What if we don't care about being richer?'

'Then think of it this way,' Ciggy said, 'if you leave the village to starve, you may find them all sleeping in your field one morning.'

Joe sat up in his chair. 'Is that a threat?'

Ciggy shook his head. 'We all know who you are, Mr Coughlin. Famous Yankee gangster. Friend of the colonel. It would be safer for a man to swim into the middle of the ocean and cut his own throat than to threaten you.' He solemnly made the sign of the cross. 'But when people starve and have nowhere to go, where would you have them end up?'

'Not on my land,' Joe said.

'But it's not your land. It's God's. You are renting it. This rum? This life?' He patted his chest. 'We are all just renting from God.'

*

The main house needed almost as much work as the farm.

While the planting season began outside, the nesting season took over on the inside. Graciela had all the walls replastered and repainted, had the flooring in half the house ripped up and replaced when they arrived. There was only one toilet; there were four by the time Ciggy started the topping process.

By then, the rows of tobacco stood about four feet high. Joe woke one morning to air so sweet and fragrant it immediately made him consider the curve of Graciela's neck with lust. Tomas lay sleeping in his crib when Graciela and Joe went to the balcony and looked out on the fields. They'd been brown when Joe went to sleep, but now a carpet of green sported pink and white blossoms that glittered in the soft morning light. Joe and Graciela looked across the breadth of their land, from the balcony of their house to the foothills of Sierra del Rosario, and the blossoms glittered as far as they could see.

Graciela, standing in front of him, reached back and placed her hand to his neck. He put his arms around her abdomen and placed his chin in the hollow of her neck.

'And you don't believe in God,' she said.

He took a deep breath of her. 'And you don't believe good deeds can follow bad money.'

She chuckled and he could feel it in his hands and against his chin.

Later that morning, the workers and their children arrived and went through the fields, stalk by stalk, removing the blossoms. Plants spread their leaves as if they were great birds, and from his window the next morning Joe could no longer see the soil, nor any blossoms. The farm, under Ciggy's stewardship, continued to work without a hitch. For the next stage, he brought in even more children from the village, dozens of them, and sometimes Tomas would laugh uncontrollably because he could hear their laughter in the fields. Joe sat up some nights, listening to the sounds of the boys playing baseball in one of the fallow fields. They'd play until the last of the light had left the sky, using only a broomstick and what remained of a regulation ball they'd found somewhere. The cowhide covering and the wool yarn was long gone, but they'd managed to salvage the cork center.

He listened to their shouts and the snap of the stick against the ball, and he thought of something Graciela had said recently about giving Tomas a little brother or little sister soon.

And he thought, Why stop at one?

Repairing the house moved more slowly than resurrecting the farm. One day Joe traveled to Old Havana, to look up Diego Alvarez, an artist who specialized in the restoration of stained glass. He and Senor Alvarez agreed on a price and a good week for him to make the hundred-mile journey to Arcenas and repair the windows Graciela had salvaged.

After the meeting, Joe visited a jeweler on Avenida de las Misiones that Meyer had recommended. His father's watch, which had been losing time for more than a year, had stopped completely a month ago. The jeweler, a middle-aged man with a sharp face and a perpetual squint, took the watch and opened the back of it, and explained to Joe that while he owned a very fine watch, it still needed to be tended to more than once every ten years. The parts, he said to Joe, all these delicate parts, you see them? They need to be reoiled.

'How long will it take?' Joe asked.

'I'm not sure,' the man said. 'I must take the watch apart and look at each piece.'

'I understand that,' Joe said. 'How long?'

'If the pieces need reoiling and nothing more? Four days.'

'Four,' Joe said and felt a flutter in his chest, as if a small bird had just flown through his soul. 'No way it could be quicker?'

The man shook his head. 'And, senor? If anything is broken, just one small part – and you see how small these parts are?'

'Yes, yes, yes.'

'I will have to send the watch to Switzerland.'

Joe looked out the dusty windows to the dusty street for a moment. He took his wallet from his inside suit pocket and removed a hundred American, placed the bills on the counter. 'I'll be back in two hours. Have a diagnosis by then.'

'A what?'

'Tell me if it'll need to go to Switzerland by then.'

'Yes, senor. Yes.'

He left the shop and found himself wandering Old Havana in all its sensual decay. Habana, he'd decided on his many trips here over the past year, wasn't simply a place; it was the dream of a place. A dream gone drowsy in the sun, fading into its own bottomless appetite for languor, in love with the sexual thrum of its death throes.

He turned one corner and then another and then a third and he was standing on the street where Emma Gould's brothel was.

Esteban had given him the address more than a year ago now, on the night before that bloody day with Albert White and Maso and Digger and poor Sal and Lefty and Carmine. He supposed he'd known he was coming here since he'd left the house yesterday, but he hadn't admitted it to himself because to come here seemed silly and frivolous, and very little of him remained frivolous.

A woman stood out front, hosing the sidewalk free of the glass that had been broken the night before. She sent the glass and dirt into the gutter and it ran down the slope of the cobblestone street. When she looked up and saw him, the hose drooped in her hand but didn't fall.

The years hadn't been horrible to her, though they hadn't exactly been fond either. She looked like a beautiful woman whose vices had failed to love her back, who'd smoked and drunk too much, and both habits had found a way to manifest themselves in crow's-feet and lines around the edges of her mouth and below her lower lip. Her lower eyelids sagged and her hair was brittle, even in all this humidity.

She raised the hose and went back to work. 'Say what you have to say.'

'You want to look at me?'

She turned toward him but kept her eyes on the sidewalk, and he had to move to keep his shoes dry.

'So you had the accident and you thought, "I'm going to take advantage of this"?'

She shook her head.

'No?'

Another shake of the head.

'Then *what*?'

'Once the coppers started chasing us, I told the driver the only way to get away was to drive off the bridge. But he wouldn't listen.'

Joe stepped out of the path of her hose. 'So?'

'So I shot him in the back of the head. We went in the water and I swam out and Michael was waiting for me.'

'Who's Michael?'

'He's the other fella I was keeping on the hook. He was waiting outside the hotel the whole night.'

'Why?'

She scowled at him. 'Once you and Albert started getting all "I can't live without you, Emma. You are my life, Emma," I needed some kind of safety net in case you blew each other up. What choice did a gal have? I knew sooner or later I'd have to get out from under your thumbs. God, the way you two would go on.'

'My apologies,' Joe said, 'for loving you.'

'You didn't love me.' She concentrated on a particularly stubborn piece of glass that had lodged itself between two stones in the street. 'You just wanted to *have* me. Like a fucking Grecian vase or a fancy suit. Show me to all your friends, say "Ain't she a dish?"' She looked at him now. 'I'm not a dish. I don't want to *be* owned. I want to own.'

Joe said, 'I mourned you.'

'That's sweet, pumpkin.'

'For years.'

'How *did* you carry such a cross? Gosh-golly, you're some man.'

He took another step back from her, even though she'd pointed the hose in the opposite direction, and he saw the whole play for the first time, like a mark who'd been grifted so many times his wife didn't allow him out of the house unless he left his watch and his pocket change behind.

'You took the money out of the bus locker, didn't you?'

She waited for the bullet she feared was behind the question, but he raised his hands to show they were empty and would stay that way.

She said, 'You *did* give me the key, remember.'

If there was honor among thieves, then she was right. He'd given her the key; from that point, it was hers to do with as she saw fit.

'And the dead girl? The one they kept finding pieces of?'

She turned off the hose and leaned against the stucco wall of her bordello. 'Remember Albert talking about how he'd found himself a new girl?'

'Not really.'

'Well, he did. She was in the car. Never got her name.'

'You kill her too?'

She shook her head, then tapped her forehead. 'Her head hit the back of the front seat during the crash. Don't know if she died then or later, but I didn't stick around to find out.'

He stood on the street feeling like a fool. A fucking fool.

'Was there a moment when you loved me?' he asked.

She searched his face with growing exasperation. 'Sure. Maybe a few moments. We had laughs, Joe. When you stopped mooning over me long enough to fuck me proper, it was really good. But you had to make it something it wasn't.'

'Which was what?'

'I dunno – something flowery. Something you can't hold in your hand. We're not God's children, we're not fairy-tale people in a book about true love. We live by night and dance fast so the grass can't grow under our feet. That's our creed.' She lit a cigarette and plucked a piece of tobacco off her tongue, gave it to the breeze. 'You don't think I know who you are now? You don't think I've been wondering when you'd show up over here, among the natives? We're free. No brothers or sisters or fathers. No Albert Whites. Just us. You want to come by? You have an open invitation.' She crossed the sidewalk to him. 'We always had a lot of laughs. We could laugh now. Spend our lives in the tropics and count our money on satin sheets. Free as birds.'

'Shit,' Joe said, 'I don't want to be free.'

She cocked her head and seemed confused to the point of genuine sorrow. 'But that's all we ever wanted.'

'It's all *you* ever wanted,' he said. 'And, hey, now you have it. Good-bye, Emma.'

She set her teeth hard and refused to say it in return, as if by not saying it she retained some power.

It was the kind of stubborn, spiteful pride you found in very old mules and very spoiled children.

'Good-bye,' he said again and walked away without a look back, without a twinge of regret, with nothing left unsaid.

*

Back at the jeweler's he was told – delicately and with great care – that the watch would need to make the trip to Switzerland.

Joe signed the release form and the repair order. He took the jeweler's scrupulously detailed receipt. He placed it in his pocket and left the shop.

He stood on the old street in the Old City and, for a moment, couldn't think of where to go next.

CHAPTER TWENTY-EIGHT

How Late It Was

All the boys who worked the farm played baseball, but some were religious about it. As the harvest came upon them, Joe noticed that several had covered their fingertips with surgical tape.

He asked Ciggy, 'Where'd they get the tape?'

'Oh, we got boxes of that, man,' Ciggy said. 'Back in Machado's days, they sent in a medical team with some newspaper writers. Show everyone how Machado loved his peasants. Soon as the newspaper writers leave, so do the doctors. They come, take all the equipment, but we hold on to a carton of that tape for the little ones.'

'Why?'

'You ever cured tobacco, man?'

'No.'

'Well, if I show you why, then will you stop asking dumb questions?'

'Probably not,' Joe said.

The tobacco stalks were now taller than most men, their leaves longer than Joe's arm. He didn't allow Tomas to run in the tobacco patch any longer for fear he could lose him. The croppers – mostly older boys – arrived one morning and picked the leaves from the ripest stalks. The leaves were piled on wooden sleds and then the sleds were unhitched from the mules and hitched to tractors. The tractors were driven to the curing barn on the western edge of the plantation, a task left to the youngest boys. Joe stepped out on the porch of the main house one morning, and a boy no older than six puttered past him on a tractor, a sledful of leaves piled high behind him. The boy gave Joe a big smile and a wave and kept puttering along.

Outside the curing barn, the leaves were pulled from the sleds and placed on stringing benches under the shade trees. The stringing benches had racks affixed to them. The stringers and the handers – all the baseball boys with the surgical tape on their fingers – would place a stick in the rack and begin tying the leaves to the sticks with twine until the leaf bunches hung from one end of the tobacco stick to the other. They did this from six in the morning until eight at night; there was no baseball those weeks. The twine had to be pulled tight while retaining pressure on the stick, so cord burns to the hands and the fingers were common. Hence, Ciggy pointed out, the surgical tape.

'Soon as this is done, *patrón*? All this 'bacco hung, one end of the barn to the other? We sit for five days while it cures. Only man has a job is the man tending the fire in the barn and the men checking it don't get too moist or too dry in there. The boys? They get to play the baseball.'

He put a quick hand on Joe's arm. 'If that's okay with you.'

Joe stood outside the barn, watching those boys string tobacco. Even with the rack, they had to raise and extend their arms to tie off the leaves – raise and extend them for pretty much fourteen hours straight. He gave Ciggy a foul look. 'Of course it's okay. Christ, that fucking work is unbearable.'

'I did it for six years.'

'How?'

'I don't like starving. You like starving?'

Joe rolled his eyes.

'Mmm hmm. Another man,' Ciggy said, 'don't like starving. Only thing the whole world agrees on – starving is no fun.'

The next morning, Joe found Ciggy in the curing barn, making sure the hangers spaced the leaves properly. Joe told him to pull himself away, and they crossed the fields and walked down the eastern ridge and stopped at the worst field Joe owned. It was rocky, it was blocked from the sun by hills and outcrops all day, and the worms and weeds loved it.

Joe asked if Herodes, their best driver, worked much during curing.

'He's still working the harvest,' Ciggy said, 'but not like the boys.'

'Good,' Joe said. 'Have him plow this field.'

'Ain't nothing going to grow here,' Ciggy said.

'No shit,' Joe said.

'So why plow it?'

'Because it's easier to build a baseball field on level ground, don't you think?'

*

The same day they constructed the pitcher's mound, Joe was walking with Tomas past the barn when he saw one of the workers, Perez, beating his son, just clouting his head like the boy was a dog he'd caught eating his supper. Kid couldn't have been any older than eight. Joe said, 'Hey,' and started toward them, but Ciggy stepped in front of him.

Perez and Perez's son looked at him, confused, and Perez hit his son in the head again and then in the ass several times.

'Is that necessary?' Joe said to Ciggy.

Tomas, oblivious, squirmed for Ciggy, to whom he'd taken a shine lately.

Ciggy took Tomas from Joe and held him high above him as Tomas giggled and Ciggy said, 'You think Perez likes to hit his boy? Think he woke up, said I want to be a bad guy, make sure the boy grows up to hate me? No, no, no, *patrón*. He woke up saying I got to put food on the table, I got to keep them warm, keep them dry, fix that roof leak, kill the rats in their bedroom, show them the right path, show my wife I love her, have five fucking minutes for myself, and sleep for four hours before I got to get up and go back into the fields. And when I leave for the fields, I can hear the littlest ones crying – "Papa, I'm hungry. Papa, there's no milk." "Papa, I feel sick." And he comes back day after day to that, goes out day after day to that, and then you give his son a job, *patrón,* and it's like you saved his life. Because maybe you did. But then his son fails at this job? *Cono.* That son gets beat. Better beat than hungry.'

'What did the boy fail at?'

'He was supposed to watch the curing fire. He fell asleep.

Could have burned the whole crop.' He handed Tomas back to Joe. 'Could have burned himself.'

Joe looked at the father and son now. Perez had his arm around the boy, the boy nodding, the father speaking in low tones and kissing the side of the boy's head several times, the lesson delivered. The boy didn't seem to soften under the kisses, though. So the father pushed his head away and they both went back to work.

The baseball field was completed the day the tobacco was moved from the barn to the pack house. Preparing the leaves for market was a job left mostly to the women, who walked up the hill to the plantation in the morning as hard-faced and hard-fisted as the men. While they sorted and graded the tobacco, Joe gathered the boys in the field and gave them the gloves and fresh balls and Louisville sluggers that had arrived two days before. He laid out three base pads and home plate.

It was as if he'd shown them how to fly.

In the early evenings, he'd take Tomas to watch the games. Sometimes Graciela would join them, but her presence often proved to be too distracting for a couple of the boys entering early adolescence.

Tomas, one of those kids who never sat still, was rapt in the presence of the game. He sat quietly, hands clasped between his knees, watching something he couldn't possibly understand yet, but which worked on him the way music and warm water did.

Joe said to Graciela one night, 'Outside of us, there's no hope in that town but baseball. They love it.'

'That's good then, yes?'

'Yeah, it's great. Shit on America all you want, honey, but we export some good things.'

She gave him a flash of wry brown eyes. 'But you charge for it.'

Who didn't? What made the world run, if not free trade? We give to you, and you give something back in return.

Joe loved his wife, but she still seemed unable to accept that her own country, while undoubtedly beholden to his, was far better off for the transaction. Before the United States had pulled their asses out of the fire, Spain had left them languishing in a cesspool of malaria and bad roads and nonexistent medical care. Machado hadn't improved on the model. But now, with General Batista, they had a surging infrastructure. They had indoor plumbing and electricity in a third of the country and half of Havana. They had good schools and a few decent hospitals. They had a longer life expectancy. They had dentists.

Yes, the United States exported some of its goodwill at the point of a gun. But all the great countries who'd advanced civilization throughout history had done the same.

And when you considered Ybor City, hadn't he? Hadn't she? They'd built hospitals with blood money. Pulled women and children off the streets with rum profits.

Good deeds, since the dawn of time, had often followed bad money.

And now, in baseball-crazy Cuba, in a region where they would have been playing it with sticks and bare hands, they had gloves so new the leather creaked and bats as blond as peeled apples. And every evening, when the work was done and the rest of the green stems had been removed from the leaves, and the crop had been sheeted and packed, and the air smelled of the remoistened tobacco and tar, he sat on a chair beside Ciggy and watched the shadows lengthen in the field, and they discussed where they'd buy the seed for the outfield grass so it would no longer be a scrabble of dirt and loose stone out there. Ciggy had heard rumors of a league near these parts, and Joe asked him to keep looking into it, particularly for the fall when the farm duties would be at their lightest.

On market day, their tobacco sold for the second-highest price at the warehouse, 400 sheets of tobacco, weighing an average of 275 pounds, went to a single buyer, the Robert Burns Tobacco Company, which manufactured the panatela, the new American sensation in cigars.

To celebrate, Joe gave bonuses to all the men and women. He gave two cases of Coughlin-Suarez rum to the village. Then on Ciggy's suggestion, he rented a bus and he and Ciggy took the baseball team to their first movie at the Bijou in Viñales.

The newsreels were all about the Nuremberg Laws taking effect in Germany – footage of anxious Jews packing up belongings and leaving furnished apartments behind to head for the first train out. Joe had read accounts recently that claimed Chancellor Hitler represented an authentic threat to the fragile peace that had held in Europe since '18, but he doubted the funny-looking little man would go much further with this lunacy, now that the world had sat up and taken notice; there just wasn't any percentage in it.

The shorts that followed were forgettable, though the boys on the team all laughed a lot, their eyes as wide as the base pads he'd bought them, and it took Joe a moment to realize that they knew so little of the movies they'd thought the newsreels about Germany *were* the feature.

Then came the main event – an oater called *Riders of the Eastern Ridge* starring Tex Moran and Estelle Summers. The credits flashed quick across the black screen and Joe, who never went to movies in the first place, couldn't have cared less who was responsible for making it. He was, in fact, starting to look down to make sure his right shoe was tied when the name that popped on the screen snapped his eyes back up:

Screenplay
Aiden Coughlin

Joe looked over at Ciggy and the boys, but they were oblivious.

My brother, he wanted to tell someone. My brother.

On the bus ride back to Arcenas, he couldn't stop thinking about the movie. A Western, yes, with gunfights galore and a damsel in distress, and a stagecoach chase along a crumbling cliff road, but something else too, if you knew Danny. The character Tex Moran had played was an honest sheriff in what turned out to be a dirty town. A town where the most prominent citizens gathered one night to plot the death of a swarthy migrant farmer who, one claimed, had ogled his daughter. In the end, the movie retreated from its own radical premise – the good townspeople learned the error of their ways – but only after the swarthy migrant farmer had been killed by a group of outsiders in black hats. The message of the movie, then, as far as Joe could tell, was that the danger from without would wash clean the danger from within. Which, in Joe's experience – and in Danny's – was bullshit.

But, either way, it was a hell of a fun time at the theater. The boys had gone wild for it; the whole bus ride home they'd talked about buying six-guns and gun belts when they grew up.

Late that summer, his watch returned from Geneva by mail. It arrived in a lovely mahogany box with velvet inlay and gleamed from a polishing.

Joe was so overjoyed that it would be days before he could admit to himself that it still ran a bit slow.

In September, Graciela received a letter informing her that the Greater Ybor Board of Overseers had elected her Woman of the Year for her work with the less fortunate in the Latin Quarter. The Greater Ybor Board of Overseers was a loose collection of Cuban, Spanish, and Italian men and women who gathered once a month to discuss their shared interests. In the first year, the group had disbanded three times while most of the meetings had ended in fights that spilled out of the restaurant of choice and into the street. The fights were usually between the Spaniards and the Cubans, but every now and then the Italians threw a punch or two so they wouldn't feel left out. After enough of the bad blood had been given full measure, the members managed to find common ground in their shared exile from the rest of Tampa and grew into a fairly powerful interest group in a very short time. If Graciela would agree, the board wrote, they would be pleased to present her with her award at a gala to be held at the Don Ce-Sar Hotel on St Petersburg Beach the first weekend in October.

'What do you think?' Graciela asked over breakfast.

Joe was groggy. He'd been having variations on the same nightmare lately. He was with his family and they were somewhere foreign, Africa he felt, but he couldn't say why exactly. Just that they were surrounded by tall grass and it was very hot. His father appeared at the limit of his vision, at the farthest edge of the fields. He said nothing. He just watched as the panthers emerged from the tall grass, sleek and yellow-eyed. They were the same shade of tan as the grass and, thus, impossible to see until it was too late. When Joe saw the first of them, he shouted to warn Graciela and Tomas, but his throat had already been removed by the cat that sat on his chest. He noticed how red his blood looked on its great white teeth and then he closed his eyes as the cat went back for seconds.

He poured himself more coffee and willed the dream from his head.

'I think,' he said to Graciela, 'that it's time for you to see Ybor again.'

The restoration of the house, much to their surprise, was mostly complete. And last week Joe and Ciggy had laid the grass sod for the outfield. There was nothing holding them to Cuba, for the time being, except Cuba.

They left near the end of September at the end of the rainy season. They left Havana Harbor and crossed the Florida Straits and steamed due north along the west coast of Florida, arriving at the Port of Tampa in the late afternoon of September 29.

Seppe Carbone and Enrico Pozzetta, both of whom had risen fast in Dion's organization, met them in the terminal, and Seppe explained that word had leaked of their arrival. He showed Joe page five of the *Tribune:*

REPUTED YBOR SYNDICATE BOSS RETURNING

The story alleged that the Ku Klux Klan was making threats again and that the FBI was mulling an indictment.

'Jesus,' Joe said, 'where do they come up with this shit?'

'Take your coat, Mr Coughlin?'

Over his suit, Joe wore a silk raincoat he'd bought in Havana. It was imported from Lisbon and sat as lightly on him as a layer of epidermis, but the rain couldn't make a dent in it. The final hour of the boat ride Joe had seen the clouds massing, which was no surprise – Cuba's rainy season might be far worse, but Tampa's was no joke, either, and judging by the clouds, it was still hanging around.

'I'll keep it on,' Joe said. 'Help my wife with her bags.'

'Of course.'

The four of them left the terminal and walked into the parking lot, Seppe to Joe's right, Enrico to Graciela's left. Tomas rode Joe's hip, his arms around his neck, Joe checking the time, when the sound of the first gunshot reached them.

Seppe died on his feet – Joe had seen it enough times. He

continued to hold Graciela's bags as the hole went straight through the center of his head. Joe turned as Seppe fell and the second gunshot followed the first, the gunman saying something in a calm, dry voice. Joe clutched Tomas to his shoulder and threw himself at Graciela and they all toppled to the ground.

Tomas cried out, more in shock than pain as far as Joe could tell, and Graciela grunted. Joe heard Enrico firing his gun. He looked over, saw that Enrico was hit in the neck, the blood coming out of him way too fast and way too dark, but he was firing his '17 Colt .45, firing it under the car nearest to him.

Now Joe heard what the shooter was saying.

'Repent. Repent.'

Tomas wailed. Not in pain but in fear, Joe knew the difference. He said to Graciela, 'You okay? Are you okay?'

'Yes,' she said. 'Wind knocked out. Go.'

Joe rolled off them, drew his .32, and joined Enrico.

'Repent.'

They fired under the car at a pair of tan boots and trouser legs.

'Repent.'

On Joe's fifth try, he and Enrico hit bull's-eyes on the same shots. Enrico's blew a hole in the shooter's left boot and Joe's snapped his left ankle in half.

Joe looked over at Enrico in time to see him cough once and die. It was that quick and he was gone, the gun in his hand still smoking. Joe jumped over the hood of the car between him and the shooter and landed on the ground in front of Irving Figgis.

He was dressed in a tan suit with a faded white shirt. He wore a straw cowboy hat and used his pistol, a long-barrel Colt, to push himself to his one good foot. Stood there on the gravel in his tan suit with his shattered foot dangling from his ankle nub like his pistol dangled from his hand.

He looked in Joe's eyes. 'Repent.'

Joe kept his own gun aimed at the center mass of Irv's chest. 'I don't follow.'

'Repent.'

'Fine,' Joe said. 'To who?'

'God.'

'Who says I don't?' Joe took a step closer. 'What I won't do, Irv, is repent to you.'

'Then repent to God,' Irv said, his breath thin and rushed, 'in my presence.'

'No,' Joe said. ''Cause then it's still about you and not about God, isn't it?'

Irv shuddered several times. 'She was my baby girl.'

Joe nodded. 'But I didn't take her from you, Irv.'

'Your kind did.' Irv's eyes opened and fixed on Joe's person, on something in the waist area.

Joe glanced down, didn't see anything.

'Your kind,' Irv repeated. 'Your kind.'

'What's my kind?' Joe asked and risked another glance down his own chest, still couldn't see anything.

'Those with no God in their heart.'

'I got God in my heart,' Joe said. 'He's just not your God. Why'd she kill herself in your bed?'

'*What?*' Irv was weeping now.

'Three bedrooms in that house,' Joe said. 'Why'd she kill herself in yours?'

'You sick and lonely man. You sick and lonely . . .'

Irv looked at something over Joe's shoulder and then back at his waistline.

And it got the better of Joe. He took a hard look at his waist and saw something that hadn't been there when he'd left the boat. Something that wasn't on his waist; it was on his coat. *In* his coat.

A hole. A perfectly round hole on the right flap, just by his right hip.

Irv met his eyes and there was a great shame there.

'I am,' Irv said, 'so sorry.'

Joe was still trying to piece it together when Irv saw what he'd been waiting for and took two one-legged hops onto the road and into the path of a coal truck.

The driver hit Irv and then he hit his brakes, but all that did was cause him to skid on the red brick and Irv went under the tires and the truck bounced when it crushed his bones and rolled over him.

Joe turned away from the road, heard the driver still skidding and he looked at the hole in his raincoat and realized the bullet had passed through from behind. Passed through clean, missed his hip by who knew how few or how many inches. The flap would have been swaying in the air at that point as he covered his family. As he . . .

He looked over the car and he saw Graciela trying to stand and the blood that poured out of her waist, out of her entire midsection. He dove over the hood of the car and landed on his hands and knees in front of her.

She said, 'Joseph?'

He could hear the fear in her voice. He could hear the *knowledge* in her voice. He tore off his coat. He found the wound just above her groin and he pressed the wadded-up coat to her midsection and he said, 'No, no, no, no, no, no, no, no.'

She wasn't trying to move anymore. She probably couldn't.

A young woman dared to stick her head out of the terminal door and Joe screamed, 'Call a doctor! A doctor!'

The woman went back inside and Joe saw Tomas staring at him, his mouth open but no sound coming out.

'I love you,' Graciela said. 'I always loved you.'

'No,' Joe said and pressed his forehead to hers. He pressed the coat as hard as he could against the wound. 'No, no, no. You're my ... you're my ... No.'

She said, 'Shhh.'

He pulled his head back from hers as she drifted off and kept drifting.

'World,' he said.

CHAPTER TWENTY-NINE

A Man in His Profession

He remained a great friend of Ybor, though few knew him. None, certainly, knew him the way he'd been known when she was alive. Then, he'd been pleasant and surprisingly open for a man in his profession. Now he was pleasant.

He grew old very fast, some said. He walked with hesitancy, as if he limped, though he didn't.

Sometimes he took the boy fishing. This was usually at sunset when the snook and redfish were most likely to bite. They'd sit on the seawall where he'd taught the boy how to tie his line, and every now and then he'd put his arm around the boy, speak softly into his ear, and point toward Cuba.

Acknowledgements

My immense gratitude to:

Tom Bernardo, Mike Eigen, Mal Ellenburg, Michael Koryta, Gerry Lehane, Theresa Milewski, and Sterling Watson for the early reads and feedback.

The folks at the Henry B. Plant Museum and the Don Vicente De Ybor Inn in Tampa.

Dominic Amenta of the Regan Communications Group for answering my questions about the Hotel Statler in Boston.

And a particular thanks to Scott Deitche for giving me the Cigar City Mafia tour of Ybor City.

Sixteen-year-old Amanda McCready has disappeared. Her anxious
aunt contacts Patrick Kenzie to investigate. It is not the first time
she has gone missing, as Patrick well knows – he was the
investigator who worked on her case when she was
kidnapped before, as a four-year-old.

But this is not a simple case of a runaway girl. In fact, nothing
in Amanda's life has been simple: brought up by the world's
worst mother, neglected throughout her childhood, she has
nonetheless blossomed into a formidably intelligent young
woman. A young woman so bright that she can seemingly
out-think and out-manoeuvre anyone ...

For Patrick, the case leads him down Boston's darkest,
most dangerous streets – and into a world of shocking secrets
that will threaten not only Amanda's life, but also his own
and that of his partner Angie Gennaro.

*

'Vintage stuff ... another dark but absurdly enjoyable tale that's so
beautifully written and so sharp in its details and atmosphere that
it's no wonder Lehane's books attract filmmakers with such ease'
Irish Voice